Addison Peale Russell

# Characteristics

Sketches and Essays

Addison Peale Russell

**Characteristics**
*Sketches and Essays*

ISBN/EAN: 9783337010492

Printed in Europe, USA, Canada, Australia, Japan

Cover: Foto ©Andreas Hilbeck / pixelio.de

More available books at **www.hansebooks.com**

# CHARACTERISTICS.

## Sketches and Essays.

BY

## A. P. RUSSELL,

AUTHOR OF "LIBRARY NOTES."

### TITLES.

BOSTON:
HOUGHTON, MIFFLIN AND COMPANY.
New York: 11 East Seventeenth Street.
The Riverside Press, Cambridge.
1884.

# CONTENTS.

# CHARACTERISTICS.

## I.

### THE CONVERSATION OF COLERIDGE.*

DE QUINCEY. It was, I think, in the month of August, but certainly in the summer season, and certainly in the year 1807, that I first saw this illustrious man, the largest and most spacious intellect, the subtlest and the most comprehensive, in my judgment, that has yet existed amongst men. . . . Little points of business being settled, Coleridge, like some great river, the Orellana, or the St. Lawrence, that had been checked and fretted by rocks, or thwarting islands, and suddenly recovers its volume of waters, and its mighty music, swept at once, as if returning to his natural business, into a continuous strain of eloquent dissertation, certainly the most novel, the most finely illustrated, and traversing the most spacious fields of thought, by transitions the most just and logical, that it was possible to conceive.

HAZLITT. I had heard a great deal of Coleridge's powers of conversation, and was not disappointed. In fact, I never met with any thing at all like them, either before or since. I could easily credit the accounts which were circulated of his holding forth to a large party of ladies and gentlemen, an evening or two before, on the Berkeleian Theory, where he made the whole material

* "Not since Pythagoras does an equal charm seem to have graced the speech of any man."

universe look like a transparency of fine words; and another story of his being asked to a party at Birmaghan's, of his smoking tobacco and going to sleep after dinner, on a sofa, where the company found him, to their no small surprise, which was increased to wonder when he started up of a sudden, and rubbing his eyes, looked about him, and launched into a three hours' description of the third heaven, of which he had had a dream.

H. N. Coleridge. Throughout a long-drawn summer's day would this man talk to you in low, equable, but clear and musical, tones, concerning things human and divine; marshaling all history, harmonizing all experiment, probing the depths of your consciousness, and revealing visions of glory and of terror to the imagination; but pouring withal such floods of light upon the mind, that you might, for a season, like Paul, become blind in the very act of conversion. And this he would do, without so much as one allusion to himself, without a word of reflection on others, save when any given act fell naturally in the way of his discourse, — without one anecdote that was not proof and illustration of a previous position;—gratifying no passion, indulging no caprice, but with a calm mastery over your soul, leading you onward and onward forever through a thousand windings, yet with no pause, to some magnificent point in which, as in a focus, all the party-colored rays of his discourse should converge in light. In all this he was, in truth, your teacher and guide; but in a little while you might forget that he was other than a fellow-student and the companion of your way, — so playful was his manner, so simple his language, so affectionate the glance of his pleasant eye. — There were, indeed, some whom Coleridge tired, and some whom he sent asleep. It would occasionally so happen, when the abstruser mood was strong upon him, and the visitor was narrow and ungenial. I have seen him at times when you could not incarnate him, — when he shook aside your petty questions or doubts, and burst with some impatience through the obstacles of common conversation. Then, escaped from the flesh, he would soar upward into an atmosphere almost too rare to breathe, but which seemed proper to him, and there he would float at ease. Like enough, what Coleridge then said, his subtlest listener would not understand as a man understands a newspaper; but, upon such a listener, there would steal an influence, and an impression, and a sympathy; there would be a gradual attempering of his body and spirit, till his total being vibrated with one pulse alone, and thought became merged in contemplation : —

> And so, his senses gradually wrapt
> In a half sleep, he 'd dream of better worlds,
> And dreaming, hear thee still, O singing lark,
> That sangest like an angel in the clouds !

But it would be a great mistake to suppose that the general character of Mr. Coleridge's conversation was abstruse or rhapsodical. . . . Mr. Coleridge's conversation at all times required attention, because what he said was so individual and unexpected. But when he was dealing deeply with a question, the demand upon the intellect of the hearer was very great; not so much for any hardness of language, for his diction was always simple and easy; nor for the abstruseness of the thoughts, for they generally explained, or appeared to explain, themselves; but pre-eminently on account of the seeming remoteness of his associations, and the exceeding subtlety of his transitional links. . . . It happened to him as to Pindar, who in modern days has been called a rambling rhapsodist, because the connections of his parts, though never arbitrary, are so fine, that the vulgar reader sees them not at all. But they are there nevertheless, and may all be so distinctly shown, that no one can doubt their existence; and a little study will also prove that the points of contact are those which the true genius of lyric verse naturally evolved, and that the entire Pindaric ode, instead of being the loose and lawless outburst which so many have fancied, is, without any exception, the most artificial and highly-wrought composition which Time has spared to us from the wreck of the Greek Muse. So I can well remember occasions, in which, after listening to Mr. Coleridge for several delightful hours, I have gone away with divers splendid ·masses of reasoning in my head, the separate beauty and coherency of which I deeply felt ; but how they had produced, or how they bore upon each other, I could not then perceive. In such cases I have mused sometimes even for days afterward upon the words, till at length, spontaneously as it seemed, " the fire would kindle," and the association which had escaped my utmost efforts of comprehension before, flashed itself all at once upon my mind with the clearness of noonday light.

MARY COWDEN CLARKE. It was in the summer of 1821 that I first met Samuel Taylor Coleridge. It was on the East Cliff at Ramsgate. He was contemplating the sea under its most attractive aspect : in a dazzling sun, with sailing clouds that drew their purple shadows over its bright green floor, and a merry breeze of sufficient prevalence to emboss each wave with a silvery foam. . . . . As he had no companion, I desired to pay my respects to one of the most extraordinary — and, indeed, in his department of genius, the most extraordinary — man of his age. And being possessed of a talisman for securing his consideration, I introduced myself as a friend and admirer of Charles Lamb. The pass-word was sufficient, and I found him immediately talking to me in the bland and frank tones of a standing acquaintance. A poor girl had that morning thrown herself from the pierhead in a pang of despair, from having been betrayed by a villain. He alluded to the event, and went on to denounce the morality of the age that will hound from the community the reputed weaker subject, and continue to receive him who has wronged her. He agreed with me, that that question will never be adjusted but by the women themselves. Justice will continue in abeyance so long as they visit with severity the errors of their own sex and tolerate those of ours. He then diverged to the great mysteries of life and death, and branched away to the sublime question — the immortality of the soul. Here he spread the sail-broad vans of his wonderful imagination, and soared away with an eagle-flight, and with an eagle eye, too, compassing the effulgence of his great argument, ever and anon stooping within my own sparrow's range, and then glancing away again, and careering through the trackless fields of ethereal metaphysics. And this he continued for an hour and a half, never pausing for an instant except to catch his breath (which, in the heat of his teeming mind, he did like a school-boy repeating by rote his task,) and gave utterance to some of the grandest thoughts I ever heard from the mouth of man. His ideas, embodied in words of purest eloquence, flew about my ears like drifts of snow. He was like a cataract filling and rushing over my penny-phial capacity. I would only gasp, and bow my head in acknowledgment. He required from me nothing more than the simple recognition of his discourse ; and so he went on like a steam-engine — I keeping the machine oiled with my looks of pleasure, while he supplied the fuel : and that upon the same theme, too, would have lasted till now. What would I have given for a short-hand report of that speech ! And such was the habit of this wonderful man. Like the old peripatetic philosophers, he walked about, prodigally scattering wisdom, and leaving it to the winds of chance to waft the seeds into a genial soil. — My first suspicion of his being in Ramsgate had arisen from my mother observing that she had heard an elderly gentleman in the public library, who looked like a dissenting minister, talking as she never heard man talk. Like his own Ancient Mariner, when he had once fixed your eye he held you spell-bound, and you were constrained to listen to his tale; you must have been more powerful than he to have broken the charm; and I know no man worthy to do that. He did, indeed, answer to my conception of a man of genius, for his mind flowed on "like the Pontick sea," that "ne'er feels retiring ebb." It was always ready for action; like the hare, it slept with its eyes open. He would at any given moment range from the subtlest and most abstruse question in metaphysics to the architectural beauty in contrivance of a flower of the fields; and the gorgeousness of his imagery would increase, and dilate, and flash forth such coruscations of similes and startling theories that one was in a perpetual aurora borealis of fancy. As Hazlitt once said of him, "He would talk on forever, and you wished him to talk on forever. His thoughts never seemed to come with labor or effort, but as if borne on the gusts of genius, and as if the wings of his imagination lifted him off his feet." ، This is truly as poetically described. He would not only illustrate a theory or an argument with a sustained and superb figure, but in pursuing the current of his thought he would bubble up with a sparkle of fancy so fleet and brilliant that the attention, though startled and arrested, was not broken. He would throw these into the stream of his argument, as waifs and strays. Notwithstanding his wealth of language and prodigious power in amplification, no one, I think, (unless it were Shakespeare or Bacon,) possessed with himself equal power of condensation. He would frequently comprise the elements of a noble theorem in two or three words; and like the genial offspring of a poet's brain, it always came forth in a golden halo. I remember once, in discoursing upon the architecture of the Middle Ages, he reduced the Gothic structure into a magnificent abstrac-

tion — and in two words. "A Gothic cathedral," he said,
"is like a petrified religion."

THOMAS CARLYLE.  Coleridge sat on the brow of Highgate Hill, in those years, looking down on London and
its smoke-tumult, like a sage escaped from the inanity of
life's battles; attracting towards him the thoughts of innumerable brave souls still engaged there. . . . A sublime man; who, alone in those dark days, had saved his
crown of spiritual manhood; escaping from the black
materialisms, and revolutionary deluges, with "God,
Freedom, Immortality" still his: a king of men. The
practical intellects of the world did not much heed him,
or carelessly reckoned him a metaphysical dreamer; but
to the rising spirits of the young generation he had this
dusky sublime character; and sat there as a kind of
Magus, girt in mystery and enigma; his Dodona oak
grove (Mr. Gillman's house at Highgate) whispering
strange things, uncertain whether oracles or jargon. . . .
Here for hours would Coleridge talk, concerning all con-
ceivable or inconceivable things; and liked nothing better than to have an intelligent, or failing that, even a
silent and patient human listener. He distinguished himself to all that ever heard him as at least the most surprising talker extant in this world, and to some small
minority, by no means at all, as the most excellent. — The
good man, he was now getting old, towards sixty, perhaps;
and gave you the idea of a life that had been full of sufferings; a life heavy-laden, half-vanquished, still swim-
ming painfully in seas of manifold physical and other
bewilderment.  Brow and head were round, and of massive weight, but the face was flabby and irresolute; expressive of weakness under possibility of strength.  He
hung loosely on his limbs, with knees bent, and stooping
attitude; in walking, he rather shuffled than decisively
stept; and a lady once remarked, he never could fix
which side of the garden walk would suit him best, but

continually shifted, in corkscrew fashion, and kept trying both. A heavy-laden, half-aspiring, and surely much suffering **man.** His **voice,** naturally soft and good, **had** contracted itself into **a** plaintive snuffle **and singsong ; he** spoke as if preaching, — you would have said, **preaching** earnestly and also hopelessly the weightiest **things. I** still recollect his " object " and " **subject,"** terms of **con**tinual recurrence in the Kantean province ; and how he sung and snuffled them into " om-m-mject," and " **summ-mject,"** with a kind of a solemn shake or quaver, as he **rolled along.** No talk in his century, or in any other, could be more surprising. . . . **"Our** interview [said Sterling in his record of his first interview with Coleridge] lasted for three hours, **during which he talked two** hours and **three quarters." Nothing could be more copious** than his **talk ; and** furthermore, it was always **virtually** or literally, **of the nature** of a monologue ; **suffering no** interruption, **however** reverent ; hastily putting **aside all** foreign additions, annotations, or most ingenuous **desires for** elucidation, as well-meant superfluities which **would never** do. Besides, **it** was talk not flowing **anywhither like** a river, but spreading everywhither in inextricable currents and regurgitations like **a** lake or sea ; terribly deficient in definite goal and **aim,** nay often in logical intelligibility ; what you were **to believe or** do, or any earthly or heavenly thing, obstinately refusing to appear from it. So that, **most** times, you felt logically lost ; swamped near to drowning in this tide of ingenious vocables, **spreading out** boundless as if to submerge the **world.** . . . **I have** heard Coleridge talk, with eager musical energy, **two** stricken hours, his face radiant and moist, and communicate no meaning whatsoever **to** any individual of his hearers, — certain of whom, **I for one,** still kept eagerly listening in hope ; the most had long before given up, and formed (if **the** room were large enough) secondary humming groups **of** their own. He began any where : you put some question to him, made some suggestive observation ; instead of answering this, or decidedly setting out towards answering it, he would accumulate formidable apparatus, logical swim-bladders, transcendental life-preservers, and other precautionary and vehiculatory gear, for setting out ; perhaps did at last get under way, — but was swiftly solicited, turned aside by the glance of some radiant new game on this hand or that, into new courses ; and ever into new ; and before long into all the universe, where it was uncertain what game you would catch, or whether any. His talk, alas, was distinguished, like himself, by irresolution : it disliked to be troubled with conditions, abstinences, definite fulfillments ;— loved to wander at its own sweet will, and make its auditor and his claims and humble wishes a mere passive bucket for itself. He had knowledge about many things and topics, much curious reading ; but generally all topics led him, after a pass or two, into the high seas of theosophic philosophy, the hazy infinitude of Kantean transcendentalism, with its " sum-m-mjects " and " om-m-mjects." Sad enough ; for with such indolent impatience of the claims and ignorances of others, he had not the least talent for explaining this or any thing unknown to them ; and you swam and fluttered in the mistiest wide unintelligible deluge of things, for the most part, in a rather profitless, uncomfortable manner. Glorious islets, too, I have seen rise out of the haze ; but they were few, and soon swallowed in the general element again. Balmy, sunny islets, islets of the blest and the intelligible ; on which occasion those secondary humming groups would all cease humming, and hang breathless upon the eloquent words ; till once your islet got wrapped in the mist again, and they could recommence humming. Eloquent artistically expressive words you always had ; piercing radiances of a most subtle insight came at intervals ; tones of noble, pious sympathy, recognizable as pious, though strangely colored, were never wanting long : but in general you could not call this aimless, cloud-capt, cloud-based, lawlessly meandering human discourse of reason by the name of "excellent talk," but only of "surprising ;" and were reminded bitterly of Hazlitt's account of it : "Excellent talker, very, — if you let him start from no premises and come to no conclusion." Coleridge was not without what talkers call wit, and there were touches of prickly sarcasm in him, contemptuous enough of the world and its idols and popular dignitaries ; he had traits even of poetic humor ; but in general he seemed deficient in laughter ; or indeed in sympathy for concrete human things, either on the sunny or on the stormy side. One right peal of concrete laughter at some convicted flesh-and-blood absurdity, one burst of noble indignation at some injustice or depravity, rubbing elbows with us on this solid earth, how strange would it have been in that Kantean haze-world, and how infinitely cheering amid its vacant air-castles and dim-melting ghosts and shadows ! None such ever came. His life had been an abstract thinking and dreaming, idealistic, passed amid the ghosts of defunct bodies and of unborn ones. The moaning sing-song of that theosophico-metaphysical monotony left on you, at last, a very dreary feeling.

LAMB. I dined yesterday in Parnassus, with Wordsworth, Coleridge, Rogers, and Tom Moore — half the poetry of England constellated and clustered in Gloucester Place ! It was a delightful evening ! Coleridge was in his finest vein of talk — had all the talk ; and let 'em talk as they will of the envy of poets, I am sure not one there but was content to be nothing but a listener. The Muses were dumb while Apollo lectured.

LEIGH HUNT. I heard him one day, under the grove at Highgate, repeat one of his melodious lamentations, as he walked up and down, his voice undulating in a stream of music, and his regrets of youth sparkling with visions **ever young. . . .** On the **same occasion he built up a metaphor out of a** flower, in a style surpassing **the famous** passage in Milton ; deducing **it** from **its root in religious** mystery, and carrying it **up into the bright, con-**summate flower, "The bridal **chamber of reproductive-**ness." Of all "the Muses' **mysteries," he was** as great a high priest **as** Spenser ; **and** Spenser himself might have gone to Highgate **to** hear him talk, **and** thank him for his Ancient **Mariner. . . .** He **recited** his Kubla Khan, one morning **to Byron, in his** lordship's house in Piccadilly, **when** I happened to **be** in another room. I **remembered the** others coming away from him, highly **struck** with **his** poem, and saying how wonderfully he **talked.** This was the impression of **every body who** heard him.

C. R. LESLIE. **Of this** extraordinary **man it might be** said, as truly as of **Burke,** that **" his stream of mind was** perpetual." His eloquence threw **a new and beautiful** light on most subjects, and when he was **beyond my com-**prehension, the melody of his voice, **and the impressive-**ness of **his** manner, held me **a** willing **listener, and** I was flattered **at being** supposed **capable of** understanding him. **Indeed, men far** advanced **beyond** myself in edu-**cation might have** felt as children **in** his presence.

JULIUS CHARLES HARE. **It is to** be regretted that **John Sterling did** not preserve an account of Coleridge's **conversations with** him ; for he was capable of represent-ing their depth, **their** ever varying lines, their sparkling lights, their ocean**ic ebb and flow;** of which **his published** Table-talk hardly **gives the slightest** conception. **Unfor-**tunately Sterling merely **took notes** of his first interview with Coleridge ; but these **are the only record** I have **seen which enables** one **at all to apprehend** how his won-derful combination of **philosophical and** poetical powers **manifested** themselves in **his discourse.**

JOHN STERLING. **Mr.** Coleridge happened to lay his

hand upon a little old engraving of Luther with four German verses above it. He said, " How much better this is than many of the butcher-like portraits of Luther, which we commonly see! He is of all men the one whom I especially love and admire." Pointing to the first words of the German verses, he explained them, " Luther, the dear hero." " It is singular," he said, " how all men have agreed in assigning to Luther the heroic character ; and indeed it is certainly most just. Luther, however wrong in some of his opinions, was always right in design and spirit. In translating his ideas into conceptions, he always understood something higher and more universal than he had the means of expressing. He did not bestow too much attention on one part of man's nature to the exclusion of the others ; but gave its due place to each, — the intellectual, the practical, and so forth. He is great, even where he is wrong." Some one mentioned Calvin. He said, " Calvin was undoubtedly a man of talent ; I have a great respect for him ; he had a very logical intellect ; but he wanted Luther's powers." He then began to speak of landscape gardening, in consequence of some remark about the beautiful view behind the house in which he resided. " We have gone too far in destroying the old style of gardens and parks. There was a great deal of comfort in the thick hedges, which always gave you a sheltered walk during winter. There is certainly a propriety in the gradual passing away of the works of man in the neighborhood of a home. The great thing is to discover whether the scenery is such that the country seems to belong to man, or man to the country. Now among the lakes of Westmoreland man evidently belongs to the country : the very cottages seem merely to rise out of, and to be growths of, the rock. But the case is different in a country where every thing speaks of man, houses, corn-fields, cattle. There your improvements ought to be in conformity with the character of the place. Man is so in love with intelligence, that where he is not intelligent enough to discover it, he will impress it. Some of the finest views about here (Highgate) are only to be seen from among the most wretched habitations. Luther said truly: ' How different is a rich country from a happy country! A rich country is always an unhappy, miserable, degraded country.'" — He then went into a long exposition of the evils of commerce and manufactures ; the argument of which, I think, is to be found in one of the Lay Sermons. In the course of it he took occasion to say that the Legislature is defective. "I don't mean any thing about the nonsense of universal suffrage ; but the land proprietors have too great a proportion of power. Land is something fixed and tangible ; if one man have more of it, another must have less. But this other kind of wealth, which is founded in the National Debt, and so forth, — one man's having a million of it does not prevent another man's getting two millions of it ; nay, it rather makes it more probable that he will do so. Thirty or forty years ago it would have been a disgrace to a merchant to be seen in the Stock Exchange. Now it is thought nothing of. There are only two remedies for the evil of our excessive increasing population. We have not virtue enough for the one, which is a plan of general and continued emigrations, in which the people would be perpetually going forth, headed by the priest and the noble. In every parish a certain portion of every family ought to live under the knowledge that at a certain age they were to emigrate. The other remedy is a perfectly free trade in corn ; but this would only do for a time. More rich men are springing up in the country than the country can support : the Regent's Park is covered as it were with an enchanted city." — "The division of labor has proceeded so far, even in literature, that people do not think for themselves ; their review thinks for them." — He said to a person in the company: "Your friend Mr. —— was here some time ago. He is evidently a man of great talent. We had a long dispute together about laughter. Mr. —— was maintaining that notion of Hobbes', that laughter arises from contempt. My theory was, that it always springs from the sudden experience of a pleasure, for which the nerves are not sufficiently prepared, and that laughter is the little convulsion by which nature gets rid of the struggle." — The population of Highgate, and the number of churches and chapels in it, happened to be mentioned, when Coleridge said: "There never was such a mistake as the government has committed in letting the population outstrip the churches to such an extent. They forgot that religion, even in its exterior forms, is the centre of gravity. Christendom is so obviously superior to all the rest of the world in every thing, — science, civilization, power, — that it is impossible to doubt of the mere external advantages of religion." But it was said how much of Christianity is there in France! "Why," replied Coleridge, "there are a great many queer Christians even here; but still religion exists as a power in the country. London has a great weight after all among mankind. People perhaps are not themselves religious; but they give their half-guineas, and they are civil. Christianity brings immense advantages to a savage. It is an evident preferment for him. The missionaries have done a great deal for us in clearing up our notions about savage nations. What an immense deal of harm Captain Cook's Voyages did in that way! Sailors, after being a long time at sea, found a fertile island, and a people of lax morals, which were just the things they wanted; and of course there never were such dear, good, kind, amiable people. We know now that they were more detestably licentious than we could have imagined. And then the romance of the Pelew Islanders! There scarcely ever existed such a set of blood-thirsty barbarians. Savages have a notion of higher powers than their own all around them ; but that is a part of superstition, not religion. The personality of the Deity is the great thing. The ancients were Spinozists : they could not help seeing an energy in nature. This was the anima mundi sine centro of the philosophers. The people, of course, changed it into all the forms that their imagination could supply. The religion of the philosophers was Pantheism, that of the people Polytheism. They knew nothing of a creative power : at first there was Chaos and Night ; and what produced the universe they could not tell. The gods were merely the first birth of Chaos. This is very evident also in the notion of the Stoics, that after ten thousand years the gods required to be formed again. Even Plato, who alone of them all had any idea of God, says that it is very hard to discover, and impossible to communicate it. And I have no doubt that the first great apostasy, the building of the Tower of Babel, consisted in erecting a temple to the heavens, to the universe. The first sovereigns of all countries were priests, and after them warriors. This is clear from the Northern traditions of Odin, the Sagas, and so forth. When the families of the priests intermarried with the children of the more ignorant people, their offspring applied their superior intelligence and knowledge to the purposes of conquest ; hence the great conquests recorded of old. We never hear of such conquests by savage nations when they are not directed by the wisdom of a priesthood." — Mr. Coleridge is not tall, and rather stout : his features, though not regular, are by no means disagreeable ; the hair quite gray ; the eye and forehead very fine. His appearance is rather old-fashioned ; and he looks as if he belonged not so much to this, or to any age, as to history. His manner and address struck me as being rather formally courteous. He always speaks in the tone and in the gesture of common conversation, and laughs a good deal, but gently. His

emphasis, though **not** declamatory, is placed with **remarkable** propriety.   **He speaks** perhaps rather slowly, **but
never stops, and seldom** ever hesitates.   There is **the**
strongest **appearance of** conviction, **without any** violence
in his manner.   **His** language is sometimes harsh, **sometimes careless,** often quaint, almost **always, I think, drawn**
from the fresh delicious fountains **of our elder** eloquence.
I have no doubt that the diction of **much** that I have re-
**ported** is different from Coleridge's, **and** always, of course,
vastly inferior.   I have treasured up as many of his
**phrases as I** could ; **they** will easily be recognized.   On
**one** occasion he quoted **a line** of his own poetry, saying,
**"If I may quote a verse of mine written when** I was a
**very young man.   It was something to this effect : '** They
kill too slow **for men to call it murder.'"   He** happened
to mention **several books in the** course **of his remarks ;**
and **he always seemed** inclined to **mention them good-
naturedly. — I was in his** company about three **hours ;**
and of **that time he** spoke during two and three quarters.
It **would have been** delightful to listen as attentively, **and**
certainly easy **for him to** speak just **as well for the next**
forty-eight hours.   **On** the whole **his conversation, or**
rather monologue, **is** by far the **most interesting I** ever
**heard** or heard of.   Dr. **Johnson's talk,** with which it is
**obvious to** compare it, seems **to me** immeasurably infe-
**rior.**   It is better balanced **and scrubbed,** and more pon-
derous with epithets ; **but the spirit and** flavor and fragrance, **the** knowledge **and the** genius are all wanting.
The one **is a house of brick,** the other a quarry of jasper.
It **is painful to observe in** Coleridge that, with **all the**
kindness **and glorious** far-seeing intelligence **of his eye,**
there is a glare in **it, a** light half **unearthly, half morbid.**
It **is the** glittering eye of the Ancient **Mariner.   His
cheek too** shows a flush of over-excitement, **the red of a**
storm-cloud at sunset.   When he dies, **another, and one
of the** greatest **of** their race, **will** rejoin the few Immor-

tals, the **ill-understood** and ill-requited, who **have walked** this earth.

PROFESSOR WILSON. If there be any man of **great and** original genius alive at this moment, in **Europe, it is S. T.** Coleridge. Nothing can surpass **the melodious** richness of words, which **he** heaps around his images ; images that are not glaring in themselves, but which are always affecting to the verge of tears, because they have all been formed **and** nourished in the recesses of one of **the most deeply** musing spirits that ever breathed forth **its inspiration, in** the majestic language of England. . . . Let the **dullest clod** that ever vegetated, provided only he **be alive** and hear, **be** shut up in **a** room with Coleridge, **or in** a wood, and **be** subjected for a few minutes **to** the ethereal influence of that wonderful man's monologue, **and** he will begin **to** believe himself **a Poet. The barren** wilderness may **not** blossom like the **rose, but it will** seem, or rather feel to do so, under **the lustre of an im-** agination exhaustless as the sun. . . . **It is easy to talk** — not very difficult to speechify — **hard to speak** ; but to "discourse" is a gift rarely bestowed by **Heaven** on mor- **tal man.** Coleridge has **it** in **perfection.** While he is discoursing **the** world loses **all its** commonplaces, and you **and** your **wife** imagine **yourself Adam and** Eve listening **to the affable** Archangel Raphael in the Garden of Eden. **You would no** more dream **of** wishing him to be mute for **a while, than you would** a river that "imposes silence with a stilly **sound."** Whether you understood two **con-** secutive sentences, **we** shall not stop too curiously **to in-** quire ; but you do something better, you **feel the whole** just like any other divine music. And 't is your own fault if you do not

"**A** wiser and a better man **arise to-morrow's** morn."

. . . **Nor are we** now **using any** exaggeration ; for if you **will but think how unutterably dull are** all the ordinary sayings and doings of this life, spent as it is with ordinary people, you may imagine how in sweet delirium you may be robbed of yourself by a seraphic tongue that has fed since first it lisped on "honey-dew," and by lips that have "breathed the air of Paradise," and learned a seraphic language, which, all the while that it is English, it is as grand as Greek and as soft as Italian. We only know this, that Coleridge is the alchemist that in his crucible melts down hours to moments — and lo ! diamonds sprinkled on a plate of gold.

DR. DIBDIN. I shall never forget the effect his conversation made upon me at the first meeting, at a dinner-party. It struck me as something not only quite out of the ordinary course of things, but an intellectual exhibition altogether matchless. The viands were, unusually costly, and the banquet was at once rich and varied ; but there seemed to be no dish like Coleridge's conversation to feed upon — and no information so instructive, as his own. The orator rolled himself up as it were in his chair, and gave the most unrestrained indulgence to his speech ; and how fraught with acuteness and originality was that speech, and in what copious and eloquent periods did it flow! The audience seemed to be wrapped in wonder and delight, as one conversation, more profound, or clothed in more forcible language than another, fell from his tongue. He spoke nearly for two hours with unhesitating and uninterrupted fluency.

TALFOURD. Instead, like Wordsworth, of seeking the sources of sublimity and beauty in the simplest elements of humanity, he ranges through all history and science, investigating all that has really existed, and all that has had foundation only in the wildest and strangest minds, combining, condensing, developing, and multiplying the rich products of his research with marvelous facility and skill ; now pondering fondly over some piece of exquisite loveliness, brought from an unknown recess, now tracing out the hidden germ of the eldest and most barbaric theories, and now calling fantastic spirits from the vasty deep, where they have slept since the dawn of reason. The term " myriad-minded," which he has happily applied to Shakespeare, is truly descriptive of himself. . . . There is nothing more wonderful than the facile majesty of his images, or rather of his world of imagery, which, whether in his poetry or his prose, start up before us self-raised, and all perfect, like the palace of Aladdin. He ascends to the sublimest truths by a winding track of sparkling glory, which can only be described in his own language :

> " The spirit's ladder
> That from the gross and visible world of dust,
> Even to the starry world, with thousand rounds
> Builds itself up ; on which the unseen powers,
> Move up and down on heavenly ministries —
> The circles in the circles, that approach
> The central sun from every narrowing orbit."

. . . The riches of his mind were developed, not in writing, but in his speech — conversation I can scarcely call it — which no one who once heard can ever forget. Unable to work in solitude, he sought the gentle stimulus of social admiration, and under its influence poured forth, without stint, the marvelous resources of a mind rich in the spoils of time — richer — richer far in its own glorious imagination and delicate fancy ! There was a noble prodigality in these outpourings ; a generous disdain of self ; an earnest desire to scatter abroad the seeds of wisdom and beauty, to take root wherever they might fall, and spring up without bearing his name or impress, which might remind the listener of the first days of poetry before it became individualized by the press, when the Homeric rhapsodist wandered through new-born cities and scattered hovels, flashing upon the minds of the wondering audience the bright train of heroic shapes, the series of godlike exploits, and sought no record more enduring than the fleshly tablets of his hearers' hearts ; no memory but that of genial tradition ; when copyright did not ascertain the reciter's property, nor marble at once perpetuate and shed chilliness on his fame ;

> "His bounty was as boundless as the sea,
> His love as deep."

Like the ocean, in all its variety of gentle moods, his discourse perpetually ebbed and flowed — nothing in it angular, nothing of set purpose, but now trembling as the voice of divine philosophy, "not harsh nor crabbed, as dull fools suppose, but musical as is Apollo's lute," was wafted over the summer wave ; now glistening, in long line of light over some obscure subject, like the path of moonlight on the black water ; and, if ever receding from the shore, driven by some sudden gust of inspiration, disclosing the treasures of the deep, like the rich strond in Spenser, "far-sunken in their sunless treasuries," to be covered anon by the foam of the same immortal tide. The benignity of his manner befitted the beauty of his disquisitions ; his voice rose from the gentlest pitch of conversation to the height of impassioned eloquence without effort, as his language expanded from some common topic of the day to the loftiest abstractions ; ascending to the highest truths which the naked eye could discern, and suggesting starry regions beyond which his own telescopic gaze might possibly decipher. If his entranced hearers often were unable to perceive the bearings of his argument — too mighty for any grasp but his own, and sometimes reaching beyond his own — they understood "a beauty in the words, if not the words ;" and a wisdom and piety in the illustrations, even when unable to connect them with the idea which he desired to illustrate. If an entire scheme of moral philosophy was never developed by him either in speaking or writing, all the parts were great : vast biblical knowledge, though sometimes eddying in splendid conjecture, was always employed with pious reverence; the morality suggested was at once elevated and genial; the charity hoped all things; and the mighty imaginative reasoner seemed almost to realize the condition suggested by the great Apostle, "that he understood all mysteries and all knowledge, and spake with the tongues both of men and angels."

SIR HUMPHRY DAVY. During his stay in London I saw him seldomer than usual; when I did see him, it was generally in the midst of large companies, where he is the image of power and activity. His eloquence is unimpaired; perhaps it is softer and stronger. His will is less than ever commensurate with his ability. Brilliant images of greatness float upon his mind, like images of the morning clouds on the waters. Their forms are changed by the motion of the waves, they are agitated by every breeze, and modified by every sunbeam.

JOHN FOSTER. Prince of magicians, Coleridge; whose mind, too, is clearly more original and illimitable than Hall's. Coleridge is indeed sometimes less perspicuous and impressive by the distance at which his mental operations are carried on. Hall works his enginery close by you, so as to endanger your being caught and torn by some of the wheels; just as one has felt sometimes when environed by the noise and gigantic movements of a great mill. . . . The eloquent Coleridge sometimes retires into a sublime mysticism of thought; he robes himself in moonlight, and moves among images of which we cannot be assured for a while whether they are substantial forms of sense or fantastic visions. . . . [His are] the most extraordinary faculties I have ever yet seen resident in a form of flesh and blood.

ROGERS. Wordsworth and myself had walked to Highgate to call on Coleridge, when he was living at Gillman's. We sat with him two hours, he talking the whole time without intermission.  When we left the house, we walked for some time without speaking.  "What a wonderful man he is!" exclaimed Wordsworth.  "Wonderful, indeed," said I.  "What depth of thought, what richness of expression!" continued Wordsworth.  "There 's nothing like him that ever I heard," rejoined I, — another pause.  "Pray," inquired Wordsworth, "did you precisely understand what he said about the Kantean philosophy?"  "Not precisely."  "Or about the plurality of worlds?"  "I can't say I did.  In fact, if the truth must out, I did not understand a syllable from one end of his monologue to the other."  "No more," said Wordsworth, "did I."

# II.

## SARAH SIDDONS.

IT will always be interesting to read of Mrs. Siddons, and of the mighty influence she exerted over multitudes of her contemporaries. Great and small vied in their admiration of her, and could not say enough in praise of her presence, her genius, and her achievements. From the meanest servant about the theatre to the most exalted personage in the realm, all London, all England, seemed to agree, and all enlightened English-speaking people everywhere accepted the verdict, that Sarah Siddons was incomparably the greatest of all actresses that had been or would be. Crowds gathered wherever and whenever she appeared in public. Every body wanted to see her, on the stage and off. The cream of London society paid obeisance to her, royalty sought her, eminent artists were ambitious to paint her, great poets to apostrophize her, and the greatest orators to enrich and adorn their orations by allusions to her.

"For my part," said De Quincey, "I shall always regard my recollections of Mrs. Siddons as those in which chiefly I have an advantage over the coming generation ; nay, perhaps over all generations ; for many centuries may revolve without producing such another transcendent creature."

Professor Wilson, who had personal knowledge of Mrs. Siddons, has this famous thing to say of her in Noctes Ambrosianæ : "Sarah was a glorious creature. Methinks I see her now in the sleep-walking scene. — SHEPHERD. As Leddy Macbeth ! Her gran' high straicht-nosed face, whiter than ashes! Fixed een, no like the een o' the dead, yet hardly mair like them o' the leevin'; dim, and yet licht wi' an obscure lustre through which the tormented sowl like in the chains o' sleep and dreams, wi' a' the distraction o' remorse and despair, — and oh! sic an expanse o' forehead for a warld o' dreadful thochts, aneath the braided blackness o' her hair, that had nevertheless been put up wi' a steady and nae uncarefu' haun' before the troubled leddy had lain doon, for it behooved ane so high-born as she, in the middle o' her ruefu' trouble, no to neglect what she owed to her stately beauty, and to the head that lay on the couch of ane o' Scotland's Thanes — noo likewise about to be, during the short space o' the passing o' a thunder-cloud, her bluidy and usurping king. — NORTH. Whisht — Tickler — whisht — no coughing. — SHEPHERD. Onwards she used to come — no Sarah Siddons — but just Leddy Macbeth hersel' — though through that melancholy masquerade o' passion, the spectator aye had a confused glimmerin' apprehension o' the great actress — glidin' wi' the ghostlike motion o' nicht - wanderin' unrest, unconscious o' surroundin' objects, — for oh! how could the glazed, yet gleamin' een, see aught in this material world? — yet, by some mysterious power o' instinct, never touchin' ane o' the impediments that the furniture o' the auld castle might hae imposed to her haunted footsteps, — on she came, wring, wringin' her hauns, as if washin' them in the cleansin' dews frae the blouts o' blood, — but wae 's me for the murderess, out they wad no be, ony mair than the stains on the spat o' the floor where some midnicht-slain Christian has groaned out his soul aneath the dagger's stroke, when the sleepin' hoose heard not the shriek o' departing life. — TICKLER. North, look at James' face. Confound me, under the inspiration of the moment, if it is not like John Kemble's! — SHEPHERD. Whether a' this, sirs, was nature's or not, ye see I dinna ken, because

I never beheld ony woman, either gentle or semple, walkin' in her sleep after having committed murder. But, Lord safe us! That hollow, broken-hearted voice, 'out, damned spot,' was o' itsell aneuch to tell to a' that heard it, that crimes done in the flesh during time will needs be punished in the spirit during eternity. It was a dreadfu' homily you, sirs ; and wha that saw 't would ever ask whether tragedy or the stage was moral, purging the soul, as she did, wi' pity and wi' terror."

Young was acting Beverley with her on the Edinburgh stage, when she gave the exclamation, " 'T is false, old man ! — they had no quarrel — there was no cause for quarrel," with such piercing grief that he said his throat swelled, and his utterance was choked. He stood unable to speak the few words which, as Beverley, he ought to have immediately delivered ; the pause lasted long enough to make the prompter several times repeat Beverley's speech, till Mrs. Siddons, coming up to her fellow-actor, put the tips of her fingers on his shoulders, and said, in a low voice, " Mr. Young, recollect yourself."

Fitzgerald mentions even a more remarkable and striking instance of this influence which was exhibited during a performance of Henry VIII., when she addressed a raw supernumerary, who was playing the Surveyor, warning him against giving false testimony against his master : —

> " If I know you well,
> You were the Duke's surveyor, and lost your office
> On the complaints of the tenants. Take good heed
> You charge not in your spleen a noble person."

Her scorn was so withering, her looks so menacing, that the actor came off literally perspiring with terror, and protesting that he would not venture again to meet her terrible look of severity. Such was her power, amid all the hackneyed associations of the side scenes, and it helps us to form an idea of what it was over an unsophisticated audience.

It was this wonderful woman's art, says Fitzgerald, in his Life of the Kembles, to stamp some remarkable image of herself on the recollection, in great plays, like Coriolanus ; and that fine actor Young, looked back with admiration and wonder to the figure of her Volumnia, as it lingered in his memory. " I remember her," he writes to Mr. Campbell, more than forty years after the performance, " coming down the stage, in 1789, in the triumphal entry of her son, Coriolanus, when her dumb-show drew plaudits that shook the building. She came alone, marching and beating time to the music ; rolling (if that be not too strong a term to describe her motion) from side to side, swelling with the triumph of her son. Such was the intoxication of joy which flashed from her eye, and lit up her whole face, that the effect was irresistible. ' She seemed to me to reap all the glory of that procession to herself. I could not take my eye from her. Coriolanus, banner, and pageant, all went for nothing to me, after she had walked to her place."

When far advanced in life, Mrs. Siddons appeared as Arpasia in Tamerlane — her brother, John Kemble, taking the part of Bajazet. It is stated that in the last act, when by order of the tyrant, her lover Moneses is strangled before her face, she worked herself up to such a pitch of agony, and gave such terrible reality to the few convulsive words she tried to utter, as she sank a lifeless heap before her murderer, that the audience for a few moments remained in a hush of astonishment, as if awe-struck ; they then clamored for the curtain to be dropped, and insisting on the manager's appearance, received from him in answer to their vehement inquiries, the assurance that Mrs. Siddons was alive, and recovering from the temporary indisposition that her exertions had caused. They were satisfied as regarded her, but would not suffer the performance to be resumed.

Macready, before he was twenty, appeared twice with

Mrs. Siddons — then in her fifty-fifth year. He says of
her in his Reminiscences : " What eulogy can do justice
to her personations. . . . How can any force of description
imprint on the imagination the sudden but thrilling
effect of tone or look, of port or gesture, or even of the
silence so often significative in the development of human
passion. . . . She stood alone on her height of excellence.
Her acting was perfection, and as I recall it I do
not wonder, novice as I was, at my perturbation when on
the stage with her. . . . In no other theatrical artist
were, I believe, the charms of voice, the graces of personal
beauty, and the gifts of genius ever so grandly and
harmoniously combined."

Godwin delighted to talk of her merits. He was an
ardent admirer of Garrick, yet he confessed to Campbell
that he thought Mrs. Siddons possessed finer powers.

Crabb Robinson bore testimony to her extraordinary
power, and it is known that he was the young man who
is described as having burst into loud laughter, in the pit,
during the most terrible portion of her performance of
the Fatal Curiosity. He was being forcibly ejected,
when it was discovered that he was in violent hysterics.

An accurate division of her tragic characters has been
made into four classes. First, it is claimed, should be
placed those of Shakespearian grandeur and dignity, like
Lady Macbeth ; secondly, those in which a classical dignity
was combined with the modern ideas of emotion,
as in The Grecian Daughter or Jane Shore ; thirdly, purely
melodramatic characters, like Mrs. Haller ; and fourthly,
characters of dignified Shakespearian comedy, like Hermione.
In each of these distinct departments one or
two characters could be named in which she was remarkable
— a singular and exceptional proof of genius.

As to her reading, Miss Edgeworth says : " I heard
Mrs. Siddons read, at her town house, a portion of Henry
VIII. I was more struck and delighted than I ever was

with any reading in my life. This is feebly expressing what I felt; I felt that I had never before fully understood or sufficiently admired Shakespeare, or known the full powers of the human voice and the English language. Queen Katharine was a character peculiarly suited to her time of life and to reading. There was nothing that required gesture or vehemence incompatible with the sitting attitude. The composure and dignity, and the sort of suppressed feeling, and touches, not bursts of tenderness, of matronly, not youthful tenderness, were all favorable to the general effect. I quite forgot to applaud — I thought she was what she appeared."

Miss Wynn, who heard her read Macbeth, said that she never knew what the play was till then. Mrs. Siddons contrived, in the sleep-walking scene, to discharge all expression from her fine eyes, leaving only a glassy stare.

Washington Irving, during his first visit to London, in 1805, saw Mrs. Siddons, and thus speaks of her in a letter to his brother: "Were I to indulge without reserve in my praises of Mrs. Siddons, I am afraid you would think them hyperbolical. What a wonderful woman! The very first time I saw her perform I was struck with admiration. It was in the part of Calista. Her looks, her voice, her gestures, delighted me. She penetrated in a moment to my heart. She froze and melted it by turns; a glance of her eye, a start, an exclamation, thrilled through my whole frame. The more I see her, the more I admire her. I hardly breathe while she is on the stage. She works on my feelings till I am like a mere child."

Northcote remarked to Hazlitt that he had seen young ladies of quality — Lady Marys and Lady Dorothys — peeping into a room where Mrs. Siddons was sitting, with all the same timidity and curiosity as if it were some preternatural being — he was sure, more than if it had been the Queen. Hazlitt said, that of all the women he had ever seen or known any thing of, Mrs. Siddons struck

him as the grandest. She appeared to him "to belong
to a superior order of beings, to be surrounded with a
personal awe, like some prophetess of old, or Roman
matron, the mother of Coriolanus and the Gracchi. Her
voice answered to her form, and her expression to both."
Northcote said if you had not seen Mrs. Siddons you
could have no idea of her, nor could you convey it to any
one who had not. She was indeed, he said, like a preternatural being descended to the earth. Byron said of
her in Lady Macbeth, that she was "something above
nature."

"I remember," says Mrs. Jameson, "that the first time
I found myself in the same room with Mrs. Siddons, I
gazed on her as I should have gazed at one of the Egyptian pyramids — nay, with a deeper awe, for what is material and physical immensity, compared with moral and
poetical grandeur? I was struck with a sensation which
made my heart pause, and rendered me dumb for some
minutes; and when I was led into conversation with her,
my first words came faltering and thick, — which never
certainly would have been the case in presence of the
autocratrix of all the Russias. The greatest, the noblest
in the land approached her with a deference not unmin-
gled with a shade of embarrassment, while she stood in
regal guise majestic, with the air of one who bestowed
and never received honor."

Tate Wilkinson, the eccentric old stage-manager, would
say of her, in his wandering, mixed way, — "To be sure,
Mrs. Siddons was all in all. Her grandeur and dignity
were indeed wonderful! and if you ask me what is a
queen? I should say Mrs. Siddons! as I said, where is
there to be found such another Mrs. Siddons? Her fine
figure and majestic mien in Elvira exceeded any thing I
ever saw." In his Memoirs he says, "Mrs. Siddons, in
a theatrical lottery, would certainly obtain fifteen prizes
out of twenty." "Certainly," he says, "where disdain,

contempt, pride, or indignation, are to be expressed, it may safely be affirmed she there stands unrivaled, and is herself alone."   "I do not mean," he says again, "to insinuate Mrs. Siddons has not foibles or faults — I can only say, if she has, I am not acquainted with them."

Of "the great queen of all actresses," Byron wrote in one of his Journals: "Of actors, Cooke was the most natural, Kemble the most supernatural — Kean the medium between the two.  But Mrs. Siddons was worth them all put together."  She took leave of the stage, he said, "to the loss of ages, — for nothing ever was, or can be, like her."

George the Fourth, after conversing with her, said, with emphasis, "She is the only real queen."

Imagine her, if you can, standing as a statue, peerless and queenly, in her part of Hermione, in Winter's Tale !

"O, royal piece,<br>
There's magic in thy majesty."

It was while she was playing this part, it is related, that Mrs. Siddons escaped death from fire, through the marvelous presence of mind of the scene-man.  As she was standing for the statue, her drapery flitted over the lamps that were placed behind the pedestal, and caught fire. The scene-man crept on his hands and knees and extinguished the flame, without discovering to her the danger she was in, a service for which she rewarded him by obtaining from the king a pardon for his son, a soldier who had incurred the death penalty for desertion from the army.

Joanna Baillie was an intimate friend of Mrs. Siddons, and wrote expressly for her the part of Jane de Montfort, in her play of De Montfort.  The poet Campbell pronounces the following passage an almost perfect picture of the great actress:

"PAGE. — Madam, there is a lady in your hall,
      Who begs to be admitted to your presence.

LADY. — Is it not one of our invited friends ?
PAGE. — No ; far unlike to them.   It is a stranger.
LADY. — How looks her countenance ?
PAGE. — So queenly, so commanding, and so noble,
    I shrank at first in awe ; but when she smiled
    Methought I could have compassed sea and land
    To do her bidding.
LADY. — Is she young or old ?
PAGE. — Neither, if right I guess ; but she is fair,
    For Time has laid his hand so gently on her,
    As he too had been awed,
    So stately and so graceful is her form.
    I thought at first her stature was gigantic,
    But, on a near approach, I found in truth
    She scarcely does surpass the middle size.
LADY. — What is her garb ?
PAGE. — I cannot well describe the fashion of it ;
    She is not decked in any gallant trim,
    But seems to me clad in the usual weeds
    Of high habitual state.
LADY. — Thine eyes deceive thee, boy,
    It is an apparition thou hast seen.
FREBERG. — It is an apparition he has seen,
    Or Jane de Montfort."

Campbell speaks of once having gone through the Louvre with Mrs. Siddons. "I observed," he says, "almost every eye in the hall was fixed upon her and followed her ; yet I could perceive that she was not known, as I could hear the spectators say, 'Who is she ? is she not an English woman ?'  At this time, though in her fifty-ninth year, her looks were so noble, that she made you proud of English beauty — even in the presence of Grecian sculpture."  This description will not seem extravagant to those who read the letters of Dr. Beattie or Washington Irving, recording the impressions made upon them by this wonderful woman, when far advanced in life.  Dr. Johnson, when asked whether he did not think her finer on the stage, where she was adorned by art, replied, "On the stage art does not adorn her ; nature adorns her there, and art glorifies her."

Davies, a contemporary and an actor, as well as a man of letters, said of her: "This actress, like a resistless torrent, has borne down all before her. Her merit, which is certainly very extensive in tragic characters, seems to have swallowed up all remembrance of present and past performers."

Henderson, not long after her first appearance on the London stage, pronounced her "an actress who never had an equal, nor would ever have a superior."

James Ballantyne gave her the name of "the Siddons," and he was pronounced by Professor Wilson "the best theatrical creetic in Embro'." She was also called the "Tragic Queen," and the "Queen of Tears."

De Quincey, who not only often saw Mrs. Siddons upon the stage, but met her privately at the house of Hannah More, has this among other quotable things to say of her: "Amongst the many pleasurable impressions which Mrs. Siddons' presence never failed to make, there was one which was positively painful and humiliating : it was the degradation which it inflicted upon other women. One day there was a large dinner-party at Barley Wood. Mrs. Siddons was present; and I remarked to a gentleman who sat next to me — a remark which he heartily confirmed — that upon rising to let the ladies leave us, Mrs. Siddons, by the mere necessity of her regal deportment, dwarfed the whole party, and made them look ridiculous ; though Hannah More, and others of the ladies present, were otherwise really women of very pleasing appearance."

Harlow, the painter, writing of Mrs. Siddons, said that when, in the character of Queen Katharine, she addressed Wolsey in the words, "Lord Cardinal, to you I speak," her statuesque attitude was the sublimest thing in ancient or modern sculpture.

The Encyclopædia Britannica pronounces her "the greatest actor that ever trod the stage. She took possession of the tragic throne, on which, **for thirty years** she **reigned without a rival.** The public were astonished **at the vastness** of her powers, and tragedy became **the fashion. The** symmetry of the great actress's person **was most** captivating. Her features were strongly **marked, but** finely harmonized ; **the** flexibility **of her countenance** was extraordinary, yielding instantaneously **to every** change of passion ; her **voice was** plaintive, yet capable of firmness and exertion ; her articulation **was** clear, penetrating, **and distinct ; above all she was** completely mistress **of her** powers ; **and** possessed that high judgment which **enabled** her to display all of her other qualifications to **the** greatest advantage. One of Mrs. Siddons' **highest** endowments, if not her very highest, was **the** power of identifying herself with the character which **she** personated. The scenes in which she acted **were to her** far from being **a mere** mimic show ; **so powerfully did her** imagination conjure up the **reality, that the tears which** she shed were those **of bitterness felt at the moment.** From her frown **of** proud **disdain and scorn, the very actors** themselves **shrank with something like terror. Her** greatest characters **were Katharine** in Henry **VIII.** (the most chaste, beautiful, **and perfect** performance **that ever** drew a tear), and Lady Macbeth, in which she **manifested a** dignity and a sensibility, a power, and a pa**thos,** never equaled **by any** female performer."

It is related, that late one night Mr. Siddons was **sitting by the fire in** the family parlor, dozing and smoking, **when** suddenly **he** was **roused,** with a start, by hurried footsteps, that were flying rather than running down **the** passage. Who could it be? he asked himself, **all in a** maze **and a wonder,** as he **jumped up and rubbed** his sleep-laden eyes. He had **hardly had time to** let the **question** go darting **through his** brain, when the door of **the room was** thrown open **quickly, as by a** hasty, trem**bling** hand, and a **female figure rushed in.** Mr. Siddons gazed in speechless astonishment, not unmixed with a touch of fear. There before him stood his wife, her fine hair disheveled, her dress all in disorder, her face all quivering with strong emotion. In bewildered alarm he asked her what was the matter, but her only answer was to throw herself into his arms, and burst into a torrent of tears. He soothed her tenderly, not knowing what to think, and gradually she grew calmer. Then her words made the mystery plain enough. Instead of going to bed, as he had bade her do, she had been sitting up studying her part as Lady Macbeth; and the character had so completely absorbed her in itself, she had so entirely realized the horror of each situation in the play, had seen it all so distinctly before her eyes, as if she had been there in the body, that a wild, unreasoning terror had seized her, and she had rushed away to seek human companionship.

The person of Mrs. Siddons, it is said by one familiar with her acting, rather courted the regal attire, and her beauty became more vivid from the decorations of her rank. The commanding height and powerful action of her figure, though always feminine, seemed to tower beyond her sex. Her walk has never been attempted by any other actress; and in deliberate dignity was as much alone, as the expression of her countenance. All accounts and pictures of her represent her nose as being very prominent. It is on record that while Gainsborough was painting that exquisite portrait of her, which is now in the South Kensington Gallery, after working in absorbed silence for some time, he suddenly exclaimed, " D—n it, madam, there is no end to your nose ! "

Speaking of the play of The Fair Penitent, one of Mrs. Siddons' admirers said that it was worth sitting out the piece for the scene with Horatio alone, and to see " such a splendid animal in such a magnificent rage." Davies noticed that in the third act she became so affected that " her paleness was seen through her rouge."

" When we have such a being as Mrs. Siddons before us in Lady Macbeth," says one who was familiar with her acting, " what signifies the order or disorder of the picture of a castle behind her, or whether the shadows be upwards or downwards on the mouldings of the midnight apartment?   It is to the terror of her eye, it is to the vehement and commanding sweep of her action — it is to the perfection of her voice that I am a captive, and I must pity the man who, not being the painter of the canvas, is at leisure to inquire how it is executed."

" The great actress steps upon the scene, and how she fills it in a moment!   Mind and majesty wait upon her in the air ; her person is lost in the greatness of her personal presence ; she dilates with thought, and a stupid giantess looks a dwarf beside her."

Of Mrs. Siddons' Mrs. Haller, one of her admirers once told Fanny Kemble that her majestic and imposing person, and the commanding character of her beauty, militated against her effect in the part.   " No man, alive or dead," said he, " would have dared to take a liberty with her ; wicked she might be, but weak she could not be, and when she told the story of her ill-conduct in the play, nobody believed her."

The stupidity of the King in not understanding her better, is past comprehension.  On one occasion, it is stated, his majesty put into her hands a sheet of paper, merely subscribed with his name, intended, it may be presumed, to afford the opportunity to Mrs. Siddons of pledging the royal signature to any provision of a pecuniary nature, which might be most agreeable to the actress herself.   This paper, with the discretion that was suited to the circumstance itself, and which was so characteristic of Mrs. Siddons, she delivered into the hands of the Queen ; upon whom conduct so delicate and dignified was not likely to be lost.

When asked as to her modes of study, discipline of

mind, etc., she replied, "When a part is first put before me for study, I look it over in a general way, to see if it is in nature, and if it is, I am sure it can be played."

"I cannot but think it a peculiar happiness to Mrs. Siddons," says Boaden, in his Memoirs of the great actress, "that she seems through life so little to have imitated what other performers did in the parts she acted. I willingly believe this not to have been sufficiency, as despising others, or disdaining help; but from a settled conviction, that she could only be great by being truly original; and that she ought to deliver her own conceptions of character with absolute indifference by what other artists they were either disputed or confirmed." Her own idea of a part she conscientiously aimed to realize in her acting, and nothing could divert her from her purpose. The same integrity marked her professional life that controlled her personal conduct. "Neither praise nor money," wrote Dr. Johnson to Mrs. Thrale, "the two powerful corrupters of mankind, seem to have depraved her."

"Have you ever heard," asked Garrick, in an unpublished letter to Moody, then at Liverpool, "of a Mrs. Siddons, who is strolling about somewhere near you?" Four months later, Garrick brought her out at Drury Lane; but she did not succeed. She returned to Bath, where she was successful. It was at Birmingham, however, in the summer of 1776, (then in her twenty-first year) that Henderson first saw the future great actress. He was immediately struck with her excellence, and declared that she would never be surpassed. One night at Bath, accident is said to have conducted into the boxes of the theatre some persons of consummate taste, and of sufficient consequence to make their opinions heard. A mysterious smile of derision, it is stated, soon announced to the votaries of fashion, that a great genius was wasting unequaled talents, without either patronage or praise, among people **who call** themselves enlightened.  **Old** Mr. Sheridan distinguished himself early **in** the list **of admirers, and asserted** that Mrs. Siddons was more pathetic **even than** Mrs. Cibber.  The prophecy of Henderson, too, was remembered, and the tide of popularity soon flowed in a stream, which was never destined to ebb.  **A** few eddies from occasional obstructions, **adds** the enthusiastic Boaden, to carry on **the** figure, hardly **merit to be** formally remembered.

**Her** second appearance at **Drury** Lane, in Southern's tragedy **of Isabella,** is thus referred **to** in her autobiographical **Memoranda** : "On the evening of the second rehearsal **I was** seized with a nervous hoarseness, which **made** me extremely wretched ; for I dreaded being obliged **to** defer my appearance, longing, as I most earnestly **did,** at least to know the worst.  I went to bed, **therefore, in a** state of dreadful suspense.  Awaking **the next morn**ing, however, though out of restless, **unrefreshing sleep, I found,** upon speaking to my husband, **that** my **voice was** very much clearer.  This, of **course, was a great comfort** to me ; and, moreover, the **sun,** which had been completely **obscured for many days, shone** brightly through **my curtains.**  I hailed **it, though tearfully, yet** thankfully, **as a** happy omen ; and even **now I am not** ashamed of **this (as** it may perhaps be called) childish superstition. **On the morning** of the 10th, my voice was, most happily, **perfectly restored,** and again 'the blessed sun shone brightly **on me.'**  On this eventful day my father arrived to comfort me, and to be a witness of my trial.  **He ac**companied me to my dressing-room at the theatre.  **There** he left me ; and **I, in one** of what I call my **desperate** tranquillities, which usually impress me under terrific cir**cumstances,** there completed my dress, **to the** astonish**ment of** my attendants, without uttering **one** word, though **often sighing** most profoundly.  **At length I** was called **to my fiery trial.**  **I found my venerable** father behind the scenes, little less agitated than myself. The awful consciousness that one is the sole object of attention to that immense space, lined as it were with human intellects from top to bottom, and all around, may perhaps be imagined, but can never be described, and by me can never be forgotten. Of the general effect of this night's performance I need not speak ; it has already been publicly recorded. I reached my own quiet fireside on retiring from the scene of reiterated shouts and plaudits. I was half dead ; and my joy and thankfulness were of too solemn and overpowering a nature to admit of words, or even tears. My father, my husband, and myself, sat down to a frugal, neat supper, in a silence uninterrupted, except by exclamations of gladness from Mr. Siddons. My father enjoyed his refreshments ; but occasionally stopped short, and laying down his knife and fork, lifting up his venerable face, and throwing back his silver hair, gave way to tears of happiness. We soon parted for the night ; and I, worn out with continually broken rest and laborious exertion, after an hour's retrospection (who can conceive the intenseness of that reverie ?) fell into a sweet and profound sleep, which lasted to the middle of the next day."

At one of her rehearsals, previous to her night of triumph at Drury Lane, an incident occurred which, though trifling enough, must have afforded her great encouragement. Her little boy, who was to be her little child in the piece, was so affected by her acting that he took the whole for reality, and burst into the most passionate flood of tears, thinking he was about to lose his mamma. This satisfactory proof of effect, it is said, deeply impressed the actors and managers, and Sheridan had the story conveyed to friendly newspapers.

Not long after, she sat for her portrait, as Isabella, to the distinguished artist Hamilton. Her immense popularity, we are told, was now shown, in the general enthusiasm to see her picture, even when it was scarcely finished. Carriages thronged the artist's door ; and, if every fine lady who stepped out of them did not actually weep before the painting, they had all of them, at least, their white handkerchiefs ready for that demonstration of their sensibility.

Notwithstanding all these evidences of her popularity, the critics, as usual, were slow to credit her with lasting excellence. Russell, the author of the History of Modern Europe, published a poem called The Tragic Muse, in which he complimented Mrs. Siddons. He was severely reproved by the critics for " wasting his verse upon excellence that was in its nature fugitive, the meteor of the moment."

In the height of her popularity she was obliged to decline all invitations to parties, routs, etc., preferring to give herself up to study, and to the duties of her family. On one occasion, at the house of a Scotch lady of high rank, but somewhat eccentric, she was conversing with three or four ladies of her acquaintance, " when," she says, " incessantly repeated thunderings at the door, and the sudden influx of such a throng of people as I had never before seen collected in any private house, counteracted every attempt that I could make for escape. I was therefore obliged, in a state of indescribable mortification, to sit quietly down, till I know not what hour in the morning ; but for hours before my departure, the room I sat in was so painfully crowded, that the people absolutely stood on the chairs, round the walls, that they might look over their neighbors' heads to stare at me ; and if it had not been for the benevolent politeness of Mr. Erskine, who had been acquainted with my arrangement (to meet a few friends only), I know not what weakness I might have been surprised into."

No actress, we are assured, was ever so gratified by the warmth of personal friendships, with attentions from persons of consideration, as Mrs. Siddons, and these were not by way of patronage, but from a sincere pleasure in her society, and respect for her character. She was to be met at Strawberry Hill, and in such company as Louis Philippe, and the Prince Regent. The latter often invited her to the Pavilion at Brighton.

A lady described to Mr. Fitzgerald a little scene which happened when she herself was very young, and when she had been taken to see "the great Mrs. Siddons." The child long after recalled the wonderful eyes, and particularly the long, silky eyelashes, which she noticed were of extraordinary length, and curled upwards in a beautiful curve. The actress was very good-natured; and on being told that the young girl was obliged to go away to the country, and would have no opportunity of seeing her, with much good-nature, she at once kindly said that the little girl should not be disappointed — that she would act for her there and then, and at once proceeded to recite from Milton and Shakespeare in her finest manner.

Boaden was present at the first appearance of Mrs. Siddons as Jane Shore. He describes the effect of her acting in that part as truly overpowering, especially at the end of the piece. I well remember, he says, (how is it possible I should ever forget?) the sobs, the shrieks, among the tender part of her audience; or those tears, which manhood at first struggled to suppress, but at length grew proud of indulging. We then, indeed, knew all the luxury of grief; but the nerves of many a gentle being gave way before the intensity of such appeals; and fainting fits, long and frequent, alarmed the decorum of the house, filled almost to suffocation.

The mother of Lord Byron, being at the Edinburgh Theatre one night, when the character of Isabella was performed by Mrs. Siddons, was so affected by the powers of the great actress, that, toward the conclusion of the play, she fell into violent fits, and was carried out of the theatre, screaming.

Her success in Ireland was very great, and in Scotland also ; but her reception there was very different. " I remember," says Campbell, " Mrs. Siddons describing to me the scene of her probation on the Edinburgh boards with no small humor. The grave attention of my Scottish countrymen, and their canny reservation of praise till they were sure she deserved it, she said had well-nigh worn out her patience. She had been used to speak to animated clay ; but she now felt as if she had been speaking to stones. Successive flashes of her elocution, that had always been sure to electrify the South, fell in vain on those Northern flints. At last, as I well remember, she told me she coiled up her powers to the most emphatic possible utterance of one passage, having previously vowed in her heart, that if this could not touch the Scotch, she would never again cross the Tweed. When it was finished, she paused, and looked to the audience. The deep silence was broken only by a single voice exclaiming, 'That 's no bad !' This ludicrous parsimony of praise convulsed the Edinburgh audience with laughter. But the laugh was followed by such thunders of applause, that amid her stunned and nervous agitation she was not without fears of the galleries coming down."

The good fortune of Mrs. Siddons, we are told, was seconded by her prudence ; she launched into no unnecessary expense ; to be herself any where implied sufficient consequence. She had genteel lodgings in the Strand ; was at the theatre in a few minutes ; and full of the best inspiration, a mother's feeling for her family, she prepared herself for a life of such exertion as even mocks the toil of mere manual art.

To give some idea of her laborious life, it may be stated that during her second season in London she acted Isabella seven times ; Mrs. Beverley, seven also ; Belvi-

dera and Lady Randolph, six times each ; Shakespeare's
Isabella and Thomson's Sigismunda, five times each ;
Euphrasia and Constance, four ; Jane Shore and the
Countess of Salisbury, three ; Zara, in the Mourning
Bride, two ; Calista, one.  In one season alone (1784–5)
she appeared seventy-one times, in as many as seventeen
different characters.  Dr. Franklin was one of her ad-
miring auditors.

The expenditure of intellect and passion in her powerful parts was prodigious.  In her personation of Constance, in King John, one familiar with her acting said
that he could point out the passages where her vicissi-   ·
tudes of hurried and deliberate gesture would have made
you imagine that her very body seemed to think.  Her
elocution varied its tones from the height of vehemence
to the lowest despondency, with an eagle-like power of
stooping and soaring, and with the rapidity of thought.
Miss Kelly told Crabb Robinson that when, as Constance,
Mrs. Siddons wept over her, her collar was wet with the
great actress' tears.  "The recollection of Mrs. Siddons
as Constance," says Robinson, "is an enjoyment in itself.
I remember one scene in particular, where, throwing herself on the ground, she calls herself 'The Queen of Sorrow,' and bids Kings come and worship her !"  He saw
her in 1811, then an old woman, in her part as Margaret
of Anjou in the play of The Earl of Warwick.  "In the
last act," he says, "her triumphant joy at the entrance of
Warwick, whom she had stabbed, was incomparable.
She laughed convulsively, and staggered off the stage as
if drunk with delight ; and in every limb showed the tu-
mult of passion.  As an actress she has left me the conviction that there never was and never will be, her equal."
In 1828 he notes reading Boaden's Life of Mrs. Siddons,
which recalled "the yet unfaded image of that most marvelous woman, to think of whom is now a greater enjoyment than to see any other actress."

Her rich emotional nature was easily aroused, and promptly responded to every phase of feeling. "During Henderson's readings from Sterne, I personally witnessed," says Campbell, "his power over the feelings of Mrs. Siddons; and the pathetic chapters of Shandy excited no few tears from the brightest eyes that I have ever seen. His alternations of humor and tenderness kept her in the situation of her own Cordelia.

> 'You have seen
> Sunshine and rain at once; her smiles and tears
> Were like, a better way. Those happy smiles
> That play'd on her ripe lip, seem'd not to know
> What guests were in her eyes, which parted thence
> As pearls from diamonds dropp'd.'"

On one occasion, after her sublime impersonation of Queen Katharine, in Henry the Eighth, she indulged her friends with a recitation of Collins' Ode to the Passions.

She has been charged with the habit of attaching dramatic tones and emphasis to commonplace colloquial subjects. She went, it is said, one day, into a shop at Bath, and after bargaining for some calico, and hearing the mercer put forth a hundred commendations of the cloth, she put the question to him, "But will it wash?" in a manner so electrifying as to make the poor shopman start back from his counter.

Moore once told a like story of her. A large party was invited to meet her. She remained silent, as was her wont, and disappointed the expectations of the whole company, who watched for every syllable that should escape her lips. At length, however, being asked if she would have some Burton's ale, she replied, with a sepulchral intonation, that she "liked ale vastly." This anecdote being told to Mr. Maturin, he said, "The voice of Mrs. Siddons, like St. Paul's bell, should never toll except for the death of kings."

In Lockhart's Life of Scott it is written that Mrs. Siddons, at the table of Sir Walter, in an eminently tragic voice, addressed a servant: "I asked for water, boy; you 've brought me beer!"

The biographer of Irving states that not long after The Sketch Book had been published in London, and made its author remarked among its literary circles, he met Mrs. Siddons in some fashionable assemblage, and was brought up to be introduced. The Queen of Tragedy had then long left the stage, but her manner and tones to the last, partook of its measured stateliness. The interview was characteristic. As he approached and was introduced, she looked at him for a moment, and then, in her clear and deep-toned voice, she slowly enunciated, "You 've made me weep." After the appearance of his Bracebridge Hall, he met her in company again, and was asked by a friend to be presented. He told him he had before gone through that ceremony, but he had been so abashed by her address, and acquitted himself so shabbily, that he was afraid to claim acquaintance. Come then with me, said his friend, and I will stand by you; so he went forward, and singularly enough, was met with an address of the self-same fashion: "You 've made me weep again."

Her manner, even at the social board, partook of the state and gravity of tragedy. Not that there was an unwillingness to unbend, but that there was a difficulty in throwing aside the solemnity of long-acquired habit. She reminded Irving's brother Peter, who dined with her at the poet Campbell's, of Walter Scott's knights, who "carved the meal with their gloves of steel, and drank the red wine through their helmets barred."

"It was a proud moment for Haydon," says Talfourd, in his Life and Letters of Lamb, "when at the opening of his Exhibition of the Entry into Jerusalem, while the crowd of visitors, distinguished in rank or talent, stood doubting whether in the countenance of the chief figure the daring **attempt to** present an aspect differing from that which **had enkindled** the devotion of ages — to **min-**gle the human **with** the Divine, resolution with **sweetness,** dignified composure with the anticipation of mighty **suf-**fering — had not failed, Mrs. Siddons walked slowly **up to** the centre of the room, surveyed it in silence **for a** minute or two, and then ejaculated **in her** deep, low, thrilling voice, ' It is perfect ! ' quelled **all** opposition, and removed the doubt from his own mind, **at least,** forever."

What peculiar **emphasis she must have** put into her words, **when the** curtain fell, at **the** end of a most un-pleasant **engagement** at Leeds ! **She** had suffered every annoyance **from** the audience ; but one of a very ludi-**crous** and distressing nature occurred, for which no part **of** the auditory was answerable. There is an amusing account of it in the Memoirs of Mathews. The **evening** was excessively hot, and Mrs. **Siddons was tempted by a** torturing thirst **to** consent to avail **herself of the only ob-**tainable relief proposed to her **at the moment. Her** dresser, therefore, despatched a boy in great **haste to** "fetch a pint of beer for Mrs. Siddons," **at the same** time charging **him** to be **quick,** as Mrs. Siddons was in a hurry for **it.** Meanwhile the **play** proceeded, and on the boy's return with the frothed pitcher, he looked about **for** the person who had sent him on **his** errand ; and not **seeing** her, inquired, " Where is Mrs. Siddons ? " The scene-shifter whom he questioned, pointing his finger to the stage where she was performing the sleeping scene **of** Lady Macbeth, replied, **" There** she is." To the surprise and horror of all the performers, the boy promptly **walked** on the stage close up to Mrs. Siddons, and **with a** total unconsciousness of the impropriety he **was** committing, presented the beer ! Her distress **may be** imagined ; she waved the boy away in her grand manner several times, without effect ; at last the people behind the scenes, by **dint of** beckoning, **stamping, and calling** in half-audible whispers, succeeded in getting him off with the beer, part of which in his exit he spilled on the stage ; while the audience were in an uproar of laughter, which the dignity of the actress was unable to quell for several minutes. It was natural that Mrs. Siddons should be disgusted with her engagement at Leeds ; and on the dropping of the curtain at the close of her last night's performance, she clasped her hands in thankfulness, ejaculating in her most tragic tones, "Farewell, ye brutes! and for ever, I trust : ye shall never torture me again, be assured."

The death of her father and of her eldest daughter had a terrible and lasting effect upon her. Suffering from the shock of these events, she wisely and profoundly wrote : "The testimony of the wisdom of all ages, from the foundation of the world to this day, is childishness and folly, if happiness be any thing more than a name ; and I am assured our own experience will not enable us to refute the opinion : no, no, it is the inhabitant of a better world. Content, the offspring of Moderation, is all we ought to aspire to here, and Moderation will be our best and surest guide to that happiness to which she will most assuredly conduct us."

Sir Joshua Reynolds often honored her with his presence at the theatre. He, it is said, always sat in the orchestra ; and in that place were to be seen Burke, Gibbon, Sheridan, Windham, and the illustrious Fox, of whom it was frequently said, that iron tears were drawn down Pluto's gloomy cheeks. Often she was heard to boast of the times when every other day she had a note or a visit from Sir Joshua Reynolds, from Mrs. Piozzi, or from Erskine, Burke, Sheridan, or Malone. Erskine, the greatest pleader of his age, said that her performance was a school for orators, — that he had studied her cadences and intonations, and that to the harmony of her periods and pronunciation he was indebted for "his best displays."

" I had frequently," she says, "the honor of dining with Sir Joshua Reynolds, in Leicester Square. At his house was assembled all the good, the wise, the talented, the rank and fashion of the age. About this time he produced his picture of me," she says, " in the character of the Tragic Muse. In justice to his genius, I cannot but remark his instantaneous decision of the attitude and expression of the picture. It was, in fact, decided within the twinkling of an eye. When I attended him for the first sitting, after more gratifying encomiums than I can now repeat, he took me by the hand, saying, ' Ascend yon undisputed throne, and graciously bestow upon me some good idea of the Tragic Muse.' I walked up the steps, and instantly seated myself in the attitude in which the Tragic Muse now appears. This idea satisfied him so well, that without one moment's hesitation he determined not to alter it. . . . I was delighted when he assured me that he was certain the colors would remain unfaded as long as the canvas would keep them together, which, unhappily, has not been the case with all his works: he gallantly added, with his own benevolent smile, ' And, to confirm my opinion, here is my name ; for I have resolved to go down to posterity on the hem of your garment.' Accordingly it appears upon the corner of the drapery."

It would not do to omit the description of her memorable call upon Dr. Johnson. " I do not exactly remember the time," she says in her Memoranda, " that I was favored with an invitation from Dr. Johnson, but I think it was during the first year of my celebrity. The Doctor was then a wretched invalid, and had requested my friend Mr. Windham to persuade me to favor him by drinking tea with him in Bolt Court. . . . The Doctor's favorite female character in Shakespeare was Katharine, in Henry VIII. He was most desirous of seeing me in that play ; but said, ' I am too deaf and too blind to see or hear it at a greater distance than the stage-box, and have little taste for making myself a public gaze, in so distinguished a situation.' I assured him that nothing would gratify me so much as to have him for an auditor, and that I could procure for him an easy-chair at the stage-door, where he would both see and hear, and be perfectly concealed. He appeared greatly pleased with this arrangement, but, unhappily for me, he did not live to fulfill our mutual wishes. Some weeks before he died I made him some morning visits. He was extremely, though formally, polite; always apologized for being unable to attend me to my carriage; conducted me to the head of the stairs, kissed my hand, and bowing, said, 'Dear madam, I am your most humble servant;' and these were always repeated without the slightest variation."

At one of these visits of Mrs Siddons to Dr. Johnson, Frank, the Doctor's servant, could not immediately provide the distinguished visitor with a chair. "You see, madam," said Johnson, "wherever you go there are no seats to be got."

Mrs. Siddons sometimes went to the theatre to see others act, but it was remarked that she always paid the greatest attention to the performance ; that she did not, like some others, sit remarkably forward, and, so to speak, throw her whole person into the lap of the audience, under the pretext of applauding strongly those whom she admired. She never applauded at all, and this was judicious. She was sitting with their judges and hers.

In acting, she seemed to forget herself wholly in her part. "It must have happened to her," said a critical contemporary, "as to every other being engaged in the concerns of life, to feel depressed by care, or absent by the rumination over probable occurrences. But on the stage, I never felt the least indication that she had a private existence, or could be any thing but the assumed character."

"When Mrs. Siddons quitted her dressing-room," says the same observing authority, " I believe she left there the last thought about herself. Never did I see her eye wander from the business of the scene — no recognizance of the most noble of her friends exchanged the character for the individual."

Mrs. Siddons' health was certainly very feeble during the winter and spring of 1804–5, and she performed only twice at Covent Garden in the whole course of the season. "Yet I suspect," says her biographer, " that bad health was not the only cause of her absence from the stage. This was the season when Master Betty made his first appearance on the London boards, and was equally the magnet of attraction at each of the great theatres. The popularity of that baby-faced boy, who possessed not even the elements of a good actor, was a hallucination in the public mind, and a disgrace to theatrical history. It enabled managers to give him sums for his childish ranting that were never accorded to the acting of a Garrick or a Siddons. His bust was cut in marble by the best sculptors ; he was painted by Opie and Northcote ; and the verses that were poured out upon him were in a style of idolatrous admiration." The young Roscius, as Master Betty was called, whom, at Belfast, Mrs. Siddons had inspired with an irresistible passion for tragedy, carried the public of London by storm, the multitude neglecting even the great actress herself for the youthful prodigy. But, making his fortune the first season, he was sent to college, and Mrs. Siddons again reigned supreme.

The last season but one (1810–11), she performed nearly the whole of her characters ; and never, it is said, did she display greater dignity and force of mind. In 1812 she was announced to appear in Lady Macbeth for the last time. The following year, however, she appeared in that part for the benefit of her brother Charles. In the year 1816 she performed Katharine once more, for the same object ; and consented to repeat her Lady Macbeth to gratify the Princess Charlotte, and her Royal Consort of Saxe-Coburg.

She gave public readings from Shakespeare at the Argyll Rooms, during two seasons, "from the two-fold inducements of personal gratification and an important addition to her income," which were now necessary to support her appropriately. " A large red screen formed what painters would call a background to the figure of the charming reader. She was dressed in white, and her dark hair, à la Grecque, crossed her temples in full masses. Behind the screen a light was placed ; and, as the head moved, a bright circular irradiation seemed to wave around its outline, which gave to a classic mind the impression, that the priestess of Apollo stood before you, uttering the inspiration of the deity, in immortal verse."

Joanna Baillie dined with Mrs. Siddons, in company with the poet Rogers and his sister. The great actress was now an old woman. " We expected," said the poetess, " to see much decay in her powers of expression, and consequently to have our pleasure mingled with pain. Judge then of our delight when we heard her read the best scenes of Hamlet, with expression of countenance, voice, and action, that would have done honor to her best days ! She was before us as an unconquerable creature, over whose astonishing gifts of nature Time had no power. At the end of the reading, Rogers said, ' Oh, that we could have assembled a company of young people to witness this, that they might have conveyed the memory of it down to another generation.' "

Campbell had once by chance the honor of seeing Mrs. Siddons and the Duke of Wellington in the same party at Paris. They were observed, after a first mutual recognizance, to stand by each other without conversing. She had very little light conversation in mixed company for any body, but when her heart was interested, she was very condescending, and would exert herself to please. She doted upon children. Some time after the poet had seen her in Paris, he visited her, with his son, who was then about six years old. He had to leave the child with her for about an hour, and in his absence he had some misgivings that it was unfair to have taxed her with the company of so young a visitant. But when he came back, he found the little fellow's face lighted up in earnest conversation with her. She had been amusing him with stories adapted to his capacity, and bestowed attentions on a child which she had refused to a conqueror.

## III.

## DOCTOR JOHNSON.

IT is impossible to think of Doctor Johnson without being struck with his prodigiousness. He was extraordinary in every way: in his mind and in his body, in his wisdom and in his prejudices, in his learning and in his superstitions, in his piety and in his bigotry: there was nothing ordinary about him. All descriptions of him are nearly alike, all impressions much the same. However excellent or mean the artist or the biographer, the picture is recognized; there is no mistaking the great lexicographer, the imperial talker; the man and the character stand before you.

In **St.** Mary's Square, Lichfield, there is a statue of "the mighty sage." "The figure," says Hawthorne, "is colossal (though perhaps not much more so than the mountainous Doctor himself). . . . The statue is immensely massive, a vast ponderosity of stone, not finely spiritualized, nor, indeed, fully humanized, but rather resembling a great stone-bowlder than a man."

Boswell's book has done more for Johnson, in the judgment of Macaulay, than the best of his own books could do. "The memory of other authors is kept alive by their works. But the memory of Johnson keeps many of his works alive. The old philosopher is still among us in the brown coat with the metal buttons and the shirt which ought to be at wash, blinking, puffing, rolling his head, drumming with his fingers, tearing his meat like a tiger, and swallowing his tea in oceans."

"To have seen such a man as Johnson," said Dr. Campbell, "was a thing to talk of a century hence."

"His person," says Lord Pembroke, "was large, robust, I may say, approaching to the gigantic, and grown unwieldy from corpulency. His countenance was naturally of the cast of an ancient statue, but somewhat disfigured by the scars of that evil, which, it was formerly imagined, the royal touch could cure. He was now [when he started on his tour to the Hebrides] in his sixty-fourth year, and was become a little dull of hearing. . . . His head, and sometimes also his body, shook with a kind of motion like the effect of a palsy : he appeared to be frequently disturbed by cramps, or convulsive contractions, of the nature of that distemper called St. Vitus' dance. He wore a full suit of plain brown clothes, with twisted hair-buttons of the same color, a large bushy grayish wig, a plain shirt, black worsted stockings, and silver buckles. Upon this tour, when journeying, he wore boots, and a very wide brown cloth great coat, with pockets which might almost have held the two volumes of his folio dictionary, and he carried in his hand a large English oak-stick."

The great oak-stick that he had brought from London he lost in the Hebrides. It had, we are informed, the properties of a measure ; for one nail was driven into it at the length of a foot ; another at that of a yard. In return for the services it had done him, he said he would make a present of it to some museum ; but he little thought he was so soon to lose it. As he preferred riding with a switch, it was intrusted to a fellow to be delivered to the baggage-man, who followed at some distance ; but he never saw it more. "I could not," said his friend, "persuade him out of a suspicion that it had been stolen. 'No, no, my friend,' said he ; 'it is not to be expected that any man in Mull, who has got it, will part with it. Consider, sir, the value of such a piece of timber here!'"

Madame D'Arblay describes him as "tall, stout, grand, and authoritative : but he stoops horribly ; his back is quite round: his mouth is continually opening and shutting, as if he were chewing something ; he has a singular method of twirling his fingers, and twisting his hands: his vast body is in constant agitation, see-sawing backward and forward: his feet are never a moment quiet; and his whole great person looked often as if it were going to roll itself, quite voluntarily, from his chair to the floor."

He held his head to one side, we are told, toward his right shoulder, and shook it in a tremulous manner, moving his body backward and forward, and rubbing his left knee in the same direction with the palm of his hand. In the intervals of articulating, he made various sounds with his mouth ; sometimes as if ruminating, or what is called chewing the cud, sometimes giving a half whistle, sometimes making his tongue play backward from the roof of his mouth, as if chuckling like a hen, and sometimes protruding it against his upper gums in front, as if pronouncing quickly under his breath, too, too, too, all this accompanied sometimes with a thoughtful look, but more frequently with a smile. Generally when he had concluded a period, in the course of a dispute, by which time he was a good deal exhausted by violence and vociferation, he used to blow out his breath like a whale. He was very near-sighted, and his big wig was often a good deal singed in consequence.

As a boy he was overgrown, if not monstrous. A lady once consulted him on the degree of turpitude to be attached to her son's robbing an orchard. " Madam," said Johnson, "it all depends upon the weight of the boy. David Garrick, who was always a little fellow, robbed a dozen of orchards with impunity; but the very first time I climbed up an apple-tree — for I was always a heavy boy — the bough broke with me, and it was called judgment. I suppose that is why Justice is represented with a pair of scales." This, it must be remembered, is in

Hood's Johnsoniana ; but it seems too characteristic and natural to be wholly apocryphal.

He is described as " a robust genius, born to grapple with whole libraries." When a child, in petticoats, he got by heart the Collect for the day from the Common Prayer-book, and repeated it distinctly, though he had read it but twice. While yet a boy, during the first interview with a tutor, in the presence of grave professors, he quoted Macrobius, to the astonishment of the company. About the same time, after a violent attack of his disorder, he communicated the state of his case to his physician, in Latin, who was struck with the "extraordinary acuteness, research and eloquence " of the paper.

It is easy for us to see him, as he has been described to us, at table. He was totally absorbed in the business of the moment ; his looks seemed riveted to his plate ; nor would he, unless in very high company, say one word, or even pay the least attention to what was said by others, till he had satisfied his appetite, which was so fierce, and indulged with such intenseness, that while in the act of eating, the veins of his forehead swelled, and generally a strong perspiration was visible. In eating and drinking he could refrain, but he could not use moderately. Every thing about his character and manners, it is stated, was forcible and violent ; there never was any moderation ; many a day did he fast, many a year did he refrain from wine ; but when he did eat, it was voraciously ; when he did drink wine, it was copiously. He could practice abstinence, but not temperance. He told Boswell that he had fasted two days without inconvenience, and that he had never been hungry but once. " Early in life," he said to Edwards, " I drank wine : for many years I drank none. I then, for several years, drank a great deal." " Some hogsheads, I warrant you," responded Edwards, daringly, and was uncontradicted. " I did not," he said, on another occasion, "leave off wine because I could not bear it. I have drunk three bottles of port without being the worse for it." We all know how copiously he drank tea at Thrale's. Sixteen cups, was it not, that he drank at a sitting?

He said when he lodged in the Temple, and had no regular system of life, he had fasted for two days at a time, during which he had gone about visiting, though not at the hours of dinner or supper; that he had drank tea, but he had eaten no bread: that this was no intentional fasting, but happened just in the course of a literary life. He closes one of his letters to Cave, "I am, sir, yours, impransus, Sam Johnson." Meaning, without breakfast. No wonder he speaks of his life, in a letter to Mrs. Thrale, as "diversified by misery, spent part in the sluggishness of penury, and part under the violence of pain, in gloomy discontent or importunate distress."

In the midst of his own distresses and pains, we are assured, he was ever compassionate to the distresses of others, and actively earnest in procuring them aid. In a note to Sir Joshua Reynolds he says: "I am ashamed to ask for some relief for a poor man, to whom, I hope, I have given what I can be expected to spare. The man importunes me and the blow goes round."

During the visit of the "Ursa Major" (as Johnson was called by Boswell's father) to the Parliament House in Edinburgh, a brother of Lord Erskine, after being presented to him by Boswell, and having made his bow, slipped a shilling into Boswell's hand, whispering that it was for the sight of his bear. "Johnson, to be sure," says Goldsmith, "has a roughness in his manner; but no man alive has a more tender heart. He has nothing of the bear but his skin."

"What a humanity the old man had!" exclaims Thackeray. "He was a kindly partaker of all honest pleasures: a fierce foe to all sin, but a gentle enemy to all sinners. 'What, boys, are you for a frolic?' he cries, when Topham **Beauclerk comes** and wakes him up at **midnight:** 'I 'm **with you.' And** away he goes, tumbles **on his** homely **old clothes,** and trundles through Covent Garden **with** the young fellows. When he used to frequent **Garrick's** theatre, and had 'the liberty **of** the **scenes, all** the actresses,' he says, **'knew me,** and dropped me **a** courtesy as they passed **to** the stage.' "

What Erasmus said of Luther may **with the** same propriety **be** said of Johnson — there **were two** natures in him. **There is** a story that **as Johnson was** riding in a **carriage through** London on a rainy day, he overtook a poor **woman** carrying a baby, without any protection from **the weather. Making** the driver stop the coach, he invited the poor woman to get in with her child, **which she did.** After she **had** seated herself, **the** Doctor said **to her,** "My good woman, I think it most likely that **the motion** of the coach **will** wake your child in **a** little while, and **I** wish you to understand **that if you talk any baby-**talk **to it,** you will have to get out **of the coach." As** the **Doctor** had anticipated, the **child soon awoke, and** the forgetful mother exclaimed **to it:** "Oh! **the** little dear, is he going to open his eyesy-pysy?" "Stop the **coach,** driver!" shouted Johnson; **and the woman** had to **get** out **and finish** her journey **on foot. What** occurred **when he went with** his sweetheart, Mrs. Porter, to Derby **on horseback to** be married, **is** familiar to every one at **all** acquainted **with** his history. Here is his own account of their journey **to** church **on** the nuptial morn: "Sir, she had read the **old** romances, and had got into her head the fantastical notion that a woman of spirit should **use** her lover like a dog. So, sir, at first, she told me that I rode too fast, and she could not keep **up with me;** and, **when I** rode a little slower, she passed **me, and** com-**plained** that I lagged behind. I was not **to be** made the **slave of caprice; and** I resolved to begin **as I** meant to **end. I therefore pushed on briskly, till I was** fairly out of her sight.  The road lay between two hedges, so I was sure she could not miss it ; and I contrived that she should soon come up with me.  When she did, I observed her to be in tears."  This, be it remembered, just before what he declared to be "a love marriage on both sides !"

His melancholy was sometimes very distressing.  One of his friends found him, on one occasion, in a deplorable state — "sighing, groaning, talking to himself, and restlessly walking from room to room.  He then used this emphatical expression of the misery he felt : 'I would consent to have a limb amputated to recover my spirits.'"  Being asked if he was really of opinion that, though in general happiness was very rare in human life, a man was not sometimes happy in the moment that was present, he answered, "Never, but when he is drunk."  A lady once said to him that she could not understand why men got drunk ; she wondered how a man could find pleasure in making a beast of himself ; and Johnson said, "He who makes a beast of himself gets rid of the pain of being a man."

We have the authority of Miss Reynolds for stating that, for the diversion of his mind, he would sometimes climb pretty large trees, and that when he was between fifty and sixty years old.  When he felt his fancy, or fancied that he felt it, disordered, his constant recurrence, says Mrs. Piozzi, was to the study of arithmetic ; and one day that he was totally confined to his chamber, and she inquired what he had been doing to divert himself, he showed her a calculation which she could scarce be made to understand, so vast was the plan of it, and so very intricate were the figures : no other, indeed, than that the National Debt, computing it at one hundred and eighty millions sterling, would, if converted into silver, serve to make a meridian of that metal, she forgot how broad (to use her own language), "for the globe of the whole earth."

His great resource of reading was generally effectual
in quieting his mind and passions when most depressed
or turbulent. An instance of his voracious reading is
given by his biographer. Before dinner Doctor Johnson seized upon Mr. Charles Sheridan's Account of the
Late Revolution in Sweden, and seemed to read it raven-
ously, as if he devoured it. " He knows how to read
better than any one," said Mr. Knowles; " he gets at the
substance of a book directly; he tears out the heart of
it." He kept it wrapped up in the table-cloth, in his lap,
during the time of dinner, from an avidity to have one
entertainment in readiness when he should have finished
another; resembling (if one may use so coarse a simile)
a dog who holds a bone in his paws in reserve, while he
eats something else which has been thrown to him.

Tate Wilkinson, in his Memoirs, relates that Johnson,
being with Foote, Holland, Woodward, and others, at a
party at Mr. Garrick's villa at Hampton, as they were
conversing on different subjects, fell into a reverie, from
which his attention was drawn by the accidentally casting
his eyes on a book-case, to which he was as naturally attracted as the needle to the pole : on perusing the title-
pages of the best bound, he muttered inwardly with in-
effable contempt, but proceeded on his exploring business
of observation, ran his finger down the middle of each
page, and then dashed the volume disdainfully upon the
floor, the which Garrick beheld with much wonder and
vexation, while the most profound silence and attention
was bestowed on the learned Doctor; but when he saw
his twentieth well-bound book thus manifestly disgraced
on the ground, and expecting his whole valuable collec-
tion would share the same fate, he could no longer restrain himself, but suddenly cried out most vociferously, —
" Why, d——n it, Doctor, you, you, you will destroy all
my books !" At this, Johnson raised his head, paused,
fixed his eyes, and replied, "Lookee, David, you do understand plays, but you know nothing about books ! "

His personal courage was prodigious. He would beat large dogs that were fighting, till they separated. To prove that a gun would not burst if charged with many balls, he put in six or seven, and fired it off against a wall. One night he was attacked in the street by four men, all of whom he kept at bay till relieved by the watch. A man, having taken possession of his seat between the side-scenes, and refusing to give it up, was tossed by the mad philosopher, chair and all, into the pit. Foote had resolved to ridicule him on the stage, but changed his mind when he heard that Johnson had been inquiring of Tom Davies, the bookseller, the price of oak-sticks. "I am told that Foote means to take me off, as he calls it, and I am determined the fellow shall not do it with impunity." He had sometime before knocked down Osborne with a folio, and put his foot upon his neck. "Sir, he was impertinent to me, and I beat him." His defiant letter to Macpherson shows how utterly impossible it was to intimidate him.

Yet he had a great horror of death. He said he never had a moment in which death was not terrible to him. Being told that Dr. Dodd seemed willing to die, and full of hopes of happiness, "Sir," said he, "Dr. Dodd would have given both his hands and both his legs to have lived. The better a man is, the more he is afraid of death, having a clearer view of infinite purity."

He defended prize-fighting. "I am sorry," he said, "that prize-fighting is gone out. Every art should be preserved, and the art of defense is surely important. Prize-fighting made people accustomed not to be alarmed at seeing their own blood, or feeling a little pain from a wound."

He hated gross flattery. When Hannah More was introduced to him she began singing his praise in the warmest manner, and continued in such an extravagant strain, that he turned suddenly to her, with a stern and angry countenance, and said, " Madam, before you flatter a man so grossly to his face, you should consider whether or not your flattery is worth his having."

Yet he thought himself very polite. Speaking of Dr. Barnard, the provost of Eton, he said, " Barnard was the only man that did justice to my good-breeding : and you may observe that I am well-bred to a degree of needless scrupulosity. No man," continued he, not observing the amazement of his hearers, "no man is so cautious not to interrupt another ; no man thinks it so necessary to appear attentive when others are speaking ; no man so steadily refuses preference to himself, or so willingly bestows it on another, as I do ; nobody holds so strongly as I do the necessity of ceremony, and the ill-effects which follow the breach of it : yet people think me rude ; but Barnard did me justice."

Boswell said that though Johnson might be charged with bad humor at times, he was always a good-natured man ; and Reynolds remarked, that when upon any occasion Johnson had been rough to any person in company, he took the first opportunity of reconciliation, by drinking to him, or addressing his discourse to him ; but if he found his dignified indirect overtures sullenly neglected, he was quite indifferent, and considered himself as having done all that he ought to do, and the other as now in the wrong.

Polite or not, he certainly excelled in compliment when he saw fit to indulge in it. His compliment to the wife of his friend Dr. Beattie is one of the prettiest we remember. It occurs in a grave letter to a friend, and is as follows : " Of Dr. Beattie I should have thought much, but that his lady put him out of my head ; she is a very lovely woman."

His royal treatment of Mrs. Siddons will be recollected by every admirer of that magnificent woman. He was an old man and a wretched invalid when the great actress became celebrated. He asked her in the most respectful and complimentary way to drink tea with him in Bolt Court. He lamented to her that his infirmities prevented him from seeing her in his favorite female character, Katharine, in Henry VIII. Some weeks before he died she made him some morning visits. He was extremely, though formally polite; always apologized for being unable to attend her to her carriage; conducted her to the head of the stairs, kissed her hand, and bowing, said, "Dear madam, I am your most humble servant;" and these, she says, were always repeated without the slightest variation.

It was at one of these visits that Frank, the Doctor's servant, could not immediately provide the distinguished visitor with a chair. "You see, madam," said Johnson, "wherever you go there are no seats to be got."

Best, in his Personal and Literary Memorials, relates this remarkable circumstance of Johnson: "After breakfast we walked to the top of a very steep hill. behind the house. When we arrived at the summit, Mr. Langton said, 'Poor dear Doctor Johnson, when he came to this spot, turned to look down the hill, and said he was determined to take a roll down. When we understood what he meant to do (said Langton) we endeavored to dissuade him; but he was resolute, saying he had not had a roll for a long time; and taking out of his lesser pockets whatever might be in them — keys, pencil, purse, or penknife — and laying himself parallel with the edge of the hill, he actually descended, turning himself over and over till he came to the bottom.' This story was told with such gravity, and with an air of such affectionate remembrance of a departed friend, that it was impossible to suppose this extraordinary freak of the great lexicographer to have been a picture or invention of Mr. Langton."

Such, it is asserted, was the heat and irritability of his

blood, that he pared his nails to the quick, and scraped the joints of his fingers with a penknife till they were red and raw. "There is no arguing with Johnson," were the words of Cibber, in one of his comedies, put, you remember, into the mouth of Goldsmith; "for when his pistol misses fire, he knocks you down with the but-end of it." Dr. Alexander McLean was so struck with his powerful conversation, that he observed, "This man is just a hogshead of sense." His laugh, too, was tremendous; not like the laugh of any other man. "He laughs," says Davies, "like a rhinoceros." Which reminds you of Hunt's observation upon the elephant: "The more you consider him, the more he makes good his claim to be considered the Doctor Johnson of the brute creation." When Hogarth first saw him, he thought he was an idiot; but when he heard him speak, he thought him inspired. Garrick said of his superlative powers of wit: "Rabelais and all the other wits are nothing, compared with him. You may be diverted by them; but Johnson gives you a forcible hug, and shakes laughter out of you, whether you will or no." Speaking of Garrick, how funny it must have been to the boys of the little school at Edial to see the future great actor, whose death, Johnson said, "eclipsed the gayety of nations, and impoverished the stock of harmless pleasures," take off the "tumultuous and awkward fondness" of their master for "Tetty," or "Tetsy," as he called his wife, — who was fat, fifty, and any thing but pretty.

That was an interesting view that Maxwell had of Johnson, when two young women visited him to consult on the subject of Methodism, to which they were inclined. It shows graphically another side of the great moralist. "Come," said he, "you pretty fools, dine with Maxwell and me at the Mitre, and we will talk over the subject;" which, said Maxwell, they did, and after dinner he took one of them upon his knee, and fondled her for half an hour together.

At the house of Lady Margaret MacDonald one of the married ladies, a lively, pretty little woman, good-humoredly sat down upon the Doctor's knee, and, being encouraged by some of the company, put her hands round his neck, and kissed him. "Do it again," said he, "and let us see who will tire first." He kept her on his knee some time, while he and she drank tea.

He was great in his self-respect, and his conduct during the famous interview with the King in the library of the Queen's house, proved that he could not, under any circumstances, be made to forget it. While he showed the profoundest respect for his majesty, his conversation was such as one gentleman would have with another. Dr. Hill, one of the King's favorites, was discussed and criticised, and the literary journals of the day were freely commented upon by both.

He had, every body knows, an extravagant regard for the hierarchy, and particularly for the dignitaries of the Church. That bow of his to the Archbishop of York, described by Mr. Seward, who witnessed it, was in character with the man, and was a thing to see. It was "such a studied elaboration of homage, such an extension of limb, such a flexion of body, as has seldom or ever been equaled." He once said that he who could entertain serious apprehensions of danger to the Church, would have "cried fire in the Deluge."

"I hold Johnson," said Thackeray, "to be the great supporter of the British monarchy and Church during the last age — better than whole benches of bishops, better than Pitts, Norths, and the great Burke himself. Johnson had the ear of the nation; his immense authority reconciled it to loyalty, and shamed it out of irreligion. When George III. talked with him, and the people heard the great author's good opinion of the sovereign, whole generations rallied to the King. Johnson was revered as a sort of oracle; and the oracle declared for Church and King."

His sense of justice, too, was generally very strong, and he supported it by his generosity. He had recommended, you remember, to Strahan, the printer, a poor boy from the country as an apprentice. Johnson, having inquired after him, said, " Mr. Strahan, let me have five guineas on account, and I 'll give this boy one. Nay, if a man recommends a boy, and does nothing for him, it is sad work. Call him down." The boy made his appearance, when Johnson gave him a guinea, and some good advice.

His charity and benevolence were unintermitted, and always beyond his means. Being asked by a lady why he so constantly gave money to beggars, he replied with great feeling, " Madam, to enable them to beg on." It was a common thing for him to empty his pockets when surrounded by beggars. We know how he took on his back the poor street-walker whom he found prostrate in the street, carried her to his home, and procured physician and nurse for her, and honorable employment. He filled up his house with a strange assortment of pensioners and dependents. Poor blind Mrs. Williams, the daughter of a Welsh physician ; Levett, " an odd little man who practiced medicine among the poorest of the poor, and often received his fees in liquor ;" Mrs. Desmoulins and her daughter, " who had no other claim upon his benevolence than the service which that lady's father, Dr. Swinfen, had rendered to Johnson in a professional capacity in his youth ;" and Francis Barber, his negro servant, were among the inmates of his house.

His prodigious pride is exhibited in his famous letter to Lord Chesterfield, — familiar to every reader, — in which he rejects the condescensions of the elegant would-be patron, and resents the seven years of cold indifference with which he had been treated. Carlyle, in his essay, characterizes it as " that far-famed Blast of Doom."

His capacity to acquire, and his ability to work, under

pressure, were extraordinary. He struck out at a single heat one hundred lines of The Vanity of Human Wishes. He wrote forty-eight of the printed octavo pages of his celebrated Life of Savage at a sitting. He wrote out whole Parliamentary debates from scanty notes furnished him by persons appointed to attend them; sometimes having nothing more communicated to him than the names of the several speakers, and the part they had taken in the debate. Sayings of his, dropped in casual conversation, about comparatively unimportant things, will live as long as the language in which they were spoken. Witness his reply, familiar to all the world, when asked, at the sale of Thrale's brewery, the value of the property to be disposed of: "We are not here," he said, "to sell a parcel of boilers and vats, but the potentiality of growing rich beyond the dreams of avarice." Who, but Johnson, in his most comfortable and self-satisfied mood, could have said it?

Having asked Langton if his father and mother had sat for their pictures, and being told that they had opposed it, he said, "Sir, among the anfractuosities of the human mind, I know not if it may not be one that there is a superstitious reluctance to sit for a picture."

On one occasion the talk had run upon fable-writing, and Goldsmith observed that in most fables the animals seldom talk in character. "For instance," said he, "the fable of the little fishes, who petitioned Jupiter to be changed into birds — the skill consists in making them talk like little fishes." This struck Johnson as very ridiculous talk, and he began to roll himself about and to shake with laughter; when Goldsmith broke in upon his entertainment by saying, "Why, Doctor Johnson, this is not so easy as you seem to think; for if you were to make little fishes talk, they would talk like whales."

An American lady was so charmed at one time by his conversation that she could not help exclaiming,

"How he does talk! Every sentence is an essay." Certainly very many of his sentences that have been reported to us are very essences of essays. Short paragraphs are sometimes whole treatises, — full of wit, wisdom, logic, and profound knowledge of human nature.

A gentleman who had been very unhappy in marriage, married immediately after his wife died; Johnson said, "It was the triumph of hope over experience."

Reynolds having observed that the real character of a man was found out by his amusements, Johnson added, "Yes, sir; no man is a hypocrite in his pleasures."

A friend mentioned to him that old Mr. Sheridan complained of the ingratitude of Mr. Wedderburne and General Fraser, who were much obliged to him when they were young Scotchmen entering upon life in London. Johnson said, "Why, sir, a man is very apt to complain of the ingratitude of those who have risen far above him. A man when he gets into a higher sphere, into other habits of life, cannot keep up all his former connexions. Then, sir, those who knew him formerly upon a level with themselves, may think that they ought still to be treated as on a level, which cannot be; and an acquaintance in a former situation may bring out things which it would be very disagreeable to have mentioned before higher company, though, perhaps every body knows of them."

"It is a very good custom," he said once, "to keep a journal for a man's own use; he may write upon a card a day all that is necessary to be written, after he has had experience of life. At first there is a great deal to be written, because there is a great deal of novelty; but when once a man has settled his opinions, there is seldom much to be set down."'

On one occasion he said, "There is nothing more likely to betray a man into absurdity, than condescension; when he seems to suppose his understanding too powerful for his company."

Of a certain lord who was something of a speaker, he said, "I never heard any thing from him in company that was at all striking; and depend upon it, sir, it is when you come close to a man in conversation, that you discover what his real abilities are; to make a speech in a public assembly is a knack."

He observed, "There is a wicked inclination in most people to suppose an old man decayed in his intellects. If a young or middle-aged man, when leaving a company, does not recollect where he laid his hat, it is nothing; but if the same inattention is discovered in an old man, people will shrug up their shoulders, and say, 'his memory is going.'"

"Sir," he said, "there is nothing by which a man exasperates most people more, than by displaying a superior ability of brilliancy in conversation. They seem pleased at the time; but their envy makes them curse him at their hearts."

"Our religion is in a book," he said; "we have an order of men whose duty it is to teach it; we have one day in the week set apart for it, and this is in general pretty well observed: yet ask the first ten gross men you meet, and hear what they can tell you of their religion."

An easy life had been imputed to clergymen. Johnson said, "Sir, the life of a parson, of a conscientious clergyman, is not easy. I have always considered a clergyman as the father of a larger family than he is able to maintain. I would rather have chancery suits upon my hands than the cure of souls. No, sir, I do not envy a clergyman's life as an easy life, nor do I envy the clergyman who makes it an easy life."

No saint, we are assured, in the course of his religious warfare, was more sensible of the unhappy failure of pious resolves, than Johnson. He said one day, talking to an acquaintance on this subject, "Sir, hell is paved with good intentions."

" He that encroaches on another's dignity," he once said, " puts himself in his power ; he is either repelled with helpless indignity, or endured by clemency and condescension."

You remember his refutation of Bishop Berkeley's ingenious sophistry to prove the non-existence of matter, and that every thing in the universe is merely ideal. It was observed that though we are satisfied the doctrine is not true, it is impossible to refute it. Johnson answered, striking his foot with mighty force against a large stone, till he rebounded from it, " I refute it thus."

Talking of a court-martial that was sitting upon a very momentous public occasion, he expressed much doubt of an enlightened decision ; and said, that " perhaps there was not a member of it, who in the whole course of his life, had ever spent an hour by himself in balancing probabilities."

Dr. Taylor commended a physician, and said, " I fight many battles for him, as many people in the country dislike him." Johnson replied, " But you should consider, sir, that by every one of your victories he is a loser ; for every man of whom you get the better will be very angry, and resolve not to employ him ; whereas if people get the better of you in argument about him, they 'll think, ' We 'll send for the doctor, nevertheless.' "

In reply to the observation that a certain gentleman had remained silent the whole evening in the midst of a very brilliant and learned society, Johnson said, " Sir, the conversation overflowed, and drowned him."

Being solicited to compose a funeral sermon for the daughter of a tradesman, he naturally inquired into the character of the deceased ; and being told that she was remarkable for her humility and condescension to inferiors, he observed that those were very laudable qualities, but it might not be so easy to discover who the lady's inferiors were.

The question, whether drinking improved **conversation and benevolence, was discussed.** Sir Joshua maintained it did. Johnson said, " No, sir ; before dinner, men meet with **great inequality of understanding; and those who are conscious of their** inferiority **have the** modesty not to talk. When they **have drunk wine, every man feels** himself happy, and loses that **modesty,** and grows impudent and vociferous ; but he is not improved : he is only not sensible of his defects."

**A pension** he defined in his Dictionary to be, " **An allowance made to any one** without an equivalent. In England it is generally under**stood to mean** pay given to a **state-hireling for treason to his country."** After such a **definition, it is scarcely to be wondered;** naturally observes the critic, **that Johnson paused, and felt some "** compunctious **visitings " before he accepted a pension him-**self.

He **loved a good hater.** " Dr. **Bathurst," he said,** " was a **man to my heart's** content : he **hated a fool, and** he hated a **rogue, and he** hated **a Whig; he was a very** good **hater."**

Every one knows the violence of his prejudices **against the** Whigs, the Americans, **the** Scotch, **and** the Presbyterians. He meant to **say a very severe** thing when he called **Burke a " bottomless Whig," and** generally spoke of **Whigs as rascals, and maintained** that the first Whig **was the devil. Hating Walpole and** the Whig excise act, he **defines Excise, " A hateful tax** levied upon commodities, **and adjudged, not** by the common judges of property, **but by** wretches hired by those to whom excise is paid." **He said, " I** am willing to love all mankind, except **an American ;" and his "** inflammable corruption bursting into horrid **fire, he** breathed **out** threatenings **and** slaughter ;" **calling them** " rascals, robbers, pirates ;" **and exclaiming, " he 'd burn and** destroy them." Miss **Seward, looking** at him with **mild but** steady astonishment, said, "Sir, this is an instance that we are always most violent against those whom we have injured." He was irritated still more by this delicate and keen reproach ; and roared out another tremendous volley, which one might fancy, imagined Boswell, could be heard across the Atlantic. The inn that the Doctor and Boswell once stayed at for a while was wretched. "Let us see now," said Boswell, "how we should describe it." "Describe it, sir," said Johnson. "Why, it was so bad that Boswell wished to be in Scotland." "Scotland is a very vile country, to be sure, sir," said Johnson to Strahan, who was also a Scotchman. "Well, sir," replied the latter, somewhat mortified, "God made it." "Certainly he did," answered Johnson, "but we must remember that he made it for Scotchmen, and comparisons are odious, Mr. Strahan ; but God made hell." Oats he defines, in his Dictionary, "A grain which in England is generally given to horses, but in Scotland supports the people." "Yes," observed Lord Elibank, when he heard the offensive definition, "and where will you find such horses and such men?" He would not allow Scotland to derive any credit from Lord Mansfield, for he was educated in England. "Much," said he, "may be made of a Scotchman if he be caught young." But we must say that we think that he was bigger in his bigotries than in any thing else. Who but "that majestic teacher of moral and religious wisdom" could have declined to hear Dr. Robertson preach, for no other reason than that he "would not be seen in a Presbyterian church"? One of the tall steeples in Edinburgh, which he was told was in danger, he wished not to be taken down ; "for," said he, "it may fall on some of the posterity of John Knox ; and no great matter." Like the detested and infamous Jeffreys, he could "smell a Presbyterian forty miles."

Not long before his death, Johnson applied to Langton for spiritual advice. "I desired him," he said, "to tell me sincerely in what he thought my life was faulty." Langton wrote upon a sheet of paper certain texts recommending Christian charity; and explained, upon inquiry, that he was pointing at Johnson's violence of vituperation and contradiction. The old Doctor began by thanking him earnestly for his kindness; but gradually waxed savage, and asked Langton, in a loud and angry tone, "What is your drift, sir?" He complained of the well-meant advice, to Boswell, with a sense that he had been unjustly treated. It was a scene for a comedy, as Reynolds observed, to see a penitent get into a passion and belabor his confessor.

Dozing one day in a railway car, in the State of Minnesota, there appeared before us, suddenly, in a seat at the other end of the carriage, a personage who seemed to be in every way familiar. His face was toward us, and he was busily engaged conversing with the man in the seat before him. The figure was enormous, and very remarkable. It filled nearly the whole seat, so gigantic it appeared. It stooped horribly; the back was round; the mouth was continually opening and shutting, as if the man were chewing something; he twisted his fingers; he twirled his hands; he see-sawed backward and forward; his feet seemed never for a moment quiet; his whole great person looked often as if it were going to roll itself quite voluntarily from his seat to the floor. Now and then he rubbed his knee with the palm of his hand, chewing his cud, and blowing out his breath like a whale. His face was disfigured by scars. His eyes were near, and otherwise imperfect. His head shook with a kind of motion like the effect of a palsy. He wore a bushy gray wig, and a brown coat, with metal buttons, and enormous pockets. Black worsted stockings and silver buckles were conspicuous. A huge English oak-stick was between his knees. He talked in a bow-wow way. He laughed like a rhinoceros. We felt sure the remarkable man was Doctor Johnson ; so sure, that we determined to approach him, whatever the risk. Respectfully, reverentially calling him by name, and apologizing for the intrusion, he said, with a sort of smile extending over his now more familiar face, "No intrusion, sir. Your approach is both natural and welcome. Let me introduce you to my friend Boswell. He is a Scotchman, sir, but he won't hurt you." In the act of extending a hand to Bozzy, and laughing at so amusing an exhibition of one of the Doctor's characteristic prejudices, the interview ended.

Cuthbert Shaw, in his poem entitled The Race, in which he whimsically made the living poets of England contend for pre-eminence of fame by running, gives an animated description of Johnson. We have only room for eight lines of it : —

> "To view him, porters with their loads would rest,
> And babes cling frighted to the nurse's breast.
> With looks convulsed, he roars in pompous strain,
> And, like an angry lion, shakes his mane.
> The Nine, with terror struck, who ne'er had seen
> Aught human with so terrible a mien,
> Debating whether they should stay or run,
> Virtue steps forth, and claims him for her son."

# IV.

## LORD MACAULAY.

AS A READER.

PERHAPS no one ever existed who was a greedier reader or who had better mental digestion than Lord Macaulay. From his infancy, he was an insatiable and omnivorous devourer of books. His nephew, in his delightful biography of him, tells us, that from the time he was three years old he read incessantly, for the most part lying on the rug before the fire, with his book in one hand, and a piece of bread and butter in the other. A woman who lived in the house as a parlor-maid, told how he used to sit in his nankeen frock, perched on the table by her as she was cleaning the plate, expounding to her out of a volume as big as himself. Hannah More, it is said, was fond of relating how she called at Mr. Macaulay's, and was met by a fair, pretty, slight child, about four years of age, with abundance of light hair, who came to the front-door to receive her, and tell her that his parents were out, but that if she would be good enough to come in he would bring her a glass of old spirits; a proposition which greatly startled the good lady, who had never aspired beyond cowslip-wine. When questioned as to what he knew about old spirits, he could only say that Robinson Crusoe often had some. In childhood he was permitted to make frequent and long visits to the Misses More, and to Hannah especially he was greatly indebted for valuable suggestions and direction in his reading. When he was six years old, she writes to him: "Though you are a little

boy now, you will one day, if it please God, be a man ;
but long before you are a man I hope you will be a
scholar. I therefore wish you to purchase such books as
will be useful and agreeable to you then, and that you
employ this very small sum in laying a little tiny corner-
stone for your future library." A year or two afterward,
she thanks him for his "two letters, so neat and free from
blots. By this obvious improvement, you have entitled
yourself to another book. You must go to Hatchard's
and choose. I think we have nearly exhausted the epics.
What say you to a little good prose? Johnson's Hebrides,
or Walton's Lives, unless you would like a neat edition
of Cowper's Poems, or Paradise Lost, for your own eating? In any case, choose something which you do not
possess. I want you to become a complete Frenchman,
that I may give you Racine, the only dramatic poet I
know in any modern language that is perfectly pure and
good."

With such intelligent and encouraging associations, and
with such healthy mental appetites, he grew every day in
intellectual capacity. While yet a boy, at school at Cambridge, he attracted the attention of Dean Milner, the
eminent President of Queen's College, then at the summit of its celebrity. The Dean "recognized the promise
of the boy, and entertained him at his college residence
on terms of friendliness and almost equality." After one
of these visits, he writes to Macaulay's father : " Your
lad is a fine fellow. He shall stand before kings. He
shall not stand before mean men." In his thirteenth
year, "the boy" wrote to his mother : " The books
which I am at present employed in reading to myself
are, in English, Plutarch's Lives, and Milner's Ecclesi-
astical History ; in French, Fénelon's Dialogues of the
Dead."

" The secret of his immense acquirements," says Trevelyan, "lay in two invaluable gifts of Nature — an un-

erring memory, and the capacity for taking in at a glance
the contents of a printed page. During the first part of
his life, he remembered whatever caught his fancy, without going through the process of consciously getting it
by heart. As a child, he accompanied his father on an
afternoon call, and found on the table the Lay of the Last
Minstrel, which he had never before met with. He kept
himself quiet with his prize while the elders were talking,
and on his return home sat down upon his mother's bed,
and repeated to her as many cantos as she had the patience or the strength to listen to. At one period of his
life he was known to say that, if by some miracle of van-
dalism all copies of Paradise Lost and the Pilgrim's Progress were destroyed off the face of the earth, he would
undertake to reproduce them both from recollection whenever a revival of learning came." Certain provincial
newspaper poems, which he happened to look once
through, while waiting in a coffee-room for a post-chaise,
and never gave a thought to for forty years, "at the end
of that time he repeated them both without missing, or,
as far as he knew, changing a single word." During his
last years he had a habit, while he was dressing in the
morning, of learning by heart one of Martial's epigrams,
of which he was very fond.

An illustration of Macaulay's preternatural quickness
is given by Caroline Fox in her Journal. A friend of his
traveling with him was reading a new book which Macaulay had not seen. The friend grew weary and indulged in a ten minutes' sleep; on awaking, they resumed
their talk, which fell on topics apropos of the book, when
Macaulay was full of quotations, judgments and criticisms.
"But I thought you had not seen it," said his friend.
"Oh, yes; when you were asleep I looked at it;" and it
seemed as if no corner of it were unexplored.

"Many Londoners — not all — (said Thackeray) have
seen the British Museum Library. . . . I have (he says)

seen all **sorts of** domes of Peters and Pauls, Sophia, **Pantheon, — what not? — and** have been struck by none **of them as much as** by that catholic dome in Bloomsbury, **under which** one million volumes are housed. . . . Under **the** dome which held Macaulay's brain, **and from** which **his** solemn eyes looked **out on** the world, **what a vast,** brilliant, and wonderful store **of** learning **was ranged!** what strange lore would **he not fetch for you at your bidding!** **A** volume **of law or history, a book** of poetry familiar or forgotten (except **by himself, who** forgot nothing), **a novel ever** so old, and he **had it at** hand."

He **was a voracious** novel-reader, and read all the romances, **good and bad, he could** lay his hands on. **He was** so familiar with **Sir** Charles Grandison that he thought it probable that **he** could rewrite it from memory. **On** the last page of a trashy sentimental **novel read** by him, "there appears **an** elaborate computation **of the number** of fainting-fits that **occur in the course of the five volumes."**

**"After all,"** he says, in **a letter to Ellis, soon after he** arrived in **India,** "the best rule **in all parts of the** world, **as** in London **itself, is to be independent of other** men's **minds.** My power of finding amusement without com**panions was pretty well tried** on my voyage. **I** read insatiably ; **the Iliad and Odyssey,** Virgil, Horace, Cæsar's **Commentaries,** Bacon, (De Augmentis,) Dante, Petrarch, **Ariosto, Tasso,** Don Quixote, Gibbon's Rome, Mill's India, all the seventy volumes of Voltaire, Sismondi's History of **France, and the** seven thick folios of the **Bio**graphia Britannica." **In a letter** written **to his sister** Margaret, soon after, **he speaks of his** "thirst **for knowledge," his** "passion for holding converse **with the** greatest **minds of** all ages and nations," his **"power of** forgetting **what surrounded** him," and of **"living with the** past, the future, the distant, and the unreal. **Books are** becoming every thing to me," he says. **"If I had at this** moment my choice of life, I would bury myself in one of those immense libraries that we saw together at the universities, and never pass a waking hour without a book before me." Conspicuous in his letters from India to Mr. Napier, the editor of the Edinburgh Review, were his requests for books, books. He writes to Ellis from Calcutta: "I have just finished a second reading of Sophocles. I am now deep in Plato, and intend to go right through all his works." In another letter to the same person, soon after, he says: "During the last thirteen months I have read Æschylus twice; Sophocles twice; Euripides once; Pindar twice; Callimachus; Apollonius Rhodius; Quintus Calaber; Theocritus twice; Herodotus; Thucydides; almost all Xenophon's works; almost all Plato; Aristotle's Politics, and a good deal of his Organon, besides dipping elsewhere in him; the whole of Plutarch's Lives; about half of Lucian; two or three books of Athenæus; Plautus twice; Terence twice; Lucretius twice; Catullus; Tibullus; Propertius; Lucan; Statius; Silius Italicus; Livy; Velleius Paterculus; Sallust; Cæsar; and, lastly, Cicero. I have, indeed, still a little of Cicero left; but I shall finish him in a few days. I am now deep in Aristophanes and Lucian." A little later, he writes to Ellis again: "My mornings, from five to nine, are quite my own. I still give them to ancient literature. I have read Aristophanes twice through since Christmas, and have also read Herodotus and Thucydides again. I got into a way last year of reading a Greek play every Sunday. I began on Sunday, the 18th of October, with the Prometheus, and next Sunday I shall finish with the Cyclops of Euripides. . . . I have read, as one does read such stuff, Valerius Maximus, Annæus Florus, Lucius Ampelius, and Aurelius Victor. I have also gone through Phædrus. I am now better employed. I am deep in the Annals of Tacitus, and I am at the same time reading Seutonius." With plenty of acute criticism following these dry lists of classical literature, showing how perfectly saturated he was with it. In another letter to Ellis, two months later, he says: "I read in the evenings a great deal of English, French, and Italian, and a little Spanish. I have picked up Portuguese enough to read Camoëns with care, and I want no more." A little later, he says : " My classical studies go on vigorously. I have read Demosthenes twice — I need not say with what delight and admiration. I am now deep in Isocrates ; and from him I shall pass to Lysias. I have finished Diodorus Siculus at last, after dawdling over him at odd times ever since last March. He is a stupid, credulous, prosing old ass; yet I heartily wish that we had a good deal more of him." And so he goes on, writing familiarly of Arrian, Quintus Curtius, Longus, Xenophon, Heliodorus, Achilles Tatius, Theocritus, Pliny, Marcellinus, Quintilian, Lucan, etc., to the bottom of his sheet.

In November, 1836, (he was then thirty-six years old,) in a letter to Napier, he says : "In little more than a year I shall be embarking for England, and I am determined to employ the four months of my voyage in mastering the German language. I should be much obliged to you to send me out, as early as you can, so that they may be certain to arrive in time, the best grammar and the best dictionary that can be procured ; a German Bible ; Schiller's works ; Goethe's works ; and Niebuhr's History, both in the orginal and in the translation. My way of learning a language is always to begin with the Bible, which I can read without a dictionary. After a few days passed in this way, I am master of all the common particles, the common rules of syntax, and a pretty large vocabulary. Then I fall on some good classical work. It was in this way that I learned both Spanish and Portuguese, and I shall try the same course with German."

His journals, after his return from India, are full of notes of his reading. His first prose letter to his little niece, Margaret, contains this sentence: "If any body would make me the greatest king that ever lived, with palaces, and gardens, and fine dinners, and wine, and coaches, and beautiful clothes, and hundreds of servants, on condition that I would not read books, I would not be a king. I would rather be a poor man in a garret, with plenty of books, than a king who did not love reading." When he was a little past fifty, he wrote to his old friend Ellis: "I do not think that I ever, at Cambridge or India, did a better day's work in Greek than to-day. I have read at one stretch fourteen books of the Odyssey, from the sixth to the nineteenth, inclusive. I did it while walking to Worcester and back." In his journal, he says: "I was afraid to be seen crying by the parties of walkers that met me as I came back; crying for Achilles cutting off his hair; crying for Priam rolling on the ground in the court-yard of his house: mere imaginary beings, creatures of an old ballad-maker, who died near three thousand years ago." In October, 1857, two years before his death, he wrote: "I walked in the portico, and learned by heart the noble fourth act of the Merchant of Venice. There are four hundred lines, of which I knew a hundred and fifty. I made myself perfect master of the whole, the prose letter included, in two hours." That "invincible love of reading," which Gibbon declared that he would not exchange for the treasures of India, was with Macaulay, says his nephew and biographer, "a main element of happiness in one of the happiest lives that has ever fallen to the lot of a biographer to record." The great reader died in his library, in his easy-chair, in his usual dress, with his book open on the table beside him.

### AS A WRITER.

When Macaulay was seven years old, he took it into his head to write a compendium of universal history, and gave, it is stated, a tolerably connected view of the leading events from the Creation to the beginning of this century, filling about a quire of paper. Before he was eight years old, he told his mother that he had been writing a paper, to be translated into Malabar, to persuade the people of Travancore to embrace the Christian religion. On reading it, she found it to contain "a very clear idea of the leading facts and doctrines of that religion, with some strong arguments for its adoption." About the same time, he determined on writing a poem in six cantos, which he called The Battle of Cheviot. After he had finished three of the cantos, of about one hundred and twenty lines each, which he did in a couple of days, he became tired of it. "I make no doubt," says his mother, "he would have finished his design, but as he was proceeding with it the thought struck him of writing an heroic poem, to be called Olaus the Great, or The Conquest of Mona, in which, after the manner of Virgil, he might introduce in prophetic song the future fortunes of his family." The clan to which the bard belonged was supposed to derive its name from Olaus Magnus, King of Norway; and so much as remains of the great family epic is an interesting treasure. The specimen stanzas given by his biographer read very well, considering the childhood of the poet. He also wrote many hymns, which Hannah More pronounced to be "quite extraordinary for such a baby." A little later, he undertook the production of an extended poem, which he entitled Fingal: a Poem in XII Books. It is described as "a vast pile of blank verse." Two of the "books" are in a "complete and connected shape, while the rest of the story is lost amidst a labyrinth of many hundred scattered lines."

The voluminous writings of his childhood, we are informed, displayed the same lucidity of meaning and scrupulous accuracy in punctuation and the other minor details of the literary art, which characterize his mature works. This was a result, doubtless, in great part, of the care in his home education, especially of the careful teaching and good advice of his mother. Here are a few advisory, encouraging sentences from one of her letters to her "dear Tom:" "I know you write with great ease to yourself, and would rather write ten poems than prune one; but remember, that excellence is not attained at first. All your pieces are much mended after a little reflection, and therefore take some solitary walks, and think on each separate thing. Spare no time or trouble to render each piece as perfect as you can, and then leave the event without one anxious thought. I have always admired a saying of one of the old heathen philosophers. When a friend was condoling with him that he so well deserved of the gods, and yet that they did not shower their favors on him, as on some others less worthy, he answered, ' I will, however, continue to deserve well of them.' So do you, my dearest."

Macaulay's father disapproved of novel-reading. While his novel-devouring son was yet a boy, he received an anonymous letter addressed to him as editor of the Christian Observer, " defending works of fiction, and eulogizing Fielding and Smollett. This he incautiously inserted in his periodical, and brought down upon himself the most violent objurgations from scandalized contributors, one of whom informed the public that he had committed the obnoxious number to the flames, and should thenceforward cease to take in the magazine. The editor replied with becoming spirit, although by that time he was aware that the communication, the insertion of which in an unguarded moment had betrayed him into a controversy for which he had so little heart, had proceeded from the pen of his son." Such, we are assured, was young Macaulay's first appearance in print.

At twenty-two, he became a contributor to Knight's Quarterly Magazine. The boldness and freedom of some of his articles were the cause of some not very agreeable correspondence with his father. About that time appeared "A Conversation between Mr. Abraham Cowley and Mr. John Milton touching the great civil war." He was now in his twenty-fifth year, and his abilities were becoming pretty well known to the literary profession. Overtures were made to him by Jeffrey, who was then the editor of the Edinburgh Review, and the result was the production of the article on Milton. The effect on the author's reputation, says his nephew and biographer, was instantaneous. Like Lord Byron, he awoke one morning and found himself famous. Murray declared that it would be worth the copyright of Childe Harold to have Macaulay on the staff of the Quarterly. The family breakfast-table in Bloomsbury was covered with cards of invitation to dinner from every quarter of London, and his father groaned in spirit over the conviction that thenceforward the law would be less to him than ever. Robert Hall, the great preacher, "then well-nigh worn out with that long disease, his life, was discovered lying on the floor, employed in learning, by aid of grammar and dictionary, enough Italian to enable him to verify the parallel between Milton and Dante." Jeffrey, in acknowledging the receipt of the manuscript, said : "The more I think, the less I can conceive where you picked up that style."

His article on Byron, too, proved to be very popular — "one among a thousand proofs," he said to his sister, "of the bad taste of the public." Blackwood's Magazine, of course, disparaged him. It described him "as a little splay-footed, ugly, dumpling of a fellow, with a mouth from ear to ear." The review of Croker's Boswell made a great sensation. "Croker," he wrote to Ellis, "looks across the House of Commons at me with a leer of hatred, which I repay with a gracious smile of pity." Busy as he was for eighteen months at the Board of Trade, he managed to supply the Edinburgh Review with the articles on **Horace** Walpole, **Lord** Chatham, and **Lord** Mahon's History. Napier, **then the** editor of the Edinburgh, **called upon him to tell him** that the sale **of the periodical was falling off, and that his articles were "the** only **things that** kept the work **up at all."** The booksellers said: " The Review sells, or **does not** sell, according as there are, or are not, articles **by Macaulay."** Napier **said of** his article on Walpole, that **it** was the best that **he had written.** Macaulay himself said of it to his sister **Margaret: " Nothing ever** cost me more pains than **the first half; I never wrote any** thing so flowingly as the latter half; and I like the latter half the best."

A few months after he arrived in India, he sent to Napier his article on Mackintosh ; and less than two years after — being then in his thirty-sixth year — he produced the more famous article on Bacon. **To Napier he says,** writing from Calcutta: " At last, I send you an article of interminable length, **about Lord Bacon.** I hardly know whether **it is not too long for an article in a Review; but** the subject **is of such vast** extent that **I could easily have made the paper twice as long as it is. . . . I never bestowed so much** care **on any thing that I have written. There** is not a sentence **in the latter half of the article** which has not been repeatedly **recast.** I have no expectation that the popularity of the article will have any proportion to the trouble which I have expended on it." The paper occupied one hundred and four of the large pages of the Review. Jeffrey saw it before it was printed, and said of it to Napier: " Since Bacon himself, I do not know that there has been any thing so fine." And marvelous the essay seems when we consider that it was written at the time when he was laboriously and exhaustively engaged upon " a complete penal code for a hundred millions of people, with a commentary explaining and defending the provisions of the text;" and in a climate that " destroys all the works of man, with scarcely one exception. Steel rusts ; razors lose their edge ; thread decays ; clothes fall to pieces ; books moulder away and drop out of their bindings ; plaster cracks ; timber rots ; matting is in shreds." All the time, too, he was devouring books, without number. The records of his Calcutta life, written in half a dozen languages, are scattered, it is said, throughout the whole range of classical literature, from Hesiod to Macrobius.

In 1840, two years after his return from Bengal, was published his essay on Lord Clive. Busy, as a member of the House of Commons, and as Secretary of War, he still found time to write essays, and plan his History. When a change of government occurred, he became engrossed with his literary work. The articles on Hastings, Frederic, Addison, etc., appeared in pretty quick succession. The Lays came out about the same time. The terrible paper on Barère a little later — "shade, unrelieved by a gleam of light." Soon he was at work on his History, the first two volumes of which were published early in 1849. His method of composition, as disclosed to us by Trevelyan, is interesting. "As soon as he had got into his head all the information relating to any particular episode in his History, he would sit down and write off the whole story at a headlong pace, sketching in the outlines under the genial and audacious impulse of a first conception, and securing in black and white each idea, and epithet, and turn of phrase, as it flowed straight from his busy brain to his rapid fingers. His manuscript, at this stage, to the eyes of any one but himself, appeared to consist of column after column of dashes and flourishes, in which a straight line, with a half-formed letter at each end and another in the middle, did duty for a word. . . . As soon as he had finished his rough draft, he began to fill it in at the rate of six sides of foolscap every morning, written in so large a hand, and with such a multitude of erasures, that the whole six pages were, on an average, compressed into **two pages of print.** This portion **he** called **his 'task,' and he was never** quite easy unless **he** completed it **daily. . . . He** never allowed a sentence **to** pass muster until it was **as good as he could** make it. **He** thought little of recasting **a** chapter **in order to obtain a** more lucid arrangement, and nothing **whatever of** reconstructing a paragraph for the sake **of one** happy stroke **or apt** illustration." He is said to have spent nineteen working days over thirty octavo pages, and ended **by** humbly acknowledging that the result was not to his mind. **"When, at length,** after repeated revisions, he had satisfied **himself that his writing** was **as** good as he could **make it, he would submit** it to the severest of **all** tests, **that of being read aloud to others. . . .** Whenever one of his books **was passing through the press,** he extended his indefatigable industry **and his scrupulous precision to** the minutest mechanical drudgery **of the literary calling.** There was no end to the trouble that **he devoted to matters** which **most** authors are only too glad **to leave to the** care and experience of their publisher. **He could not** rest until the lines were level to a hair's **breadth, and the** punctuation correct to **a comma; until** every paragraph **concluded** with a telling sentence, and every sentence **flowed** like running water."

During the later years **of his life,** Macaulay sent articles on Atterbury, Bunyan, Goldsmith, Dr. Johnson, and William **Pitt, to the** Encyclopædia Britannica. The last of these, which is little more than seventy octavo pages in **length, was on** hand, he tells us, for three quarters of a year. **Early in** November, 1857, he writes : " The plan of a good character of Pitt is forming in my mind ;" and on the 9th **of** August, 1858 : **"I** finished and sent **off the** paper which has caused me **so much** trouble. I began it, I see, in last November. **What a time to have been** dawdling over such a trifle !"

**His fame was** hardly earned. " Take at hazard," says

Thackeray, "any three pages of the Essays or History, and, glimmering below the stream of the narrative, you, an average reader, see one, two, three, a half score allusions to other historic facts, characters, literature, poetry, with which you are acquainted. Your neighbor, who has his reading and his little stock of literature stowed away in his mind, shall detect more points, allusions, happy touches, indicating not only the prodigious memory and vast learning of this master, but the wonderful industry, the honest, humble, previous toil of this great scholar. He reads twenty books to write a sentence ; he traveled a hundred miles to make a line of description."

"My task ;" "Did my task ;" "My task, and something over," continually occur in his diary. July 28, 1850, he says : "To-morrow I shall begin to transcribe again, and to polish. What trouble these few pages will have cost me !" February 6, 1854, he says : "I worked hard at altering the arrangement of the first three chapters of the third volume. What labor it is to make a tolerable book, and how little readers know how much trouble the ordering of parts has cost the writer !" In 1858, he made this entry : "I read my own writings during some hours, and was not ill-pleased on the whole. Yet, alas ! how short life, and how long art ! I feel as if I had just begun to understand how to write ; and the probability is that I have very nearly done writing." The next year, the pen dropped from his hand for ever, leaving his great "task"-work — his History — unfinished.

### AS A SPEAKER AND AS A TALKER.

It is as a writer that Lord Macaulay is famous, and it is not often that he is thought of as a speaker or as a talker. Proverbially, the world is slow to credit any one with more than one excellence. The mighty Cæsar, even, is rarely thought of but as a great general.

"When I praise an author," Macaulay used to say, "I

love to give a sample of his wares." It would be a
pleasure to copy, as it would be to read, samples of Macaulay's speeches, but there is not room enough for them
in one short article. Any one of many passages that
might be produced would give convincing proof of his
great powers as a speaker.

When a little child, he had an uncommon way of speaking, which foretold his future extraordinary power of expression. On one occasion a servant blunderingly spilled
hot coffee over his legs. The hostess, after a while, asked
him how he was feeling. The little fellow looked up in
her face, and replied: "Thank you, madam, the agony
is abated." He had, it is stated, a little plot of ground at
the back of the house marked out as his own by a row
of oyster-shells, which a maid one day threw away as
rubbish. He went straight to the drawing-room, where
his mother was entertaining some visitors, walked into
the circle, and said, very solemnly: "Cursed be Sally;
for it is written, 'Cursed is he that removeth his neighbor's landmark.'" In later years, his father was often
heard to exclaim: "If I had only Tom's power of
speech!"

His first public speech was made when he was not
twenty-four years old, at the annual anti-slavery meeting
in London, and all accounts agree in the statement that
its brilliancy confirmed the reputation he had acquired
in the debating societies of Cambridge and the metropolis. The Edinburgh Review described it as "a display
of eloquence so signal for rare and matured excellence,
that the most practiced orator may well admire how it
should have come from one who then for the first time
addressed a public assembly." His first speech in the
House of Commons was made five or six years afterward,
in support of the bill to repeal the civil disabilities of the
Jews of Great Britain, and his second on Slavery in the
West Indies. The next year he delivered the first of what

are known as his Reform speeches. When he sat down, it is said, the Speaker sent for him, and told him that, in all his prolonged experience, he had never seen the House in such a state of excitement. Portions of the speech, said a distinguished opponent, "were as beautiful as any thing I have ever heard or read. It reminded one of the old times." The names of Fox, Burke, and Canning, it is stated, were during that evening in every body's mouth; and Macaulay overheard with delight a knot of old members illustrating their criticisms by recollections of Lord Plunket. It was no easy thing to achieve such extraordinary success in such a peculiar place. "A place," to use Macaulay's own language, "where Walpole succeeded and Addison failed; where Dundas succeeded and Burke failed; where Peel now succeeds and Mackintosh fails; where Erskine and Scarlett were dinner-bells; where Lawrence and Jekyll, the two wittiest men, or nearly so, of their time, were thought bores, is surely a very strange place." Peel described the speech as a "wonderful flow of natural and beautiful language," richly freighted with "thought and fancy." Jeffrey said of it: "It was prodigiously cheered, as it deserved, and, I think, puts him clearly at the head of the great speakers, if not the debaters, of the House." Cockburn, who sat under the gallery for twenty-seven hours during the last three nights of the Reform bill, pronounced Macaulay's speech to have been "by far the best." Mackintosh writes from the library of the House of Commons: "Macaulay and Stanley have made two of the finest speeches ever spoken in Parliament." The bill was carried by one vote. In a letter to his old friend Ellis, Macaulay gives an animated description of the effect of its passage. "If I should live fifty years," he says, "the impression of it will be as sharp in my mind as if it had just taken place. It was like seeing Cæsar stabbed in the Senate-house, or seeing Oliver taking the mace from the table; a sight to be seen only once, and never to be forgotten." You might, he says, have heard a pin drop as Duncannon declared the result. "Then again the shouts broke out, and many of us shed tears. I could scarcely refrain. And the jaw of Peel fell; and the face of Twiss was as the face of a damned soul; and Herries looked like Judas taking his neck-tie off for the last operation."

His speeches in behalf of the Jews, the Slaves in the West Indies, and the Catholics, must stand as fine specimens of a high order of eloquence. His whole heart was in every word of them. By nature and by education he bitterly hated every form of injustice and oppression. The orator, it should be remembered, was a son of Zachary Macaulay, the philanthropist, one of the chiefs of the Clapham sect, and an active associate of Clarkson and Wilberforce. The inscription on the pedestal of the eminent man's bust in Westminster Abbey characterizes him as one "who during forty successive years, partaking in the counsels and the labors which, guided by favoring Providence, rescued Africa from the woes, and the British empire from the guilt, of slavery and the slave-trade, meekly endured the toil, the privation, and the reproach, resigning to others the praise and the reward." Living in the moral atmosphere of such a man, Macaulay imbibed his convictions and enthusiasm, and was fully prepared, when the time came, to assist in finishing the work which the little despised band of reformers had so inauspiciously begun.

His set speeches were of course carefully prepared; yet, it is said, when he rose in his place to take part in a discussion which had been long foreseen, he had no notes in his hand and no manuscript in his pocket. "If a debate was in prospect, he would turn the subject over while he paced his chamber or tramped along the streets. Each thought, as it rose in his mind, embodied itself in phrases, and clothed itself in an appropriate drapery of images, instances, and quotations ; and when, in the course of his speech, the thought recurred, all the words which gave it point and beauty spontaneously recurred with it."

"A torrent of words," said a critical listener, "is the only description of Macaulay's style, when he has warmed into speed. And such words!" "In all probability," said another, "it was that fullness of mind, which broke out in many departments, that constituted him a born orator. Vehemence of thought, vehemence of language, vehemence of manner, were his chief characteristics. The listener might almost fancy he heard ideas and words gurgling in the speaker's throat for priority of utterance. There was nothing graduated or undulating about him. He plunged at once into the heart of the matter, and continued his loud resounding pace from beginning to end, without halt or pause." When highly excited in speech, his mind might have been likened — as somebody has compared Napoleon's at times — to " a volcano, surcharged with molten granite." Of his most tremendous bursts might have been said what Jeffrey once said of Chalmers' eloquence, — " he buried his adversaries under the fragments of burning mountains."

As a talker, Macaulay must have been very extraordinary, judging even from the accounts of associate talkers, who, wanting their own share in the conversation, found it difficult to give due credit to a brilliant competitor. Crabb Robinson met him at a dinner-party, about the time he began to be famous, and described him in his diary as " very eloquent and cheerful. Overflowing with words, and not poor in thought. Liberal in opinion, but no radical. He seems a correct as well as a full man. He showed a minute knowledge of subjects not introduced by himself." A high compliment, certainly, to be paid by one wit to another. Sumner, the first time he was in England, dined with Macaulay. He speaks of "the incessant **ringing of** Macaulay's voice," in contrast with Bulwer's "**lisping, slender,** and effeminate tones." Altogether, he thought Macaulay "oppressive." **Perhaps,** bred **under Puritan influence, and imbibing some of the** same tastes and convictions, **they both wanted to** talk of the same things at the same time. **S**ydney Smith, we suspect, was a little inclined to disparage him for a **like reason.** With such great conversers as Rogers, Luttrell, Sydney Smith, Tom Moore, Mackintosh, and Conversa- tion Sharp, it was a bitter thing to be put out in conver- sation. **Any** thing might be forgotten before that. Hardly **any loss** was more serious, for the time being, than the **loss** of opportunity to say **a good thing.** He was a favor- ite at Holland **House. L**ady Holland, we know, listened to him with **unwonted deference, and scolded him** with a circumspection that **was in itself a compliment.** Rogers spoke of him with friendliness, **and to him with positive** affection. Sharp treated him **with great kindness and** consideration. For the space of three **seasons, we are** informed, he dined out almost nightly, and **spent many** of his Sundays in the suburban mansions **of his friends.** It would have been interesting to have heard him converse with Talleyrand, at Holland House, about Metternich and **Cardinal Mazarin. If** some Boswell had followed him **about,** what an interesting book we should have had! **Lord** Carlisle, in his journal, mentions having met Ma- caulay **at a** dinner-party. "Never," **he** says, "were such torrents **of good** talk as burst and sputtered over from Macaulay **and Hallam."** He notes another occasion when he breakfasted with Macaulay in his rooms at the top **of** the Albany — their walls covered with seven **to ten thou- sand** books. Macaulay's conversation, he says, "**ranged** the world."

"If a company of giants **were** got together," **says** Thackeray, in one of his Roundabout Papers, "**very** likely one or two of the mere six-feet-six people might be angry at the incontestable superiority of the very tallest of the party; so I have heard some of the London wits, rather peevish at Macaulay's superiority, complain that he occupied too much of the talk, and so forth. Now that that wonderful tongue is to speak no more, will not many a man grieve that he no longer has the chance to listen? To remember the talk is to wonder: to think not only of the treasures he had in his memory, but of the trifles he had stored there, and could produce with equal readiness. . . . Every man who has known him has his story regarding that astonishing memory. It may be that he was not ill-pleased that you should recognize it; but to those prodigious intellectual feats, which were so easy to him, who would grudge his tribute of homage?"

Hawthorne, you remember, in one of his English Note-Books, speaks of having met Macaulay at Milnes'. "All through breakfast," he says, "I had been more and more impressed by the aspect of one of the guests, sitting next to Milnes. He was a man of large presence, — a portly presence, gray-haired, but scarcely as yet aged; and his face had a remarkable intelligence, not vivid nor sparkling, but conjoined with great quietude, — and if it gleamed or brightened at one time more than another, it was like the sheen over a broad surface of sea. There was a somewhat careless self-possession, large and broad enough to be called dignity; and the more I looked at him, the more I knew that he was a distinguished person, and wondered who. He might have been a minister of state; only there is not one of them who has any right to such a face and presence. At last, — I do not know how the conviction came, — but I became aware that it was Macaulay, and began to see some slight resemblance to his portraits. But I have never seen any that is not wretchedly unworthy of the original. As soon as I knew him, I began to listen to his conversation, but he did not talk a great deal."

In one of his letters to his sisters, he speaks of an occasion when he dined with the two wits, Rogers and Sydney Smith. Two or three sentences are worth quoting, though a little out of the way, to show how different and incompatible they were. "Singly," says Macaulay, "I have often seen them; but to see them both together was a novelty, and a novelty not the less curious because their mutual hostility is well known, and the hard hits which they have given to each other are in every body's mouth. They were very civil, however. But I was struck by the truth of what Matthew Bramble says in Smollett's Humphry Clinker — that one wit in a company, like a knuckle of ham in soup, gives a flavor, but two are too many. Rogers and Sydney Smith would not come into conflict. If one had possession of the company, the other was silent; and, as you may conceive, the one who had possession of the company was always Sydney Smith, and the one who was always silent was Rogers." The conversation of Rogers, he informs us, was remarkably polished and artificial. What he said seemed to have been long meditated, and might have been published with little correction. Sydney talked from the impulse of the moment, and his fun was quite inexhaustible. No wonder such opposites could never agree. No intellectual or moral amalgam — not even Macaulay, with all his genius and good-nature — could have fused them together.

At the Palace of the Queen his powers of conversation were as well known and as fully appreciated as at the house of his sisters. A lady who met him frequently at the Palace, whether in the character of a cabinet minister or of a private guest, said of him: "Mr. Macaulay was very interesting to listen to; quite immeasurably abundant in anecdote and knowledge."

"Years ago," says Thackeray, "there was a wretched outcry raised because Mr. Macaulay dated a letter from

Windsor Castle, where he was staying. Immortal gods! Was this man not a fit guest for any palace in the world? or a fit companion for any man or woman in it?"

His appearance and bearing in conversation are described as singularly effective. " Sitting bolt upright, his hands resting on the arms of his chair, or folded over the handle of his walking-stick ; knitting his great eyebrows if the subject was one which had to be thought out as he went along, or brightening from the forehead downward when a burst of humor was coming ; his massive features and honest glance suited well with the manly, sagacious sentiments which he set forth in his pleasant, sonorous voice, and in his racy and admirably intelligible language. To get at his meaning, people had never the need to think twice, and they certainly had seldom the time. And with all his ardor, and all his strength and energy of conviction, he was so truly considerate toward others, so delicately courteous with the courtesy which is of the essence, and not only in the manner. However eager had been the debate, and however prolonged the sitting, no one in the company ever had personal reasons for wishing a word of his unsaid, or a look or a tone recalled."

Great, however, as were his gifts as a talker and as a speaker, he surrendered them all finally to literature. " At a period," says his biographer, "when the mere rumor of his presence would have made the fortune of any drawing-room in London, Macaulay consented to see less and less, and at length almost nothing, of general society, in order that he might devote all his energies to the work which he had in hand. He relinquished that House of Commons which the first sentence of his speeches hushed into silence, and the first five minutes filled to overflowing." He gave up all to devote himself to his History.

### AS A MAN.

Carlyle once said of Macaulay, that he was " an honest,

good sort of fellow, made out of oatmeal." In other words, that he was of good Scotch stock, and had been generously brought up on good air, simple food, and sound instruction. The qualities that he had inherited and scrupulously cultivated, were genuine, and of the highest manhood. The "pith o' sense," and "pride o' worth," and books, made him so much a man, and so different from other men, that independence was a necessity to him. If he was to be a man, and fight the battle of life on his own ground, it must be his, without any question of title. Believing that in the hour in which a man "mortgages himself to two, or ten, or twenty, he dwarfs himself below the stature of one;" and being determined that he would not be "cramped and diminished of his proportions," the desire, not for riches, but for independence, took deep root within him. He felt that he had much to say in this world, and would say it, without fear or favor. He felt, too, there is reason to believe, as a late writer expresses it, that "good work, as a rule, is only done by people who have paid their bills. Why was Shakespeare so far ahead of all contemporary dramatists? Because Shakespeare had the good sense to make money, and was therefore able to command the market, and write his late works without undue pressure. Others could only write in a tavern, or to get out of a creditor's clutches. Shakespeare's mind was at ease by the consciousness of his comfortable investments at Stratford. Hamlet was written because Shakespeare was solvent."

Just before going to India, Macaulay wrote to Lord Lansdowne: "I feel that the sacrifice which I am about to make is great. But the motives which urge me to make it are quite irresistible. Every day that I live, I become less and less desirous of great wealth. But every day makes me more sensible of the importance of a competence. Without a competence, it is not very easy for a public man to be honest : it is almost impossible for him to be thought so. I am so situated that I can subsist only in two ways : by being in office, and by my pen. Hitherto literature has been merely my relaxation — the amusement of perhaps a month in the year. I have never considered it as the means of support. I have chosen my own topics, taken my own time, and dictated my own terms. The thought of becoming a bookseller's hack ; of writing to relieve, not the fullness of the mind, but the emptiness of the pocket ; of spurring a jaded fancy to reluctant exertion ; of filling sheets with trash merely that the sheets may be filled ; of bearing from publishers and editors what Dryden bore from Tonson, and what, to my own knowledge, Mackintosh bore from Lardner, is horrible to me. Yet thus it must be if I should quit office. Yet to hold office merely for the sake of emolument would be more horrible still. The situation in which I have been placed, for some time back, would have broken the spirit of many men. It has rather tended to make me the most mutinous and unmanageable of the followers of the Government. I tendered my resignation twice during the course of the last session. I certainly should not have done so if I had been a man of fortune."

Not long after he arrived in India, he wrote familiarly to two of his sisters : " Money matters seem likely to go on capitally. My expenses, I find, will be smaller than I anticipated. The rate of exchange, if you know what that means, is very favorable indeed ; and, if I live, I shall get rich fast. I quite enjoy the thought of appearing in the light of an old hunks who knows on which side his bread is buttered ; a warm man ; a fellow who will cut up well. This is not a character which the Macaulays have been much in the habit of sustaining ; but I can assure you that, after next Christmas, I expect to lay up, on an average, about seven thousand pounds a year, while I remain in India. At Christmas, I shall send home a thousand or twelve hundred pounds for my father, and you all. I cannot tell you what a comfort it is to me to find that I shall be able to do this. It reconciles me to all the pains — acute enough, sometimes, God knows — of banishment. In a few years, if I live — probably in less than five years from the time at which you will be reading this letter, — we shall be again together in a comfortable, though modest, home ; certain of a good fire, a good joint of meat, and a good glass of wine ; without owing obligations to any body, and perfectly indifferent, at least as far as our pecuniary interest is concerned, to the changes of the political world."

The sacrifice he made for independence was indeed great. He wrote to one of his sisters from Calcutta : " I have no words to tell you how I pine for England, or how intensely bitter exile has been to me, though I hope that I have borne it well. I feel as if I had no other wish than to see my country again, and die. Let me assure you that banishment is no light matter. No person can judge of it who has not experienced it. A complete revolution in all the habits of life ; an estrangement from almost every old friend and acquaintance ; fifteen thousand miles of ocean between the exile and every thing that he cares for ; all this is, to me at least, very trying. There is no temptation of wealth or power which would induce me to go through it again." But, back again in London, two or three years after his return — his object accomplished, — he wrote to Napier : " I can truly say, that I have not, for many years, been so happy as I am at present. Before I went to India, I had no prospect of a change of government, except that of living by my pen, and seeing my sisters governesses. In India I was an exile. When I came back, I was for a time at liberty ; but I had before me the prospect of parting in a few months, probably forever, with my dearest sister and her children. That misery was removed ; but I found myself in office, a member of a Government wretchedly weak, and struggling for existence. Now I am free. I am independent. I am in Parliament, as honorably seated as man can be. My family is comfortably off. I have leisure for literature, yet I am not reduced to the necessity of writing for money. If I had to choose a lot from all that are in human life, I am not sure that I should prefer any to that which has befallen me. I am sincerely and thoroughly contented."

To his sisters, especially to Margaret and Hannah, he was warmly attached. Although younger than himself by ten and twelve years respectively, they were on terms of the most intimate companionship with him. Afternoons he took long walks with them. "We traversed," says one of them, "every part of the city, Islington, Clerkenwell, and the parks, returning just in time for a six o'clock dinner. What anecdotes he used to pour out about every street, and square, and alley. There are many places I never pass without the tender grace of a day that is dead coming back to me. Then, after dinner, he always walked up and down the drawing-room between us, chatting till tea-time. Our noisy mirth, his wretched puns, so many a minute, so many an hour ! Then we sung, none of us having any voices, and he, if possible, least of all ; but still the old nursery songs were set to music and chanted." "When alone with his sisters," says Trevelyan, "and, in after years, with his nieces, he was fond of settling himself deliberately to manufacturing conceits resembling those on the heroes of the Trojan war which have been thought worthy of publication in the collected works of Swift. When walking in London [he had Dr. Johnson's passion for the great town] he would undertake to give some droll turn to the name of every shopkeeper in the street, and, when traveling, to the name of every station along the line. At home, he

would run through the countries of Europe, the States
of the Union, the chief cities of our Indian Empire, the
provinces of France, the Prime Ministers of England, or
the chief writers and artists of any given century; striking off puns, admirable, endurable, and execrable, but
all irresistibly laughable, which followed each other in
showers like sparks from flint.  Capping verses was a
game of which he never tired."   Such entries as this
occur in Margaret's diary: "Jan'y 8th, 1832.  Yesterday
Tom dined with us, and staid late.  He talked almost
uninterruptedly for six hours.   In the evening he made a
great many impromptu charades in verse."  He read his
works to them in manuscript, and when they found fault,
as they often did, with his being too severe upon people,
he took it with the greatest kindness, and often altered
what they did not like.  After a visit to Holland House,
he writes to Hannah: "But for all this, I would much
rather be quietly walking with you : and the great use of
going to these fine places is to learn how happy it is possible to be without them."  In another letter to Hannah,
after speaking of the compliments showered upon him
by Althorp, Graham, Stanley, Russell, O'Connell, and
the newspaper press, he says : "My greatest pleasure, in
the midst of all this praise, is to think of the pleasure
which my success will give to my father and my sisters.
It is happy for me that ambition has in my mind been
softened into a kind of domestic feeling, and that affection has at least as much to do as vanity with my wish to
distinguish myself.  This I owe to my dear mother, and
to the interest which she always took in my childish successes.  From my earliest years, the gratification of those
whom I love has been associated with the gratification of
my own thirst for fame, until the two have become inseparably joined in my mind."  After reciting his engage-
ments to dine with lords and ladies, every day for a fortnight, he writes : "Yet I would give a large slice of my

quarter's salary, which is now nearly due, to be at the Dingle. I am sick of lords with no brains in their heads, and ladies with paint on their cheeks, and politics, and politicians, and that reeking furnace of a House. As the poet says:

> ' Oh ! rather would I see this day
> My little Nancy well and merry,
> Than the blue ribbon of Earl Grey,
> Or the blue stockings of Miss Berry.' "

Writing anxiously to Hannah about her health, he says: "I begin to wonder what the fascination is which attracts men, who could sit over their tea and their books in their own cool, quiet room, to breathe bad air, hear bad speeches, lounge up and down the long gallery, and doze uneasily on the green benches till three in the morning. Thank God, these luxuries are not necessary to me. My pen is sufficient for my support, and my sister's company is sufficient for my happiness. Only let me see her well and cheerful, and let offices in Government and seats in Parliament go to those who care for them." Again he says: "The Tories are quite welcome to take every thing, if they will only leave me my pen and my books, a warm fireside, and you chattering beside it. This sort of philosophy, an odd kind of cross between Stoicism and Epicureanism, I have learned where most people unlearn all their philosophy — in crowded senates and fine drawing-rooms." "There are not ten people in the world whose deaths would spoil my dinner ; but there are one or two whose deaths would break my heart. The more I see of the world, and the more numerous my acquaintance becomes, the narrower and more exclusive my affection grows, and the more I cling to my sisters, and to one or two old tried friends of my quiet days." The marriage of Margaret, and his separation from her, were serious things to Macaulay. Hannah (Nancy) he took with him to India, where she met and married Trevelyan. He wrote to Margaret (Mrs. Cropper) from Calcutta : " My parting from you almost broke my heart. But when I parted from you I had Nancy ; I had all my other relations ; I had my friends ; I had my country. Now I have nothing except the resources of my own mind, and the consciousness of having acted not ungenerously." Next came Margaret's death. One of the many painful references he makes to it is in a letter to his dear old friend Ellis, nearly a year after the event : " I have but very lately begun to recover my spirits. The tremendous blow which fell on me at the beginning of this year has left marks behind it which I shall carry to my grave. Literature has saved my life and my reason. Even now, I dare not, in the intervals of business, remain alone for a minute without a book in my hand."

After his departure to India, writes one of his sisters : " You can have no conception of the change which has come over this household. It is as if the sun had deserted the earth. The chasm Tom's departure has made can never be supplied. He was so unlike any other being one ever sees, and his visits among us were a sort of refreshment which served not a little to enliven and cheer our monotonous way of life ; but now day after day rises and sets without object or interest, so that sometimes I almost feel aweary of this world."

" He was peculiarly susceptible," says Lady Trevelyan, " of the feeling of ennui when in society. He really hated staying out, even in the best and most agreeable houses. It was with an effort that he even dined out, and few of those who met him, and enjoyed his animated conversation, could guess how much rather he would have remained at home, and how much difficulty I had to force him to accept invitations and prevent his growing a recluse. But though he was very easily bored in general society, I think he never felt ennui when he was alone, or when he was with those he loved. Many people are very fond of children, but he was the only person I ever knew who never tired of being with them. Often has he come to our house, at Clapham or in Westbourne Terrace, directly after breakfast, and finding me out, he dawdled away the whole morning with the children ; and then, after sitting with me at lunch, has taken Margaret a long walk through the city, which lasted the whole afternoon. Such days are always noted in his journals as especially happy."

All this of the man who was so severe upon Robert Montgomery, Croker, Barère, and others, that his severity has become famous. He had no mercy for bad, loose, or inaccurate writing. His models were classics. "See," he says, referring to Croker, "see whether I do not dust that varlet's jacket for him in the next number of the Blue and Yellow. I detest him more than cold boiled veal." Again he says: "I have, though I say it who should not say it, beaten Croker black and blue." Of Barère, he wrote to Napier: "If I can, I will make the old villain shake, even in his grave." What he said of Churchill was perhaps more or less applicable to himself: "There was too great a tendency to say with willing vehemence whatever could be eloquently said." There is something in the prolonged pounding he gave Walpole that reminds us of Walpole's blow or two at Johnson. Bold, too, he was, as well as severe. In his famous review of Ranke's History of the Popes, "he contrived," says one who knew, "to offend all parties — Romanist, Anglican, and Genevan." But all the boldness he ever evinced would have appeared timidity, and all his severity gentleness, if he had once fallen upon Brougham, who bitterly hated him, and whom Macaulay cordially disliked in return, and would have delighted beyond measure, we believe, in combating to the death. He was perfectly aware of Brougham's jealousies, insincerities, and cruelties, and would have exhausted upon him all the prodigious resources of his genius and passions. "I do not think it possible," he said to Ellis, "for human nature, in an educated, civilized man — a man, too, of great intellect — to have become so depraved." "Strange fellow!" he characterized him, more than twenty years afterward. "His powers gone. His spite immortal. A dead nettle." What a contest there would have been had the two giants come together!

Of Macaulay's public life and character, Sydney Smith expressed the truth in a few words: "I believe Macaulay to be incorruptible. You might lay ribbons, stars, garters, wealth, title, before him in vain. He has an honest, genuine love of his country, and the world could not bribe him to neglect her interests."

The last use the great man made of his pen was to sign a letter he had dictated, inclosing twenty-five pounds to a poor curate.

## V.

### LAMB.

SOME one has said, that to have a true idea of man, or of life, one must have stood himself on the brink of suicide, or on the door-sill of insanity, at least once. It does seem impossible that easy-going people, who have been easily prosperous, who have uniformly enjoyed good health, who have always been free from distressing care, should know at all what is inevitably and perfectly known by being between the millstones. "We learn geology," says Emerson, "the morning after the earthquake, on ghastly diagrams of cloven mountains, upheaved plains, and the dry bed of the sea." It is only an experience of the awful that fully opens the eyes of the understanding upon the dread abysses of extremity and possibility. To know life, it is necessary to have struggled hard in the midst of it ; to feel for the suffering, we must have suffered acutely ourselves. "Before there is wine or there is oil, the grape must be trodden and the olive must be pressed." The sweetest characters, we know, often result from the bitterest experiences. The weight of great misfortunes, and the perpetual annoyance of petty evils, only tend to make them stronger and better. Patience and resignation under multiplied ills can hardly be conceived by those who have only trodden at will, without burdens, over safe and pleasant ground in easy sandals. They look upon life ·and inquire, "What would the possession of a hundred thousand a year, or fame, and the applause of one's countrymen, or the loveliest and best-beloved woman — of any glory and happiness, or good fortune, avail to a man, who was allowed to enjoy them only with the condition of wearing a shoe with a couple of nails or sharp pebbles inside of it?" Good men, knowledge of the world teaches us, are not easily found amongst those who have never known misfortune: "the heart must be softened by sufferings, to make it constant, firm, patient, and wise." As there are fishes which are intended by nature for great sea-depths, so there are human beings to whom severe pressure seems to be suited, and who seem to thrive best when every weight is upon them. Birds of paradise, from the very nature of their plumage, cannot fly except against the wind. One of the most marvelously beautiful of all the many species of the humming-bird is only to be found in the crater of an extinguished volcano.

That Charles Lamb ever contemplated suicide, we do not know; but we do know, that he was, early in life, confined in an insane asylum for a short period. Once, alas! he not only stood upon, but passed, the door-sill of madness, and was ever after indeed wise in a wisdom unknowable but by those who dwell long enough in the midst of mental chaos for the impression of the dreadful situation ineradicably to infix itself. No wonder, knowing what we do of his wretched experiences, the best picture we have of him should show to us a face full of all endurable suffering, all possible pain, awful in its expression of wretchedness, and looking, for all the world — we cannot help saying it — like a skillful limner's painstaking study of madness.

Life very early taught him the bitter lesson that the ancient Mexicans taught their children: so soon as a child was born they saluted it, "Child, thou art come into the world to endure, suffer, and say nothing." Lamb endured, and suffered, how long! and was dumb beyond comprehension. When his wretchedness voiced itself, it was unconsciously or inevitably. When the burden was unbearable, merciless, the cry announcing it was but the creak of the timber before breaking — the echo of the agony within his soul.

Is it too much to say, that his peculiar genius was in great part a direct result of his supreme wretchedness? His humor, his wit, his wisdom, his very style, seem indeed to be, literally, expression — to have been forced out of him by pressure, as juices and oils are forced from plants. We know how much mere physical suffering has had to do with the most famous productions of literature. We know that the Caudle Lectures, which, as social drolleries, set all the world laughing, were written to dictation on a bed of sickness, racked by rheumatism. We know that Scott dictated that fine love story, the Bride of Lammermoor, from a bed of torment ; and that so great was his suffering that when he rose from his bed, and the published book was placed in his hands, he did not recollect one single incident, character, or conversation it contained. We know that Heine, for several years preceding his death, was a miserable paralytic. All that time he lay upon a pile of mattresses, racked by pain and exhausted by sleeplessness, till his body was reduced below all natural dimensions. The muscular debility was such that he had to raise the eyelid with his hands when he wished to see the face of any one about him ; and thus in darkness, he thought, and listened, and dictated, preserving to the very last his clearness of intellect, his precision of diction, and his invincible humor. The wretchedness of Scarron, at whose jests, burlesques, and buffooneries all France was laughing, may be guessed from his own description. His form, to use his own words, "had become bent like a Z." "My legs," he adds, "first made an obtuse angle with my thighs, then a right, and at last an acute angle ; my thighs made another with my body. My head is bent upon my chest ; my arms are contracted as well as my legs, and my fingers as well as my arms.

I am, in truth, a pretty complete abridgment of human misery." His days were passed in a chair with a hood, and his wife had to kneel to look in his face. He could not be moved without screaming from pain, nor sleep without taking opium. Balzac said of him, "I have often met in antiquity with pain that was wise, and pain that was eloquent ; but I never before saw pain joyous, nor found a soul merrily cutting capers in a paralytic frame." He continued to jest to the last ; and seeing the by-standers in tears, he said, "I shall never, my friends, make you weep as much as I have made you laugh." Pascal, we know, was pitifully feeble, and constantly in pain, at the same time that he "fixed," to use the glowing words of Châteaubriand, "the language which Bossuet and Racine spoke, and furnished a model of the most perfect wit as well as of the closest reasoning ; and in the brief intervals of his pain solved by abstraction the highest problems of geometry, and threw on paper thoughts which breathe as much of God as of man." We know, too, that many of Hood's most humorous productions were dictated to his wife, while he himself was in bed from distressing and protracted sickness. His own family was the only one which was not delighted with the Comic Annual, so well thumbed in every house. "We ourselves," said his son, "did not enjoy it till the lapse of many years had mercifully softened down some of the sad recollections connected with it." It is recorded of him, that upon a mustard plaster being applied to his attenuated feet, as he lay in the direst extremity, he was heard feebly to remark, that there was "very little meat for the mustard."

Physical suffering having had so much to do with so many of the productions of genius, is it hard to believe that mental anguish may not have contributed even more and to a greater number ? Literature is full of instances to enforce the conclusion. Mental wretchednesses of every description connect themselves inseparably with the memory of many of the most illustrious names, and with their greatest achievements. Curran, for instance, at the very time he was one of the most unhappy and melancholy of men, was one of the most delightful and wonderful. What a talker he was! Such imagination! "There never was any thing like it," said Byron, "that I ever saw or heard of. His published life, his published speeches, give you no idea of the man — none at all. He was a machine of imagination. The riches of it were exhaustless. I have," said the poet, "heard that man speak more poetry than I have ever seen written, though I saw him seldom, and but occasionally. I saw him presented to Madame de Staël. It was the great confluence between the Rhone and the Saone." Cervantes, from all accounts, dragged on a most wretched and melancholy existence. He was groaning and weeping while all Spain was laughing at the adventures of Don Quixote and the wise sayings of Sancho Panza. The great Swift, we know, was never known to smile. Butler's private history was but a record of his miseries. Burns confessed that his design in seeking society was to fly from constitutional melancholy. "Even in the hour of social mirth," he tells us, "my gayety is the madness of an intoxicated criminal under the hands of the executioner." The author of John Gilpin said of himself and that humorous poem, "Strange as it may seem, the most ludicrous lines I ever wrote have been when in the saddest mood, and but for that saddest mood, perhaps, would never have been written at all." While it was being read by Henderson, in London, to large audiences, its author was mad. Jean Paul wrote a great part of a comic romance in an agony of heart-break from the death of his son. Washington Irving completed that most extravagantly humorous of all his works — The History of New York — while suffering from the death of his sweetheart, which nearly broke his heart. The fact, therefore, that the most facetious of all Lamb's letters was written in a paroxysm of melancholy, amounting almost to madness, does not deserve to be called curious, but is only another instance added to the list that might easily be extended, if not to the point of tediousness, certainly beyond the purposes of this paper.

The circumstances of Lamb's life were awfully depressing. Conceive them if you can. Himself, as we have said, in a mad-house for a short time at the end of his twentieth year; his sister insane at intervals throughout her life; his mother hopelessly bedridden till killed by her daughter in a fit of frenzy; his father pitifully imbecile; his old maiden aunt home from a rich relation's to be nursed till she died — all dependent upon him, his more prosperous brother declining to bear any part of the burden; his·work for more than thirty years distasteful and monotonous, and most of it performed at the same desk in the same office. Imagine his loneliness during all those thirty dreary years, with no one in the vast establishment at all congenial to him that we hear of; indeed we do not remember that he any where refers by name to any one employed there with him. Dr. James Alexander, describing a visit to the India House, says he inquired for Charles Lamb of the doorkeeper, who replied he had been there since he was sixteen years old, and had never heard of any Mr. Lamb. But the doorkeeper of the British Museum knew him very well.

It is now well-known that Lamb's description of Lovel, in one of his essays, is an accurate description of his own father. It helps us to a better understanding of himself, besides being good enough to read over and over. " I knew this Lovel," he says. "He was a man of an incorrigible and losing honesty. , A good fellow withal, and 'would strike.' In the cause of the oppressed he never considered inequalities, or calculated the number of his opponents. He once wrested a sword out of the hand of a man of quality that had drawn upon him, and pommeled him severely with the hilt of it. The swordsman had offered insults to a female — an occasion upon which no odds against him could have prevented the interference of Lovel. He would stand next day bareheaded to the same person, modestly to excuse his interference — for L. never forgot rank, where something better was not concerned. L. was the liveliest little fellow breathing, had a face as gay as Garrick's, whom he was said greatly to resemble (I have a portrait of him which confirms it), possessed a fine turn for humorous poetry — next to Swift and Prior — moulded heads in clay or plaster of Paris to admiration, by the dint of natural genius merely; turned cribbage boards, and such small cabinet toys, to perfection; took a hand at quadrille or bowls with equal facility; made punch better than any man of his degree in England; had the merriest quips and conceits; and was altogether as brimful of rogueries and inventions as you could desire. He was a brother of the angle, moreover, and just such a free, hearty, honest companion as Mr. Izaak Walton would have chosen to go a-fishing with. I saw him in his old age and the decay of his faculties, palsy-smitten, in the last sad stage of human weakness — 'a remnant most forlorn of what he was,' — yet even then his eye would light up upon the mention of his favorite Garrick. He was greatest, he would say, in Bayes — 'was upon the stage nearly throughout the whole performance, and as busy as a bee.' At intervals, too, he would speak of his former life, and how he came up a little boy from Lincoln to go to service, and how his mother cried at parting with him, and how he returned, after some few years' absence, in his smart new livery, to see her, and she blessed herself at the change, and could hardly be brought to believe that it was 'her own bairn.' And then, the excitement subsiding, he would weep, till I have wished that sad second childhood might have a mother still to lay its head upon her lap.  But the common mother of us all in no long time after received him gently into hers."

The circumstances attending the death of Lamb's mother, by the hand of his sister, were reported by the coroner : " It appeared, by the evidence adduced, that, while the family were preparing for dinner, the young lady seized a case-knife, lying on the table, and in a menacing manner pursued a little girl, her apprentice, round the room.  On the calls of her infirm mother to forbear, she renounced her first object, and with loud shrieks, approached her parent.  The child, by her cries, quickly brought up the landlord of the house, but too late.  The dreadful scene presented to him the mother lifeless, pierced to the heart, on a chair, her daughter yet wildly standing over her with the fatal knife, and the old man, her father, weeping by her side, himself bleeding at the forehead from the effects of a severe blow he received from one of the forks she had been madly hurling about the room. . . .  The jury, of course, brought in their verdict — Lunacy." .

Lamb's own account of the dreadful event, to Coleridge, is extremely touching : — " My Dearest Friend : White, or some of my friends, or the public papers, by this time may have informed you of the terrible calamities that have fallen on our family.  I will only give you the outlines : My poor dear, dearest sister, in a fit of insanity, has been the death of her own mother.  I was at hand only time enough to snatch the knife out of her grasp.  She is at present in a mad-house, from whence I fear she must be moved to an hospital.  God has preserved to me my senses — I eat and drink, and sleep, and have my judgment, I believe, very sound.  My poor father was slightly wounded, and I am left to take care of him and my aunt. . . .  Write as religious a letter as possible, but no mention of what is gone and done with.  With me, 'the former things are passed away,' and I have something more to do than to feel. . . . Mention nothing of poetry. I have destroyed every vestige of past vanities of that kind. Do as you please, but if you publish, publish mine (I give free leave) without name or initial, and never send me a book, I charge you. . . . I charge you, don't think of coming to see me. Write. I will not see you if you come. God Almighty love you and all of us."

Whenever, we are told, the approach of one of her fits of insanity was announced by some irritability or change of manner, he would take her under his arm to Hoxton Asylum. It was very afflicting to encounter the young brother and his sister walking together (weeping together) on this painful errand; Mary herself, although sad, very conscious of the necessity for temporary separation from her only friend. They used to carry a strait-jacket with them.

Dr. Weddell, in the account of his travels and adventures in South Africa, speaks of a species of variegated woodpecker, called the carpenter. If one is killed, it is rare that its mate does not come and place itself beside the dead body, as if imploring a similar fate. Such touching fidelity on the part of a bird, but feebly and imperfectly suggests the perpetual, unwearying, undying devotion of Lamb to his poor sister. He was always at her side, in any and every extremity, and there was no sacrifice that he did not stand ready to make. Year after year for years, he was father, mother, brother, sister, friend, nurse, comforter — every thing to her.

"I do not observe," says Barry Cornwall, "more than one occasion on which (being then himself ill) his firmness seemed altogether to give way. In 1798, indeed, he had said, 'I consider her perpetually on the brink of madness.' But in May, 1800, his old servant Hetty having died, and Mary (sooner than usual) falling ill again, Charles was obliged to remove her to an asylum; and was left in the house alone with Hetty's dead body. 'My heart is quite sick (he cries), and I don't know where to look for relief. My head is very bad. I almost wish that Mary were dead.' This was the one solitary cry of anguish that he uttered during his long years of anxiety and suffering. At all other times he bowed his head in silence, uncomplaining."

To Coleridge he wrote, "Mary will get better again, but her constantly being liable to such relapses is dreadful; nor is it the least of our evils [they were then at Pentonville, in the neighborhood of Holborn] that her case and all our story is so well known around us. We are in a manner marked." To Manning he wrote, about the same time, "It is a great object to me to live in town, where we shall be much more private, and to quit a house and a neighborhood, where poor Mary's disorder, so frequently recurring, has made us a sort of marked people. We can be nowhere private except in the midst of London."

Sensitive natures, like Lamb's, are wretched under the social microscope. Hawthorne, nearly alike sensitive, wrote of the Eternal City, "Rome is not like one of our New England villages, where we need the permission of each individual neighbor for every act that we do, every word that we utter, and every friend that we make or keep." It is rather a weary thing for any one to live under the microscope. In every man's life are there not apartments he would have forever locked, the keys forever lost, into which he himself never enters but by a skeleton? It is pleasant sometimes to get where no one knows you, nor cares a brass farthing what you say or do. No one knew better than Lamb, shrinking from microscopic observation, what a perfect place for any wretchedness is a great city.

No man, we imagine, ever suffered more from compassion, than Lamb, unless it was Steele. The latter, out of

his bitter experience called it shrewdly the best disguise
of malice, and said that the most apposite course to cry
a man down was to lament him. Lamb had a great dread
of being lectured, as all sensitive people have naturally.
A lady, we are told — a sort of social Mrs. Fry — had
been for some time lecturing him on his irregularities.
At last, she said: "But, really, Mr. Lamb, I'm afraid all
that I'm saying has very little effect on you. I'm afraid
from your manner of attending to it, that it will not do
you much good." "No, ma'am," said Lamb, "I don't
think it will. But as all that you have been saying has
gone in at this ear (the one next her) and out at the
other, I dare say it will do this gentleman a great deal of
good," turning to a stranger who stood on the other side
of him. The advice — ill-timed and ill-applied, no doubt
— had much the same effect that the whipping had upon
the German soldier, who laughed all the time he was being flogged. When the officer, at the end, inquired the
cause of his mirth, he broke out into a fresh fit of laughter, and cried, " Why, I'm the wrong man ! "

Impertinence, or offensive interference of any sort,
Lamb could not brook. An unpopular head of a department in the India House came to him one day (perhaps
at the very time he was engaged on one of his inimitable
essays or letters) and inquired, "Pray, Mr. Lamb, what
are you about?" "Forty, next birthday," said Lamb.
"I don't like your answer," said the man. "Nor I your
question," was Lamb's reply.

He did not like to have the epithet "gentle" applied
to him. Coleridge, in a poem, had characterized him as
" My gentle-hearted Charles." Lamb replied, " For God's
sake (I never was more serious), don't make me ridiculous any more by terming me gentle-hearted in print, or
do it in better verses. It did well enough five years ago
when I came to see you, and was moral coxcomb enough
at the time you wrote the lines, to feed upon such epi-

thets ; but, besides **that, the** meaning of gentle **is** equiv-ocal at best, and **almost** always means poor spirited ; **the** very quality **of gentleness** is abhorrent to such vile **trump-etings.** My sentiment is long since banished. I hope **my virtues have** done sucking. **I can** scarce think but **you meant it** in joke. I hope you **did, for I** should be **ashamed** to think you could think **to** gratify me by **such praise, fit** only to be a cordial to **some** green-sick son-neteer."

The immediate **cause** of Lamb's insanity was his **love** for his **sweetheart,** Alice W., as he delicately calls her. **He** says that his sister would often "lend an ear to his desponding, **love-sick lay."** After he had **been** in the asylum, he writes **to Coleridge that his** "**head ran** upon him, in **his madness, as much almost as** on another per-son [meaning the **dear one**] who was the more immediate cause of my frenzy." **Later,** he burned **the** "little jour-nal," **as he called it,** " of his foolish **passion."**

It must have been at about this time that Coleridge **had** a **call from** Lamb, which he speaks of in a letter to **Ma-**tilda Betham. "**I had," he** says, "just **time** enough **to** have half an hour's mournful conversation with him. **He** displayed such fortitude in his manners, and such a rav-**age** of mental suffering in his countenance, that I walked **off,** my head throbbing with long weeping."

**Wretched man !** In his disordered state — a tempest of agitation — **events** sometimes affected him most strangely. **In a letter** to Southey he says, "**I** was at Hazlitt's marriage, and had like to have been turned out several **times** during the ceremony. Any thing **awful** makes me laugh."

**Ah !** poor humanity — in extremity — what are **you to say of it ?** The plague, **says Bulwer,** breaks out at Flor-ence, — all the **pious virgins, the** religious matrons, and even the sacred sisters, devoted **to** seclusion and God, **give themselves up** in a species of voluptuous delirium to the wildest excesses of prostitution and debauch. The same pestilence visits Aix, and the oldest courtezans of the place rush in pious frenzy to the hospitals, and devote themselves to the certain death which seizes those who attend upon the sick.

Yet, who but Lamb could have said so tender a word for an unfortunate man as this? — addressed also to Southey : " Your friend John May has formally made kind offers to Lloyd of serving me in the India House, by the interest of his friend, Sir Francis Baring. It is not likely that I shall ever put his goodness to the test on my own account, for my prospects are very comfortable. But I know a man, a young man, whom he could serve through the same channel, and, I think, would be disposed to serve if he were acquainted with his case. This poor fellow (whom I know just enough of to vouch for his strict integrity and worth) has lost two or three employments from illness, which he cannot regain. He was once insane, and, from the distressful uncertainty of his livelihood, has reason to apprehend a return of that malady. He has been for some time dependent on a woman whose lodger he formerly was, but who can ill afford to maintain him ; and I know that on Christmas night last he actually walked about the streets all night, rather than accept of a bed, which she offered him, and offered herself to sleep in the kitchen ; and in consequence of that severe cold, he is laboring under a bilious disorder, besides a depression of spirits, which incapacitates him from exertion when he most needs it. For God's sake, Southey, if it does not go against you to ask favors, do it now ; ask it as for me ; but do not do a violence to your feelings, because he does not know of this application, and will suffer no disappointment."

You know what he did for John Morgan — Coleridge's friend — whose name deserves to go down with the Thrales, the Shaftesburys, the Abneys, the Gillmans, the

Unwins, and others who have afforded kindly shelter to illustrious men of excellence, learning, or genius. Morgan was the only child of a retired spirit merchant of Bristol, who left him a handsome independence. He was, according to Cottle, a worthy kind-hearted man, possessed of more than an average of reading and good sense; generally respected, and of unpresuming manners. He was a great friend and admirer of Coleridge; deploring his habits, and laboring to correct them. Except Mr. Gillman there was no individual with whom Coleridge lived gratuitously so much, during Morgan's residence in London, extending to a domestication of several years. When Morgan removed to Calne, in Wiltshire, for a long time he gave Coleridge an asylum, and till his affairs, through the treachery of others, became involved, Coleridge, through him, never wanted a home. Morgan, after the turn of the wheel of fortune till the day of his death, was supported by a subscription, set on foot, and contributed to — too liberally, no doubt — by Lamb.

To be taken into Lamb's favor and protection, it was said, you had only to get discarded, defamed, and shunned by every body else; and if you deserved this treatment, so much the better. "If I may venture so to express myself," says Patmore, "there was in Lamb's eye a sort of sacredness in sin, on account of its sure ill-consequences to the sinner; and he seemed to open his arms and his heart· to the rejected and reviled of mankind in a spirit kindred at least with that of the Deity."

"Take life too seriously, and what is it worth?" asks Goethe, in Egmont. "If the morning wake us to no new joys, if in the evening we have no pleasures, is it worth the trouble of dressing and undressing?" Lamb, under the most discouraging circumstances, tried always to make the best of life. You remember the Spaniard that Southey tells us about, who always put on his spectacles when about to eat cherries, that they might look bigger and more tempting. In like manner Lamb made the most of his enjoyments, and though he did not cast his eyes away from his troubles, he packed them in as little compass as he could for himself, and never let them annoy others.

What a resource to him Rickman was ! — a clerk in the House of Commons, introduced to him by George Dyer. "This Rickman," says Lamb, describing him, " lives in our Buildings, immediately opposite our house ; the finest fellow to drop in o' nights, about nine or ten o'clock — cold bread-and-cheese time — just in the wishing time of the night, when you wish for some body to come in, without a distinct idea of a probable any body. Just in the nick, neither too early to be tedious, nor too late to sit a reasonable time. He is a most pleasant hand ; a fine rattling fellow, has gone through life laughing at solemn apes ; — himself hugely literate, oppressively full of information in all stuff of conversation, from matter of fact to Xenophon and Plato — can talk Greek with Porson, politics with Thelwall, conjecture with George Dyer, nonsense with me, and any thing with any body ; a great farmer, somewhat concerned in an agricultural magazine — reads no poetry but Shakespeare, very intimate with Southey, but never reads his poetry, relishes George Dyer, thoroughly penetrates into the ridiculous wherever found, understands the first time (a great desideratum in common minds) — you need never twice speak to him ; does not want explanations, translations, limitations, as Professor Goodwin does when you make an assertion ; up to any thing ; down to every thing ; whatever sapit hominem. A perfect man. . . . a species in one. A new class. . . . The clearest-headed fellow. Fullest of matter, with least verbosity."

And here a word or two about Lamb's friends — mostly an odd set of intellectual worthies. Coleridge — deep in metaphysical subtleties, or up in the empyrean ; scholarly

George Dyer — simple-hearted as my Uncle Toby — always conjecturing and always absent-minded — at one time emptying the contents of his snuff-box into the tea-pot, at another walking straight into the river at noonday; Barton — the healthful friend, and good Quaker poet; Hazlitt — passionate and untamable — with a face as pale as marble, yet pointed at as the "pimpled Hazlitt" — who never tasted any thing but water, yet was held up as an habitual gin-drinker; Crabb Robinson — with the most hospitable of intellects — who had seen every thing and every body, and was always entertaining; Talfourd — full of law and literature, and ever ready with his reason or his rhetoric; Rickman — bounding, as you have seen, as a roe, and as fresh as the morning; Rough — a chronic and incurable borrower, to whom some of Lamb's most amusing letters were written; Manning — the most wonderful of all, Lamb said; Barry Cornwall — who wrote sea songs, yet was rarely if ever on the tossing element — whose poetry, it was said, is a record of the extravagances of one who was habitually sober, the audacities of one who was habitually cautious, the eloquence of one who was habitually reserved; Godwin — who wrote against matrimony and was twice married, and while scouting all commonplace duties, was a good husband and kind father; Lloyd — an insane poet, who took lodgings at a working brazier's shop to distract his mind from melancholy and postpone his madness; Southey — a bookworm and a bookmaker — who loved books so well that some of his last hours were spent caressing them; De Quincey — who had made himself famous by inimitably confessing to the sin of opium; Hammond — an incomprehensible character, who journalized his food, his sleep, and his dreams — who had a conviction that he was to have been, and ought to have been, the greatest of men, but was conscious in fact that he was not — and who said, the chief philosophical value of his papers consisted in the fact that they recorded something of a mind that was very near taking a station far above all that had hitherto appeared in the world ; Blake — artist, genius, mystic, madman — of whom it was said, he possessed the highest and most exalted powers of the mind, but not the lower — who could fly, but could not walk — who had genius and inspiration, without the prosaic balance-wheel of common sense — who all his life was a victim of poverty and privation, but who, in his old age, put his hands on ·the head of a little girl, and said, " May God make this world to you, my child, as beautiful as it has been to me ;" and Wordsworth — who heard and saw in abounding nature what nobody saw or heard but himself without his assistance — who loved himself chiefly, and disparaged Burns, and even Shakespeare, as we shall see ; and Hood — "so grave, and sad, and silent " — one of Lamb's youngest friends ; and Cottle, the kind old bookseller ; and Munden, his favorite comedian ; and Liston ; and Charles Kemble ; and Morgan ; and Jem White, " the drollest of fellows," the author of the Falstaff Letters ; and the passionate Thelwall ; and Clarkson, the destroyer of the slave-trade ; and Basil Montagu, the constant opponent of the judicial infliction of death ; and scholarly Barnes, the editor of the Times newspaper ; and the turbulent, ambitious Haydon ; and the frank-hearted Captain Burney, who voyaged round the world with Captain Cook ; and stalwart Allan Cunningham ; and Cary, "pleasantest of clergymen," who "rendered the adamantine poetry of Dante into English ;" and the Reverend Edward Irving ; and the easy-going, delightful Leigh Hunt ; and ever so many more, only a little more obscure, — all of whom were visitors, friends, associates, favorites, or pets, of Lamb — walking with him in London streets — talking with him in quiet upper rooms, all about books and authors, plays and players, pictures and artists — any thing about which any one of them was interested. Nothing is easier than to gossip about these interesting characters, — always interesting in themselves, but especially so to us now, on account of their acquaintance and association with Lamb.

His literary work was mostly done for occupation, although he did hope — occasionally, at least — for considerable pecuniary remuneration from it. His plays disappointed him — they did not take with the public. The same may be said of his essays. "Present time and future," says Sir Joshua Reynolds, "are rivals; he who solicits the one, must expect to be discountenanced by the other." Willis, breakfasting at the Temple with a friend, met Lamb. He mentioned having bought a copy of Elia the last day he was in America, to send as a parting gift to a lady. "What did you give for it?" said Lamb. "About seven and sixpence." "Permit me to pay you that," said he; and with the utmost earnestness he counted out the money upon the table. "I never yet wrote any thing that would sell. I am the publishers' ruin." "To be neglected by his contemporaries," said Macaulay, speaking of Milton, "was the penalty which he paid for surpassing them."

His literary expedients were many, and some of them were very curious. "Coleridge," he says, in a letter to Manning, "has lugged me to the brink of engaging to a newspaper, and has suggested to me for a first plan, the forgery of a supposed manuscript of Burton, the anatomist of melancholy. I have even written the introductory letter; and, if I can pick up a few guineas in this way, I feel they will be most refreshing, bread being so dear."

Although he felt the need of money, and was constantly in some literary employment, he fully realized the miseries of subsisting by authorship. "'T is a pretty appendage to a situation like yours or mine," he wrote to Barton; "but a slavery, worse than all slavery, to be a bookseller's dependent, to drudge your brains for pots of ale, and breasts of mutton, to change your free thoughts and voluntary numbers for ungracious task-work. These fellows hate us. The reason I take to be, that contrary to other trades, in which the master gets all the credit, (a jeweler or silversmith for instance,) and the journeyman, who really does the fine work, is in the background; in our work the world gives all the credit to us, whom they consider as their journeymen, and therefore do they hate us, and cheat us, and oppress us, and would wring the blood of us out, to put another sixpence in their mechanic pouches."

The best of his literary achievements, no doubt, are owing to the very necessity of occupation. In his isolation and dreariness and gloom, he wrote and wrote to keep his mind from preying on itself. You remember the story of the black pin which the lady wore as a brooch — repeated some time ago by Holmes in one of his happy little speeches. Her husband had been confined in prison for some political offense. He was left alone with his thoughts to torture him. No voice, no book, no implement — silence, darkness, misery, sleepless self-torment; and soon it must be madness. All at once he thought of something to occupy these terrible unsleeping faculties. He took a pin from his neckcloth and threw it upon the floor. Then he groped for it. It was a little object, and the search was a long and laborious one. At last he found it, and felt a certain sense of satisfaction in difficulty overcome. But he had found a great deal more than a pin — he had found an occupation, and every day he would fling it from him and lose it, and hunt for it, and at last find it, and so he saved himself from going mad: and you will not wonder that when he was set free and gave the little object to which he owed his reason and, perhaps, his life, to his wife, she had it set round with pearls and wore it next her heart.

His monotonous, uninteresting, tread-mill work at the office, it is easy to understand, became very oppressive to him, and finally nearly unendurable. "My head is in such a state from incapacity for business," wrote he to Miss Betham, "that I certainly know it to be my duty not to undertake the veriest trifle in addition. I hardly know how I can go on. I have tried to get some redress by explaining my health, but with no great success. No one can tell how ill I am because it does not come out to the exterior of my face, but lies in my skull deep and invisible. I wish I was leprous, and black-jaundiced skin-over, and that all was as well within as my cursed looks. You must not think me worse than I am. I am determined not to be over-set, but to give up business rather, and get 'em to allow me a trifle for services past. O that I had been a shoemaker or a baker, or a man of large independent fortune. O darling laziness ! heaven of Epicurus ! Saints' Everlasting Rest ! that I could drink vast potations of thee through unmeasured Eternity — Otium cum vel sine dignitate. Scandalous, dishonorable, any kind of repose. I stand not upon the dignified sort. Accursed, damned desks, trade, commerce, business. Inventions of that old original busy-body, brain-working Satan — Sabbathless, restless Satan. A curse relieves : do you ever try it ?"

In a letter to Barton he thus wails out his distresses : "Of time, health, and riches, the first in order is not last in excellence. Riches are chiefly good, because they give us Time. What a weight of wearisome prison-hours have I to look back and forward to, as quite cut out of life ! and the sting of the thing is, that for six hours every day I have no business which I could not contract into two, if they would let me work task-work."

But, let us say, for the "weight of wearisome prison-hours," we should never have had his precious letters. To Walter Wilson, one of the friends of his youth, he wrote :

"I have a habit of never writing letters but at the office ; 't is so much time cribbed out of the company." He sometimes spent a week at a time in elaborating a single humorous letter. He was hunting the brooch.

Release came at length, but it was no better with him. He found no-work worse even than over-work. To Barton he wrote : "I pity you for over-work, but, I assure you, no work is worse. The mind preys on itself, the most unwholesome food. I bragged formerly that I could not have too much time. I have a surfeit. With but few years to come, the days are wearisome. But weariness is not eternal. Something will shine out to take the load off that flags me, which is at present intolerable. I have killed an hour or two in this poor scrawl."

As to his indulgences, regrets, and indecision, he has spoken for himself. He wrote to Manning, "I have been ill more than a month, with a bad cold, which comes upon me (like a murderer's conscience) about midnight, and vexes me for many hours. . . . I am afraid I must leave off drinking." To Hazlitt he said, at the end of a letter, "I am going to leave off smoke. In the meantime I am so smoky with last night's ten pipes, that I must leave off."

Ah! these medicines for the mind. Easily indulged, bitterly lamented, hardly avoided. In such cases as poor Lamb's, a sentence from one of his own favorite authors is peculiarly fitting : "In speaking of the dead, so fold up your discourse that their virtues may be outwardly shown, while their vices are wrapped up in silence." "He shall be immortal," said old Thomas Fuller, "who liveth to be stoned by one without fault."

He drank wine only during dinner — none after it. Over him, at one period of his life, "there passed regularly," says De Quincey, "after taking wine, a brief eclipse of sleep. It descended upon him as softly as a shadow. In a gross person, laden with superfluous flesh, and sleeping heavily, this would have been disagreeable ; but in Lamb, thin even to meagreness, spare and wiry as an Arab of the desert, or as Thomas Aquinas, wasted by scholastic vigils, the affection of sleep seemed rather a net-work of aërial gossamer than of earthly cobweb — more like a golden haze falling upon him gently from the heavens than a cloud exhaling upwards from the flesh. Motionless in his chair as a bust, breathing so gently as scarcely to seem certainly alive, he presented the image of repose midway between life and death, like the repose of sculpture ; and to one who knew his history, a repose affectingly contrasting with the calamities and internal storms of his life. I have heard more persons," continues De Quincey, "than I can now distinctly recall, observe of Lamb when sleeping, that his countenance in that state assumed an expression almost seraphic, from its intellectual beauty of outline, its childlike simplicity and its benignity. It could not be called a transfiguration that sleep had worked in his face ; for the features wore essentially the same expression when waking ; but sleep spiritualized that expression, exalted it, and also harmonized it."

It was Coleridge, who, after smoking tobacco after dinner, went to sleep on a sofa, where the company found him, to their no small surprise, which was increased to wonder, when he started up of a sudden, and rubbing his eyes, looked about him, and launched into a three hours' description of the third heaven, of which he had had a dream.

All accounts represent Lamb as one of the most punctual of men, although he never carried a watch. A friend observing the absence of this usual adjunct of a business man's attire, presented him with a new gold one, which he accepted (no doubt reluctantly) and carried for one day only. A colleague asked him what had become of it. "Pawned," was the reply. He had actually pawned the watch, finding it a useless encumbrance. Nobody knows how much his necessities had to do with that manner of disposing of the article ; or perhaps pride, which, you remember, made proud old Sam Johnson reject the new shoes which an officious or inconsiderate friend had placed at his chamber door.

Lamb was never introduced to Scott ; but we are told he used to speak with gratitude and pleasure of the circumstances under which he saw him once in Fleet-street. A man, in the dress of a mechanic, stopped him just at Inner Temple-gate, and said, touching his hat, "I beg your pardon, sir, but perhaps you would like to see Sir Walter Scott ; that is he just crossing the road ;" and Lamb stammered out his hearty thanks to his truly humane informer.

He literally loved books, and every thing pertaining to them. Sometimes — in a way scarcely discernible — he would kiss a volume of Burns ; as he would also a book by Chapman, or Sir Philip Sidney, or any other which he particularly valued. "I have seen him," said Procter, "read out passages from the Holy Dying and the Urn Burial, and express in the same way his devotion and gratitude."

We all know his supreme devotion to Shakespeare. In a letter to Talfourd, he says that Wordsworth, who worshiped nobody but himself, affected to slight Shakespeare — said he was a clever man, but his style had a great deal of trick in it, and that he could imitate him if he had a mind to. "So you see," said Lamb, "there's nothing wanting but the mind."

Of Lamb's pathos, and deep religious feeling, we give one interesting example, recorded by Hazlitt. Speaking, in conversation, of Judas Iscariot, Lamb said : "I would fain see the face of him, who, having dipped his hand in the same dish with the Son of Man, could afterward betray him. I have no conception of such a thing ; nor have **I ever seen any** picture (not even Leonardo's very fine one) **that gave me the least** idea of **it."** . . . "There is only **one** other **person I can ever** think of after this," continued **Lamb ; but without mentioning a name that** once put on a semblance of mortality. **"If Shakespeare** was **to** come into the room, we **should all rise** up **to meet** him ; **but** if that person was to **come into it,** we should **all** fall down and try to kiss the hem **of** his garment."

"Lamb's essays, the gossip of creative genius," says **an acute critic, "are** of a piece with the records of his **life and conversation.** Whether saluting his copy of Chapman's **Homer** with **a kiss, —— or saying a** grace before reading **Milton, ——** or going to **the theatre** to see his own farce acted, and **joining in the hisses of the pit** when it fails, —— or eagerly **wondering if the Ogles of** Somerset are not descendants **of King Lear, —— or telling** Barry Cornwall not to invite **a lugubrious gentleman to dinner** because **his face would cast a** damp **over a funeral, —— or** giving as a reason **why he did** not leave **off smoking, the** difficulty of finding **an** equivalent vice, **—— or striking into a** hot controversy between Coleridge **and** Holcroft, as to whether man as he is, **or** man as he **is to be, is** preferable, **and** settling the dispute by saying, **'Give me** man as he **is not to be,' —— or** doing some deed of kindness and **love with tears in his eyes and a** pun on his lips, **—— he is always the same dear,** strange, delightful companion and friend. **He is** never —— the rogue —— without **a** scrap of logic **to** astound common sense. **'Mr.** Lamb,' says the head **clerk at** the India House, 'you come down **very late in the morning!'** 'Yes, sir,' Mr. Lamb replies, 'but then you know I go home very early in the afternoon !'"

When reminded by his **sister of** the days when they were poor, and capable of enjoying every little treat with **the** keenest **relish,** so different from **the days when they** were rich, stately and dull, he said, "Well, Bridget, **since** we **are** in **easy** circumstances, we must just endeavor to put up with it." On a certain occasion he blandly proposed to his friend who offered to wrap up for him a bit of old cheese which he had seemed to like at dinner, to let him have a bit of string with which he could probably "lead it home." He said to Coleridge, "You are one of the most perfect of men, with only this one slight fault, that if you have any duty to do, you never do it." You remember his objection to brandy-and-water, — "It spoiled two good things." Crabb Robinson, just called to the bar, told Lamb exultingly, that he was retained in a cause in the King's Bench. "Ah," said Lamb, "the great first cause, least understood." Some one spoke of a Miss Pate, when Lamb inquired if she was any relation of Mrs. John Head of Ipswich. A person in his company said something about his grandmother. "Was she a tall woman?" said Lamb. "I don't know; no. Why do you ask?" "Oh, mine was; she was a granny dear." Running on ludicrously about some lady who had died of love for him, he said, he "was very sorry, but we could not command such inclinations." A lady who had been visiting in the neighborhood of Ipswich, on her return could talk of nothing else but the beauty of the country and the merits of the people. Lamb remarked that she was "Suffolk-ated." Like Dr. Johnson, he disliked the country. "A garden," he said, "was the primitive prison, till man, with Promethean felicity and boldness, luckily sinned himself out of it." One of his odd sayings is reported by Macready, — that "the last breath he drew in he wished might be through a pipe and exhaled in a pun." You have heard of his defense of lying, related by Leigh Hunt, that "Truth was precious, and not to be wasted on every body." "Hang the age," he wrote after one of his literary failures, "I will write for antiquity." "One cannot bear," he said, "to pay for articles he used to get for nothing. When Adam laid out his first penny for nonpareils at some stall in Mesopotamia, I think it went hard with him, reflecting upon his old goodly orchard, where he had so many for nothing."  "The water-cure," he said, "is neither new nor wonderful, but it is as old as the Deluge, which, in my opinion, killed more than it cured."

But Lamb's "witty and curious sayings," says Talfourd, "give no idea of the general tenor of his conversation, which was far more singular and delightful in the traits, which could never be recalled, than in the epigrammatic turns which it is possible to quote.  It was fretted into perpetual eddies of verbal felicity and happy thought, with little tranquil intervals reflecting images of exceeding elegance and grace."

His serious conversation, like his serious writing, is said to have been his best.  Yet no one, it is stated, "ever stammered out such fine, piquant, deep, eloquent things in half-a-dozen half sentences ; his jests scald like tears, and he probes a question with a play on words."

"Charles Lamb is gone," lamented De Quincey ; "his life was a continued struggle in the service of love the purest, and within a sphere visited by little of contemporary applause.  Even his intellectual displays won but a narrow sympathy at any time, and in his earlier period were saluted with positive derision and contumely on the few occasions when they were not oppressed by entire neglect.  But slowly all things right themselves.  All merit, which is founded in truth, and is strong enough, reaches by sweet exhalations in the end a higher sensory ; reaches higher organs of discernment, lodged in a selecter audience.  But the original obtuseness or vulgarity of feeling that thwarted Lamb's just estimation in life, will continue to thwart its popular diffusion.  There are even some that continue to regard him with the old hostility.  And we, therefore, standing by the side of Lamb's grave, seemed to hear, on one side, (but in abated tones,) strains of the ancient malice — 'This man, that thought himself to be somebody, is dead — is buried — is forgotten !' and, on the other side, seemed to hear ascending, as with the solemnity of an anthem — 'This man, that thought himself to be nobody, is dead — is buried ; his life has been searched ; and his memory is hallowed forever !' "

# VI.

## BURNS.

A DISTINGUISHED gentleman asked a poor man, whom he overtook on a visit to the birth-place of Robert Burns, — "Can you explain to me what it is that makes Burns such a favorite with you all in Scotland? Other poets you have, and great ones, but I do not perceive the same instant flash, as it were, of an electric feeling when any name is named but that of Burns." "I can tell you," said the man, "what it is. It is because he had the heart of a man in him. He was all heart and all man; and there's nothing, at least in a poor man's experience, either bitter or sweet, which can happen to him, but a line of Burns springs into his mouth, and gives him courage and comfort if he needs it. It is like a second Bible."

The reply of the peasant explains, in a few words, the popularity and growing fame of the poet. Everywhere, wherever men live and Burns is known, he is and will be, we believe, the acknowledged poet of humanity. Scotchmen especially, — on every spot of civilized earth, the same as in Scotland, — love him and quote him, and ever will love and quote him, particularly in every extremity of ill-fortune. He was the one exceptional fearless man, conceived by one of his countrymen, who had uttered feelings and thoughts participated in by the whole human race, and was the mouth of a dumb humanity.

When a very young man it was our good fortune to receive occasional nocturnal visits from an itinerant Scotch clock-tinker, who highly entertained us with readings and recitations from Burns. He was very poor, but seemed content with the very scanty living that his humble occupation brought him. His figure we can see now, in all its proportions, as we saw it then, by the light of a tallow candle, in a little upper room in an Ohio village. His head, especially, is vividly in memory. It was colossal, in comparison with common heads, and would have been picked out from an hundred thousand as in every way remarkable. It was one of those two-storied heads that Holmes talks so suggestively about, with the advantage or disadvantage of having its upper story most commodious and best occupied. The top of it rose like Walter Scott's, and his brow had the expression that Socrates' had, as shown in the bust we have of the philosopher. His face, though rather a hard one in repose, warmed and glowed under the inspiration of his beloved poet, as the great Stockton's did in the sublime passages of his sermons. The subtlest meanings were echoed by his varying emphasis; and responsive tears flowed down his weather-beaten cheeks. When he gave a convivial song, your ear caught the resounding laughter; when he recited a love ditty, you heard the

> " Youthful, loving, modest pair,
> In other's arms breathe out the tender tale,
> Beneath the milk-white thorn that scents the evening gale ; "

when he read a pitiless satire, you saw the miserable pretender writhing under the poet's lash; when he repeated a passage full of all humanity and Christian charity, the pathetic tenderness of his accents stirred the very fountains of feeling; when he read a lamentation upon poverty, you understood at once the reconcilement the poet so feelingly expresses of penury with death; and when he sang, with prodigious emphasis and spirit, that best of all war-songs, Bruce's Address, you felt the truth of the tradition, that the famous air was indeed the hero's march at the battle of Bannockburn, and that the words were

the veritable language addressed by the gallant royal
Scot to his heroic followers on that eventful morning.
The honest old man, who was so kind as to seek us out
in that solitary upper room, always met with a generous
welcome, a warm fire, and a pot of good ale from Father
Bowers', which helped him, for the time being, to forget
his patches and his hard lot, and to

> " Snatch a taste
> Of truest happiness."

Burns, to him — the good clock-tinker — was indeed "like
a second Bible."

The learned Judge Rodgers once related to us a death-
bed incident of a neighbor of his, — another poor, honest
Scotchman, a woodsawyer, — whose inspiration and solace, all through his hard life, had been Scotia's great
poet. ´ The good man, worn out and weary, was told by
his physician that his last hour had come — that he must
soon die.  He received the announcement philosophically ; and after naming a few things for which he expressed a desire to live, he said to the judge — about the
last thing he said on earth — " Yes," (with a glowing face
and a grasp of the hand,) " for these things I should like
to live ; but — but — judge " (they had many a time
read the poet together,) — " I shall see — Burns ! "  To
the honest woodsawyer also, Burns was "like a second
Bible."

In the Central Park, New York, is a piece of statuary
(removed, we believe, from its conspicuous place, on account of injury by the weather, and suffering somewhat
by fire in the building where it was placed for protection)
representing the meeting of two friends — Scotchmen.
The figures, as we remember them, are about half natural size, cut in light-colored sandstone.  Traveling-bag,
hat, and dog, are hard by.  The friends are seated at a
table, and are taking

> " A cup o' kindness yet,
> For auld lang syne."

And they are grasping hands, — the whole illustrating the verse —

> "An' here 's a hand, my trusty fiere,
>   An' gie 's a hand o' thine ;
> An' we 'll tak' a right guid willie-waught,
>   For auld lang syne."

Happy the sculptor so fortunate as to choose a subject expressing the friendly feeling of all mankind ; especially happy in wedding his art to Burns' immortal verse. Go when you would, early or late, you always found a rapt crowd surrounding the interesting work.

All his life in the jaws of need, Burns knew how to feel for the poor and poverty-stricken. The circumstances even of his birth, were wretched. While his mother was yet on the straw, the miserable clay cottage fell above her and the infant bard, who both narrowly escaped, first being smothered to death, and then of being killed by cold, as they were conveyed through frost and snow by night to another dwelling. Every day the poverty of the family increased. The cattle died, the crops failed, debts accumulated. They lived so sparingly that butchers'-meat was nearly unknown to the family for years. The poet describes his life, until his sixteenth year, as "the cheerless gloom of a hermit, with the unceasing moil of a galley-slave." "Stubborn, ungainly integrity, and headlong ungovernable irascibility," interfered seriously with his father's success in the world ; they made him poor and kept him so. At the age of twenty-three Robert set out for himself. He "joined a flaxdresser in a neighboring town to learn his trade. This was an unlucky affair, and, to finish the whole, as we were giving," he says, " a welcome to the New Year, the shop took fire and burnt to ashes, and I was left like a true poet, not worth a sixpence." And so all the way through ; he had little of thrift at any time. His business enterprises failed ; nothing he touched turned into gold.

The pictures he drew were of life as he had seen it and felt it. He had experienced its ills, and had realized their benefits. Who but one who had known misfortunes could have said of them so wisely? —

> "I, here, wha sit, ha'e met wi' some,
>   An 's thankfu' for them yet.
> They gie the wit of age to youth ;
>   They let us ken oursel' ;
> They mak' us see the naked truth,
>   The real guid and ill.
>     Though losses and crosses
>       Be lessons right severe,
>     There 's wit there, ye 'll get there,
>       Ye 'll find nae other where."

Who but one who had himself known "the miseries of man " could so sympathizingly remember and immortalize an old granduncle, with whom his mother lived while in her girlish years? The good old man was long blind ere he died ; during which time his highest enjoyment was to sit down and cry, while the poet's mother would sing the simple old song of the Life and Age of Man. From that pitiful scene in real life, and from his own bitter experiences, he produced those immortal lines — so consolatory to poverty and wretchedness : —

> "O Death ! the poor man's dearest friend —
>   The kindest and the best !
> Welcome the hour my aged limbs
>   Are laid with thee at rest !
> The great, the wealthy, fear thy blow,
>   From pomp and pleasure torn ;
> But, oh ! a blest relief to those
>   That weary-laden mourn ! "

George Sand, in the introduction to one of her novels, has been looking at an engraving of Holbein's Laborer. "An old, thick-set peasant, in rags, is driving his plow in the midst of a field. All around spreads a wild landscape, dotted with a few poor huts. The sun is setting behind a hill ; the day of toil is nearly over. It has been hard; the ground is rugged and stony; the laborer's horses are but skin and bone, weak and exhausted. There is but one alert figure, the skeleton Death, who with a whip skips nimbly along at the horse's side and urges the team. Under the picture is a quotation in old French, to the effect that after the laborer's life of travail and service, in which he has to gain his bread by the sweat of his brow, here comes Death to fetch him away. And from so rude a life does Death take him, says George Sand, that Death is hardly unwelcome ; and in another composition by Holbein, where men of almost every condition — popes, sovereigns, lovers, gamblers, monks, soldiers — are taunted with their fear of Death, and do indeed see his approach with terror, Lazarus alone is easy and composed, and sitting on his dunghill at the rich man's door, tells Death that he does not mind him."

What a picture the poet makes of

"Age and Want, oh ! ill-matched pair !"

further back in the poem last quoted.  See !

> "On the edge of life,
> With cares and sorrows worn ;
> Then Age and Want — oh ! ill-matched pair ! —
> Show man was made to mourn."

Dr. Hooker, a traveler in Thibet, describes it as a mountainous country, and inconceivably poor. There are no plains save flats in the bottom of the valleys, and the paths lead over lofty mountains. Sometimes, when the inhabitants are obliged from famine to change their habitations in winter, the old and feeble are frozen to death standing and resting their chins on their staves ; remaining as pillars of ice, to fall only when the thaw of the ensuing spring commences ! — Ah !

> "Age and Want — oh ! ill-matched pair !"

a terrible illustration : too terrible to be contemplated. It proves, that in life there are extremities of distress and wretchedness inconceivable, even to poetic fancy.   Dante, amongst the damned, saw nothing more dreadful.

"We talk," said Douglas Jerrold, "of the intemperance of the poor ; why, when we philosophically consider the crushing miseries that beset them — the keen suffering of penury, and the mockery of luxury and profusion with which it is surrounded — the wonder is, not that there are so many who purchase temporary oblivion of their misery, but that there are so few."

Living in London streets accounts for the younger Weller's shrewdness ; but the pretended advantages of poverty are not to the poor themselves so easy to see, nor so pleasant to contemplate.   If success hath crowned the struggle, the battle may be calculatingly, perhaps complacently, remembered.   "I would not," said Jean Paul, "for any money, have had money in my youth ;" but Jean Paul, no doubt, when he wrote the quaint words, was looking back over the rugged way to eminence attained.   Looking up at the precipitous, jagged path, he would have cried out in quite other words, if not too dumb by despairing discouragement to utter them.

"Moralists tell you," said Sydney Smith, "of the evils of wealth and station, and the happiness of poverty.   I have been very poor the greatest part of my life, and have borne it as well, I believe, as most people, but I can safely say that I have been happier every guinea I have gained."

The advantages of poverty, at best but remote and fortuitous, are sometimes subject to facetious illustration. For instance, it is said that amongst the higher classes in Constantinople, the mortality is out of proportion great, owing to two facts ; first, whenever a person is unwell he calls in a doctor, and the doctor as sure as fate calls in a barber, and has the patient bled ; then, between doctors, barbers, bleedings, and leechings, the patient stands a fair chance of being soon carried to the burying-ground. Poor folks cannot afford all this expense, and they live.

Asa, King of Judah, Bible readers remember, " was diseased in his feet, until his disease was exceeding great: yet in his disease he sought not to the Lord, but to the physicians. And Asa slept with his fathers."

No man ever existed who better understood the uses of money than Burns ; else could he have written those oft-quoted lines ? They occur in The Epistle to a Young Friend, — Mr. Andrew H. Aikin of Ayr, to whose father the Cotter's Saturday Night is inscribed. Andrew is said to have profited by the advice, as he lived and died a prosperous man. Better did he " reck the rede than ever did the adviser."

> " To catch dame Fortune's golden smile,
>    Assiduous wait upon her ;
> And gather gear by ev'ry wile
>    That 's justified by honor ;
> Not for to hide it in a hedge,
>    Nor for a train attendant,
> But for the glorious privilege
>    Of being independent."

Sir James Mackintosh returned to England from India in broken health. He had enjoyed opportunities for accumulating a competency. He was judge of the admiralty court, besides being recorder of Bombay. " He had been," he said, " to El Dorado ; but he had forgotten the gold ; and was obliged to confess to his friends that he was ashamed of his poverty, since it showed a want of common sense."

Burns, no doubt, often lamented his situation in the same self-upbraiding spirit ; though the independence he enjoyed was of the genuine sort, and altogether agreed with his theory of life. It was that kind of independence inculcated in the Oriental story. They asked the famous Hatim Tayi, the most generous of mankind, " Have you ever met any one more independent than yourself ? " He replied : " Yes ! One day I gave a feast to the whole neighborhood, and had fifty oxen roasted. As I was proceeding to the place, I found a woodcutter tying up his fagots. I said, 'Why do you not go to Hatim's feast, which is open to all?' But he answered, 'Whoever can eat the bread earned by his own labor will not put himself under obligation to Hatim Tayi.' Then I knew that I had found one more independent than myself."

Burns had a proud hatred of patronage. He would not, like Samson's bees, "make honey in the bowels of a lion, and fatten on the offal of a rich man's superfluities."

Charlemagne had the habit of impressing the seal upon treaties which he had concluded with the pommel of his sword, upon which was engraved, "Thus with the pommel of my sword I seal this act, the conditions of which I will execute with its point." Burns, with a like sense of personal responsibility, swore "by that honor which crowns the upright statue of Robert Burns' Integrity." Like Voltaire, he perceived very early that every man must be hammer or anvil, and he determined with the great Frenchman to become a hammer. With what effect he hammered injustice, falsehood, and hypocrisy, and struck for liberty, equality, and the rights of man, all the world will attest till the last day.

For his boldness he was, of course, hated. The hurt cried out. Enemies were as hostile as friends were faithful. The division was natural. Tze-Kung asked Confucius, "What do you say of a man who is loved by all the people of his village?" The Master replied, "We may not for that accord an approval of him." "And what do you say of him who is hated by all the people of his village?" The Master said, "We may not for that conclude that he is bad. It is better than either of these cases that the good in the village love him, and the bad hate him."

Said old Daniel, enthusiastically, in his Epistle to Lady Margaret, Countess of Cumberland,

> "Unless above himself he can
> Erect himself, how poor a thing is man."

Like all enthusiasts, Burns' standards, in his exalted moments, were apt to be too high. The pattern was inimitable, and approximations only were discouraging. Socrates' precept to attain honest fame — "Study to be what you wish to seem "— was to him disheartening. His self-reverence was shaken ; and he felt himself as much worse than himself as he had purposed being better. Self-reverence! You remember how it was urged upon every one by the elder Cato, as every one is always in his own presence.

"I was a lad of fifteen," said Scott to Lockhart, "when Burns came to Edinburgh. The only thing I remember which was remarkable in his manner was the effect produced upon him by a print, representing a soldier lying dead on the snow, his dog sitting in misery on one side — on the other, his widow with a child in her arms. These lines of Langhorne's were written beneath : —

> "Cold on Canadian hills, or Minden's plain,
> Perhaps that parent wept her soldier slain —
> Bent o 'er the babe, her eye dissolved in dew,
> The big drops mingling with the milk he drew,
> Gave the sad presage of his future years,
> The child of misery baptized in tears."

Burns seemed much affected by the print: he actually shed tears. There was a strong expression of sense and shrewdness in all his lineaments ; the eye alone, I think, indicated the poetical character and temperament. It was large, and of a dark cast, which glowed (I say literally glowed) when he spoke with feeling or interest. I never saw such another eye in a human head, though I have seen the most distinguished men of my time."

Of Jeffrey, when a lad in his teens, it is recorded that one day, as he stood on the High street of Edinburgh, staring at a man whose appearance struck him, a person at a shop door tapped him on the shoulder, and said, "Aye, laddie, ye may weel look at that man. That's Robbie Burns."

"I have been in the company of many men of genius, some of them poets," said Ramsey, a laird, to Dr. Currie, "but I never witnessed such flashes of intellectual brightness as from him, the impulse of the moment, sparks of celestial fire. When I asked whether the Edinburgh literati had mended his poems by their criticisms, 'Sir,' said he, 'these gentlemen remind me of some spinsters in my country, who spin their thread so fine, that it is neither fit for weft nor woof.'"

The scholarly and refined Edinburghers rigidly scrutinized the rustic poet, but all accounts warrant the statement that he paid them back in their own coin. His natural penetration was too keen to be blinded by a learned look, a haughty bearing, or the glitter of a fashion. One of his remarks, when he first went to Edinburgh was, that "between the men of rustic life and the polite world he observed little difference; that in the former, though unpolished by fashion, and unenlightened by science, he had found much observation and intelligence." "He manifested," says Lockhart, "in the whole strain of his bearing and conversation, a most thorough conviction, that in the society of the most eminent men of his nation, he was exactly where he was entitled to be; hardly deigned to flatter them by exhibiting even an occasional symptom of being flattered by their notice; by turns calmly measured himself against the most cultivated understandings of his time in discussion; overpowered the witty sayings of the most celebrated convivialists by broad floods of merriment, impregnated with all the burning fire of genius; astounded persons habitually enveloped in the thrice-piled folds of social reserve, by compelling them to tremble, nay to tremble visibly beneath the fearless touch of natural pathos; and all this without indicating the smallest willingness to be ranked among those professional ministers of excitement, who are content to be paid in money and smiles for doing what the specta-

tors and auditors would be ashamed of doing in their own
persons, even if they had the power of doing it."

Now and again, it is said, the homage to genius would
assume the character of the patronage of dependence,
and then Burns' proud spirit would break through the
very courtesies of society, and lash the offender against
his jealous sense of independence with sarcasm or satire.
From this it has been judged by an English critic that
pride was the key to the personal character of Burns,
sometimes manifesting itself in what appeared to be arrogance and injustice. Pride he had undoubtedly, says one
of his biographers, but it was the pride of a man — an
honest uncompromising pride, that scorned the arrogance
and injustice of those who dared to obtrude their petty
conventional honors or social position before one who
knew their unreality. Could he have mounted a little of
the furnishings of the artful hypocrite, or the pliant syco-
phant, he might have slipped into the robes and dignity
of some lucrative office.

What a talker he must have been! All accounts agree
in representing his conversation as wonderful. It was
better even than his verse. Sir Richard Phillips once
went up to Coleridge, after hearing him talk in a large
party, and offered him nine guineas a sheet for his conversations. If any enterprising publisher had been fortunate enough to secure a few hundred pages of Burns'
conversation, he might have dreamed of building another
Abbotsford. If another Boswell had followed him about,
what a book we should have!

We have an account of a call that two Englishmen
made upon him. They found him fishing. He received
them with great cordiality, and asked them to share his
humble dinner. He was in his happiest mood, and the
charm of his conversation was altogether fascinating.
He ranged over a variety of topics, illuminating whatever
he touched. He related the tales of his infancy and

youth; he recited some of his gayest and some of his tenderest poems; in the wildest of the strains of his mirth he threw in some touches of melancholy, and spread around him the electric emotions of his powerful mind. The Highland whiskey improved in its flavor; the marble bowl was again and again emptied and replenished; the guests of the poet forgot the flight of time and the dictates of prudence; at the hour of midnight they lost their way to Dumfries, and could scarcely distinguish it when assisted by the morning's dawn. No wonder that "nicht wi' Burns" was so vividly remembered and so vividly narrated.

In his fifteenth summer he first fell in love with a "bonnie, sweet, sonsie lass." The tones of her voice made his "heart-strings thrill like an Æolian harp," and made his pulse beat a "furious ratan," when he "looked and fingered over her little hand, to pick out the cruel nettle-stings and thistles." To her he wrote his first song, Handsome Nell. In it occurs this felicitous verse:

> "She dresses aye sae clean and neat,
>   Baith decent and genteel,
> And then there 's something in her gait
>   Gars ony dress look weal."

"I composed it," he says, "in a wild enthusiasm of passion, and to this hour I never recollect it but my heart melts, my blood sallies at the remembrance."

In his nineteenth summer he fell in love again, "which ebullition," he says, "ended the school business at Kirkoswold. It was in vain to think of doing any more good at school. The remaining week I stayed," he says, "I did nothing but craze the faculties of my soul about her, or steal out to meet her; and the two last nights of my stay in the country, had sleep been a mortal sin, the image of this modest and innocent girl had kept me guiltless." From that time on, we are told, for several years, love-making was his chief amusement, or rather most serious business. His brother tells us that he was in the secret of half the love affairs of the parish of Tarbolton, and was never without at least one of his own. There was not a comely girl in the parish on whom he did not compose a song, and then he made one which included them all.

At twenty-three he had an affair which turned out to be serious. Ellison Begbie, whom he "adored," and who had "pledged her soul" to meet him "in the field of matrimony," jilted him, "with peculiar circumstances of mortification." His constitutional melancholy was increased to such a degree, that "for three months," he says, "I was in a state of mind scarcely to be envied by the hopeless wretches who have got their mittimus, Depart from me, ye accursed!" To the cause of all this distress he wrote some of his finest songs, especially that of Mary Morison.

> "Yestreen when to the trembling string
>   The dance gaed thro' the lighted ha',
> To thee my fancy took its wing,
>   I sat, but neither heard nor saw:
> Tho' this was fair, an' that was braw,
>   An' yon the toast of a' the town,
> I sighed, an' said amang them a',
>   'Ye are na Mary Morison.'
>
> O Mary, canst thou wreck his peace,
>   Wha for thy sake would gladly dee?
> Or canst thou break that heart of his,
>   Whase only faut is loving thee?
> If love for love thou wilt nae gie,
>   At least be pity on me shown;
> A thought ungentle canna be
>   The thought o' Mary Morison."

In these lines to Clarinda, Mrs. M'Lehose, with whom he had the famous correspondence, are concentrated, Scott and Byron both thought, "the essence of a thousand love tales:"

> "Had we never loved so kindly,
>  Had we never loved so blindly;
>  Never met, or never parted,
>  We had ne'er been broken-hearted."

What a favorite he was with the fair! It is said that Abdallah, the father of Mahomet, the most admirable of the Arabian youths, when he consummated his marriage with Amina, of the noble race of Zahrites, two hundred virgins died of jealousy and despair. Burns! such a splendid fellow! such a hearty lover! what wonder that he also was the admiration of hosts of sighing maidens. Salvini, magnificent histrionic lover that he is, were tame indeed in comparison with Burns as an incarnation of the tender passion.

He yielded to woman as Hercules yielded to Omphale, or Samson to Delilah. His love was not platonic, but, "the love of human passion, burning with the warmth of human affection." Lovely woman inspired him. He told Thomson that when he wished to compose a love-song, his recipe was to put himself on a "regimen of admiring a beautiful woman." When Aristotle was asked why people liked to spend a great deal of time in the presence of beauty, he said, "That is a question for a blind man to ask."

His intense earnestness put him often at loggerheads with the universe. The Orientalists have a saying, that when a word has once escaped, a chariot with four horses cannot overtake it. He had opinions, and was unwise enough to express them. Wise men, said old John Selden, say nothing in dangerous times. The Lion, you know, called the Sheep to ask her if his breath smelt: she said Aye; he bit off her head for a fool. He called the Wolf and asked him: he said No; he tore him in pieces for a flatterer. At last he called the Fox and asked him: Truly he had got a cold and could not smell.

Joubert has said, that we use up in the passions the

stuff that was given us for happiness. It is accounted a melancholy fact by Madame de Staël, that from the influence of the passions, the human race is doomed to move in the same circle of error, notwithstanding its advancement by the acquisition of intellect. To most men, "experience is like the stern lights of a ship, which illumine only the track it has passed."

Memnon, in the story, conceived the insensate idea of becoming perfectly wise. He said to himself, To become very wise, all which is necessary is to control the passions, and that may be easily done. The day after, on his way home from the Palace, he reflected on the excellent resolutions he had formed — to defy the power of women ; to guard against intemperance and quarrels ; preserve his independence, and not solicit favors at court : yet in one day, he had suffered himself to be duped by a woman, and robbed, been intoxicated, lost deeply at play, had his eye knocked out in a quarrel, was reduced to poverty, and had solicited a favor at court, where he had received nothing but contempt.

The ways of men will be awry. They will not straighten them, nor let you, without resistance. Remember the battle ! It is in cracking the bad nuts that you hurt your fingers. Charles the Fifth, Emperor of Germany, when he abdicated a throne, and retired to the monastery of Yuste, amused himself with the mechanical arts, and particularly with that of watch-making. He one day exclaimed, "What an egregious fool must I have been to have squandered so much blood and treasure, in an absurd attempt to make all men think alike, when I cannot even make a few watches keep time together."

Men mean better than they do ; and pride of opinion will account for most of their differences. For fifteen hundred years, the story is, two sects in Babylon had maintained a violent contest. One said it was proper to enter the Temple with the right foot foremost; the other insisted that it should be with the left foot foremost; and both sects impatiently expected the day on which the festival of the sacred fire was to be celebrated to see which of them Zadig would favor. Zadig, you must know, had acquired the admiration and love of the people; his name was celebrated throughout the empire. The learned considered him as an oracle; the priests confessed that he was wiser than the old archmagi Yebor; and they believed only what he thought was probable. The people were all in suspense and perturbation. The day arrived, and every eye was fixed on the feet of Zadig. He placed them close together, and jumped into the Temple.

Genius is bold, and strikes to the core. Talent hesitates, and stops short. There is said to be a species of cactus from whose outer bark, if torn by some ignorant person, there exudes a poisonous liquid; but the natives, who know the plant, strike to the core, and thus find a sweet, refreshing juice, that renews their strength.

Talent busies itself with modes and accommodations, and the purpose is apt to be obscured in a chaos of details. We have an analysis of one of the most pathetic of Balzac's minor stories, which describes the fate of a poor painter, who had labored for years at a picture destined to create a new era in art. All his hopes in life, his love and his ambition, were involved in his success. No one had been admitted to the room in which he labored with unremitting devotion. At last, the day came when the favored person stood before the curtain which concealed the masterpiece. The painter drew it aside, slowly and solemnly, and revealed a meaningless confusion of chaotic coloring. The artist's mind was unhinged, and had been nearly destroyed by endless refinements and details. Recalling the statement made by Dr. Johnson, that Mallet, though pensioned for the purpose, never wrote a single line of his projected life of Marlborough, — groping for materials, and thinking of it, till he exhausted his mind.

The rapidity of Burns' genius may be imagined from the production of some of his poems — Tam o' Shanter, for instance — which, we are told by Mrs. Burns, was the work of a single day. She retained a vivid recollection of it. Her husband had spent most of the day by the river side, and in the afternoon she joined him with her two children. He was busily engaged crooning to himself; and Mrs. Burns perceiving that her presence was an interruption, loitered behind with her little ones among the broom. Her attention was presently attracted by the strange and wild gesticulations of the bard, who was now seen at some distance, agonized with an ungovernable access of joy. He was reciting very loud, and with tears rolling down his cheeks, those animated verses which he had just conceived :

> " Now Tam ! **O Tam ! had** thae been queans,
> A' plump and strapping, in their teens."

" I wish ye had seen him," said his wife; " he was in such ecstasy that the tears were happing down his cheeks." Some passages of that poem, produced that day by the river side, appear to us as the figures of Michel Angelo appeared to Castelar — " as if they had issued from the flashes of a tempest, and been produced from the fury of a giant." The rapidity of his genius may be illustrated by a tradition of Mahomet, who, his followers believe, was conveyed by the angel Gabriel through the seven heavens, paradise, and hell, and held fifty-nine thousand conferences with God, and was brought back to his bed before the water had finished flowing from a pitcher which he upset as he departed.

In sight of the Mexicans, who had a vast superiority of men and artillery, General Taylor held a council of war, and the nearly unanimous opinion was, that he should not risk a contest. "Gentlemen," said Taylor, "I adjourn this council, until to-morrow — after the battle," — which, it is hardly necessary to say, he won, against the great odds.　Burns had like confidence in his abilities, and knew what he could do.　Scott told Leslie, the artist, that he had known a laboring man who was with Burns when he turned up the mouse with his plow.　The poet's first impulse was to kill it, but checking himself, as his eye followed the little creature, he said, " I 'll make that mouse immortal."　In connection with this, how amusing the letter received by Goethe, from a conceited student, who begged of him the plan for the second part of Faust, with the design of completing the work himself !

The first object that strikes the eye on approaching Palermo is the Monte Pellegrino, whose square and isolated mass shelters the town from the north-westerly winds, and makes the sirocco still more oppressive.　When the great Napoleon was in power, the people believed, it is said, so great was their confidence in his supernatural power, that if he made himself master of Sicily, he would cause this mountain to be thrown into the sea. The ruder country lads and the lower peasantry, looked upon Burns as more than a man — with something like supernatural power.　Especially they dreaded "lest he should pickle and preserve them in sarcastic song."　Once at a penny wedding, when two wild lads quarreled, and were about to fight, Burns rose up and said, " Sit down, or I 'll hang you up like potato-bogles in sang to-morrow." They ceased, and sat down, it is stated, as if their noses had been bleeding.

It is an observation of Lord Halifax that a man has rarely one good quality but he possesses too much of it. Burns' detestation of falsehood, injustice, and hypocrisy, sometimes made him merciless in assaulting them.　Hypocrites, especially, trembled and winced under his lash. He was well aware, with Molière, of the marvelous advantages that the profession of hypocrisy possesses, and the fact angered him.　It is an act, says the French dramatist, of which the imposture is always respected ; and though it may be discovered, no one dares to do any thing against it. All the other vices of man are liable to censure, and every one has the liberty of boldly attacking them, but hypocrisy is a privileged vice, which with its hand closes everybody's mouth, and enjoys its repose with sovereign impunity.

> " The tender creature's eyes with sweetness swell :
> Heaven 's in those eyes, and in his heart is hell."

" There is some hypocrisy," says Thackeray, " of which one does not like even to entertain the thought ; especially that awful falsehood which trades with divine truth, and takes the name of Heaven in vain." Kossuth had a similar horror of the same awful falsehood, when he spoke of one who had climbed to the top of the altar of God to light the torch of Satan.

Burns hated lying, and had a conscience toward God, which, says George Macdonald, is the guide to freedom, but conscience toward society is the slave of a fool. "Any man may put himself in training for a liar by doing things he would be ashamed to have known." You remember the philosopher in Lucian, who was present at Jupiter's whispering place, and heard one pray for rain, another for fair weather ; one for his wife's, another for his father's death, etc., — all asking that at God's hand which they were ashamed any man should hear.

Peasantry and gentry, saint and sinner, alike knew, and alike dreaded, his ridicule. And what is there, pray, that is more dreadful than the ridicule of genius? Nothing so much put Napoleon in a rage : it made him drive Madame de Staël out of his empire. Nobody likes it, for the reason that nobody likes to be exposed, and all the world is ready to unite in punishing it. The Koran threatens that on the day of resurrection, those who have indulged in ridicule will be called to the door of Paradise, and hear it shut in their faces, when they reach it. Again, on their turning back they will be called to another door, and again, on reaching it, will see it closed against them ; and so on without end.

Burns, for his disposition to satire, was bitterly punished by his neighbors, in the only way they could punish one so superior to them. They exaggerated his follies, and scandalized his name. "The disposition," says Froude, speaking of a certain scandal relating to Cæsar, "to believe evil of men who have risen a few degrees above their contemporaries, is a feature of human nature as common as it is base ; and when to envy there are added fear and hatred, malicious anecdotes spring like mushrooms in a forcing-pit." Arthur Helps remarks, in reference to the accusation against Cortez of having poisoned Ponce de Leon, that "any man who is much talked of will be much misrepresented. Indeed, malignant intention is unhappily the least part of calumny, which has its sources in idle talk, playful fancies, gross misrepresentations, utter exaggerations, and many other rivulets of error that sometimes flow together in one huge river of calumniation, which pursues its muddy, mischievous course unchecked for ages."

Admire him, however, they would, abuse him as they might. They were proud of him, even those who hated him. Moore records in his Diary, that when a number of persons in his presence were speaking of O'Connell, — of the mixture there was in the great Irishman of high and low, formidable and contemptible, mighty and mean, Bobus Smith summed up all by saying : "The only way to deal with such a man is to hang him up, and erect a statue to him under his gallows."

Speaking his mind, as freely as Burns did, has ruined many a man. It is an extravagance that few men can afford. Sydney Smith, at a meeting of the clergy to petition parliament against the passage of the Catholic emancipation bill, found himself in a minority of one. A poor clergyman whispered to him that he was quite of his way of thinking, but had nine children. The witty and humane parson begged he would remain a Protestant.

They pronounced him irreligious, because he hated and scourged hypocrisy. Full as he was of religious feeling, they were ready to deny him belief in God ; — the truth being that no one exceeded him in reverence of the Deity, nor had a greater horror of atheism or an atheist. Who could ever forget his expression ? —

> " An atheist's laugh 's a poor exchange
> For Deity offended."

Few really great men have been professed atheists. Voltaire, it will be remembered, said to the atheist Damilaville, " My friend, after you have supped on well-dressed partridges, drank your sparkling champagne, and slept on cushions of down in the arms of your mistress, I have no fear of you, though you do not believe in God. But if you are perishing of hunger, and I meet you in the corner of a wood, I would rather dispense with your company."

His hatred of injustice, cant, and hypocrisy, had the effect no doubt to put him often into too intimate relation and association with those who were really uncongenial to him, but who had like aversions with himself. It has been said, somewhat cynically perhaps, "That we must have the same enmities to be united in spirit. In order to love one another, we must have hatreds in common." Some strange friendships in political life might be cited in illustration. Literature, too, could produce some proofs. We know, for instance, how, on account of the satire of Fielding, the moral Richardson and the dissolute Cibber became lasting friends.

But, in mixing with all, he found many advantages. Meeting freely the low and the mean, as well as the high and influential, he had every view of man, and was enabled to know the possibilities of so great a composition. The good and the evil lie close together ; the virtues and the vices **alternate : so is** power accumulated ; alternately metals **and rags —a terrible voltaic** pile.   To know man, you must **know men — all sorts of** men.   Nothing, it has been **truly said, more conducts to** liberality **of** judgment than **facile** intercourse **with various minds.**   The commerce **of** intellect loves **distant shores.**   The small retail **dealer** trades only with his neighbor ; **when** the great merchant trades, he links the four quarters of the globe.

**But** with all his gettings, he did not get the wisdom **of** silence.   **He** knew it, **but** could not put it in practice. He advised it, **but did not** act upon it.

> " Aye free, aff han' your story tell,
>      When wi' a bosom crony ;
>      But still keep something to yoursel'
>      Ye scarcely tell to ony."

And **here we may profit by an observation of Leigh** Hunt's — which **Burns above all** men realized — **that the** great **secret** of **giving advice** successfully **is to mix up** with **it something** that implies **a real** consciousness **of the** adviser's **own defects,** and as much **as possible of an ac-** knowledgment **of the other party's merits.**   Most advisers sink both the one **and the other ; and hence the failure** which they meet with, **and deserve.**   Burns knew too well his own habit of talking **right out of** his mind, and mem- orably warned against **the** dangers of so easy and **costly** an indulgence.   The **law of** the Pundits he should have nailed **on his door-post :** "The **Magistrate, at** what time he **is desirous to consult with his** counselors, should choose **a retired** place, **on the top of the** house, or on the top of a mountain, or in **the desert, or** some such secret recess, and **shall hold his council there ;** and **in places** where there are parrots, **or other** talkative birds, **he shall** not hold his council, **while they** are present."

**He was a** born convivialist, **and they pronounced him** a drunkard.   Drinking was very general **in his day,** and **we** imagine he drank little if any more than **those who**

drank less publicly. "It is a current story in Teviot-dale," says Scott, "that in the house of an ancient family of distinction, much addicted to Presbyterianism, a Bible was always put into the sleeping apartment of the guests, along with a bottle of strong ale. On some occasion there was a visiting of clergymen in the vicinity of the castle, all of whom were invited to dinner by the worthy baronet, and several abode all night. According to the fashion of the times, seven of the reverend guests were allotted to one large barrack-room, which was used on such occasions of extended hospitality. The butler took care that the divines were presented, according to custom, each with a Bible and a bottle of ale. But after a little consultation amongst themselves, they are said to have recalled the domestic as he was leaving the apartment. 'My friend,' said one of the venerable guests, 'you must know, when we meet together as brethren, the youngest minister reads aloud a portion of Scripture to the rest;— only one Bible, therefore, is necessary; take away the other six, and in their place bring six more bottles of ale.'"

It is yet not an uncommon thing, we believe, in Scotland, for the clergyman, upon returning with the gentlemen to the dining-hall, after dinner, to ask a blessing, the same as at dinner when the ladies were present, although only the bottles and the necessary conveniences for drinking have a place upon the table.

Alcohol is as old as Satan. Klopstock, in his Messiah, indulges the speculation that the loved and hated thing was introduced by Satan into the tree of knowledge before our first parents partook of it, and was attended with the same effects that have followed it ever since. One of the tales in Gesta Romanorum is to the effect that Noah discovered the wild vine, and because it was bitter, he took the blood of four animals,— of a lion, of a lamb, a pig, and a monkey; this mixture he united with earth, and made a kind of **fertilizer, which** he put at the roots of **the** vines. Thus **the blood** sweetened the fruit, with which he afterward **intoxicated** himself, and lying naked in his tent, was derided by his younger **son.**

The excuse generally given for drinking is, **that** it unclogs the wheels of life, and sets them **running faster** than **usual.** A zest in that way is given **to it, for** the time being, **in** spite of all its impediments and burdens. Blackstone composed his Commentaries with a bottle of **port before him.** Addison's conversation is reported as not **good for much till he** had taken a similar dose. Byron's **account of a party with** Sheridan is picturesque. It was, he says, first **silent, then talky, then argumentative,** then disputatious, **then unintelligible, then altogethery, then inarticulately,** then **drunk. Irving used to tell a witty anec**dote of one of his early **friends, Henry Ogden, illustrative** of the convivial feature **of the dinners in New York when** he was a **young man. Ogden had been at one of these** festive meetings on the evening **before, and had left with** a brain half bewildered **by the number** of bumpers **he had been** compelled **to drink. He told** Irving the next **day that** in going home he had fallen through a grating, **which** had carelessly been left open, into a vault beneath. **The** solitude, he said, was rather dismal at first, but **sev**eral other of the guests fell in, in the course of the even**ing,** and they had on the whole quite **a** pleasant night of it.

The implicit faith the Scotch have **in their** clergy, in all things, is sometimes a great protection to the cloth. Fifty years ago, **we are told,** when most of the good folk in Scotland **esteemed going to** the theatre **as entirely** analogous to going to **destruction, a** popular Edinburgh preacher, being in London, **was** surreptitiously entering with the multitude into the pit of Drury Lane. **Sud**denly a hand was laid upon him, and an awe-stricken **voice** said, **"Oh,** Doctor MacGrugar, what would the congregation in

Tolbooth Kirk say if I told them I saw you here?"
"Deed," replied the ready-witted divine, "they wadna
believe you, and so you needna tell them."

Dr. Alexander Webster, also of Edinburgh, was remarkable, according to Scott, for the talent with which
he at once supported his place in convivial society, and a
high character as a leader of the strict and rigid Presbyterian party in the Church of Scotland, which certainly
seemed to require very different qualifications. He was
ever gay amid the gayest. When it once occurred to
some one present to ask, what one of his elders would
think, should he see his pastor in such a merry mood: —
"Think!" replied the doctor; "why he would not believe
his own eyes."

Johnson and Boswell were told in Sky, that every week
a hogshead of claret was drunk at the table of Sir Alexander MacDonald — kinsman of the romantic and heroic
Flora, the guide and companion of Charles Edward
Stuart, after his defeat at Culloden, disguised as a woman.

That for which a laird or a doctor of divinity was excused, was punished with severity in a peasant. Burns
was, and is, bitterly censured, for what were, in his day,
common sins of society. It is too much the way of the
world, savage or civilized, and, we fear, ever will be. It
is the Feejeean idea of justice, where the criminality of an
act is in proportion to the rank of the offender. Murder
by a chief is less heinous than petty larceny committed
by a man of low rank. It is the universal rule, to estimate men, and respect them, according to circumstances.
Pope was one day with Sir Godfrey Kneller, when his
nephew, a Guinea-trader, came in. "Nephew," said Sir
Godfrey, "you have the honor of seeing the two greatest
men in the world." "I don't know how great you may
be," said the slave-trader, "but I don't like your looks:
I have often bought a man, much better than both of you
together, all muscles and bones, for ten guineas."

"It is a folly," said Publius Syrus, "to punish your neighbor by fire when you live next door." "If he that were guiltless himself," said old Burton, "should fling the first stone at thee, and he alone should accuse thee that were faultless, how many executioners, how many accusers, wouldst thou have? If every man's sins were written in his forehead, and secret faults known, how many thousands would parallel, if not exceed thy offense? It may be the judge that gave you sentence, the jury that condemned thee, the spectators that gazed on thee, deserved much more, and were far more guilty than thou thyself. But it is thine infelicity to be taken, to be made a public example of justice, to be a terror to the rest; yet should every man have his desert, thou wouldst peradventure be a saint in comparison."

Say the Buddhists, "This is an old saying, O Atula! this is not only of to-day: 'They blame him who sits silent, they blame him who speaks much, they also blame him who says little; there is no one on earth who is not blamed.'"

Archibald Prentice could not bear to hear any one speak evil of his friend Burns. Once at a meeting of ministers and elders, some of them began to denounce Burns' works as immoral. "I tell you what," said the old man, "if you had a' his ill and the half o' his gude amang ye, ye 'd be a' better men than ye are."

"Since Adam," said Margaret Fuller, "there has been none that approached nearer fitness to stand up before God and angels in the naked majesty of manhood than Robert Burns; — but there was a serpent in his field also! Yet but for his fault we could never have seen brought out the brave and patriotic modesty with which he owned it. Shame on him who could bear to think of faults in this rich jewel, unless reminded by such confession."

Ah! the chances and accidents and risks of life! We never can estimate them. The Duke of Wellington was accustomed to say that the stumbling of a horse in a charge of cavalry might lose a battle ; and, mindful of these chances, Sir Charles Napier wrote, "I am as sure of a victory as a man who knows that victory is an accident can be." Julius Cæsar owed two millions when he risked the experiment of being General in Gaul. If Julius Cæsar, reflected Bulwer, had not lived to cross the Rubicon, and pay off his debts, what would his creditors have called Julius Cæsar?

There is a novel by Émile Souvestre, in which all the warm-hearted people come to grief, and the cold-hearted calculating monopolize all the honors and riches of this world. But the balance is restored in the next, when all hearts being laid bare, in those of the prosperous appears a serpent, and in those of the reprobates a star.

## VII.

### THE CHRISTIANITY OF WOOLMAN.

In the year of our Lord 1720, in the province of New Jersey, was born into the world, in the judgment of a very high literary and critical authority of Great Britain, "the man, who, in all the centuries since the advent of Christ, lived nearest to the Divine pattern." John Woolman was the name of the remarkable man. He was a Quaker, who lived a quiet, somewhat ascetic life, and left behind him some simple, unrhetorical writings, all of which together would make no more than one ordinary volume. The chief and best known of his published works is the Journal of his Life and Travels. It is one of those little books that have had incalculable good influence. "Remember," says Joubert, "what St. Francis of Sales said, in speaking of the Imitation of Christ,— 'I have sought repose every where, and have only found it in a little corner, with a little book.' Happy is the writer who can make a beautiful little book!" Woolman's Journal is such another beautiful little book, and deserves to be read and cherished along with the immortal Imitation. The one, indeed, is a constant reminder of the other, as the same spirit of purity, humility, and devotion characterizes both.

"Get the writings of John Woolman by heart," is the emphatic advice of Charles Lamb, in one of his essays. Dr. Channing, not long before his death, expressed his very great surprise that the writings of Woolman were so little known. His countenance lighted up as he pronounced Woolman's Journal "beyond comparison the sweetest and purest autobiography in the language." "I should almost despair of that man," said Coleridge, "who could peruse the Life of John Woolman without an amelioration of heart." Crabb Robinson, after referring to a sermon by the distinguished Edward Irving, which he feared would deter rather than promote belief, said: "How different this from John Woolman's Journal I have been reading at the same time! A perfect gem! His is a beautiful soul. An illiterate tailor, he writes in a style of the most exquisite purity and grace. His moral qualities are transferred to his writings. His religion was love. His whole existence and all his passions were love. If one could venture to impute to his creed, and not to his personal character, the delightful frame of mind he exhibited, one could not hesitate to be a convert. His Christianity is most inviting, — it is fascinating." Theodore Parker was in like manner impressed with the extraordinary qualities of the Journal, and the Christian character of its author. "This is one of the most encouraging books," he wrote, "that I ever read. What depths of insight into divine things! How lowly and meek! How lofty, too, his aspirations! What gentle courage — what faith!"

The most encouraging of all the thousands and thousands of books the great reader and scholar and thinker had read! Why? Because, the Christianity inculcated in it, illustrated in it, incarnated in its author, is apprehensible, comprehensible — more than all, it is practical and practicable. That, we take to be the reason, and a reason sufficient, why the Journal of John Woolman is so encouraging to Christians and so unique in religious literature. The religion it inculcates and illustrates is a religion for men, not for angels — for human creatures, not for celestial intelligences — very human creatures, with appetites, and passions, and naked bodies — only a little while on the earth at the longest, and not long

enough to know any thing that is really worth knowing
except by suffering and blundering — creatures that are
not only sinners, but born sinners — of infinitely long
lines of sinners — sinners from the foundation — blind,
ignorant, and erring — for such human creatures — and
all human creatures are such — is the Christianity of
Woolman adapted. He did not understand Christianity
to be for the super-terrestrial, to whom sin is known only
by wisdom. He understood it to be for men, needing it,
and showed its adaptability by accepting it — its practi-
cableness by practicing it. His Christianity was encouraging, in that it did not require absolute imitation of, but
some slight approximation to the Divine Founder.

The discouraging mistake too commonly made by the
preacher is to set up standards of conduct unattainable
by himself or by any of his hearers. He turns the key
of heaven against himself and all mankind. He preaches
an empty heaven, when an empty heaven, in his reflective
moments, he no more believes in than any of his hearers.
His logic and his law, he perceives, exclude him as certainly from paradise as they exclude all the myriads of
mankind. He knows, if he has observed, that no man
is so bad but that there is some good in him, and that no
man is so good but that he might be better. The good
and the bad, too, appear to him, the more he observes, so
much worse or better according to situation and circumstances, that his abstract estimates of them become confused, and require constant revision. The differences
between the good and the bad, which appeared to him so
great, as he knows more of man and men — more of the
weaknesses and distresses and ignorances of his fellows
— seem less and less to him ; and he reflects how, in the
eye of the Maker, who knows every thing of every one
of his creatures — every besetment and every infirmity —
how impossible, with all his efforts, to accomplish very
much — how next to impossible to use at all his imper-

fectly developed wings — the good and the bad must appear pitifully alike, if not the same. The moral distinctions which appear to the preacher, with his imperfect vision, so very definite, may in the eye of God, who sees all, be nearly invisible. But for every little departure from his rigidly straight line, the preacher has a penalty ready-made — to be found in his own inflexible little code, if not in the New Testament. As if the creature, who knows next to nothing, should judge for the Creator, who knows every thing! Ah! justly is it said, our measure of rewards and punishments is most partial and incomplete, absurdly inadequate, utterly worldly, and we wish to continue it into the next world. Into that next and awful world we strive to pursue men, and send after them our impotent party verdicts, of condemnation or acquittal. We set up our paltry little rods to measure Heaven immeasurable, as if, in comparison to that, Newton's mind, or Pascal's, or Shakespeare's, was any loftier than mine; as if the ray which travels from the sun would reach me sooner than the man who blacks my boots. Measured by that altitude, the tallest and the smallest among us are so alike diminutive and pitifully base that we should take no count of the calculation, and it is a meanness to reckon the difference.

A religion that is discouraging to hope, is a poor religion for men; and a religion that requires of them the impossible, is such. For some it may be easy to be good — very good — as we understand goodness; for others it is nearly impossible to be good at all, according to pulpit standards. To the former it may seem easy to believe that Christ should be imitated; to the latter it seems to be only possible he should be approximated. He is the Great Exemplar, the Divine, to be approached, and only approached, as nearly as possible, by the creature. Now and then, it may be, a man is born into the world in whom are all the virtues so admirably mixed that it is possible for him to approach very near to the Divine Founder — so near as almost to touch the hem of His garment ; the many, however, are unable to approach so near by a very great way ; while the great multitudes are so far off that, instead of seeing the light of His countenance, they only see the reflection of it as it appears faintly, very faintly, in the comparatively few, very few, alas ! who are able to approach near enough to feel a little the direct rays of the Divine Effulgence. After a poor human creature has done all that it is possible for him to do, it is discouraging to be told that he has not done enough ; that after he has done all that it is possible for him to do, he shall be damned. He knows himself what he can do and what he cannot do ; and finds himself unable to accept a faith which offers rewards for the impracticable and impossible only. If the gate of paradise is to remain shut against him, for what he could not help, it must remain shut against all mankind, as he is not able to see the mighty difference in men that their hopeless separation implies ; — a separation inconceivable to a vast number of sincere believers in a future state, — believers in Christ, and heirs to heaven under his Testament.

The Christianity of Woolman is a practical, practicable Christianity. It is broad enough to meet the wants of every human being, and generous enough to encourage every human being to accept it, and, to the extent of possibility, to shape his life by it. Nowhere in all his writings do we find a single word discouraging to any human creature. The life he recommended he lived ; the wisdom he taught he illustrated ; the Christianity he preached he incarnated. Without violence or passion, he was commanding ; without great intellect or learning, he was convincing. His simplicity was more than eloquence ; his goodness was power. Humble, sincere, and devoted, there was no trace of selfishness visible in his transparent character.  He was what he wished to seem, and seemed to be what he was.

Whittier, in his Introduction to the Journal, has some just observations upon Woolman's writings in general, — the larger portion of which are devoted to the subjects of slavery, uncompensated labor, and the excessive toil and suffering of the many to support the luxury of the few.  "The argument running through them is searching, and in its conclusions uncompromising, but a tender love for the wrong-doer as well as the sufferer underlies all.  They aim to convince the judgment and reach the heart without awakening prejudice and passion.  To the slaveholders of his time they must have seemed like the voice of conscience speaking to them in the cool of the day.  One feels, in reading them, the tenderness and humility of a nature redeemed from all pride of opinion and self-righteousness, sinking itself out of sight, and intent only upon rendering smaller the sum of human sorrow and sin by drawing men nearer to God and to each other.  The style is that of a man unlettered, but with natural refinement and delicate sense of fitness, the purity of whose heart enters into his language.  There is no attempt at fine writing, not a word or phrase for effect ; it is the simple unadorned diction of one to whom the temptations of the pen seem to have been wholly unknown.  He wrote as he believed from an inward spiritual prompting ; and with all his unaffected humility he evidently felt that his work was done in the clear radiance of 'the light which never was on land or sea.'  It was not for him to outrun his Guide, or, as Sir Thomas Browne expresses it, to 'order the finger of the Almighty to his will and pleasure, but to sit still under the soft showers of Providence.'  Very wise are these essays, but their wisdom is not altogether that of this world.  They lead one away from all the jealousies, strifes, and competitions of luxury, fashion, and gain, out of the close air of parties and sects, into a region of calmness, — 'the haunt of every gentle wind whose breath can teach the wild to love tranquillity;'—a quiet habitation where all things are ordered in what he calls 'the pure reason;' a rest from all self-seeking, and where no man's interest or activity conflicts with that of another. Beauty they certainly have, but it is not that which the rules of art recognize; a certain indefinable purity pervades them, making one sensible, as he reads, of a sweetness as of violets. "The secret of Woolman's style,' said Dr. Channing, 'is that his eye was single, and that conscience dictated his words.' Of course we are not to look to the writings of such a man for tricks of rhetoric, the free play of imagination, or the unscrupulousness of epigram and antithesis. He wrote as he lived, conscious of 'the great Task-master's eye.' With the wise heathen Marcus Aurelius Antoninus he had learned to 'wipe out imaginations, to check desire, and let the spirit that is the gift of God to every man, as his guardian and guide, bear rule.'"

John Woolman's gift, it has been well and justly said, by an appreciating religious writer, was love, — "a charity of which it does not enter into the natural heart of man to conceive, and of which the more ordinary experiences, even of renewed nature, give but a faint shadow. Every now and then, in the world's history, we meet with such men, the kings and priests of Humanity, on whose heads this precious ointment has been so poured forth that it has run down to the skirts of their clothing, and extended over the whole of the visible creation; men who have entered, like Francis of Assisi, into the secret of that deep amity with God and with his creatures which makes man to be in league with the stones of the field, and the beasts of the field to be at peace with him. In this pure, universal charity there is nothing fitful or intermittent, nothing that comes and goes in showers and gleams and sunbursts. Its springs are deep and constant, its rising is like that of a mighty river, its very overflow calm and steady, leaving life and fertility behind it."

"Looking at the purity, wisdom, and sweetness of his life, who shall say," asks a distinguished admirer, " that his faith in the teaching of the Holy Spirit — the interior guide and light — was a mistaken one ? Surely it was no illusion by which his feet were so guided that all who saw him felt that, like Enoch, he walked with God. 'Without the actual inspiration of the Spirit of Grace, the inward teacher and soul of our souls,' says Fénelon, 'we' could neither do, will, nor believe good. We must silence every creature, we must silence ourselves also, to hear in a profound stillness of the soul this inexpressible voice of Christ. The outward word of the gospel itself without this living efficacious word within would be but an empty sound.' 'I am sure,' says Sir Thomas Browne, 'that there is a common spirit that plays within us, and that is the Spirit of God. Whoever feels not the warm gale and gentle ventilation of this Spirit, I dare not say he lives ; for truly without this to me there is no heat under the tropic, nor any light though I dwelt in the body of the sun.' 'Thou Lord,' says Augustine, 'communicatest thyself to all: thou teachest the heart without words ; thou speakest to it without articulate sounds.' Never was this divine principle more fully tested than by John Woolman ; and the result is seen in a life of such rare excellence that the world is still better and richer for its sake, and the fragrance of it comes down to us through a century, still sweet and precious."

At twenty-one he became a clerk and book-keeper in a small store kept by a tailor at Mount Holly. During the second year of his employment there, his employer, "having a negro woman, sold her, and desired me," he says, " to write a bill of sale, the man being waiting who bought her. The thing was sudden ; and though I felt uneasy at the thoughts of writing an instrument of slavery for one of my fellow-creatures, yet I remembered that I was hired by the year, that it was my master who directed me to do it, and that it was an elderly man, a member of our Society, who bought her; so through weakness I gave way, and wrote it; but at the executing of it I was so afflicted in my mind, that I said before my master and the Friend, that I believed slave-keeping to be a practice inconsistent with the Christian religion. This, in some degree, abated my uneasiness; yet as often as I reflected seriously upon it I thought I should have been clearer if I had desired to be excused from it, as a thing against my conscience; for such it was. Some time after this a young man of our Society spoke to me to write a convey-ance of a slave to him, he having lately taken a negro into his house. I told him I was not easy to write it; for, though many of our meeting and in other places kept slaves, I still believed the practice was not right, and de-sired to be excused from the writing. I spoke to him in good-will; and he told me that keeping slaves was not altogether agreeable to his mind; but that the slave being a gift made to his wife he had accepted her."

This circumstance was the beginning of a life of quiet but persistent opposition to slavery. Not long afterward he visited Maryland, Virginia, and North Carolina. He was afflicted by the prevalence of the sin of slavery. It appeared to him, in his own words, "as a dark gloominess overhanging the land." On his return he wrote an essay on the subject, which was published in 1754, bearing the imprint of Benjamin Franklin. Three years later he made a second visit to the Southern meetings of Friends. "Traveling as a minister of the gospel, he was compelled to sit down at the tables of slaveholding planters, who were accustomed to entertain their friends free of cost, and who could not comprehend the scruples of their guest against receiving as a gift food and lodging which he re-garded as the gain of oppression. He was a poor man, but he loved truth more than money.   He therefore either placed the pay for his entertainment in the hands of some member of the family, for the benefit of the slaves, or gave it directly to them, as he had opportunity."   "When I expected," he says, "soon to leave a friend's house where I had entertainment, if I believed that I should not keep clear from the gain of oppression without leaving money, I spoke to one of the heads of the family privately, and desired them to accept of pieces of silver, and give them to such of their negroes as they believed would make the best use of them ; and at other times I gave them to the negroes myself, as the way looked clearest to me.   Before I came out, I had provided a large number of small pieces for this purpose, and this offering them to some who appeared to be wealthy people was a trial both to me and them.   But the fear of the Lord so covered me at times that my way was made easier than I expected ; and few, if any, manifested any resentment at the offer, and most of them, after some conversation, accepted of them."

He also journeyed through New York and the New England States in the same unostentatious but earnest way, bearing his testimony as he went against sinfulness of every sort, especially against the sin of slavery.   The object of his travels was of course to meet with the members of his Society ; but, says a distinguished anti-slavery leader, "the influence of the life and labors of John Woolman has by no means been confined to the religious society of which he was a member.   It may be traced wherever a step in the direction of emancipation has been taken in America or in Europe.   During the war of the Revolution many of the noblemen and officers connected with the French army became, as their journals abundantly testify, deeply interested in the Society of Friends, and took back to France with them something of its growing anti-slavery sentiment.   Especially was this the case with Jean Pierre Brissot, the thinker and statesman of the Girondists, whose intimacy with Warner Mifflin, a friend and disciple of Woolman, so profoundly affected his whole after life. He became the leader of the Friends of the Blacks, and carried with him to the scaffold a profound hatred of slavery. To his efforts may be traced the proclamation of Emancipation in Hayti by the commissioners of the French convention, and indirectly the subsequent uprising of the blacks and their successful establishment of a free government. The same influence reached Thomas Clarkson and stimulated his early efforts for the abolition of the slave-trade ; and in after life the volume of the New Jersey Quaker was the cherished companion of himself and his amiable helpmate. It was in a degree, at least, the influence of Stephen Grellet and William Allen, men deeply imbued with the spirit of Woolman, and upon whom it might almost be said his mantle had fallen, that drew the attention of Alexander I. of Russia to the importance of taking measures for the abolition of serfdom, an object the accomplishment of which the wars during his reign prevented, but which, left as a legacy of duty, has been peaceably effected by his namesake, Alexander II. In the history of Emancipation in our own country evidences of the same original impulse of humanity are not wanting. . . . Looking back to the humble workshop at Mount Holly from the standpoint of the Proclamation of President Lincoln, how has the seed sown in weakness been raised up in power ! "

" Having now been several years with my employer," he says, " and he doing less in merchandise than heretofore, I was thoughtful about some other way of business, perceiving merchandise to be attended with much cumber in the way of trading in these parts. My mind, through the power of truth, was in a great degree weaned from the desire of outward greatness, and I was learning to be content with real conveniences, that were not costly, so that a way of life free from much entanglement appeared best for me, though the income might be small. I had several offers of business that appeared profitable, but I did not see my way clear to accept of them, believing they would be attended with more outward care and cumber than was required of me to engage in. I saw that an humble man, with the blessing of the Lord, might live on a little, and that where the heart was set on greatness, success in business did not satisfy the craving ; but that commonly with an increase of wealth the desire of wealth increased. There was a care on my mind so to pass my time that nothing might hinder me from the most steady attention to the voice of the true Shepherd. My employer, though now a retailer of goods, was by trade a tailor, and kept a servant-man at that business ; and I began to think about learning the trade, expecting that if I should settle I might by this trade and a little retailing of goods get a living in a plain way, without the load of great business. I mentioned it to my employer, and we soon agreed on terms, and when I had leisure from the affairs of merchandise I worked with this man. I believed the hand of Providence pointed out this business for me, and I was taught to be content with it, though I felt at times a disposition that would have sought for something greater ; but through the revelation of Jesus Christ I had seen the happiness of humility, and there was an earnest desire in me to enter deeply into it ; at times this desire arose to a degree of fervent supplication, wherein my soul was so environed with heavenly light and consolation that things were made easy to me which had been otherwise."

A person at some distance lying sick, his brother came to Woolman to write his will. " I knew he had slaves," writes Woolman, " and, asking his brother, was told he intended to leave them as slaves to his children. As writing is a profitable employ, and as offending sober people was disagreeable to my inclinations, I was straitened in my mind; but as I looked to the Lord, he inclined my heart to his testimony. I told the man that I believed that the practice of continuing slavery to this people was not right, and that I had a scruple in my mind against doing writings of that kind; that though many in our Society kept them as slaves, still I was not easy to be concerned in it, and desired to be excused from going to write the will. I spake to him in the fear of the Lord, and he made no reply to what I said, but went away; he also had some concerns in the practice, and I thought he was displeased with me. In this case I had fresh confirmation that acting contrary to present outward interest, from a motive of Divine love and in regard to truth and righteousness, and thereby incurring the resentments of people, opens the way to a treasure better than silver, and to a friendship exceeding the friendship of men."

His persistence in declining to write wills bequeathing human beings, and his mild and sincere manner — Christian manner — of advocating emancipation, resulted sometimes in the freedom of those whose enslavement it was intended to perpetuate.

The increase of business soon became a burden. "Though my natural inclination," he says, "was towards merchandise, yet I believed truth required me to live more free from outward cumbers; and there was now a strife in my mind between the two. In this exercise my prayers were put up to the Lord, who graciously heard me, and gave me a heart resigned to his holy will. Then I lessened my outward business, and, as I had opportunity, told my customers of my intentions, that they might consider what shop to turn to; and in a while I wholly laid down merchandise, and followed my trade as a tailor by myself, having no apprentice. I also had a nursery of apple-trees, in which I employed some of my time in hoeing, grafting, trimming, and inoculating." "He seems," says Whittier, "to have regarded agriculture as the business most conducive to morals and physical health.    He thought 'if the leadings of the spirit were more attended to, more people would be engaged in the sweet employment of husbandry, where labor is agreeable and healthful.'    He does not condemn the honest acquisition of wealth in other business free from oppression ; even 'merchandising,' he thought, might be carried on innocently and in pure reason.    Christ does not forbid the laying up of a needful support for family and friends ; the command is, 'Lay not up for yourselves treasures on earth.'    From his little farm on the Rancocas he looked out with a mingled feeling of wonder and sorrow upon the hurry and unrest of the world ; and especially was he pained to see luxury and extravagance overgrowing the early plainness and simplicity of his own religious society. He regarded the merely rich man with unfeigned pity. With nothing of his scorn, he had all of Thoreau's commiseration, for people who went about bowed down with the weight of broad acres and great houses on their backs."    "Though trading in things useful," he says, "is an honest employ, yet through the great number of superfluities which are bought and sold, and through the corruption of the times, they who apply to merchandise for a living have great need to be well experienced in that precept which the Prophet Jeremiah laid down for his scribe : 'Seekest thou great things for thyself? seek them not.' "

Writing to Friends at their monthly meeting in North Carolina, he says : " First, my dear friends, dwell in humility ; and take heed that no views of outward gain get too deep hold of you, that so your eyes being single to the Lord, you may be preserved in the way of safety. Where people let loose their minds after the love of outward things, and are more engaged in pursuing the profits and seeking the friendships of this world than to be inwardly acquainted with the way of true peace, they walk in a vain shadow, while the true comfort of life is wanting. Their examples are often hurtful to others ; and their treasures thus collected do many times prove dangerous snares to their children. . . . Treasures, though small, attained on a true principle of virtue, are sweet ; and while we walk in the light of the Lord there is true comfort and satisfaction in the possession ; neither the murmurs of an oppressed people, nor a throbbing, uneasy conscience, nor anxious thoughts about the events of things, hinder the enjoyment of them. When we look towards the end of life, and think on the division of our substance among our successors, if we know that it was collected in the fear of the Lord, in honesty, in equity, and in uprightness of heart before him, we may consider it as his gift to us, and, with a single eye to his blessing, bestow it on those we leave behind us. Such is the happiness of the plain ways of true virtue."

How strange this old-fashioned Christian philosophy seems to us, in these feverish days of greed and desperate competition ! How strange to us this pious "taste for poverty," as Souvestre calls it, when gold, more than ever, is an object of worship, and poverty so generally is thought to be, and sometimes admits itself to be, criminal.

"Having at times," he says, "perceived a shyness in some Friends of considerable note towards me, I found an engagement in gospel love to pay a visit to one of them ; and as I dwelt under the exercise, I felt a resignedness in my mind to go and tell him privately that I had a desire to have an opportunity with him alone ; to this proposal he readily agreed, and then, in the fear of the Lord, things relating to that shyness were searched to the bottom, and we had a large conference, which, I believe, was of use to both of us, and I am thankful that way was opened for it."

In a debate in one of the church meetings on the subject of lotteries, he took decided grounds against them. "In the heat of zeal," he says, " I made reply to what an ancient Friend said, and when I sat down I saw that my words were not enough seasoned with charity. After this I spoke no more on the subject. Some time after the minute was made I remained uneasy with the manner of my speaking to an ancient Friend, and could not see my way clear to conceal my uneasiness, though I was concerned that I might say nothing to weaken the cause in which I had labored. After some close exercise and hearty repentance for not having attended closely to the safe guide, I stood up, and, reciting the passage, acquainted Friends that though I durst not go from what I had said as to the matter, yet I was uneasy with the manner of my speaking, believing milder language would have been better. As this was uttered in some degree of creaturely abasement after a warm debate, it appeared to have a good savor amongst us."

Thinking of "hats and garments dyed with a dye hurtful to them," and of "wearing more clothes in summer than are useful," made him "uneasy," "believing them to be customs which have not their foundation in pure wisdom. The apprehension," he says, "of being singular from my beloved friends was a strait upon me, and thus I continued in the use of such things contrary to my judgment." Pretty soon, however, his "mind was settled in relation to hurtful dyes," having determined that all new garments should be of the natural color. "Then I thought," he says, "of getting a hat the natural color of the fur, but the apprehension of being looked upon as one affecting singularity felt uneasy to me." On this account he was "under close exercise of mind, greatly desiring to be rightly directed," "when," he says, "being deeply bowed in spirit before the Lord, I was made willing to submit to what I apprehended was required of me, and when I returned home got a hat of the natural color of the fur. In attending meetings this singularity was a trial to me, and more especially at this time, as white hats were used by some who were fond of following the changeable modes of dress, and as some Friends who knew not from what motives I wore it grew shy of me, I felt my way for a time shut up in the exercise of the ministry."

He was greatly distressed on account of the sale by white people of rum to the Indians, and his Journal, during a missionary visit to the natives, contains some noteworthy observations growing out of it. "I was," he says, "renewedly confirmed in a belief that if all our inhabitants lived according to sound wisdom, laboring to promote universal love and righteousness, and ceased from every inordinate desire after wealth, and from all customs which are tinctured with luxury, the way would be easy for our inhabitants, though they might be much more numerous than at present, to live comfortably on honest employments, without the temptation they are so often under of being drawn into schemes to make settlements on lands which have not been purchased of the Indians, or of applying to that wicked practice of selling rum to them." "A weighty and heavenly care came over my mind, and love filled my heart towards all mankind, in which I felt a strong engagement that we might be obedient to the Lord while in tender mercy he is yet calling to us, and that we might so attend to pure universal righteousness as to give no just cause of offense to the Gentiles, who do not profess Christianity, whether they be the blacks from Africa, or the native inhabitants of this continent."

The circumstance of having joined with another executor in selling a negro lad till he might attain the age of thirty years, was the cause of great sorrow to him. "With abasement of heart I may now say," he says, "that sometimes as I have sat in a meeting with my heart exercised towards that awful Being who respecteth not persons nor colors, and have thought upon this lad, I have felt that all was not clear in my mind respecting him; and as I have attended to this exercise and fervently sought the Lord, it hath appeared to me that I should make some restitution. My mind for a time was covered with darkness and sorrow. Under this sore affliction my heart was softened to receive instruction, and I now first perceived that as I had been one of the two executors who had sold this lad for nine years longer than is common for our children to serve, so I should now offer part of my substance to redeem the last half of the nine years; but as the time was not yet come, I executed a bond, binding myself and my executors to pay to the man to whom he was sold what to candid men might appear equitable for the last four and a half years of his time, in case the said youth should be living, and in a condition likely to provide comfortably for himself."

In 1772, in the fifty-second year of his age, he visited England, with a certificate directed to Friends in Great Britain. He declined a passage in the cabin for the reasons (to use his own language) "That on the outside of that part of the ship where the cabin was I observed sundry sorts of carved work and imagery; that in the cabin I observed some superfluity of workmanship of several sorts; and that according to the ways of men's reckoning, the sum of money to be paid for a passage in that apartment has some relation to the expense of furnishing it to please the minds of such as give way to a conformity to this world; and that in this, as in other cases, the moneys received from the passengers are calculated to defray the cost of these superfluities, as well as the other expenses of their passage. I therefore felt a scruple with regard to paying my money to be applied to such purposes."

Lodging in the steerage, he was much among the seamen, and, "from a motion of love," took "sundry opportunities with one of them at a time," and "labored," "in free conversation," "to turn their minds towards the fear of the Lord." Deeply he grieved over their oppression and distresses, and his lamentations, as set down in his Journal, are profoundly touching. "They mostly," he says, "appeared to take kindly what I said to them; but their minds were so deeply impressed with the almost universal depravity among sailors that the poor creatures in their answers to me have revived in my remembrance that of the degenerate Jews a little before the captivity, as repeated by Jeremiah the prophet, 'There is no hope.'"

Arriving in London, he went straight to the Quaker meeting, which he knew to be in session. Coming in late and unannounced, his peculiar dress and manner naturally excited attention, and apprehension that he was an itinerant enthusiast. He presented his certificate from Friends in America, but the dissatisfaction still remained, and some one remarked that perhaps the stranger Friend might feel that his dedication of himself to this apprehended service was accepted, without further labor, and that he might now feel free to return to his home! John Woolman sat silent, it is stated, for a space, seeking the unerring counsel of Divine Wisdom. He was profoundly affected by the unfavorable reception he met with, and his tears flowed freely. The words, however, which he was permitted to utter, made a different impression on the meeting. A deep silence, it is said, prevailed over the assembly, many of whom were touched by the wise simplicity of the stranger's words and manner. At the conclusion, "the Friend who had advised against his further service rose up and humbly confessed his error, and avowed his full unity with the stranger."

The low wages paid to English laborers, and the poverty and wretchedness visible on every hand, caused him to cry out, "Oh may the wealthy consider the poor!" It gave him also great distress of mind to discover that in many instances members of his Society "mixed with the world in various sorts of traffic, carried on in impure channels." He found them loading ships engaged in the slave-trade, and trading as others in all kinds of super-fluities, till, he said, "dimness of sight came over many." " I have felt," he says, " in that which doth not deceive, that if Friends who have known the truth keep in that tenderness of heart where all views of outward gain are given up, and their trust is only in the Lord, he will gra- ciously lead some to be patterns of deep self-denial in things relating to trade and handicraft labor ; and others who have plenty of the treasures of this world will be ex-amples of a plain frugal life, and pay wages to such as they may hire more liberally than is now customary in some places."

He " saw that people setting off their tables with silver vessels at entertainments was often stained with worldly glory," and he preferred not to drink from them. His sense of cleanliness was also affected as he traveled through the kingdom. "Some of the great," he says, "carry delicacy to a great height themselves, and yet real cleanliness is not generally promoted. Dyes being in-vented partly to please the eye and partly to hide dirt, I have felt, when traveling in dirtiness, and affected with unwholesome scents, a strong desire that the nature of dyeing cloth to hide dirt may be more fully considered. Real cleanliness becometh a holy people ; but hiding that which is not clean by coloring our garments seems con-trary to the sweetness of sincerity." He declined to travel in stage-coaches, because the horses and drivers were cruelly used ; the former sometimes being killed by hard driving, and the latter sometimes frozen to death by exposure. "So great," he says, "is the hurry in the spirit of this world, that in aiming to do business quickly and to gain wealth, the creation at this day doth loudly groan." For the **reasons** mentioned, his travels in **England** were entirely **on foot.** Sickness came upon him; the climate **and every thing** seemed **to be** against him; he was even sometimes **in need.** " I have," he says, near the **end of his Journal,** " known **poverty of late.**" His mind, it appears, was greatly exercised **by a sense** of the intimate connection of luxury **and** oppression; **the burden** of the laboring poor rested heavily **upon** him. **In his lonely** wanderings on foot through the rural districts, **or in** his temporary sojourn in crowded manufacturing towns, **the eager** competitions and earnest pursuit of gain of one **class, and the poverty and** physical and moral degradation **of another, so oppressed him** that his health suffered and his strength failed. In his frequent mention throughout **his** Journal **of trials and afflictions, he nowhere betrays any** personal **solicitude, any merely selfish anxiety.** He offered **no prayers for special personal favors.** He was, to use his own words, mixed with his fellow-creatures in their misery, and could not consider himself **a distinct** and separate being. **His last** public **labor, says his eminent** biographer, was **a** testimony in **the York Meeting in** behalf of the poor and enslaved. **His last** prayer **on his** death-bed **was a** commendation **of** his **"** fellow-creatures separated from the Divine harmony" **to the** Omnipotent **Power, whom** he had learned **to call** his Father. He died **of small-pox in the city of** York, **on** the 7th day of October, 1772, aged fifty-two **years.**

His simple words have **a precious flavor of** sweetness and purity and genuineness that **is not** surpassed, we believe, in **the** whole **range of** literature. Passages like these, for instance: **how delicious!** how Christlike!

" Selfish men may possess the earth: **it is the meek** alone who inherit **it** from the Heavenly **Father free from all** defilements and perplexities **of unrighteousness.**"

" Whoever rightly advocates the **cause** of some, thereby promotes **the** good of the whole."

"If one suffers by the unfaithfulness of another, the mind, the most noble part of him that occasions the discord, is thereby alienated from its true happiness."

"There is harmony in the several parts of the Divine work in the hearts of men. He who leads them to cease from those gainful employments which are carried on in the wisdom which is from beneath delivers also from the desire of worldly greatness, and reconciles to a life so plain that a little suffices."

"Oppression in the extreme appears terrible; but oppression in more refined appearances is nevertheless oppression. To labor for a perfect redemption from the spirit of it is the great business of the whole family of Jesus Christ in this world."

"There is a principle which is pure, placed in the human mind, which in different places and ages hath had different names; it is, however, pure, and proceeds from God. It is deep and inward, confined to no forms of religion nor excluded from any, when the heart stands in perfect sincerity. In whomsoever this takes root and grows, they become brethren."

What precious society a man capable of so generous, so comprehensive, so profound a sentiment would have been to Buddha, Confucius, Plato, Marcus Aurelius, Thomas à Kempis, Fénelon, or Sir Thomas Browne!

"He who professeth to believe in one Almighty Creator, and in his Son Jesus Christ, and is yet more intent on the honors, profits, and friendships of the world than he is, in singleness of heart, to stand faithful to the Christian religion, is in the channel of idolatry; while the Gentile, who, notwithstanding some mistaken opinions, is established in the true principle of virtue, and humbly adores an Almighty Power, may be of the number that fear God and work righteousness."

"To treasure up wealth for another generation, by means of the immoderate labor of those who in some measure depend upon us, is doing evil at present, without knowing that wealth thus gathered may not be applied to evil purposes when we are gone. To labor hard, or cause others to do so, that we may live conformably to customs which our Redeemer discountenanced by his example, and which are contrary to Divine order, is to manure a soil for propagating an evil seed in the earth."

" When house is joined to house, and field laid to field, until there is no place, and the poor are thereby straitened, though this is done by bargain and purchase, yet so far as it stands distinguished from universal love, so far that woe predicted by the prophet will accompany their proceedings. As he who first founded the earth was then the true proprietor of it, so he still remains, and though he hath given it to the children of men, so that multitudes of people have had their sustenance from it while they continued here, yet he hath never alienated it, but his right is as good as at first ; nor can any apply the increase of their possessions contrary to universal love, nor dispose of lands in a way which they know tends to exalt some by oppressing others, without being justly chargeable with usurpation."

" I find that to be a fool as to worldly wisdom, and to commit my cause to God, not fearing to offend men, who take offense at the simplicity of truth, is the only way to remain unmoved at the sentiment of others."

" Deep humility is a strong bulwark, and as we enter into it we find safety and true exaltation. The foolishness of God is wiser than man, and the weakness of God is stronger than man. Being unclothed of our own wisdom, and knowing the abasement of the creature, we find that power to arise which gives health and vigor to us."

" The love of ease and gain are the motives in general of keeping slaves, and men are wont to take hold of weak arguments to support a cause which is unreasonable. I have no interest on either side, save only the interest which I desire to have in the truth.   I believe liberty is their right, and as I see they are not only deprived of it, but treated in other respects with inhumanity in many places, I believe he who is a refuge for the oppressed will, in his own time, plead their cause, and happy will it be for such as walk in uprightness before him."

How like the sentiment and thought of John Brown, who died a martyr on the scaffold a little more than a hundred years after this prophecy was uttered !

"The natural man loveth eloquence, and many love to hear eloquent orations, and if there be not a careful attention to the gift, men who have once labored in the pure gospel ministry, growing weary of suffering, and ashamed of appearing weak, may kindle a fire, compass themselves about with sparks, and walk in the light, not of Christ, who is under suffering, but of that fire which they in departing from the gift have kindled, in order that those hearers who have left the meek, suffering state for worldly wisdom may be warmed with this fire and speak highly of their labors.   That which is of God gathers to God, and that which is of the world is owned by the world."

A little while before he died he asked for pen and ink, and wrote : " I believe my being here is in the wisdom of Christ ; I know not as to life or death."

It will not lessen the value of these detached passages in the minds of the true disciples of our Divine Lord, that they are manifestly not written to subserve the interests of a narrow sectarianism.   They might have been penned, says his brother Whittier, by Fénelon in his time, or Robertson in ours, dealing as they do with Christian practice, — the life of Christ manifesting itself in purity and goodness, — rather than with the dogmas of theology. The underlying thought of all is simple obedience to the Divine word in the soul.   " Not every one that saith unto me Lord, Lord, shall enter into the kingdom of heaven, but he that doeth the will of my Father in heaven." John Woolman's faith, like the Apostle's, is manifested by his labors, standing not in words but in the demonstration of the spirit, — a faith that works by love to the purifying of the heart. The entire outcome of this faith was love manifested in reverent waiting upon God, and in that untiring benevolence, that quiet but deep enthusiasm of humanity, which made his daily service to his fellow-creatures a hymn of praise to the common Father.

John Woolman's religion was real Christianity, "which being too spiritual to be seen by us," saith old Dr. Donne, "doth therefore take an apparent body of good life and works." His life was religion incarnate, of perpetual good works, that had but little time to voice itself but in acts, — like the good woman's, who, after having bred a large family, and led a long life of devotion and self-sacrifice — worn out by care, and weary of her burdens — came at length to what was supposed to be her death-bed. A clergyman in the neighborhood thought it to be his duty to call upon her. He asked her in language usual with his sect if she had made her peace with her Maker; to which she replied that she was not aware that there had been any trouble. John Woolman lived his religion, and so the world had faith in it. "Preachers say," said old John Selden, "Do as I say, not as I do. But if a physician had the same disease upon him that I have, and he should bid me do one thing, and he do quite another, could I believe him?"

"To the multitude," says the author of Ecce Homo, "religion will always mean what parsons talk about, what goes on in churches and chapels. . . . Religion, many will insist, means, and must mean, churches and clergymen, and you determine the condition of it by ascertaining what proportion of the population goes to church, and whether the number of candidates for orders increases or diminishes, just as you ascertain the state of trade by looking at the returns of export and import. . . . Religion has been so defined, that morality can be separated from it, that the laws of the universe can be separated from it, that all noble and elevated acts can be separated from it ; what wonder then that nothing but a caput mortuum seems to remain?" "All Christians believe," says another eminent English writer, "that the blessed are the poor and humble, and those who are ill-used by the world ; that it is easier for a camel to pass through the eye of a needle than for a rich man to enter the kingdom of heaven ; that they should judge not, lest they be judged ; that they should swear not at all ; that they should love their neighbor as themselves ; that if one take their cloak, they should give him their coat also ; that they should take no thought for the morrow ; that if they would be perfect, they should sell all that they have and give it to the poor. They are not insincere when they say that they believe these things. They do believe them, as people believe what they have always heard lauded and never discussed. But in the sense of that living belief which regulates conduct, they believe these doctrines just up to the point to which it is usual to act upon them. Whenever conduct is concerned, they look round for Mr. A. and B. to direct them how far to go in obeying Christ." By such sort of mere nominalism we are apt to get as far away from Christ as possible, and possibly without knowing it. A writer in Temple Bar states that the native trading community in Cyprus consists of Moslems, Jews, and Christians. Of these he says a European merchant can nearly always believe the first upon his simple word, the two latter he can rarely credit on oath, and the harder they swear the more certain one may be that they are stating what is not true.

Theology is one thing and religion another. "Travelers have often observed," says Archibald Alison, in his essay on Châteaubriand, "that in a certain rank in all countries manners are the same ; naturalists know, that at a certain elevation above the sea in all latitudes, we meet with the same vegetable productions ; and philosophers have often remarked, that in the highest class of intellects, opinions on almost every subject in all ages and places are the same. A similar uniformity may be observed in the principles of the greatest writers of the world on religion ; and while the inferior followers of their different tenets branch out into endless divisions, and indulge in sectarian rancor, in the more lofty regions of intellect the principles are substantially the same, and the objects of all identical. So small a proportion do all the disputed points in theology bear to the great objects of religion, love to God, charity to man, and the subjugation of human passion." There is, we are compelled to believe, a respectable amount of truth in the two familiar lines of Pope :

> " For forms and creeds let graceless bigots fight ;
> He can't be wrong whose life is in the right."

Dr. Holmes, expatiating in the Professor on the possible church of the future, says : "The Broad Church, I think, will never be based on any thing that requires the use of language. Free Masonry gives an idea of such a church, and a brother is known and cared for in a strange land where no word of his can be understood. The apostle of this church may be a deaf mute carrying a cup of cold water to a thirsting fellow-creature. The cup of cold water does not require to be translated for a foreigner to understand it. I am afraid the only Broad Church possible is one that has its creed in the heart, and not in the head, — that we shall know its members by their fruits, and not by their words."

John Woolman's religion was as broad as the brotherhood of man, and as boundless as Christian charity. Wherever there was a man, there was a brother, good

enough for him to love and worship with: alone, he
communed with God.   As with the hermit in Italy, who
lived in a simple cottage on the top of a mountain, a mile
from any habitation, Providence was his very next-door
neighbor.   His happiness was in duty.   It is said of Col-
lingwood that he never saw a vacant place in his estate
but he took an acorn out of his pocket and popped it in.
Woolman, also, wherever he found a human soul in which
he thought the seed of practical Christianity would grow
he planted it there.   Not noisily or aggressively.   He
had nothing of the vice of rectitude.   He did not insist
authoritatively that you should ever and forever walk in
his own remorselessly  strait path.   He did not discharge his moral pistol at you and knock you down with
the but-end of it if you failed to pronounce him infalli-
ble.   He had not a particle of what has been called the
wrath of celestial minds.   Nor was he a motive-monger,
like Walter Shandy, — a very dangerous sort of person
for a man to sit by, either laughing or crying.   He was
most concerned about his own motives, and the good of
his acts.   He was never ill-humored or rude from an
ostentatious love of speaking truth.   He knew as well as
any man the truth of the inscription upon one of the
seals of the Mogul Sultan Achar, that " never a man was
lost upon a straight road."   He knew at the same time
that the ways of men are crooked and will be ; that his
own way was not perfectly straight, and could not be.
Self he kept out of view as far as possible, but not osten-
tatiously.   In these days, it has been very truly said, part
of the stock in trade of the unscrupulous self-seeker is
sometimes a great parade of unselfishness : the man who
never in his life really exerted himself for any other end
than the advantage of number one, requests you to take
notice that his sole end is the glory of God and the good
of mankind.   And the transparent pretext, which infuri-
ates the perspicacious few, is found to succeed with the

undiscerning many. In John Woolman there was no parade of unselfishness, though unselfish he was as few men in this world have been or will be. His peculiar self-sacrifice and self-denial were too genuine to be mistaken; they commanded reverence without exciting derision. He possessed to a remarkable degree that quality which Dr. Arnold calls moral thoughtfulness, which makes a man love Christ instead of being a fanatic, and love truth without being cold or hard. In Norse mythology, Odin's ravens, memory and reflection, are perched upon the god's shoulders, and whisper into his ear what they see and hear. He sends them out at daybreak to fly over the world, and they come back at eve towards meal-time. Hence it is that Odin knows so much, and is called the raven-god. Woolman's quiet reflection and boundless charity opened the windows of his mind to all wingéd suggestions, and his heart abounded in true wisdom. Peaceful and unaggressive, the way was sure to be opened to whatever he conceived to be his duty, and his very peacefulness preserved him in the discharge of it. Every good influence stands round such a man in any extremity. Three cubs, say the Buddhists, the lioness brings forth, five the tigress, but one the cow; yet many are the meek cattle, few the beasts of prey. The fierce and grasping soon decay; the universe preserves to the peaceful the heritage of the earth.

The quiet influence of one wise man, who never bullies the world with his own excellence, may not be calculated. Confucius seldom claimed any superiority above his fellow-creatures. He offered his advice to those who were willing to listen; but he never spoke dogmatically; he never attempted to tyrannize over the minds or hearts of his friends. "If we read his biography," says a distinguished Orientalist, "we can hardly understand how a man whose life was devoted to such tranquil pursuits, and whose death scarcely produced a ripple on the smooth

and silent surface of the Eastern world, could have left
the impress of his mind on millions and millions of human beings — an impress, which even now, after more
than two thousand three hundred years, is clearly discernible in the national character of the largest empire
in the world." The lives and teachings of such men are
like the mighty, noiseless influences of nature. In Java
the vegetation has forced asunder and thrown down the
largest blocks of masonry, and has inflicted no little dam-
age upon the Hindoo ruins : literally has " the wild fig-tree
split their monstrous idols." The Brighton emeralds, originally bits of the thick bottoms of broken bottles, thrown
purposely into the sea by the lapidaries of the place, are by
the attrition of the shingle speedily converted into the
form of natural pebbles, and sold at high prices. The Chinese are in the habit of producing pearls artificially by the
introduction of small images of Buddha into the mussels,
which in the course of time are covered with the pearly
substance. We hardly think of the prodigious work of
those quiet subsoilers, the common earth-worms. The
ground is almost alive with them. Wherever mould is
turned up, there these sappers and miners are turned up
with it. They have been called nature's plowmen. They
bore the stubborn soil in every direction, and render
it pervious to air, rain, and the fibres of plants. Without these auxiliaries the farmer, says Gilbert White,
would find that his land would become cold, hard-bound,
and sterile. The green mantle of vegetation which covers the earth is dependent upon the worms which bur-
row in the bowels of it. When the rose bud blossomed
in the bower, the Persians have it, a nightingale said to
the falcon, " How is it that thou, being silent, bearest the
prize from all birds? Thou hast not spoken a pleasing
word to any one ; yet thy abode is the wrist of the king,
and thy food the delicate partridge. I who produce a
hundred musical gems in a moment have the worm for

my food and the thorn for my mansion." The falcon replied, "For once be all ear. I who perform a hundred acts repeat not one. Thou who performest not one deed displayest a thousand. Since I am all intelligence in the hunt, the king gives me dainty food and his wrist. Since thou art one entire motion of a tongue, eat worms and sit on thorns ; and so peace be with you." The Turks have a tale, that as a king of Bactria was pursuing the chase one day, he felt hungry, and sat down to eat. And while he was eating, a bee came, seized a morsel of bread, and flew slowly away with it. Wondering thereat, the king followed the bee, which led him to where sat on a bough a sparrow blind of both eyes, which opened its beak wide as soon as it heard the bee's humming. And the bee broke the bread into three pieces, fed the bird with them, and then flew away. When the king saw this wondrous work of God he renounced all earthly ties, and gave himself up to the All-True.

John Woolman's kindness went hand in hand with his quietness. He saw some good in every body, and was careful not to extinguish it. He never scolded. A saint would be damned by unintermitted scolding. It was Mary Lamb, we believe, who said that a babe is fed with milk and praise. John Woolman did not blame whom he sought to benefit, if he did not praise. No man was so bad as to appear in his eyes wholly blameworthy, and so he easily gained the ears of the most abandoned. In Sir William Jones's Persian grammar may be found the beautiful story from Nizami. It cannot be too often repeated for the lesson it teaches. One evening Jesus arrived at the gates of a certain city, and sent his disciples forward to prepare supper, while he himself, intent on doing good, walked through the streets into the market-place. And he saw at the corner of the market some people gathered together, looking at an object on the ground ; and he drew near to see what it might be. It was a dead dog, with a halter round his neck, by which he appeared to have been dragged through the dirt ; and a viler, a more abject, or more unclean thing never met the eyes of man. And those who stood by looked on with abhorrence. "Faugh !" said one, stopping his nose, "it pollutes the air !"  "How long," said another, "shall this foul beast offend our sight ?"  "Look at his torn hide," said a third ; "one could not even cut a shoe out of it." "And his ears," said a fourth, "all draggled and bleeding !"  "No doubt," said a fifth, "he has been hanged for thieving."  And Jesus heard them, and looking down compassionately on the dead creature, he said, "Pearls are not equal to the whiteness of his teeth !"  Then the people turned towards him with amazement, and said among themselves, "Who is this?  It must be Jesus of Nazareth, for only he could find something to pity and approve in a dead dog."  And being ashamed, they bowed their heads before him, and went each on his way.

We all know how even brutes are influenced by kindness.  A market-gardener had a very fine cow that was milked week after week by hired men.  He observed that the amount of butter he carried to market weighed about a pound more on each alternate week.  He watched the men, and tried the cow after they had finished milking, but always found that there was no milk to be had.  He finally asked the Scotch girl who took care of the milk if she could account for the difference.  "Why, yes," she said.  "When Jim milks he says to the cow, 'So, my pretty creature, so !'  But when Sam milks he hits her on the hips with the edge of the pail, and says, 'Hoist, you old brute !'"  Hawthorne, in his English Note-Books, speaks of a donkey that stubbornly refused to come out of a boat which had brought him across the Mersey ; at last, after many kicks had been applied, and other persecutions of that kind, a man stepped forward, addressing him affectionately, "Come along, brother," and the donkey obeyed at once.

"I once asked a successful peach-grower," said Professor Venable, "how it was that he always had plenty of excellent fruit, while his neighbors, with apparent equal facilities, failed more than half the time to obtain any crop at all, and always failed to raise first-rate peaches. Said he: 'I know my trees; they tell me what they need; I have a special interest in every twig of this orchard. A peach-tree will not produce unless you love it.'"

Some years ago a pretty French girl sold violets at the steps of one of the New York hotels. She had her regular customers, who could always be counted upon to purchase. One morning very early we happened to be passing just when she was taking her flowers out of her basket to display them on the table. "Your violets look very beautiful this morning," we said. "Yes," she answered, with a glow upon her face; "when I went out into the garden at day-break, they were all talking to one another!" Then we knew why her violets were always so beautiful. She loved them, and they grew better for her.

Moral honesty was a conspicuous trait in the character of John Woolman. A religion without it he could not comprehend; certainly it was not the religion of Christ. "They that cry down moral honesty," said old John Selden, "cry down that which is a great part of religion, my duty towards God, and my duty towards man. What care I to see a man run after a sermon, if he cozens and cheats as soon as he comes home?" The integrity of John Woolman was complete: it was so perfect as to appear "a law of nature with him, rather than a choice or a principle."

His good influence, everywhere that he went — in his own America and in London streets — amongst slave-drivers and sailors — the worst men and the most abandoned women — reminds us, in some respects, of the monk

Basle, of whom it is related that, being excommunicated by the Pope, he was, at his death, sent in charge of an angel to find a fit place of suffering in hell ; but such was the excellence of his manner that, wherever he went, he was received gladly, and civilly treated, even by the most uncivil angels ; and, when he came to discourse with them, instead of contradicting or forcing him, they took his part and adopted his manners : and even good angels came from far to see him, and take up their abode with him. The angel that was sent to find a place of torment for him attempted to remove him to a worse pit, but with no better success ; for such was the spirit of the monk, that he found something to praise in every place and company, though in hell, and made a kind of heaven of it. At last the escorting angel returned with his prisoner to them that sent him, saying, that no phlegethon could be found that would burn him ; for that, in whatever condition, Basle remained incorrigibly Basle. The legend says, his sentence was remitted, and he was allowed to go into heaven, and was canonized as a saint.

John Woolman was pure, and in every situation remained pure. It has been said by naturalists that hunters, when in pursuit of the ermine, spread with mire all the passes leading to its haunts, to which they drive it, knowing that it will submit to be taken rather than defile itself. John Woolman was so pure that in any extremity he would have suffered everything rather than be defiled.

He was a Christian, and lived very near the Divine pattern. He loved God and his fellow-man. The Golden Rule was his rule of life : he applied it, and lived by it. Christian Faith, such as his, is " a grand cathedral, with divinely pictured windows. Standing without, you see no glory, nor can possibly imagine any ; standing within, every ray of light reveals a harmony of unspeakable splendors."

Two miles out of Cracow, the ancient capital of Poland, stands the Hill of Kosciuszko.  It has received its name from a lofty mound of earth which was heaped up on the top of it in honor of the patriot after his death. Nobles, burghers, ladies, labored with their own hands in piling it up ; bags and baskets filled with earth were brought from every part of the dominions of the ancient Polish kingdom to be added to the heap ; and thus it was raised in a steep grass-covered cone, to a height of more than eighty feet above the top of the hill.  Some such everlasting monument should be erected to the memory of Woolman.  A vast plateau might be selected, sacred forever to the purpose, and upon it, if possible, might be deposited, by every Christian, every struggling poor man, every man who has been a serf or a slave, his tribute of earth, that so a mighty mountain might be raised, to tell to all the world that such a man as John Woolman had lived.

# VIII.

## JOHN RANDOLPH AND JOHN BROWN.

Two of the really great men that America has produced were John Randolph and John Brown. We speak of them in the order of chronology. Two more antithetic types could hardly be named. One was a born aristocrat, the other a born democrat, and as such they incarnated the two civilizations that have been in irreconcilable conflict since the foundation of the Nation, and that finally produced the Civil War.

John Randolph of Roanoke, to use his own language, "was ushered into this world of woe" on the second day of June, 1773. The mansion-house in which he was born is described as of ample proportions, with offices and extended wings, and as not an unworthy representative of the baronial days in which it was built — when Virginia cavaliers, under the title of gentlemen, with their broad domain of virgin soil, and long retinue of servants, lived in a style of elegance and profusion, not inferior to that of the barons of England. The first of his name that emigrated to Virginia was Colonel William Randolph, an English gentleman, who died in 1711. He was the father of seven sons and two daughters, who became the progenitors of a widespread and numerous race, embracing the most wealthy families, and many of the most distinguished names in Virginia history. His descendants were active promoters of the Revolution. John, the father of John of Roanoke, with two other relatives, sold forty slaves, and with the money purchased powder for the use of the colony. He married Jane Bolling, a descendant of Pocahontas, the beautiful Indian princess, daughter of Powhatan, between whom and Randolph there was said to be a striking resemblance.

The birthplace of Randolph, before referred to, was consumed by fire, also, the home of his childhood, also, the house where he spent the first fifteen years of his manhood. He was asked by a friend, after the latter place was burned, why he did not write something to leave behind him. "Too late, sir, too late," was the reply; "all I ever wrote perished in the flames; it is too late to restore it now." He felt and owned himself to be a child of destiny; he had a work given him to do, but some cross fate prevented; he failed to fulfill his destiny, and was wretched. "My whole name and race," he was heard to say, "lie under a curse. I am sure I feel the curse cleaving to me."

As a child, he is described as delicate, reserved, and beautiful. He said of himself that "but for a spice of the devil in his temper," his delicacy and effeminacy of complexion would have consigned him to the distaff or the needle. Before he was four years old, he was known to swoon away in a fit of passion, and with difficulty could be restored: "an evidence of the extreme delicacy of his constitution, and the uncontrollable ardor of a temper that required a stronger frame to repress and restrain it." In those fits of passion, his mother only, by her caresses, was able to soothe him. She was the one only human being, he said, who understood him. She was a woman, we are informed, not only of superior personal attractions, but excelled all others of her day in strength of intellect. Her death, when he was fifteen years old, nearly broke his heart. She was a member of the Church of England, a faith from which, we are assured, her son never long departed. She carefully guarded his associations. "He was allowed," it was said, "to come in contact with nothing low, vulgar, or mean." So, by training, as well as by natural bent, the child became "father of the man."

Some attention was paid to his education at home by his step-father and by his mother. He was too delicate, however, to be confined to study, and having "a spice of the devil in his temper," not much progress was made. But he was not idle. There was a certain closet, it is known, to which he stole away and secreted himself whenever he could. It was well stored with good books. Before he was eleven years of age he had read Voltaire's History of Charles XII. of Sweden, Humphry Clinker, Reynard the Fox, Shakespeare, the Arabian Nights, Goldsmith's Roman History, an old History of Braddock's War, Don Quixote, Gil Blas, Quintus Curtius, Plutarch, Pope's Homer, Robinson Crusoe, Gulliver, Tom Jones, Orlando Furioso, and Thomson's Seasons! Fit resource for the "thin-skinned, sensitive, impulsive, imaginative boy," subject to "fits of passion and swooning." "I have been all my life," he said, "the creature of impulse, the sport of chance, the victim of my own uncontrolled and uncontrollable sensations; of a poetic temperament. I admire and pity all who possess this temperament."

In the year 1781 the family were hastened from their home by the invasion of Virginia by Benedict Arnold,— Mr. Tucker, young Randolph's step-father, joining General Greene, then manœuvring before Cornwallis's army on the borders of North Carolina and Virginia, and afterward joining La Fayette, with whom he continued until the capture of Cornwallis at Yorktown. John was left with his mother during this stirring period. Her precepts, it is easy to believe, were law to his plastic mind. When riding over the vast Roanoke estates one day, she took John up behind her, and waving her hand over the broad acres spread before them, she said, " Johnny, all this land belongs to you and your brother Theodorick; it is your father's inheritance. When you get to be a man you must not sell your land ; it is the first step to ruin for a boy to part with his father's home : be sure to keep it as long as you live.  Keep your land and your land will keep you."  In relating this anecdote, Mr. Randolph said it made such an impression on his mind that it governed his future life.  He was confident it saved him from many errors.  " He never did part with his father's home.  His attachment to the soil, the old English law of inheritance, and a landed aristocracy, constituted the most remarkable trait in his character."  After the Virginia law of descents was changed, he said, " The old families of Virginia will form connections with low people, and sink into the mass of overseers' sons and daughters ; and this is the legitimate, nay, inevitable conclusion to which Mr. Jefferson and his leveling system has brought us."

The next two years, from nine till eleven, he spent at schools in Orange county and the city of Williamsburg. At the latter, it is related, the boys were in the habit of acting plays in the original language from Plautus and Terence.  John was always selected to perform the female parts.  His feminine appearance, and the "spice of the devil in his temper," rendered him, it was said, peculiarly fitted for that purpose, and his performance was admirable.  His proud temper and reserved manners prevented him from forming any intimate associations with his school-fellows.  He, it is stated, "shunned vulgar society, and repelled familiarity."

At eleven he went with his parents to the island of Bermuda, where he remained eighteen months.  While there he read Chatterton and Rowley, Young and Gay. Percy's Reliques and Chaucer became his favorites.  A year or two after his return from Bermuda, he went to Princeton, thence to Columbia College, in New York. " At Princeton College," he says, " where I spent a few months, the prize of elocution was borne away by mouthers and ranters.  I never would speak if I could possibly avoid it, and when I could not, repeated without gesture, the shortest piece that I had committed to memory. I was then as conscious of my superiority over my competitors in delivery and elocution, as I am now that they are sunk in oblivion ; and I despised the award and the umpires in the bottom of my heart. I believe that there is nowhere such foul play as among professors and schoolmasters ; more especially if they are priests. I have had a contempt for college honors ever since."

In New York he took much interest in passing events. His letters were considered very extraordinary for a boy of fifteen. One of them was upon " alien duties " exacted by the custom-house there ; another described with particularity the first inauguration of Washington as President.

At sixteen he had abandoned classical study, turning his attention and reflection to other fields. While yet a youth, he was in daily intercourse with statesmen and men of learning. He enjoyed great and rare opportunities for acquiring information on those subjects towards which his mind, he said, had "a precocious proclivity." He was a constant attendant on the sittings of the first Congress, which sat in New York. "I was at Federal Hall," he said long afterwards, in a speech ; "I saw Washington, but could not hear him take the oath to support the Federal Constitution. The Constitution was in a chrysalis state. I saw what Washington did not see ; but two other men in Virginia saw it — George Mason and Patrick Henry — the poison under its wings " — meaning too great a consolidation of power in the General Government, and too small a recognition of the rights of the States. With Henry, also, he saw the " awful squintings towards monarchy " in the Executive. He was, says his biographer, bred up in the school of Mason and of Henry. His step-father, his uncles, his brother, and all with whom he associated, imbibed the sentiments

of those statesmen, shared their devotion to the principles and the independence of the Commonwealth of Virginia, and participated in all their objections to the new
government.   Young Randolph, as we have seen, was a
constant attendant on the debates of the first Congress,
which had devolved on it the delicate task of organizing
the government, and setting its wheels in motion.   It was
amid these scenes, and by associating with such men,
that his political principles were formed and established,
and from which he never swerved.   His jealousy of the
power of the Federal Government, and his zeal for the
rights of the States, increased rather than diminished.
Upon the removal of the seat of government to Philadelphia, he went with it, where he remained, with short
intervals, till the spring of 1794, when he returned to Virginia.

He became extremely fond of the writings of Edmund
Burke, and they are said by Garland, in his careful history of his character, proclivities, and career, to have
been the key to his political opinions.   In after life, we
are told, as he grew in experience, those opinions became
more and more assimilated to the doctrines of his great
master.   His position in society, his large hereditary
possessions, his pride of ancestry, his veneration for the
Commonwealth of Virginia, her ancient laws and institutions; his high estimation of the rights of property in
the business of legislation, — all conspired to shape his
thoughts, and mould them in matters pertaining to domestic polity after the fashion of those who have faith in
the old, the long-established, and the venerable.

While in Philadelphia, he attended several courses of
lectures on anatomy and physiology.   In April, 1794, he
returned to Virginia.   In June he was twenty-one years
old, when he took upon himself the management of his
vast patrimonial estates.   At twenty-three he had the
appearance of a youth of sixteen, and was not grown.

He grew, it is said, a full head taller after this period. The death of his oldest brother at about this time, was a terrible blow to him. A relative, who slept in the room under his, said she never waked in the night that she did not hear him moving about, sometimes striding across the floor, and exclaiming, "Macbeth hath murdered sleep! Macbeth hath murdered sleep!" She knew him to have his horse saddled in the dead of night, and ride over the plantation with loaded pistols. His natural temper, we are informed, became more repulsive; he had no confidential friend, nor would any tie, however sacred, excuse inquiry. He was never in one place long enough to study much, yet he was known to turn over the leaves of a book carelessly, then lay it down, and tell more about it than those who had studied it.

In the winter of 1799, in the twenty-sixth year of his age, he was announced as a candidate for Congress. On March court day, the venerable Patrick Henry and the youthful John Randolph met, for the first time, at Charlotte Court House — the one to make his last speech, the other his first — the one the candidate of George Washington for a seat in the legislature of Virginia, the other a self-announced candidate for Congress — the one the champion of the Federal, the other the champion of the Republican cause. The occasion and event will long be memorable. The young man, says the historian of the contest, who was to answer the venerable orator, if indeed the multitude suspected that any one would dare venture on a reply, was unknown to fame. A tall, slender, effeminate-looking youth was he; light hair, combed back into a well-adjusted cue — pale countenance, a beardless chin, bright, quick, hazel eye, blue frock, buff smallclothes, and fair-top boots. He was doubtless known to many on the court green as the little Jack Randolph they had frequently seen dashing by on wild horses, from one of his estates to another. A few knew him more intimately, but none had ever heard him speak in public, or even suspected that he could make a speech. His friends knew his powers, his fluency in conversation, his ready wit, his polished satire, his extraordinary knowledge of men and affairs; but still he was about to enter on an untried field, and all those brilliant faculties might fail him, as they had so often failed men of genius before.

Henry, old and feeble, spoke first, in his usual eloquent manner, for two hours. Randolph followed. He spoke, it is said, for three hours; all that time the people, standing on their feet, hung with breathless silence on his lips. His youthful appearance, boyish tones, clear, distinct, thrilling utterance; his graceful action, bold expression, fiery energy, and manly thoughts, struck the multitude with astonishment. A bold genius and an orator of the first order had suddenly burst upon them, and dazzled them with his power and brilliancy. The orators, both of whom were elected, dined together after the contest, and Randolph ever after venerated the memory of Henry, who died in a few weeks.

Randolph's first speech in Congress was on a resolution to repeal an act to augment the army. It was energetic and fierce, and in it he applied the epithet "ragamuffins" to the soldiers enlisted in the army; which caused him to be insulted by two young officers in the theatre, of which insult he complained in plain language to the President, John Adams. The President enclosed Randolph's letter to the House of Representatives, with a not very agreeable intimation as to its "matter and style." The affair created much excitement throughout the country, and was considered by Randolph and his friends "as but one of a series of events that had for their end the subjugation of the people to the will of the federal oligarchy."

He was too impatient and violent to be trusted as a

leader. He suspected corruption in many men connected with the administration, and he denounced them unsparingly. What had been called the "colossus of turpitude, the Yazoo speculation," was the especial object of his violent denunciation.

In the midst of all this fever and distraction, the issue of an unfortunate love affair with one whom he said he loved more than his "own soul, or the God that made it," nearly unhinged his mind. His letters to his friends about this time are full of wretchedness and misery. He purposed flying across the sea, but stayed at home to brood. To a friend who was miserable, he said and wrote, "I, too, am wretched."

Notwithstanding, he took a leading part in every debate on the floor of Congress. The first fourteen years of his public service covered discussions of an exciting nature relating to our affairs with France, Spain, and England, the Embargo, the Gunboat scheme, and the war with Great Britain. The latter he opposed with all the vehemence and vigor of his mind and passions. For that opposition and for other reasons he was driven into retirement. The election in the spring of 1813 resulted in his defeat, after a contest of prodigious energy and desperation.

He said the defeat relieved him "from an odious thralldom." He retired to his home at Roanoke, which he described as "a savage solitude," where he lived in the utmost seclusion. The only companion of his solitude was a young relative he had taken to live with him, whom he educated with much care and at great expense. "It is indeed," he wrote to a friend, "a life of seclusion that I live here, uncheckered by a single ray of enjoyment. I try to forget myself in books; but that 'pliability of man's spirit' which yields him up to the illusions of the ideal world, is gone from me forever." "For my part," writing again to the same friend, "it requires an effort to take an interest in any thing ; **and** it seems to be strange that there should be found inducements strong **enough to** carry on the **business of the** world." He complained of violent palpitations **of the heart.** "When the fit is **on,"** he said, "it **may be seen through my** dress **across the** room." Some months afterward **he wrote,** "Since the hot weather set in, I have been **in a state** of collapse, **and** am as feeble as an infant — **with all this** I am tortured with rheumatism, or gout, a wretched cripple, and **my** mind is yet more weak and diseased than my body. **I hardly** know myself, so irresolute and timid have I become. **In short, I hope** that there is not another creature **in the world as unhappy as myself.** This **I can** say to **you. To the world I endeavor to put** on a different countenance, and **hold a bolder language ; but it is** sheer hypocrisy, assumed, **to guard against the pity of** mankind." About the same time **he wrote to the same friend,** "On the terms by which I hold **it, life is a curse, from which** I would willingly escape, if I knew where **to fly.** I have lost my relish for reading ; indeed, **I could not devour** even the Corsair with the zest that Lord Byron's pen generally inspires."

Two years after his defeat for Congress he was elected **again.** His candidacy brought out a swarm of detractors, **whom** he refused to answer. "It is too late in the day," **he said,** "to vindicate my public character before a people whom I** represented fourteen years, and **whom,** if they do not now **know me, never will.** I therefore abstain from **all** places of public **resort, as well from** inclination as principle." After the **election,** he said, "I do assure you with the **utmost** sincerity, that, so far as I am personally concerned, I cannot but regret the partiality **of** my friends, who insisted on holding **me up on this occasion.** I am engrossed by sentiments **of a far different** character, and **I** look forward to **the future in this** world, **to** say nothing of the next, with anticipations that forbid **any idle expression of** exultation."

Mr. Clay was his great antagonist. Although a Republican, he was accused of being a Federalist at heart, and opposed to the doctrine of State rights. For that, above every thing, Randolph was ever the bold champion. He thus refers to a memorable effort, in a letter dated Feb'y 23, 1820, the day after the speech was delivered: " Yesterday I spoke four hours and a half to as attentive an audience as ever listened to a public speaker. Every eye was riveted upon me, save one, (Mr. Clay's,) and that was sedulously and affectedly turned away. The ears, however, were drinking up the words as those of the royal Dane imbibed the ' juice of cursèd hebenon,' though not, like his, unconscious of the ' leperous distilment.' "

The peculiar state of his health, the excitement incident to the settlement of the Missouri question, and the death of his friend Commodore Decatur — who fell in a duel with Commodore Barron, March 20, 1820 — all contributed to produce a state of mind bordering on insanity. He went into the United States Branch Bank at Richmond and asked for writing materials to write a check. He dipped his pen in the ink, and finding that it was black, asked for red ink, saying, " I now go for blood." He filled the check up, and asked the cashier to write his name to it. The cashier refused to write his name ; and after importuning him for some time, he called for black ink, and signed John Randolph, of Roanoke, ✕ his mark. At about the same time, as the same person, the cashier, was passing along the street, Mr. Randolph hailed him in a louder voice than usual. The first question he asked the gentleman was, whether he knew of a good ship in the James River in which he could get a passage for England. He said he had been sick of a remittent and intermittent fever for forty days, and his physician said he must go to England. He was told there were no ships there fit for his accommodation, and that he had better go to New York, and sail from that port. " Do you think," said he, "I would give my money to those who are ready to make my negroes cut my throat? If I cannot go to England from a Southern port I will not go at all." A ship in the river was then recommended to him. He asked the name of it, and was told it was the "Henry Clay." He threw up his arms and exclaimed, "Henry Clay! No, sir! I will never step on the planks of a ship of that name." Soon after, he drew all his funds out of the bank, and put them in English guineas, — saying there was no danger of them. His "madness," as they called it, lasted but for a few months. In the autumn his understanding was as good as ever.

The summer he had spent at Roanoke. "The boys," as he called his wards, were off at school, and he found the solitude as usual, nearly intolerable. His letters written at this time abound in wise thoughts. "The true cure for maladies like yours," he says to one who had written in a desponding tone, "is employment. 'Be not solitary; be not idle!' was all that Burton could advise." "One of the best and wisest men I ever knew has often said to me, that a decayed family could never recover its loss of rank in the world, until the members of it left off talking and dwelling upon its former opulence." "Nothing can be more respectable than the independence that grows out of self-denial. The man who, by abridging his wants, can find time to devote to the cultivation of his mind, or the aid of his fellow-creatures, is a being far above the plodding sons of industry and gain. He is a spirit of the noblest order." "You know my opinion of female society. Without it, we should degenerate into brutes. To a young man, nothing is so important as a spirit of devotion (next to his Creator) to some virtuous and amiable woman, whose image may occupy his heart, and guard it from the pollution which besets it on all sides." "If matrimony has its cares, celibacy has no pleasures. A Newton, or a mere scholar, may find employment in study; a man of literary taste can receive, in books, a powerful auxiliary; but a man must have a bosom friend, and children around him, to cherish and support the dreariness of old age." Before leaving home he wrote his will, which emancipated all of his slaves, and provided for their maintenance.

In the spring of 1822, immediately after a speech of two hours against the Bankrupt Bill, he set out for New York to embark for Liverpool. The sea seemed to stimulate him. His social talents were exhibited in a manner highly delightful to the passengers. "He proposed one fine morning," said one of them, "to read (Halleck's) Fanny to me aloud, and on deck, where we were enjoying a fine breeze and noonday sun. It was the most amusing 'reading' I ever listened to. The notes were much longer than the poem; for, whenever he came to a well-known name, up went his spectacles and down went the book, and he branched off into some anecdote of the person or of his family. Thus we 'progressed' slowly from page to page, and it actually consumed three mornings before we reached —

> ' And music ceases when it rains
> In Scudder's balcony.' "

His visit to the House of Lords was characteristic. He refused to be admitted at the lower door. "Do you suppose," he said to the friend who held the tickets, "that I would consent to struggle with and push through the crowd of persons who, for two long hours, must fight their way in at the lower door? Oh, no sir! I shall do no such thing; and if I cannot enter as a gentleman commoner I go not at all." They separated — the friend to struggle in with the crowd, half suffocated by the long and perilous exertion. "Casting a glance toward the throne," said he, "soon after my entrance, to my no small surprise and envy, I beheld 'Randolph of Roanoke' in all his glory, **walking in most** leisurely, and perfectly **at** home, alongside **of** Canning, Lord Castlereagh, Sir Robert Peel, and many other distinguished members of **the House** of Commons."

While **in** England he had **interviews** of the most interesting character with **Mrs.** Fry, **Moore, Miss Edgeworth,** Wilberforce, and others, besides **making a** speech **at a meeting** of the African Institution **in London,** expressing in **his** usual vigorous way an abhorrence of the slave-trade.

**The following winter,** from his place on the floor **of Congress, he spoke a** cheering word for the Greeks. The speech **was one of his best, and** attracted great attention. Other **speeches followed on Internal** Improvements, the Tariff, and other **public questions. The** next summer he made another voyage **to Europe. In the spring of 1825** he was again a candidate for **Congress —** "that **bear gar-**den," he called it, **" of** the House **of Representatives."** On the 18th **of** April — the day **of the election —** he made a speech at Prince Edward **Court House, which is** referred to by Garland **— who was then a boy —** in his biography of Randolph. **The theme of his discourse was** the " alarming encroachments of the General **Gov-**ernment upon **the** rights of the States." " I shall never **forget** the manner of **the** man," says Garland. " The **tall, slender** figure, swarthy complexion, animated counte-**nance ; the solemn** glance, that passed leisurely over the audience, **hushed into deep** silence before him, and bend-ing forward to catch every look, every motion and every word of the **inspired orator ; the clear,** silver tones of his voice ; the distinct **utterance — full,** round expression, and emphasis of his words ; the graceful bend **and easy** motion of the person, as he turned from side **to side ; the** rapid, lightning-like sweep of the **hand** when **something** powerful **was** uttered ; the earnest, fixed **gaze,** that followed, as if searching into the **hearts of his** auditors, while his words were telling upon them ; then, the ominous pause, and the movement of that long, slender forefinger, that accompanied the keen, cutting sarcasm of his words — all these I can never forget."

The following December he was elected to the Senate. In his speech before that body upon the message of the President, John Quincy Adams, in answer to resolutions relating to the Panama Mission, Mr. Randolph said: ' Who made him a judge of our usages? Who constituted him? He has been a professor, I understand. I wish he had left off the pedagogue when he got into the Executive chair. Who made him the censor morum of this body? Will any one answer this question? Yes or no? Who? Name the person. Above all, who made him the searcher of hearts, and gave him the right, by an innuendo black as hell, to blacken our motives? Blacken our motives! I did not say that then. I was more under self-command ; I did not use such strong language. I said, if he could borrow the eye of Omniscience himself, and look into every bosom here ; if he could look into that most awful, calamitous, and tremendous of all gulfs, the naked unveiled human heart, stripped of all its covering of self-love, exposed naked, as to the eye of God — I said if he could do that, he was not, as President of the United States, entitled to pass upon our motives, although he saw and knew them to be bad. I said, if he had converted us to the Catholic religion, and was our father confessor, and every man in this House at the footstool of the confessional had confessed a bad motive to him by the laws of his church, as by this Constitution, above the law and above the church, he, as President of the United States, could not pass on our motives, though we had told him with our own lips our motives, and confessed they were bad. I said this then, and I say it now. Here I plant my foot ; here I fling defiance right into his teeth before the American people ; here I throw the gauntlet to

him and the bravest of his compeers, to come forward
and defend these miserable lines: 'Involving a departure,
hitherto, as far as I am informed, without example, from
that usage, and upon the motives for which, not being informed of them, I do not feel myself competent to decide.'
Amiable modesty!  I wonder we did not, all at once, fall
in love with him, and agree, una voce, to publish our proceedings, except myself, for I quitted the Senate ten minutes before the vote was taken.  I saw what was to follow;
I knew the thing would not be done at all, or would be
done unanimously.  Therefore, in spite of the remonstrance of friends, I went away, not fearing that any one
would doubt what my vote would have been, if I had
stayed.  After twenty-six hours' exertion, it was time to
give in.  I was defeated, horse, foot, and dragoons — cut
up, and clean broke down by the coalition of Blifil and
Black George — by the combination, unheard of till then,
of the puritan with the blackleg."

The epithet "blackleg," as every body knew, referred
to Clay, and resulted in a duel.  Randolph did not deny
the use of the offensive word.  The parties met the suc-
ceeding evening at four o'clock on the banks of the Po-
tomac.  The sun was just setting behind the blue hills.
An accident occurred by which Randolph's pistol dis-
charged, with the muzzle down, before the word was given.
Clay at once exclaimed that it was an accident.  On the
word being given, Clay fired, without effect, Randolph
discharging his pistol in the air.  The moment Clay saw
that Randolph had thrown away his fire, "with a gush of
sensibility," he instantly approached Randolph, and said
with emotion, "I trust in God, my dear sir, you are un-
touched; I would not have harmed you for a thousand
worlds."

One of his greatest speeches was on Negro Slavery in
South America.  His views were radical on every thing
relating to slavery.  He said in a letter to a friend, "From

the institution of the Passover to the latest experience of man, it would be found, that no two distinct people could occupy the same territory, under one government, but in the relation of master and vassal."

Early in May, 1826, before the adjournment of Congress, he went to Europe for a third time. He traveled extensively in England, Wales, and on the Continent. The next year he was defeated for the Senate, but was re-elected by his old district to a seat in the House. The summer was spent, as usual, at Roanoke. "I am dying," he said, "as decently as I can."

In January, 1829, he wrote from Washington, "It won't do for a man, who wishes to indulge in dreams of human dignity and worth, to pass thirty years in public life. Although I do believe that we are the meanest people in the world — I speak of this 'court' and its retainers and followers. I am super-saturated with the world, as it calls itself, and have now but one object, which I shall keep steadily in view, and perhaps some turn of the dice may enable me to obtain it : it is to convert my property into money, which will enable me to live, or rather to die, where I please ; or rather where it may please God."

The same year he retired from the public service, as he supposed, forever ; but a Convention had been called to amend the Constitution of Virginia, and he was elected a member of it without consulting him. He watched the proceedings of that body with unremitting attention, and spoke to it upon important questions with quite his usual power.

Before Mr. Randolph took his seat in the Convention he had been offered the mission to Russia by President Jackson. He was not, however, called upon to assume the duties of his mission till the May following. In June he set sail. In the autumn of the following year (1832) he returned to the United States, much reduced in health. His friends were shocked at his emaciated appearance.

Some misapprehension as to his conduct in St. Petersburgh, caused him to make a speech in explanation. But his last energies were to be expended in a conflict more serious than any in which he had been engaged. The authority of the General Government and the rights of the States were fairly in antagonism. Congress had passed a new tariff law, and South Carolina had proclaimed by ordinance that she would not obey it. General Jackson proclaimed that the law should be obeyed. Randolph, the champion of State rights, justified South Carolina in her attitude of nullification. Although he had to be lifted into his carriage like an infant, he went from county to county, speaking to the people in his old tones with his accustomed fire. His only hope of salvation for the country was in his old antagonist, Henry Clay. "I know he has the power," he said, "I believe he will be found to have the patriotism and firmness equal to the occasion."

On his way to Philadelphia, whence he expected to be able to embark for Europe, he visited the Senate Chamber, and took his seat in the rear of Mr. Clay, who happened to be on his feet addressing the Senate. "Raise me up!" said Randolph; "I want to hear that voice again." When Mr. Clay had concluded his remarks, which were very few, he turned round, to see from what quarter that singular voice proceeded. Seeing Mr. Randolph, and that he was in a dying condition, he left his place and went to speak to him; as he approached, Mr. Randolph said to the gentleman with him, "Raise me up!" As Mr. Clay offered his hand, he said, "Mr. Randolph, I hope you are better, sir." "No, sir," replied Randolph, "I am a dying man, and I came here expressly to have this interview with you."

He was indeed a dying man. He managed, however, to get to Philadelphia, where he soon died, at the City Hotel. Not long before his death he had been lying perfectly quiet, with his eyes closed. He suddenly roused up and exclaimed — "Remorse! remorse!" It was twice repeated — the last time at the top of his voice, with great agitation. He cried out — "Let me see the word. Get a dictionary. Let me see the word." "There is none in the room, sir." "Write it down, then — let me see the word." The doctor picked up one of his cards, " Randolph of Roanoke " — " Shall I write it on this card?" "Yes, nothing more proper." The word remorse was then written in pencil. He took the card in a hurried manner, and fastened his eyes on it with great intensity. "Write it on the back," he exclaimed — it was so done and handed him again. He was extremely agitated — "Remorse! you have no idea what it is; you can form no idea of it whatever; it has contributed to bring me to my present situation — but I have looked to the Lord Jesus Christ, and hope I have obtained pardon. Now let John take your pencil and draw a line under the word," which was accordingly done. "What am I to do with the card?" inquired the doctor. "Put it in your pocket — take care of it — when I am dead, look at it."

In a few minutes — after a few hurried words relating to his will — John Randolph was no more.

JOHN BROWN was born on the 9th day of May, 1800. His parents were poor, but eminently of good repute. The first of his ancestry on the paternal side that we have any account of came over on the Mayflower. His mother was a descendant of Peter Miles, an early emigrant from Holland, a tailor by trade, who died in 1754, at the advanced age of eighty-eight. His father and grandfather, and his mother's father and grandfather, all served in the war of the Revolution. His grandfather died in a barn near New York, while in the service. This is the inscription on his grave-stone: "The memory of Captain John Brown, who died in the Revolutionary army, at New York, September 3, 1776. He was of the fourth generation, in regular descent, from Peter Brown, one of the Pilgrim Fathers, who landed from the Mayflower at Plymouth, Massachusetts, December 22, 1620." He left a widow and eleven children. It is believed that she reared these children with singular taste and judgment, to habits of industry and principles of virtue, as all became leading citizens in the communities in which they resided. One of the sons became a judge in one of the courts of Ohio. One of the daughters gave to one of the most flourishing of New England's colleges a president for twenty years, in the person of her son. She is described as a woman of great energy and economy — the economy being a needful virtue. She cooked "always just what the children needed, and no more, and they always 'licked their trenchers,' when they had done with knife and fork."

John Brown lived at Torrington, Connecticut, his birthplace, until he was five years old, when he emigrated with his father to Hudson, Ohio. The latter soon became one of the principal pioneer settlers of the new town; was ever respected for his probity and honor; was commonly called 'Squire Brown, and was one of the Board of Trustees of Oberlin College; was endowed with energy and enterprise, and went down to his grave honored and respected, about the year 1852, at the ripe age of eighty-seven. He was an earnestly devout and religious man, of the old Connecticut fashion. He was an inveterate and most painful stammerer — "the first specimen of that infirmity that I had seen," says an early friend of the Brown family, "and, according to my recollection, the worst that I have ever known to this day; and I have never seen a man struggling and half strangled with a word stuck in his throat, without remembering good Mr. Owen Brown, who could not speak without stammering — except in prayer."

When John was four years old, he tells us himself, in the little sketch he made for the amusement of a child, that "he was tempted by three large brass pins belonging to a girl in the family, and stole them. In this he was detected by his mother, and, after having a full day to think of the wrong, received from her a thorough whipping." He preferred, he says, remaining at home to work hard, rather than to go to school. In warm weather, he says, he "might generally be seen barefooted and bareheaded, with buckskin breeches, suspended with one leather strap over his shoulder, but sometimes with two." He delighted to be sent great distances through the wilderness alone. Sometimes he was sent a hundred miles, all alone, in charge of herds of cattle. He says he "would have thought his character much injured had he been obliged to be helped in such a job." This life in the woods gave him the habits and the keen senses of a hunter or an Indian. He told a friend that he became remarkably clear-sighted and quick of ear, and that he had smelled the frying of doughnuts, when he was very hungry, at five miles distance. He knew all the devices of woodcraft ; declared he could make a dinner for forty men out of the hide of one ox, and thought he understood how to provide for an army's subsistence. During the war with England, his father furnished the troops with beef cattle, the collecting and driving of which afforded John opportunity, which he enjoyed, of chasing the wild cattle, when they broke away, panic-stricken, through the unbroken forest.

At the age of ten years, an old friend induced him to read a little history, and offered him the free use of his library ; in that way he acquired some taste for reading, which formed, he says, the principal part of his early education. He became very fond of the company and conversation of old and intelligent persons. "He learned nothing of grammar, nor of composition ; nor did he get at school so much knowledge of common arithmetic as the four ground rules. This will give the reader some general idea of the first fifteen years of his life; during which time he became very strong and large of his age, and ambitious to perform the full labor of a man, at almost any kind of hard work. By reading the lives of great, wise, and good men — their sayings and writings — he grew to a dislike of vain and frivolous conversation and persons; and was often greatly obliged by the kind manner in which older and more intelligent persons treated him at their homes." He joined the Congregational Church at the age of sixteen, with which, and the Presbyterian Church, he was connected till the day of his death.

The years from fifteen to twenty were mostly spent in acquiring the trade of a tanner and currier — a part of the time acting in the capacity of foreman. His attention to business, and success in its management, made him a favorite with older and graver persons. From the age of fifteen he felt a great anxiety to study; but an inflammation of the eyes prevented close application. He managed, however, to become pretty well acquainted with arithmetic and surveying, which latter he practiced more or less for the rest of his life. At nineteen or twenty, he left Ohio and went East, to acquire a liberal education. His ultimate design, it is stated, was the ministry. At Plainfield, Massachusetts, he was fitted or nearly fitted for college. A brother of his teacher thus describes John Brown as he appeared at that time: "He was a tall, sedate, dignified young man. He had been a tanner, and relinquished a prosperous business for the purpose of intellectual improvement, but with what ultimate end I do not now know. He brought with him a piece of soleleather, about a foot square, which he himself had tanned for seven years, to resole his boots. He had also a piece of sheep-skin which he had tanned, and of which he cut some strips about an eighth of an inch wide for other students to pull upon. My father took one string, and, winding it around his fingers, said, ' I shall snap it.' The very marked, yet kind unmovableness of the young man's face on seeing my father's defeat — my father's own look, and the position of the people and things in the old kitchen — somehow gave me a fixed recollection of the little incident." While pursuing his studies, he was again attacked with inflammation of the eyes, and he returned to Ohio. "God," says his admiring biographer, "had higher work for this sedate, dignified young man than to write and deliver sermons to a parish. He was raising him up as a deliverer of captives and a teacher of righteousness to a nation ; as the conserver of the light of true Christianity, when it was threatened with extinction, under the rubbish of creeds and constitutions, and iniquities enacted into laws."

When he was just entering upon his twenty-first year he was married. He describes his young wife as remarkably plain ; neat, industrious, and economical ; of excellent character ; earnest piety ; good practical common sense ; and about one year younger than himself. This woman, he says, by her mild, frank, and, more than all else, very consistent conduct, acquired and maintained while she lived a powerful and good influence over him. Her plain but kindly admonitions generally had the right effect, without arousing his haughty, obstinate temper. Her name was Dianthe Lusk, by whom he had seven children. Some time after her death, he married Mary A. Day, by whom he had thirteen children — twenty in all.

From his twenty-first to his twenty-sixth year, John Brown was engaged in the tanning business, and as a farmer in Ohio. In 1826 he went to Pennsylvania, where he carried on the tanning business for nine years. One of his apprentices at this period informed his biographer that he was characterized by singular probity of life, and by his strong and "eccentric" benevolent impulses. He refused to sell leather until the last drop of moisture had been dried from it, "lest he should sell his customer water, and reap the gain." He is said to have caused a man to be arrested, or rearrested, for some small offense, simply because he thought the crime should be punished; and his benevolence induced him to supply the wants of the offender out of his private means, and to provide for the family until the trial.

He returned to Ohio in 1835, where he again engaged in tanning, and trading in real estate. The latter turned out to be unfortunate. He then took a drove of cattle to Connecticut, and returned with a flock of sheep,— his first purchases in that business, in which afterward he became pretty largely interested. In 1840 he went to Hudson again, and engaged in the wool business. His partner there says of him: "From boyhood I have known him through manhood; and through life he has been distinguished for his truthfulness and integrity; he has ever been esteemed, by those who have known him, as a very conscientious man."

It was, we are told, in 1839 that he conceived the idea of becoming a liberator of the Southern slaves. He had been an abolitionist since he was twelve years old, but now he determined to devote his life, as far as possible, to the cause of liberty against slavery, and to the rescue of slaves. His devotion to the cause was intensely earnest and heroic. "He had elements of character," said one who knew him well, "which, under circumstances favorable to their proper development and right direction, would have made him one of the greatest men of the world. Napoleon himself had no more blind and trusting confidence in his own destiny and resources; his iron will and unbending purpose were equal to that of any man, living or dead; his religious enthusiasm and sense of duty were earnest and sincere, and not excelled by that of Oliver Cromwell or any of his followers ; while no danger could for a moment alarm or disturb him. His manner, though conveying the idea of a stern and self-sustaining man, was yet gentle and courteous, and marked by frequent and decided manifestations of kindness ; and it can probably be said of him, with truth, that, amid all his provocations, he never perpetrated an act of wanton or unnecessary cruelty. He was scrupulously honest, moral, and temperate, and never gave utterance to a boast."

He was a very early riser, and a very hard worker. His dress is described as extremely plain ; never in the fashion, and never made of fine cloth. But he was always scrupulously clean and tidy in his personal appearance. "When first I saw him," says Redpath, "at his camp in Kansas, although his clothing was patched and old, and he was almost barefooted, he was as tidy, both in person and dress, as any gentleman of Boston."

He was extremely fond of music. "I once saw him," said a friend, "sit listening with the most rapt attention to Schubert's Serenade, played by a mutual acquaintance, and, when the music ceased, tears were in the old man's eyes. He was indeed most tender-hearted — fond of children and pet creatures, and always enlisted on the weaker side. The last time I saw him in Boston, he had been greatly annoyed by overhearing in the street some rude language addressed to a black girl, who, he said, would never have been insulted if she had been white."

"John Brown was always very agreeable," said Judge Russell, of Boston, in a recent address. "He used to hold up my little girl, eighteen months old, and say: ' Now, when I am hung for treason, you can say that you used to stand on old Captain Brown's hand.' He walked the floor at night with his hands behind him, and occasionally brought out an idea. One I remember very distinctly : 'It would be better that a whole generation should perish from the earth, than that one truth in the Sermon on the Mount or the Declaration of Independence should be forgotten among men.'"

He went to Springfield, Massachusetts, in 1846, and engaged again in the wool business. His book-keeper describes him as a quiet and peaceable citizen, whose integrity was never doubted ; honorable in all his dealings, but peculiar in many of his notions, and adhering to them with great obstinacy. He and his eldest son discussed slavery by the hour in the counting-room ; he said it was right for slaves to kill their masters and escape, and thought slaveholders were guilty of a very great wickedness. While at Springfield he went to Europe to look after his wool interests. He interested himself in agriculture, but particularly in the armies of Great Britain and the Continent. He visited several of the battle fields of Napoleon : he thought him wrong in several points of strategy, particularly in his choice of ground for a strong position ; which Brown maintained should be a ravine rather than a hill-top. He said that a ravine could be held by a few men against a larger force ; that he had acted on this principle in Kansas, and never suffered from it. He ascribed his winning the battle of Black Jack to his choice of ground.

In 1849, he removed his family to North Elba, in Essex County, New York. It was at about this time, as stated by his biographer, that Gerritt Smith offered to colored settlers his wild lands in that district of the Adirondack wilderness. Many of them accepted the offer, and went there to make the experiment. At this period, it is related, John Brown appeared one day at Peterboro', and said to Mr. Smith, " I see, by the newspapers, that you have offered so many acres of wild land to each of the colored men, on condition that they cultivate them. Now, they are mostly inexperienced in this kind of work, and unused to the climate, while I am familiar with both.  I

propose, therefore, to take a farm there myself, clear it
and plant it, showing the negroes how such work should
be done. I will also employ some of them on my land,
and will look after them in all ways, and will be a kind of
father to them." Mr. Smith accepted the humane proposal, gave John Brown the land, and allowed him to make
the experiment, although he had never before seen him.
So far as the negroes were concerned, this proved a failure, but, it is believed, through no fault of Brown's. He
did his part faithfully by them. He had, it is known,
a higher notion of the capacity of the negro race than
most white men. He was often heard to dwell on this
subject, and mention instances of their fitness to take care
of themselves. He thought that "perhaps a forcible separation of the connection between master and slave was
necessary to educate the blacks for self-government;"
but this he threw out as a suggestion merely.

The John Brown farm is described as a wild place;
cold and bleak. It is too cold to raise corn there; they
can scarcely, in the most favorable seasons, obtain a few
ears for roasting. Stock must be wintered for almost
six months in the year. I was there, says Higginson, on
the first day of November; the ground was snowy, and
winter had apparently begun — and it would last until the
middle of May. They never raised any thing to sell off
the farm, except sometimes a few fleeces. It was well,
the family said, if they raised their own provisions, and
could spin their own wool for clothing. "I was the
first person," said Higginson, "who had penetrated their
solitude from the outer world since the thunderbolt had
fallen. Do not imagine that they asked, What is the world
saying of us? Will justice be done to the memory of our
martyrs? Will men build the tombs of the prophets?
Will the great thinkers of the age affirm that our father
'makes the gallows glorious, like the cross'? Not at
all; they asked but one question after I had told them

how little hope there was of acquittal or rescue. Does it seem as if freedom were to gain or lose by this? That was all. Their mother spoke the spirit of them all to me, next day, when she said, 'I have had thirteen children, and only four are left; but if I am to see the ruin of my house, I cannot but hope that Providence may bring out of it some benefit to the poor slaves.'" "People are surprised," said Annie Brown, "at father's daring to invade Virginia with only twenty-three men; but I think if they knew what sort of men they were, there would be less surprise. I never saw such men."

In 1854, four sons of John Brown determined to remove to Kansas. In the summer of 1855, in a county adjoining Essex, in New York, a meeting of abolitionists was held. John Brown appeared in that convention, and made a very fiery speech, in which he said he had four sons in Kansas, and had three others who were desirous of going there, to aid in fighting the battles of freedom. He could not consent to go unless he could go armed, and he would like to arm all his sons; but his poverty prevented him from doing so. He stated that he had only two objects in going to Kansas: first, to begin the work for which, as he believed, he had been set apart, by so acting as to acquire the confidence of the friends of freedom, who might thereby subsequently aid him; and, secondly, because, to use his own language, "with the exposure, privations, hardships, and wants of pioneer life, he was familiar, and thought he could benefit his children, and the new beginners from the older parts of the country, and help them to shift and contrive in their new home."

The first that we hear of him there was in a caucus at Ossawattomie. A resolution had been offered that aroused the old man's anger. It declared that Kansas should be a free white State, thereby favoring the exclusion of negroes and mulattoes, whether slave or free. He rose to speak, and, it is stated, soon alarmed and disgusted the politicians present by asserting the manhood of the negro race, and expressing his earnest, anti-slavery convictions with great force and vehemence.

In camp, it is further stated, he permitted no manner of profane language; no man of immoral character was allowed to stay, excepting as a prisoner of war. He made prayers in which all the company united, every morning and evening; and no food was ever tasted by his men until the divine blessing had been asked on it. It is said also that he would retire into the densest solitudes for secret prayer. One of his company said that after these retirings he would say that the Lord had directed him in visions what to do; that, for himself, he did not love warfare, but peace, — only acting in obedience to the will of the Lord, and fighting God's battles for His children's sake.

At the battles of Black Jack and Ossawattomie his reputation as a guerrilla commander was established. At Black Jack, with a squad of only a few men, after a three hours' fight, he succeeded in killing, scattering, and capturing a superior force. Only two of the Free State men were wounded — one of them a son-in-law of the commander. At Ossawattomie, with a force of not more than thirty men, against a formidable enemy — nearly five hundred it is stated — he came out of the conflict with one dead, two wounded, and two missing, while the loss of the other side was "thirty-one or two killed, and from forty to fifty wounded." The old man, we are informed, stood near a sapling during the whole of the engagement, quietly giving directions to his men, and "annoying the enemy" with his own steady rifle, indifferent to the grape shots and balls which whizzed around him, and hewed down the limbs, scattered the foliage, and peeled off the bark from the trees on every side.

His conduct at the defense of Lawrence was characterized by the same courage and ability. Mounting a dry-goods box in the main street, he addressed the excited citizens as follows : "Gentlemen, it is said there are twenty-five hundred Missourians down at Franklin, and that they will be here in two hours. You can see for yourselves the smoke they are making by setting fire to the houses in that town. Now this is probably the last opportunity you will have of seeing a fight ; so that you had better do your best. If they should come up and attack us, don't yell and make a noise, but remain perfectly silent and still. Wait till they get within twenty-five yards of you ; get a good object ; be sure you see the hind sight of your gun : then fire. A great deal of powder and lead, and very precious time, are wasted by shooting too high. You had better aim at their legs than at their heads. In either case, be sure of the hind sights of your guns. It is from this reason that I myself have so many times escaped ; for, if all the bullets which have ever been aimed at me had hit me, I should have been as full of holes as a riddle."

After the retreat from Franklin, Brown and his four sons left Lawrence for the East. Encountering a fugitive slave at Topeka, they covered him up in their wagon, and carried him along with them. We hear of him in Iowa, in Cleveland, then in Boston — in January, 1857 — where he made a speech, recounting his experiences and views, to the Massachusetts legislature. As to his appearance at that time, an acquaintance said : "His brown coat of the fashion of ten years before, his waistcoat buttoning nearly to the throat, and his wide trowsers, gave him the look of a well-to-do farmer in his Sunday dress ; while his patent leather stock, gray surtout, and fur cap, added a military air to his figure. At this time he wore no beard." The next we hear of him is at New York, at the Metropolitan Hotel, on his way to Philadelphia and Washington. He objected to the show and extravagance of such an establishment as the Metropolitan, and said he preferred a plain tavern, where drovers and farmers lodged in a plain way. Next he is at his home at North Elba. In February, in Collinsville, Connecticut, he contracted for the manufacture of his pikes. Every thing he did now bore as directly as possible upon the final result, so rapidly approaching. He visited Kansas again, and Iowa, and Canada, where he conveyed some fugitive slaves. Here the conspiracy against Harper's Ferry was organized, but the attack was not made until the night of the 17th day of October, 1859. The night before the attack, he said to his men : " Let me press this one thing on your minds. You all know how dear life is to you, and how dear your lives are to your friends ; and, in remembering that, consider that the lives of others are as dear to them as yours are to you. Do not, therefore, take the life of any one if you can possibly avoid it ; but if it is necessary to take life, in order to save your own, then make sure work of it."

The Governor of the State of Virginia visited him in prison, after his capture, and said of him : " They themselves are mistaken who take him to be a madman. He is a bundle of the best nerves I ever saw, cut, and thrust, and bleeding, and in bonds. He is a man of clear head, of courage, fortitude, and simple ingenuousness. He is cool, collected, and indomitable. The gamest man I ever saw."

On the scaffold, at midday, under the shining sun, on the second day of December, in the year of our Lord one thousand eight hundred and fifty-nine, he died.

* John Brown, when he was twelve years old, on seeing a negro slave of his own age cruelly beaten, began to hate slavery and love the slaves so intensely that he sometimes asked himself the question, Is God their Father ? At forty, he conceived the idea of becoming a liberator of the Southern slaves ; at the same time he determined to

* Library Notes.

15

let them know that they had friends, and prepared himself to lead them to liberty. From the moment that he formed this resolution, he engaged in no business which he could not, without loss to his friends and family, wind up in fourteen days. His favorite texts of Scripture were, "Remember them that are in bonds, as bound with them;" "Whoso stoppeth his ear at the cry of the poor, he also shall cry himself, but shall not be heard;" "Whoso mocketh the poor reproacheth his Maker, and he that is glad at calamities shall not be unpunished;" "Withhold not good from them to whom it is due, when it is in the power of thine hand to do it." His favorite hymns were, "Blow ye the trumpet, blow!" and "Why should we start and fear to die?" A child asked him how he felt when he left the eleven slaves, which he had taken from Missouri to Canada? His answer was, "Lord, permit now thy servant to die in peace, for mine eyes have seen thy salvation. I could not brook the idea that any ill should befall them, or they be taken back to slavery. The arm of Jehovah protected us." Upon one occasion, when one of the ex-governors of Kansas said to him that he was a marked man, and that the Missourians were determined, sooner or later, to take his scalp, the old man straightened himself up, with a glance of enthusiasm and defiance in his gray eye: "Sir," said he, "the Angel of the Lord will camp round about me." On leaving his family the first time he went to Kansas, he said, "If it is so painful for us to part, with the hope of meeting again, how dreadful must be the separation for life of hundreds of poor slaves." He deliberately determined, we are assured, twenty years before his attack upon Harper's Ferry, that at some future period he would organize an armed party, go into a slave State, and liberate a large number of slaves. Soon after, surveying professionally in the mountains of Virginia, he chose the very ground for the purpose. He said, "God had established the Alleghany Mountains from the foundation of the world that they might one day be a refuge for fugitive slaves." Visiting Europe afterward, he studied military strategy, and made designs for a new style of forest fortifications, simple and ingenious, to be used by parties of fugitive slaves when brought to bay. He knew the ground, he knew his plans, he knew himself; but where should he find his men? Such men as he needed are not to be found ordinarily; they must be reared. John Brown did not merely look for men, therefore; he reared them in his sons. Mrs. Brown had been always the sharer of his plans. "Her husband always believed," she said, "that he was to be an instrument in the hands of Providence, and she believed it too. This plan had occupied his thoughts and prayers for twenty years. Many a night he had lain awake and prayed concerning it." He believed in human brotherhood, and in the God of battles; he admired, he said, Nat Turner, the negro patriot, equally with George Washington, the white American deliverer. He secretly despised even the ablest of the anti-slavery orators. He could see "no use in this talking," he said. "Talk is a national institution; but it does no manner of good to the slaves." The year before his attack upon Harper's Ferry, he uttered these sentences in conversation: "Nat Turner, with fifty men, held Virginia five weeks. The same number, well organized and armed, can shake the system out of the State." "Give a slave a pike, and you make him a man. Deprive him of the means of resistance, and you keep him down." "The land belongs to the bondsman. He has enriched it, and been robbed of its fruits." "Any resistance, however bloody, is better than the system which makes every seventh woman a concubine." "A few men in the right, and knowing they are, can overturn a king. Twenty men in the Alleghanies could break slavery to pieces in two years." "When the bondsmen stand like men, the nation

will respect them. It is necessary to teach them this."
About the same time he said, in another conversation,
that "it was nothing to die in a good cause, but an eternal disgrace to sit still in the presence of the barbarities
of American slavery." "Providence," said he, "has
made me an actor, and slavery an outlaw." "Duty is the
voice of God, and a man is neither worthy of a good
home here, or a heaven, that is not willing to be in peril
for a good cause." He scouted the idea of rest while he
held "a commission direct from God Almighty to act
against slavery." After his capture, and while he lay in
blood upon the floor of the guard-house, he was asked by
a bystander upon what principle he justified his acts?
"Upon the Golden Rule," he answered. "I pity the
poor in bondage that have none to help them. That is
why I am here; it is not to gratify any personal animosity, or feeling of revenge, or vindictive spirit. It is my
sympathy with the oppressed and the wronged, that are
as good as you, and as precious in the sight of God. I
want you to understand, gentlemen, that I respect the
rights of the poorest and weakest of the colored people,
oppressed by the slave system, just as much as I do those
of the most wealthy and powerful. That is the idea that
has moved me, and that alone. We expected no reward
except the satisfaction of endeavoring to do for those in
distress — the greatly oppressed — as we would be done
by. The cry of distress, of the oppressed, is my reason,
and the only thing that prompted me to come here. I
wish to say, furthermore, that you had better, all you
people of the South, prepare yourselves for a settlement
of this question. It must come up for settlement sooner
than you are prepared for it, and the sooner you com-
mence that preparation, the better for you. You may
dispose of me very easily. I am nearly disposed of now;
but this question is still to be settled — this negro question, I mean. The end of that is not yet." In his "last

speech," before sentence of death was passed upon him, he said, "This court acknowledges, as I suppose, the validity of the law of God. I see a book kissed here which I suppose to be the Bible, or, at least, the New Testament. That teaches me that all things 'whatsoever I would that men should do unto me I should do even so to them.' It teaches me further to 'remember them that are in bonds, as bound with them.' I endeavored to act up to that instruction. I say, I am yet too young to understand that God is any respecter of persons. I believe that to have interfered as I have done, as I have always freely admitted I have done, in behalf of his despised poor, was not wrong, but right. Now, if it is deemed necessary that I should forfeit my life for the furtherance of the ends of justice, and mingle my blood further with the blood of my children, and with the blood of millions in this slave country whose rights are disregarded by wicked, cruel, and unjust enactments — I submit: so let it be done." In a postscript to a letter to a half-brother, written in prison, he said, "Say to my poor boys never to grieve for one moment on my account; and should any of you live to see the time when you will not blush to own your relation to old John Brown, it will not be more strange than many things that have happened." In a letter to his old schoolmaster, he said, "I have enjoyed much of life, as I was enabled to discover the secret of this somewhat early. It has been in making the prosperity and happiness of others my own; so that really I have had a great deal of prosperity." To another he wrote; "I commend my poor family to the kind remembrance of all friends, but I well understand that they are not the only poor in our world. I ought to begin to leave off saying our world." In his last letter to his family, he said, "I am waiting the hour of my public murder with great composure of mind and cheerfulness, feeling the strong assurance that in no other possible way could I be used to so much advantage to the cause of God and of humanity, and that nothing that I or all my family have sacrificed or suffered will be lost. Do not feel ashamed on my account, nor for one moment despair of the cause, or grow weary of well-doing. I bless God I never felt stronger confidence in the certain and near approach of a bright morning and glorious day than I have felt, and do now feel, since my confinement here." In a previous letter to his family, he said, "Never forget the poor, nor think any thing you bestow on them to be lost to you, even though they may be as black as Ebed-melech, the Ethiopian eunuch, who cared for Jeremiah in the pit of the dungeon, or as black as the one to whom Philip preached Christ. 'Remember them that are in bonds, as bound with them.'" As he stepped out of the jail-door, on his way to the gallows, "a black woman, with a little child in her arms, stood near his way. The twain were of the despised race for whose emancipation and elevation to the dignity of the children of God he was about to lay down his life. His thoughts at that moment none can know except as his acts interpret them. He stopped for a moment in his course, stooped over, and with the tenderness of one whose love is as broad as the brotherhood of man, kissed the child affectionately. As he came upon an eminence near the gallows, he cast his eye over the beautiful landscape, and followed the windings of the Blue Ridge Mountains in the distance. He looked up earnestly at the sun, and sky, and all about, and then remarked, 'This is a beautiful country. I have not cast my eyes over it before.'" "You are more cheerful than I am, Captain Brown," said the undertaker, who sat with him in the wagon. "Yes," answered the old man, "I ought to be." "'Gentlemen, good-by,' he said to two acquaintances, as he passed from the wagon to the scaffold, which he was first to mount. As he quietly awaited the necessary arrangements, he surveyed the scenery unmoved, looking principally in the direction of the people, in the far distance. 'There is no faltering in his steps,' wrote one who saw him, 'but firmly and erect he stands amid the almost breathless lines of soldiery that surround him. With a graceful motion of his pinioned right arm he takes the slouched hat from his head and carelessly casts it upon the platform by his side. His elbows and ankles are pinioned, the white cap is drawn over his eyes, the hangman's rope is adjusted around his neck. 'Captain Brown,' said the sheriff, 'you are not standing on the drop. Will you come forward?' 'I can't see you, gentlemen,' was the old man's answer, unfalteringly spoken; 'you must lead me.' The sheriff led his prisoner forward to the centre of the drop. 'Shall I give you a handkerchief,' he then asked, 'and let you drop it as a signal?' 'No; I am ready at any time; but do not keep me needlessly waiting.'"

John Randolph and John Brown! Remarkable men! and peculiarly interesting, as characters and types, to all Americans. What contrasts! The first, an aristocrat — born, as we have seen, in a mansion-house, not unworthy of the baronial days in which it was built; the inheritor of an honored name and of vast estates; proud of his cavalier descent, and proud of his princely possessions; surrounded, from his birth, with an atmosphere of refinement and intelligence; with every accessory and auxiliary, it would appear, to make him supremely happy; with every body to do for him, and every thing to do with; "thin-skinned, sensitive, impulsive, and imaginative," but with an accomplished and tender mother to soothe him, and a quiet closet to resort to, stored with the wisdom of all ages; flattered, caressed, and petted; in his youth at the capital, enjoying daily intercourse with statesmen and men of learning; in his early manhood elected to Congress, and kept there, nearly the remainder of his life, by

an admiring and generous constituency ; a student of the
Constitution with the makers of it ; a traveler abroad,
with every advantage of society, study, and observation ;
commanding, as a man and as a statesman ; distressed,
after all, in body and in mind, and going to his grave re-
morseful, and despairing of his country.  The second,
a democrat, the product of poverty and hope ; of a long
line of indigence, industry, and honesty ; knowing life at
its hardest, from the beginning ; dressing in skins, like a
savage ; stealing a pin, and getting a whipping for it ;
loving the wilderness, for its immensity and loneliness,
and driving wild cattle through it for a hundred miles ;
growing up illiterate, but intelligent ; a tanner, and learning how to make a dinner for forty men out of the hide
of an ox ; married at twenty, and the father of twenty
children — all Browns — every inch ; on his feet, struggling abreast with poor men, remembering those that are
in bonds, as bound with them ; inspired, twenty years before his death, with the idea of becoming a liberator of
slaves ; from that moment bending every effort of his life
to that end ; visiting Europe on business, and studying
military strategy ; encouraging emigration, and protect-
ing the immigrants ; fighting slavery, and rescuing slaves ;
on the border, with a reward offered for his head ; in
Boston, with an officer after him with a warrant ; shunned
and forsworn by multitudes of sympathizers ; by slavery
made an outlaw, and by Providence an actor ; avoided,
suspected, and hunted, but vindictive never ; scouting the
idea of rest, holding, as he believed, a commission direct
from Almighty God ; cheerful and composed in the teeth
of need and of vengeance ; never querulous or complaining, even when in prison and in chains ; but serenely
going to his death, with still a conscience toward God.
Both were honest men, to the core.  Both were brave, to
a fault.  Each was the peer of any, and a natural ruler
over many.  Each was true to what he believed to be his

mission.   One was a born hater of caste, and a staunch believer in the equality of all men, without distinction ; the other a born believer in radical differences of blood and race, — declaring, as we have seen, that " no two distinct people could occupy the same territory, under one government, but in the relation of master and vassal." One gave the efforts of his life to his idea ; the other gave all his efforts, and his life too, to his.   One went discouraged to his grave, with remorse lingering on his tongue and preying at his heart ; the other serenely riding to the scaffold, smiling with the sun and the morning, and confidently hoping for a better day.

# IX.

## THE AUDACITY OF FOOTE.

Was ever wit more audacious than Foote? Perspicacious and bold — seeing every thing and stopping at nothing, — no wonder the great town shook with terror and laughter at his daring personalities and mimicries. As quick to say as to see, the strokes of his humor were as surprising as they were instantaneous, and his victims fell without staggering. There was no threatening, to forewarn or alarm ; no noisy brewing of elements ; no waste by elaboration ; and when the mischief was done, there was no smell of spent forces. On the stage, at the club, at the coffee-house, he took off every body of prominence or eminence. Nobody seemed to escape him. At the Haymarket, for forty nights in succession, he imitated Whitefield. "There is hardly a public man in England," said Davies, "who has not entered Mr. Foote's theatre with an aching heart, under the apprehension of seeing himself laughed at." His rule was, that you ought not to run the chance of losing your friend for your joke unless your joke happens to be better than your friend. Imagine how the sensitive Goldsmith must have shrunk from his aggressive wit, and insolent, impudent, swaggering animal spirits. Johnson alone, of all that were about him, seemed able to keep the brilliant, audacious outlaw within bounds. The great moralist was but too conscious of his peculiarities and deformities, and if Foote had dared to mimic them publicly he would have broken his bones.

"Foote," said Johnson, "is the most incompressible

fellow that I ever saw : when you have driven him into a corner, and think you are sure of him, he runs through between your legs, or jumps over your head, and makes his escape. Then he has a great range for wit ; he never lets truth stand between him and a jest, and he is sometimes mighty coarse. . . . The first time I was in company with Foote, was at Fitzherbert's. Having no good opinion of the fellow, I was resolved not to be pleased ; and it is very difficult to please a man against his will. I went on eating my dinner pretty sullenly, affecting not to mind him. But the dog was so very comical that I was obliged to lay down my knife and fork, throw myself back upon my chair, and fairly laugh it out. No, sir, he was irresistible. He upon one occasion experienced, in an extraordinary degree, the efficacy of his powers of entertaining. Amongst the many and various modes which he tried of getting money, he became a partner with a small-beer brewer, and he was to have a share of the profits for procuring customers amongst his numerous acquaintance. Fitzherbert was one who took his small-beer ; but it was so bad that the servants resolved not to drink it. They were at some loss how to notify their resolution, being afraid of offending their master, who they knew liked Foote much as a companion. At last they fixed upon a little black boy, who was rather a favorite, to be their deputy, and deliver their remonstrance ; and having invested him with the whole authority of the kitchen, he was to inform Mr. Fitzherbert, in all their names, upon a certain day, that they would drink Foote's small-beer no longer. On that day, Foote happened to dine at Fitzherbert's, and this boy served at table ; he was so delighted with Foote's stories, and merriment, and grimace, that when he went down stairs, he told them, 'This is the finest man I have ever seen. I will not deliver your message. I will drink his small-beer.' "

Foote went to Ireland, and took off a celebrated Dublin printer.  The printer stood the jest for some time, but found at last that Foote's imitations became so popular, and drew such attention to himself, that he could not walk the streets without being pointed at.  He bethought himself of a remedy.  Collecting a number of boys, he gave them a hearty meal, and a shilling each for a place in the gallery, and promised them another meal on the morrow if they would hiss off the scoundrel who turned him into ridicule.  The injured man learned from his friends that Foote was received that night better than ever.  Nevertheless, in the morning, the ragged troop of boys appeared to demand their recompense, and when the printer reproached them for their treachery, their spokesman said : " Plase yer honor, we did all we could, for the actor man had heard of us, and did not come at all at all.  And so we had nobody to hiss.  But when we saw yer honor's own dear self come on, we did clap, indeed we did, and showed you all the respect and honor in our power.  And so yer honor won't forget us because yer honor's enemy was afraid to come, and left yer honor to yer own dear self."  For this story we are indebted to Crabb Robinson, to whom Incledon, the singer, related if one day when they were traveling in a stage-coach together — the garrulous fellow all the time rattling away about Garrick and Mrs. Siddons and every body — himself especially.

On one occasion, some one said to Johnson, " If Betterton and Foote were to walk into this room, you would respect Betterton much more than Foote."  Johnson replied, " If Betterton were to walk into this room with Foote, Foote would soon drive him out of it.  Foote, sir, has powers superior to them all."

Successful mimicry is more generally pleasing than any other kind of amusement : it amuses every one but the victim of it.  Mathews, the elder, when a boy, successfully imitated the cry of a perambulating fishmonger, and was severely punished for it. "Next time," said the huge monster, as he felled the youthful comedian to the earth, "next time as you twists your little wry mouth about, and cuts your mugs at a respectable tradesman, I'll skin you like an e — e —"; and seizing his whole shop up in his Brobdingnagian arms, he finished the monosyllable not much less than a square away. "For weeks — nay months " — says Mathews — "did I suffer from the effects of this punishment." At a later period — soon after he made his appearance on the stage — his imitations of a fellow-actor — Lee Sugg — were punished even more severely. Sugg, it is stated, trusting not too implicitly to his own personal strength, which was very great, called in to his aid an auxiliary in the shape of an iron bar ; and thus doubly armed, he lay in wait one night in a dark corner for the young offender's approach, who, in passing, received a blow across his back, which, had it alighted on his head, would have cured him of all further attempts to take others off. He felt the effects of the ruffianly attack for a long while. Still later — at the very height of his reputation — he writes to his wife from Edinburgh : "I was placed in a most awkward situation in the Courts of Law on Saturday. Erskine, while pleading, glanced his eye toward me, stopped, laughed, and shook his fist at me. This drew the eyes of about two hundred people upon me. I blushed up to the eyes. When he sat down, I observed he wrote a note with a pencil to the judge, Lord Gillies. He craned his neck directly to look at me, and when he came out of court, Erskine said, 'What the devil brings you here, mon, — you spoilt my speech, — I canna afford to be taken off. Did you observe Lord Gillies look at you ? I wrote him a caird, and told him to be on his guard, as I was, or we should both be upon the stage before supper to-night."

Very early in life Foote's peculiar genius began to show itself. There is, it is related, a tradition remaining in the

school at Oxford that the boys often suffered on a Monday
for preferring Sam's laughter to their lessons, for, whenever he had dined on a Sunday with any of his relatives,
his jokes and imitations next day at the expense of the
family entertaining him had all the fascination of a stage-
play. When brought before the provost, who is represented as a pedant of the most uncompromising school,
Foote would present himself to receive his reprimand
with great apparent gravity and submission, but with a
large dictionary under his arm ; when, on the doctor beginning in his usual pompous manner with a surprisingly
long word, he would immediately interrupt him, and,
after begging pardon with great formality, would produce
his dictionary, and pretending to find the meaning of the
word, would say, " Very well, sir ; now please to go on."
His first essay as an author, Murphy tells us, was "a
pamphlet, giving an account of one of his uncles who
was executed for murdering his other uncle," for which
he received ten pounds of an Old Bailey bookseller.
Such was the extremity of his need at the time, that on
the day he sold his manuscript, he was, we are told by
Cooke, actually obliged to wear his boots without stockings, and on his receiving his ten pounds he stopped at a
hosier's in Fleet Street to remedy the defect ; but hardly
had he issued from the shop when two old Oxford associates, arrived in London on a frolic, recognized him and
bore him off to dinner at the Bedford ; where, as the glass
began to circulate, the state of his wardrobe came within
view, and he was asked what the deuce had become of
his stockings? " Why," said Foote, unembarrassed, " I
never wear any at this time of the year, till I am going
to dress for the evening ; and you see," pulling his purchase out of his pocket, and silencing the laugh and the
suspicion of his friends, " I am always provided with a
pair for the occasion."

Forster, in his delightful monograph of the English

Aristophanes, as Foote was sometimes called, gives some anecdotes to show the remarkable readiness of his humor. He was talking away one evening, at the dinner-table of a man of rank, when, at the point of one of his best stories, one of the party interrupted him suddenly, with an air of most considerate apology, "I beg your pardon, Mr. Foote, but your handkerchief is half out of your pocket." "Thank you, sir," said Mr. Foote, replacing it ; "you know the company better than I do," and finished his joke. At one of Macklin's absurd Lectures on the Ancients, the lecturer was solemnly composing himself to begin, when a buzz of laughter from where Foote stood ran through the room, and Macklin, thinking to throw the laugher off his guard, and effectually for that night disarm his ridicule, turned to him with this question, in his most severe and pompous manner : "Well, sir, you seem to be very merry there ; but do you know what I am going to say, now?" "No, sir," at once replied Foote ; "pray, do you?" The then Duke of Cumberland came one night into the green-room of the Haymarket Theatre. "Well, Foote," said he, "here I am, ready, as usual, to swallow all your good things." "Really," replied Foote, "your Royal Highness must have an excellent digestion, for you never bring any up again." "Why are you forever humming that air?" he asked a man without a sense of tune in him. "Because it haunts me." "No wonder," said Foote; "you are forever murdering it." One of Mrs. Montagu's bluestocking ladies fastened upon him at one of the routs in Portman Square with her views of Locke on the Understanding, which she protested she admired above all things ; only there was one particular word very often repeated which she could not distinctly make out, and that was "the word (pronouncing it very long) ide-a ; but I suppose it comes from a Greek derivation." "You are perfectly right, madam," said Foote; "it comes from the word ideaowski." "And pray, sir, what does that mean?" "The feminine of idiot, madam." Much bored by a pompous physician of Bath, who confided to him as a great secret that he had a mind to publish his own poems, but had so many irons in the fire he really did not know what to do: "Take my advice, doctor," says Foote, "and put your poems where your irons are." Selwyn mentioned that Foote, having received much attention from the Eton boys, in showing him about the college, collected them round him in the quadrangle, and said, "Now, young gentlemen, what can I do for you to show you how much I am obliged to you?" "Tell us, Mr. Foote," says the leader, "the best thing you ever said." "Why," says Foote, "seeing once a little blackguard imp of a chimney-sweeper mounted on a noble steed, prancing and curveting in all the pride and magnificence of nature, — 'There,' cried I, 'goes Warburton on Shakespeare.'" "Pray, sir," asked a lady of fashion, referring to his play of the Puppet-show, "are your puppets to be as large as life?" "Oh dear, madam, no," replied Foote; "not much above the size of Garrick." A country farmer who had just buried a rich relation, an attorney, complained to him of the very great expense of a country funeral, in respect to carriages, scarfs, hat-bands, etc. "Why, do you bury your attorneys here?" asked Foote. "Yes, to be sure we do: how else?" "Oh! we never do that in London." "No!" said the other, much surprised; "how do you manage?" "Why, when the patient happens to die, we lay him out in a room over night by himself, lock the door, throw open the sash, and in the morning he is entirely off." "Indeed!" said the other, in amazement; "what becomes of him?" "Why, that we cannot exactly tell; all we know is, there's a strong smell of brimstone in the room the next morning."

He was notorious as a spendthrift, having spent three handsome fortunes before he became noted as a player.

The success of one of his comedies having recruited his finances, he made alterations both in his town and country house, enlarged his hospitalities, and laid out twelve hundred pounds in a magnificent service of plate. When he was reminded by some friends of these extravagances, and particularly the last, he turned it off by saying, he acted from a principle of economy; for as he knew he could never keep his gold, he very prudently laid out his money in silver, which would not only last longer, but in the end sell for nearly as much as it originally cost.

One of his noble friends, a paymaster of the forces, having observed how grossly he was plundered at play, made so bold as to say to him, that from his careless manner of playing and betting, and his habit of telling stories when he should be minding his game, he must in the long run be ruined, let him play with whom he would. Foote resented this advice. He told his friend with sharpness, that although he was no politician by profession, he could see as soon as any into any sinister designs laid against him; that he was too old to be schooled; and that as to any distinction of rank between them to warrant this liberty, he saw none; they were both the king's servants, with this difference in his favor,— that he could always draw upon his talents for independence, when perhaps a courtier could not find the king's treasury always open to him for support.

In his stage mimicries he was merciless on some of his fellow-actors. Even their infirmities were made the subject of his ridicule. Delane had only one eye. He brought him on as a beggar-man in St. Paul's Churchyard : " Would you bestow your pity on a poor blind man?" Ryan had met with an injury to the mouth, which gave his utterance a peculiar discordance. This infirmity was also fair game ; and he was held up as a razor-grinder,— "Razors to grind, scissors to grind, pen-knives to grind !"

16

Foote's " enmity," as Fitzgerald calls the feeling toward
Garrick, had, in the judgment of the fore-mentioned partial biographer, the happy effect of showing the man he
hated in a superior light. Foote, very short of money,
had accepted a Scotch engagement. " But where's the
means?" he said to Wilkinson. " D—n it, I must solicit that hound, Garrick." He did so; and the " hound"
Garrick at once lent him one hundred pounds. He was
aggrieved because Garrick did not give it him " off-hand,"
but said instead that he must " see Pritchard, the treas-
urer, first," on whom Foote might call in the evening, and
leave his note. These were not very hard conditions; but
it was a little homage which Garrick was not disinclined
to exact. That very evening the borrower laid out some
of his cash on a feast, at which he told the most comic
stories of the lender. He never was so fertile as on this
theme. He ridiculed his poetry, and added that " David's
verses were so bad, that if he (Foote) died first, all he
dreaded was that Garrick would undertake his epitaph."

Tate Wilkinson, who knew both Garrick and Foote very
well, viewed them and their relations with each other dif-
ferently. His rambling gossip about them and himself is
entertaining. In his Memoirs he gives an interesting
account of his first introduction to Garrick. He went
armed with letters from Lord Mansfield and the sister of
Lord Foley. " I marched," he says, " up and down -
Southampton Street three or four times before I dared
rap at this great man's door, as fearing instant dismission
might follow; or. what appeared to me almost as dreadful, if graciously admitted, how I should be able to walk,
move, or speak before him. However, the rap was at last
given, and the deed was done past all retreating. 'Is
Mr. Garrick at home?' 'Yes.' Then delivering the letters, and after waiting in a parlor for about ten minutes,
I was ordered to approach. Mr. Garrick glanced his
scrutinizing eye first at me, then at the letters, and so al-

ternately ; at last — ' Well, sir — Hey!—What, now you are a stage candidate ?  Well, sir, let me have a taste of your quality.'  I distilled almost to jelly with my fear, attempted a speech from Richard, and another from Essex; which he encouraged by observing I was so much frightened that he could not form any judgment of my abilities ; but assured me it was not a bad omen, as fear was by no means a sign of want of merit, but often the contrary. We then chatted for a few minutes, and I felt myself more easy, and requested leave to repeat a few speeches in imitation of the then principal stage representatives. ' Nay — now,' says Garrick ; ' sir, you must take care of this, for I used to call myself the first at this business.'  I luckily began with an imitation of Foote.  It is difficult here to determine whether Garrick hated or feared Foote the most ; sometimes one, sometimes the other was predominant ; but from the attention of a few minutes, his looks brightened — the glow of his countenance transfused to mine, and he eagerly desired a repetition of the same speech.  I was animated — forgot Garrick was present, and spoke at perfect ease. ' Hey, now! Now — what — all '— says Garrick ; ' how — really this — this — is — (with his usual hesitation and repetition of words) why — well — well — do call on me again on Monday at eleven, and you may depend upon every assistance in my power. I will see my brother manager, Mr. Lacey, to-day, and let you know the result.'"

" I would wish," says Wilkinson, " to avoid meanness, abuse, or falsehood, and give an exact and candid trait of Mr. Garrick and Mr. Foote, with their shades ; but by no means to obscure their lights and good qualities, and hope I shall prove my words on the examination of the sum total, and that my accounts are given in like a just steward, and with these gentlemen and myself the reckoning shall be fairly balanced.

" If any one person possessed the talent of pleasing

more than another," continues the garrulous Tate, "Mr.
Foote was certainly the **man**.  I can aver in all my observations that **I never met with** his equal.  Mr. **Garrick,**
whom I have **dined and** supped with, was far inferior to
him in wit or repartee, as indeed **were persons of** rank
and degree; for Nature bestows not **all her graces on the
great** or opulent.  Mr. Foote **was not** confined to any
particular topic; he was equal **to all**; religion, law, poli-
**tics,** manners of this or any age, and the stage of course.
**Indeed a** polished stranger would find it **rare to meet
with so** many agreeable qualities for the conviviality of
**any company** so combined as in the society of Mr. Foote.
**This** is not the tribute **of flattery** to his manner, but a
**piece of** justice **my own impartiality demands; for it**
would be despicable **indeed to point out his foibles, and**
not be ready to attest **his good qualities.  As a wit he is**
too well remembered, and **far beyond my abilities to de-**
scribe.  As a blemish to **his entertaining and improving**
qualities I must, **as a** relater of truth **remark, that all these**
shining talents did not dazzle **or answer the eager** expectation, unless he himself **was the sole** object of **every**
directed eye; for if **a man of genius** (I will **suppose a**
Murphy or a Henderson) **had** slipt in **a** good story, or
**had** given any entertaining information, and **thereby
gained the** approbation and merit **of the** flowing **souls,
Foote not** only immediately felt lessened, but could not
**easily recover** his **chagrin and jealousy;** and **the** instant
the guest **had** taken **his leave** and departed, he could **not**
help expressing himself **with** great contempt, and asking
the person or persons remaining **if** they had ever heard
such nonsense **as** that man **had** been uttering.  And
added expressions of wonder **how** the persons at **table
could** be entertained with such absurdity.  But, indeed,
to give the just picture, **I must add, as a true historian —**
**had the company** left him in the best humor, these **very**
spirits were only reserved for the **exposure of each per-**

son's failure or particular manner, and which most people, more or less, have, as a certain appendage, tagged to human nature; nor did that happen in a less but even in a stronger degree to himself; for his own peculiarities were more extravagant than any person's whose gait, or gesture, or history he might choose to record or divert himself with; and if not given immediate credit for what he asserted against the absentee, he would vigorously fly to his happy reserve of never-failing fiction, which was veiled under such an appearance of truth, aided by wit, humor, and great vivacity, that he generally made converts, who, from irresistible impulse, obeyed his laughing mandates. It was policy to defer, as long as possible, quitting the room where he was monarch, as it was certain, the instant of any one's exit, without loss of time, he would be served up, raw or roasted, to the next comer, and that without mercy, although he had at the hour of his adieu conferred on Mr. Foote an obligation of the utmost necessary service. . . .

"Mr. Foote possessed, with all his foibles, mingled excellences, generosity and humanity; but vast ostentation was annexed to them. His table was open — he loved company at that table, and if they pronounced his wine had a superior flavor, they could not drink too much, nor could he himself be gratified till he had produced his claret of the best vintage.

"Now Garrick was always in a fidget, eager for attention and adulation, and when he thought himself free and adored, would prattle such stuff as would disgrace a child of eight years old in conversation with its admiring and doting grandmamma. His hesitation and never giving a direct answer, arose from two causes — affectation, and a fear of being led into promises which he never meant to perform. . . . As to money, he seldom, when walking the streets, had any, therefore could only lament his inability to give to a distressed supplicant; but if greatly touched — 'Why, Holland,' or any other person that was with him, 'cannot you now advance half a crown ? ' which if Holland did, was a very good joke, and for fear of spoiling the jest, he never paid Holland again."

One day in Dublin, as Wilkinson was pursuing his walk, a strong voice issued from a dining-room window, with great vehemence calling out, "Wilkinson! Wilkinson! Wilkinson!" "I looked round," said Wilkinson, " and soon spied my Master Foote, as he was termed. He insisted on my staying to dinner, which invitation I could not refuse ; after dinner, and while the glass was circulating, he intimated a wish I would make my first appearance at Drury Lane as his pupil, in a farce he had newly furbished up, and titled the Diversions of the Morning ; and added, 'You must, Wilkinson, plainly see and be convinced that dirty hound Garrick does not mean to do you any service or wish you success ; but on the contrary he is a secret enemy, and if he can prevent your doing well be assured he will.  I know his heart so well, that if you give me permission to ask for your first attempt on his stage, and to be in my piece, the hound will refuse the moment I mention it ; and though his little soul would rejoice to act Richard III. in the dogdays, before the hottest kitchen fire for a sop in the pan, yet I know his mean soul so perfectly, that if, on his refusal, I with a grave face tell him, I have his figure exactly made and dressed as a puppet in my closet, ready for public admiration, the fellow will not only consent to your acting, but what is more extraordinary, his abject fears will lend me money, if I should say I want it.' "

Foote having been publicly ridiculed, time and again, by Wilkinson, broke friendship with him, and they remained apart for five years, at the end of which time Foote made generous overtures, and they became friends again.  It hurt Foote to be taken off as much as any of his fellows.  Wilkinson, in the farce of High Life Below

Stairs, had been particularly severe upon him. "Before my benefit happened," says Wilkinson, "Mr. Foote (who of all men in the world ought not to have been offended) found himself much hurt and wounded, and so little master of himself, that, notwithstanding the unbounded liberties he had taken, not only with the players, but others, to the disturbance of the peace of private families, he actually visited me in great wrath, attended by Mr. Larry Kennedy, and in Pistol-like manner protested, 'If I dare take any more liberties on the stage in future with him, he was determined the next day to call me to account.' But I pursued my plan, and was obliged, amongst other favors to Mr. Foote, that he was not observant, but let me rest in quiet. We often met drawn up at noon in different parties in the Trinity College Gardens, as perfect strangers, but never at any house of visiting; if we had, his talent of wit would have forced me to have felt the severity of his lash."

A project of Foote's to publicly ridicule Garrick, fell through in a singular manner. The parties met, as if by accident, at the house of a nobleman, the common friend of both; when alighting at the same time from their chariots at his lordship's door, and exchanging significant looks at each other, Garrick broke silence first by asking, "Is it war or peace?" "Oh! peace, by all means," said Foote, with apparent good will; and the two spent the day together cordially.

Foote had an especial aversion to attorneys. One of this profession, not remarkable for the integrity of his character, having a dispute with a bailiff, brought an action against him, which Foote recommended to be compromised. The parties agreed to do it, but differed as to who should be arbitrator, and at length requested Foote to act in that capacity. "Oh! no!" said Foote, "I might be partial to one or other of you, but I tell you what, I 'll do better — I 'll recommend a thief, as a common friend to both."

Dining while in **Paris** with Lord Stormont, that thrifty Scotch peer, **then ambassador,** as usual produced his wine in the smallest **of decanters,** and dispensed **it in the** smallest **of** glasses, **enlarging all the time on its exquisite** growth and enormous age. **"It is very** little of **its age,"** said Foote, holding up his diminutive **glass.**

Quin, it is known, was one of **the few** men who could **stand** a fall with Foote, and come **off** the better man. **Foote,** who, as we have seen, could not endure a joke **made on** himself, broke friendship with Quin on account **of such** offense. Ultimately they were reconciled ; **but even then Foote** referred to **the** provocation. "Jemmy, **you should not have said that I** had but one shirt, **and** that **I lay abed while it was washed."** "Sammy," replied Quin, **"I never could have said so, for I never knew** that you had a shirt **to wash ! "**

When down at Stratford, on the **occasion of the Shake-** speare Jubilee, **Garrick's success** embittered **Foote's nat-** urally bitter spirit. **A** well-dressed gentleman **there civilly** spoke **to him** on the proceedings. **"Has** Warwickshire, sir," said Foote, **"the advantage** of having produced **you as well as** Shakespeare ?" **"Sir,"** replied the gentleman, **"I come** from Essex." "Ah !" rejoined Foote, remembering that county was famous for calves, — "from Essex. **Who** drove you ? "

**"One may,"** said **Doran,** "forgive Foote for his remark to **Rich, who had been** addressing him curtly as 'Mister.' Perceiving that Foote **was** vexed, Rich apologized by saying, 'I sometimes forget **my own** name.' 'I am astonished you could **forget** your **own** name,' said Foote, 'though **I know very** well that you are not able to write **it ! ' "**

Amongst the fairest of Foote's sayings was **the** reply **to Mr.** Howard's intimation that he was **about to** publish a second edition of his Thoughts **and Maxims.** "Ay ! **second** thoughts are best." Fair, **too, was his retort on** the person who alluded to his "game leg." "Make no allusion to my weakest part. Did I ever attack your head?"

Cooke, in his Memoirs, has preserved many examples of Foote's wicked wit. In a song sung by Mrs. Cibber, there was this line:

"The roses will bloom when there 's peace in the breast."

Foote parodied it:

The turtles will coo when there 's pease in their craws; "

and actually destroyed the popularity of the song.

A person talking of an acquaintance of his, who was so avaricious as even to lament the prospect of his funeral expenses, though a short time before he had been censuring one of his own relatives for his parsimonious temper: "Now is it not strange," said the person, "that this man would not take the beam out of his own eye before he attempted the mote in other people's?" "Why, so I dare say he would," cried Foote, "if he was sure of selling the timber."

On his return from Scotland, being asked by a lady whether there was any truth in the report that there were no trees in Scotland: "A very malicious report indeed, my lady," said he; "for just as I was crossing Portpatrick to Donaghadee, I saw two blackbirds perched on as fine a thistle as ever I saw in my life."

Foote, who lived in habits of intimacy with Lord Kellie, took as many liberties with his face (which somewhat resembled in appearance a meridian sun) as ever Falstaff did with his friend Bardolph's. One day his lordship choosing to forget his promise to dine with him, it piqued Foote so, that he called out, loud enough to be heard by the whole coffee-house where they were sitting, "Well, my lord, since you cannot do me the honor of dining with me to-day, will you be so good, as you ride by, just to look over against my south wall? for, as we have had little or no sun for this fortnight past, my peaches will want the assistance of your lordship's countenance."

His lordship having cracked some jokes upon one of his friends rather too coarsely, an Irish gentleman, who heard of it, said, "if he had treated him so he would pull him by the nose." "Pull him by the nose," said Foote; "you may as well thrust your hand into a furnace."

The same noble lord coming into the club, on a hot summer night, dressed in a somewhat tarnished suit of laced clothes, the waiter announced "Lord Kellie!" "Lord Kellie!" repeated Foote, looking him full in the face at the same time, "I thought it was all Monmouth street in flames."

A country squire just come to town, was bragging of the great number of fashionable people he had visited that morning; "and among the rest," said he, in a pompous deliberate manner, "I called upon my good friend the Earl of Chol-mon-dely, but he was not at home." "That is rather surprising," said Foote: "what! nor none of his pe-o-ple?"

Being on a visit at Crabbe Boulton's (chairman of the East India Company) during a frosty season, where they kept very bad fires, Foote found himself so uncomforta-ble, that he prepared next morning for setting off to town. "Eh!" said his host, seeing the chaise at the door, "Why think of going so soon?" "Because, if I stay any longer, perhaps I shall not have a leg to stand upon." "Why, we don't drink so hard." "No; but it freezes so hard, and your servants know the value of a good bit of timber so well, that I'm in hourly dread of losing my wooden leg."

Paul Hiffernan, a mendicant author who attended Foote's levees, was fond of laying, or rather offering, wagers. One day, in the heat of argument, he cried out, "I'll lay my head you are wrong upon that point." "Well," said Foote, "I accept the wager; any trifle among friends has a value."

"Pray," said a lady to Foote, "what sort of a man is Sir John D.?" "Oh! a very good sort of man." "But what do you call a good sort of man?" "Why, madam, one who preserves all the exterior decencies of ignorance."

An author left a comedy with Foote for perusal; and on the next visit asked for his judgment on it, with rather an ignorant degree of assurance. "If you looked a little more to the grammar of it, I think," said Foote, "it would be better." "To the grammar of it, sir! What! Would you send one to school again?" "And pray, sir," replied Foote very gravely, "would that do you any harm?"

A clergyman in Essex, not much celebrated as a preacher, used to wear boots generally on duty; and gave as a reason for it, that "the roads were so deep in some places, that he found them more convenient than shoes." "Yes," said Foote; "and I dare say, equally convenient in the pulpit; for there the doctor is generally out of his depth too."

Foote called upon a gentleman of the law who did not live happily with his wife. The servant maid soon afterward came into the room to look for her mistress. "What do you want your mistress for?" asked the barrister. "Why, indeed, sir, to tell you the truth, she scolds me so from morning to night, I come to give her warning." "What, then you mean to leave us?" "Certainly, sir," said she, shutting the door after her. "Happy girl!" exclaimed Foote; "I most sincerely wish your poor master could give warning too."

A conceited young man asking Foote what apology he should make for not being one of the party the day before to which he had a card of invitation; "Oh, my dear sir!" replied the wit; "say nothing about it; you were never missed."

You remember Foote's advice to the Duke of Norfolk. On a masquerade night, his Grace consulted the famous actor as to what character he should appear in. "Don't go disguised," said Foote, "but assume a new character —go sober." (It was the successor of the Duke of Norfolk in question who consulted Abernethy for some ailment, and was asked whether he had ever tried the remedy of a clean shirt.)

Foote, being notoriously lavish with his money, was fond of taking off Garrick's reputed niggardliness. Here is an anecdote that Rogers was fond of relating, and which he is said to have told with infinite humor. At the Chapter Coffee-house, Foote and his friends were making a contribution for the relief of a poor fellow, a decayed player, who was nicknamed the Captain of the Four Winds, because his hat was worn into four spouts. Each person of the company dropped his mite into the hat, as it was held out to him. "If Garrick hears of this," exclaimed Foote, "he will certainly send us his hat." "There is a witty satirical story of Foote," said Johnson to Boswell. "He had a small bust of Garrick placed upon his bureau. 'You may be surprised,' said he, 'that I allow him to be so near my gold; but you will observe he has no hands!'" Foote and Garrick were leaving the Bedford one night when Foote had been the entertainer, and on his pulling out his purse to pay the bill, a guinea dropped. Impatient at not immediately finding it, "Where on earth can it be gone to?" he said. "Gone to the devil, I think," rejoined Garrick, who had sought for it everywhere. "Well said, David," cried Foote; "let you alone for making a guinea go farther than any body else." "Garrick and Foote," says Forster, "were among the company one day at the dinner-table of Lord Mansfield. Many grave people were there, and the manager of Drury Lane was on his best good company behavior. Every one listened deferentially to him as he enlarged on the necessity of prudence in all the relations of life, and drew his illustration from Churchill's death, which was then the talk of the town. No one would have supposed it possible to dislodge him from such vantage-ground as this, surrounded by all the decorums of life, and with a Lord Chief Justice at the head of the table. But Foote suddenly struck in. He said that every question had two sides, and he had long made up his mind on the advantages implied in the fact of not paying one's debts. In the first place, it presupposed some time or other the possession of fortune to be able to get credit. Then, living on credit was the art of living without the most troublesome thing in the whole world, which was money. It saved the expense and annoyance of keeping accounts, and made over all the responsibility to other people. It was the panacea for the cares and embarrassments of wealth. It checked and discountenanced avarice ; while, people being always more liberal of others' goods than their own, it extended every sort of encouragement to generosity. And would any one venture to say that payment of one's debts could possibly draw to us such anxious attention from our own part of the world while we live, or such sincere regrets when we die, as not paying them. All which, Foote put with such whimsical gravity, and supported with such a surprising abundance of sarcastic illustration, that in the general laughter against Garrick no laugh was heartier than Lord Mansfield's."

Macklin's topic, we are told, at one of his evening lectures, was the employment of memory in connection with the oratorical art, in the course of which, as he enlarged on the importance of exercising memory as a habit, he took occasion to say, that to such perfection he had brought his own he could learn any thing by rote on once hearing it. Foote waited till the conclusion of the lecture, and then handing up the subjoined sentences, desired that Mr. Macklin would be good enough to read and afterward repeat them from memory. More amazing nonsense never was written. " So she went into the garden to cut a cabbage-leaf, to make an apple-pie; and at the same time a great she-bear, coming up the street, pops its head into the shop. 'What! no soap?' So he died, and she very imprudently married the barber; and there were present the Picninnies, and the Joblillies, and the Garyulies, and the Grand Panjandrum himself, with the little round button at top; and they all fell to playing the game of catch as catch can, till the gunpowder ran out at the heels of their boots."

One of the many victims of Foote's humor and mimicry was Alderman George Faulkner. He took off the Alderman, wooden leg and all, under the name of Peter Paragraph. Soon afterward he went on a visit with the Duke of York to Lord Mexborough's, where, in hunting, he rode a too spirited horse, and received so severe a hurt that his left leg had to be amputated. Old Lord Chesterfield, who had sympathized with Faulkner in his bitterness toward Foote, eagerly informed Faulkner of the accident, and expressed his satisfaction that Heaven had avenged his cause by punishing his adversary in the part offending. The same thought had of course occurred to the satirist himself. "Now I shall take off old Faulkner indeed to the life!" was the first remark he made when what he had to suffer was announced to him. Time, for once at least, had his revenge, and mercilessly made things even.

# X.

## HABIT.

Nothing is becoming, it is said, which is not habitual. It may be said as well, that life would be intolerable if habit did not relieve it. Think of thinking of every thing you do! Life is so made up of infinite little things, that the infinite little things must of necessity be done as they have been done before. Almost mechanically, so habitually most of them are done: they seem even to do themselves. Life itself goes on: breath following breath —almost as unconsciously waking as sleeping. Pretty certainly, if almost any human being were compelled, for a single day, to think, to reason originally of his every act, even for that short period, he would lose the power of reasoning. Habitually, almost every one dresses one foot before the other, without thinking of it. When a hand goes to the face, it touches, almost invariably, one part before another. When you climb the stairs, the left foot or the right begins the process. And so of a hundred things you do every day. Think of them: one will suggest another. You will be surprised to see how your life is made up of unconsciously formed habits — small and great — for better or for worse. That you are good or bad from habit mainly, a little self-observation and reflection will reveal to you. "All is habit in mankind," exclaimed Metastasio, — "even virtue itself."

"I trust every thing under God," said Lord Brougham, "to habit, upon which in all ages, the lawgiver as well as the schoolmaster, has mainly placed his reliance; habit, which makes every thing easy, and casts all difficulties upon the deviation·from a wonted course. Make sobriety a habit, and intemperance will be hateful; make prudence a habit, and reckless profligacy will be as contrary to the nature of the child, grown or adult, as the most atrocious crimes. Give a child the habit of sacredly regarding the truth; of carefully respecting the property of others; of scrupulously abstaining from all acts of improvidence which can involve him in distress, and he will just as likely think of rushing into an element in which he cannot breathe, as of lying, cheating, or swearing."

One of the wisest and most suggestive precepts to be found in Plutarch's Morals cannot be too often repeated: "Choose but the best condition you can, and custom will make it pleasant to you." "You may take my word," says Sterne, in the opening chapter of Tristram Shandy, "that nine parts in ten of a man's sense, or his nonsense, his successes and miscarriages in this world, depend upon the motions and activity of the animal spirits, and the different tracks and trains you put them into; so that when they are once set a-going, whether right or wrong, 't is not a half-penny matter, — away they go clattering like hey-go mad; and by treading the same steps over and over again, they presently make a road of it, as plain and as smooth as a garden-walk, which when they are once used to, the devil himself shall not be able to drive them off it." So great is the power of habit, that it has been often remarked, says Scott, in one of his romances, that when a man commences by acting a character he frequently ends by adopting it in good earnest. So soon as Ravenswood had determined upon giving the Lord Keeper such hospitality as he had to offer, he deemed it incumbent on him to assume the open and courteous brow of a well-pleased host. In the course of an hour or two, Ravenswood, to his own surprise, found himself in the situation of one who frankly does his best to entertain welcome and honored guests.

**Dr. Johnson was of opinion** that the force of our early **habits was so great, that though** reason approved, nay, **though** our senses relished a different course, almost **every man** returned to them.

Layard relates **an** incident of a party of **Arabs which** for some time had been employed **to assist him in** excavating among the ruins of Nineveh. **One** evening, after their day's work, he **observed them** following **a** flock of sheep belonging **to the** people **of the** village, shouting their **war-cry,** flourishing their swords, and indulging in the **most extravagant** gesticulations. He asked one **of the most active of the** party to explain to him the cause **of such** violent proceedings. "**O Bey!**" they exclaimed, almost together, "**God be** praised, **we** have eaten butter **and** wheaten bread **under** your shadow, and are content ; **but an** Arab is **an Arab.** It is **not for a man to carry** about dirt **in baskets, and** to use **a spade all his life ; he** should be **with** his sword and his **mare in the desert.** We are sad as we think of the days **when we plundered** the Anayza, and we must have excitement or our hearts **must** break. Let us then believe **that these** are the sheep **we have taken** from the enemy, **and** that we are driving **them to our tents."** And off they **ran, raising** their wild **cry, and flourishing** their swords, to the no small alarm **of the shepherd, who saw his sheep** scampering in all **directions.**

"**I have," says** Montaigne, "picked up boys from begging, to serve me, who soon after have quitted both my kitchen and livery, only that they might return to **their** former course of life ; and I found one afterward picking up mussels **in our** neighborhood for his dinner, **whom I** could **neither by** entreaties nor threats reclaim **from the** sweetness he found in indigence."

Habit sometimes produces curious and amusing physical adaptations. "The police of Naples," says Hillard, in his Six Months in Italy, "**are** said **to** practice a singular test, to ascertain whether a lad accused of picking a pocket be guilty or not. The culprit is required to place his hand upon a table with his fingers outstretched, and if the forefinger and middle finger be of the same length, the case goes against him, and judgment is passed accordingly; for, in the exercise of this profession, these two fingers are made use of like a forceps, and the young ragamuffins in the streets are said to encourage the growth of the forefinger by habitually pulling it."

"On Sundays, at noon," says the same interesting writer, "the pigeons of St. Mark's are fed. As the hour approaches, flock after flock of hungry expectants comes wheeling in, and the air is filled with the rustling of innumerable wings, from which the sunshine is flung in dazzling beams." The pigeons of Venice know when Sunday at noon comes.

A clergyman who filled one of the Boston pulpits, drove every morning into the city. His horse, from habit, and without any suggestion from his master, went, week-day mornings, directly to the post-office; Sundays, he went straight to the church. A friend once told us of a dog belonging to one of his relations — a Quaker. First-days and fifth-days the dog always went to meeting. If the family went, he went with them; if not, he went alone. And he always occupied the same spot in the meeting-house.

Lord Thurlow habituated himself to such a majestic air, that it came to be asked whether any one could really be as wise as Lord Thurlow always seemed. Talleyrand's habit of mind was so wary and suspicious, that, when a celebrated diplomatist fell ill, he inquired, "What does he mean by it?"

The power of habit is exemplified in the case of Jonathan Wild and Count Fathom: Wild could not keep his hands out of the Count's pockets, although he knew they were empty; nor could the Count abstain from palming a card, although he was well aware Wild had no money to pay him. In his last hours, whilst the ordinary was busy in his ejaculations, Wild, in the midst of the shower of stones, etc., which played upon him, applied his hand to the parson's pocket, and emptied it of his corkscrew, which he carried out of the world in his hand.

The practice of hanging in chains, although discontinued before its formal abolition, lasted far into the present century. Within living memory, it is stated, a batch of pirates was hung in chains in the marshes before Woolwich. A farmer and his son who rented the ground happening to take a close inspection of the victims, saw symptoms of life in one, took him down, carried him home with them, and employed him as a farm servant; till one night, finding him at his old trade of thieving, they laid hold of him, twisted his neck, and replaced him on the gallows; not at all imagining that they had been guilty of any description of irregularity.

After Gulliver had been snatched from Brobdingnag by the eagle, and rescued from the sea, he astonished Captain Wilcocks by the loudness of his voice. He explained it by saying that he had been used to that tone for two years; that "when he spoke in that country, it was like a man talking in the streets, to another looking out from the top of a steeple."

"A tallow chandler," says Southey, in The Doctor, "having amassed a fortune, disposed of his business, and took a house in the country, not far from London, that he might enjoy himself; but, after a few months' trial of a holiday life, requested permission of his successor to come into town and assist him on melting-days. The keeper of a retail spirit-shop, having in like manner retired from trade, used to employ himself by having one puncheon filled with water, and measuring it off by pints into another. A butcher in a small town, for some little

time after he had left off business, informed his old customers that he meant to kill a lamb once a week, just for
amusement."

Sergeant Ballantine commenced practice in Inner Temple Lane. His father furnished his chambers, and one of
the principal articles he sent him was a horse-hair arm-
chair with only three legs, upon which the future great
barrister got so accustomed to balance himself that he
scarcely felt safe on one furnished with the proper com-
plement.

Avarice is a vice that is especially the product of habit ;
and it grows and grows to the end. "Other vices," says
St. Ambrose, " decay with our age ; but avarice renews
its youth." An epitaph on a rude grave-stone in Cali-
fornia puts it more forcibly if not so philosophically and
elegantly :

> " Here lies old Thirty-five per cent. !
> The more he got the more he lent ;
> The more he got the more he craved ;
> The more he made the more he shaved —
> Good God ! can such a soul be saved ? "

Foster, in his famous essay On Decision of Character,
mentions a young man " who wasted in two or three
years a large patrimony in profligate revels with a number of worthless associates who called themselves his
friends, and who, when his last means were exhausted,
treated him of course with neglect or contempt. Reduced
to absolute want he one day went out of the house with
an intention to put an end to his life ; but wandering
awhile, almost unconsciously, he came to the brow of an
eminence which overlooked what were lately his estates.
Here he sat down, and remained fixed in thought a number of hours, at the end of which he sprang from the
ground with a vehement, exulting emotion. He had
formed his resolution, which was, that all these estates
should be his again ; he had formed his plan too, which

he instantly began to execute. He walked hastily forward, determined to seize the very first opportunity, of however humble a kind, to gain any money, though it were ever so despicable a trifle, and resolved absolutely not to spend, if he could help it, a farthing of whatever he might obtain. The first thing that drew his attention was a heap of coals shot out of carts on the pavement before a house. He offered himself to shovel or wheel them into the place where they were to be laid, and was employed. He received a few pence for the labor ; and then, in pursuance of the saving part of his plan, requested some small gratuity of meat and drink, which was given him. He then looked out for the next thing that might chance to offer ; and went, with indefatigable industry, through a succession of servile employments, in different places, of longer and shorter duration, still scrupulously avoiding, as far as possible, the expense of a penny. He promptly seized every opportunity which could advance his design, without regarding the meanness of occupation or appearance. By this method he had gained, after a considerable time, money enough to purchase, in order to sell again, a few cattle, of which he had taken pains to understand the value. He speedily but cautiously turned his first gains into second advantages ; retained without a single deviation his extreme parsimony ; and thus advanced by degrees into larger transactions and incipient wealth." The essayist did not hear, or had forgotten, the continued course of his life ; but the final result was, that he more than recovered his lost possessions, and died an inveterate miser, worth hundreds of thousands of dollars.

The avarice of the great Duke of Marlborough is historical. "One day," said Pope to Spence, "as the duke was looking over some papers in his scrutoire with Lord Cadogan, he opened one of his little drawers, took out a green purse, and turned some broad pieces out of it.

After viewing them for some time, with a satisfaction that appeared very visibly in his face; 'Cadogan,' said he, 'observe these pieces well! They deserve to be observed; there are just forty of them: 't is the very first sum I ever got in my life, and I have kept it always unbroken from that time to this day.' This shows how early, and how strongly, this passion must have been upon him."

You recollect that fine passage of Macaulay's in his History: "Avarice is rarely the vice of a young man; it is rarely the vice of a great man; but Marlborough was one of the few who have, in the bloom of youth, loved lucre more than wine or women, and who have, at the height of greatness, loved lucre more than power or fame. All the precious gifts which nature had lavished on him he valued chiefly for what they would fetch. At twenty he made money of his beauty and his vigor. At sixty he made money of his genius and his glory. The applauses which were justly due to his conduct at Walcourt could not altogether drown the voices of those who muttered that, wherever a broad piece was to be saved or got, this hero was a mere Euclio, a mere Harpagon; that, though he drew a large allowance under pretense of keeping a public table, he never asked an officer to dinner; that his muster rolls were fraudulently made up; that he pocketed pay in the names of men who had long been dead, of men who had been killed in his own sight four years before at Sedgemoor; that there were twenty such names in one troop; that there were thirty-six in another."

A beggar once asked an alms of Lord Peterborough, and called him by mistake "My Lord Marlborough." "I am not Lord Marlborough," replied the earl, "and to prove it to you, here is a guinea." Lord Bolingbroke, writing to one of his friends, said, "I am very sorry my Lord Marlborough gives you so much trouble. It is the only thing he will give you." The duke, some years before his death, retired occasionally to Bath, and often amused himself with cards, though he seldom ventured to play high. One night he was engaged at piquet with Dean Jones, from whom he had won sixpence, and exacted payment. The dean declared he had no silver, but borrowed the money, as the duke said he wanted it to pay for his sedan chair. The dean, knowing the duke's avarice, watched him, and saw him actually walking home, in order to save the sixpence. Pope speaks of him as one who would " Now save a sixpence, and now save a groat."

" You don't say that your husband the duke is without faults ? " said Lady Sunderland to the Duchess of Marlborough. "By no means," was the reply : " I knew them better than he did himself, or even than I do my own. He came back one day from my poor misled mistress Queen Anne (I believe when he resigned his commission), and said he had told her, that he thanked God, with all his faults, neither avarice nor ambition could be laid to his charge."

Crabb Robinson, in his Diary, speaks of one of these habitual accumulators for whom his nephew made a will. The man was supposed to be at the point of death, and he produced from under his bed, in gold and silver, upwards of fifteen hundred dollars. A banker's clerk was sent for, and the money was secured. When the old wife found out what had taken place, she scolded him with such fury that she went into a fit and died. The man in great agitation produced an additional one thousand and forty dollars ; but this he insisted on giving away absolutely to some poor people who were near him, and had served him. The money was tied up in old stockings and filthy rags. When he was informed of his wife's death, he eagerly demanded her pockets, and took from them a few shillings with great avidity. The accumulation was the result of a life of continued abstinence.

There is an account of a millionaire who was accused

of wishing to invest the accumulations of more than half a century in one big bank-note, and carry it out of the world with him. When Lord Erskine heard that somebody had died worth two hundred thousand pounds, he observed, " Well, that 's a very pretty sum to begin the next world with."

Rousseau went to Venice as Secretary to the French ambassador, the Count of Montaign. Avarice was the count's most remarkable trait. Careful observation had persuaded him that three shoes are equivalent to two pairs, because there is always one of a pair which is more worn than the other ; and hence he habitually ordered his shoes in threes.

La Fontaine was always forgetting himself. Having attended the funeral of a friend, he was so absent-minded as to call upon him a short time afterwards. Being reminded of the fact, he was at first greatly surprised, but recollecting himself, said : " It is true enough, for I was there."

Ampère, the great mathematician, wrote rather by moving his arm than his fingers, and in a hand so immense that a gentleman sent him an invitation to dinner penned within the outline of the first letter of his signature.

The attendant of the elder Mathews in his last illness intended to give his patient some medicine ; but a few minutes afterward it was discovered that the medicine was nothing but ink, which had been taken from the phial by mistake, and his friend exclaimed, " Good Heavens, Mathews, I have given you ink ! " " Never mind, my boy," said Mathews, faintly (joking to the last), " I 'll swallow a bit of blotting paper."

People objected (in Bleak House) to Professor Dingo (Mrs. Badger's second husband), that he disfigured some of the houses and other buildings by chipping off fragments of those edifices with his little geological hammer. But the professor replied that he knew of no building, save the Temple of Science. In his last illness (his mind wandering), he insisted on keeping his little hammer under the pillow, and chipping at the countenances of the attendants.

Kant, to aid his thoughts, had a habit of fixing his attention closely on some one auditor, and judged by him whether he was understood. Once a button on a student's coat, which he had made his fixed point of vision, being lost, disconcerted the philosopher and interrupted the lecture. A tower on which he used to gaze, in his reveries at home, having become hidden by the growth of trees, he could not rest until the foliage was cut away. Neander had a habit, when he was lecturing, of playing with a goose-quill which his amanuensis always provided for him, constantly crossing and recrossing his feet, his figure bent forward, and his head down, except when excited, when it suddenly went up, at such times, we are told, fairly threatening to turn the desk over. Madame de Staël, it is stated, had a way, while she discoursed, of taking a scrap of paper and a pair of scissors, and snipping it to bits, as an employment for her fingers. Once she was observed to be at a loss for this her usual mechanical resource, when a gentleman quietly placed near her the back of a letter from his pocket: afterward she earnestly thanked him for this timely supply of the means she desired as a needful aid to thought and speech. Gibbon held a pinch of snuff between his finger and thumb while he told an anecdote, invariably dropping the pinch at the point of the story. Lord Bacon had a habit of "wringing his speeches from the strings of his bands," and Ben Jonson of "drawing poetic inspiration from his great toe." "He hath," says Drummond of Hawthornden, "consumed a whole night in lying looking to his great toe, about which hé hath seen Tartars and Turks, Romans and Carthaginians, fight in imagination." Schiller kept a drawer in his work-room always filled with rotten apples. " I called on him one day," said Goethe, " and as I did not find him at home, and his wife told me that he would soon return, I seated myself at his work-table to note down various matters. I had not been seated long before I felt a strange indisposition steal over me, which gradually increased, until at last I nearly fainted. At first I did not know to what cause I should ascribe this wretched and, to me, unusual state, until I discovered that a dreadful odor issued from a drawer near me. When I opened it, I found to my astonishment that it was full of rotten apples. I immediately went to the window and inhaled the fresh air, by which I felt myself instantly restored. In the mean time his wife had re-entered, and told me that the drawer was always filled with rotten apples, because the scent was beneficial to Schiller, and he could not live or work without it."

One day they were waiting dinner at Charles Sheridan's for Dr. Johnson. " Take out your opera-glass," said the host to one of his guests ; " Johnson is coming ; you may know him by his gait." " I passed him," responded the guest, " at a good distance, working along with a peculiar solemnity of deportment, and an awkward sort of meas-ured step. At that time the broad flagging at each side the streets was not universally adopted, and stone posts were in fashion to prevent the annoyance of carriages. Upon every post, as he passed along, I could observe, he deliberately laid his hand : but missing one of them, when he had got at some distance, he seemed suddenly to rec-ollect himself, and immediately returning back, carefully resumed his former course, not omitting one till he gained the crossing." This, Mr. Sheridan stated, however odd it might appear, was his constant practice ; but why or wherefore he could give no information.

" Dr. Johnson had another particularity," says Bos-well, " of which none of his friends ever ventured to ask an explanation. It appeared to me some superstitious habit, which he had contracted early, and from which he had never called upon his reason to disentangle him. This was his anxious care to go out or in, at a door or passage, by a certain number of stages from a certain point, or at least so as that either his right or his left foot (I am not certain which) should constantly make the first actual movement when he came close to the door or passage. Thus I conjecture; for I have, upon innumerable occasions, observed him suddenly stop, and then seem to count his steps with a deep earnestness; and when he had neglected or gone wrong in this sort of magical movement, I have seen him go back again, put himself in a proper posture to begin the ceremony, and, having gone through it, break from his abstraction, walk briskly on, and join his companion." Sir Joshua Reynolds had observed him to go a good way about, rather than cross a particular alley; but this Sir Joshua imputed to his having had some disagreeable recollection associated with it.

Malherbe, the French poet, on account of a delicate ear and refined taste, and a habit of criticising every thing that he saw or heard, was called "the tyrant of words and syllables." When dying, his confessor, in speaking of 'the happiness of heaven, expressed himself inaccurately. "Say no more about it," said Malherbe, "or your style will disgust me with it."

Readers of Rabelais will remember that on one occasion Gargantua could not sleep by any means, on which side soever he turned himself. Whereupon Friar John said to him, I never sleep soundly but when I am at sermon or prayers. Let us therefore begin, you and I, the Seven Penitential Psalms, to try whether you shall not quickly fall asleep. The conceit pleased Gargantua very well, and, beginning the first of these psalms, as soon as they came to the words, Beati quorum, they fell asleep both the one and the other.

The detestable habit of fault-finding — too common in this world, as all good-natured people know — was once, we remember, most effectually rebuked by Crabb Robinson. It was during one of his visits to Paris. A great part of a day had been spent sight-seeing with a London acquaintance, who said to him at parting, "I will call for you to-morrow." "I will thank you not to call," replied the kindly and philosophic barrister. "I would rather not see any thing else with you, and I will tell you frankly why. I am come to Paris to enjoy myself, and that enjoyment needs the accompaniment of sympathy with others. Now, you dislike every thing, and find fault with every thing. You see nothing which you do not find inferior to what you have seen before. This may be all very true, but it makes me very uncomfortable. I believe, if I were forced to live with you, I should kill myself. So I shall be glad to see you in London, but no more in Paris."

In contrast with this habit of fault-finding is the philosophic turn of mind that finds the bright side of things, and turns even misfortunes into blessings. Nathan James, of the Alamo, once owned a large merino ewe which he valued highly. His son informed him one morning that his favorite ewe had twins. Mr. James said he "was glad; she could bring up two as well as one." Soon after, the son reported one of the twins dead. The father said, "the one left would be worth more in the autumn than both." In the afternoon the boy told his father that the other lamb was dead. "I am glad," said he; "I can now fatten the old sheep for mutton." In the morning the boy reported the old ewe dead. "That is just what I wanted," said the old farmer; "now I am rid of the breed."

The rapid growth of a habit of committing improper or unlawful acts, is shown in an instance given by Dr. Hammond, in a recent interesting article entitled A

Problem for Sociologists. A lady came under his observation who was subject to no delusion, and who had never exhibited any evidence of mental alienation except in showing an impulse, which she declared she could not control, to throw valuable articles into the fire. At first, as she said in her confession to the doctor, the impulse was excited by the satisfaction she derived from seeing an old pair of slippers curl up into fantastic shapes after she had thrown them into a blazing wood-fire. She repeated the act the following day, but, not having a pair of old shoes to burn, she used instead a felt hat which was no longer fashionable. But this did not undergo contortions like the shoes, and therefore she had no pleasurable sensations like those of the day before, and thus, as far as any satisfaction was concerned, the experiment was a failure. On the ensuing day, however, she felt, to her great surprise, that it would be a pleasant thing to burn something. She was very clear that this pleasure consisted solely in the fulfillment of an impulse which, to a great extent, had been habitual. She therefore seized a handsomely bound prayer-book which lay on the table, and throwing it into the fire, turned away her face, and walked to another part of the room. It was very certain, therefore, that she was no longer gratified by the sight of the burning articles. She went on repeating these acts with her own things, and even with those which did not belong to her, until she became a nuisance to herself, and to all those with whom she had any relations. Her destructive propensities stopped at nothing which was capable of being consumed. Books, bonnets, shawls, laces, handkerchiefs, and even table-cloths and bed-linen, helped to swell the list of her sacrifices. As soon as she had thrown the articles into the fire, the impulse was satisfied. She did not care to see them burn ; on the contrary, the sight was rather disagreeable to her than otherwise. But the power which affected her the way it did, she represented as being imperative, and, if not immediately allowed to act, giving rise to the most irritable and unpleasant sensations, which she could not describe otherwise than by saying that she felt as if she would have to fly, or jump, or run, and that there was a feeling under the skin all over the body as though the flesh were in motion. As soon as she had yielded to the impulse, these sensations departed.

The habit of scolding, it may not be improper to say, is of like rapid growth, and soon ends in a species of noxious insanity, which few persons in this world are happy enough to avoid seeing frequent exhibitions of, to say nothing of the supreme delectation of being able altogether to escape being its victims. Husbands, wives, schoolmasters, clergymen, unmarried men and unmarried women of a certain age — all are liable to this distressing, detestable, nearly incurable mental and moral malady. God help us !

Perhaps no really great man ever existed who had the habit of detraction and vituperation to compare with Thomas Carlyle. To him, the Edinburgh clergy were "narrow, ignorant, and barren without exception." He rode sixty miles to consult an eminent Edinburgh physician. "Found," he says, "after long months, that I might as well have ridden sixty miles in the opposite direction, and poured my sorrows into the long hairy ear of the first jackass I came upon, as into the select medical man's." "I knew Robert Burns," he says, "and I knew my father. Yet were you to ask me which had the greater natural faculty, I might actually pause before replying." "It was not with aversion that my father regarded Burns ; at worst, with indifference and neglect." "Intrinsically a poor creature this Bulwer," he wrote ; "has a bustling whisking agility and restlessness which may support him in a certain degree of significance with some, but which partakes much of the nature of levity.

Nothing truly notable can come of him or of it." "One of the wretchedest Phantasms I had yet fallen in with." De Quincey was "a pretty little creature, full of wire-drawn ingenuities, bankrupt enthusiasm, bankrupt pride," etc. "Poor, fine-strung weak creature, launched so into the literary career of ambition and mother of dead dogs" (as he called London). "Shaped like a pair of tongs." Leigh Hunt, who was very useful and kind to him in many ways, "had to be associated with on cautious terms." "Good humor and no common sense." "Hug-germugger was the type of his economies, in all respects, financial and other." (This of the "beautiful old man," as Hawthorne calls him, who, when he told the news of his pension, received the kiss from Mrs. Carlyle which he immortalized in the improvisation: —

> "Jenny kissed me when we met,
>     Jumping from the chair she sat in.
> Time, you thief ! who love to get
>     Sweets into your list, put that in.
> Say I 'm weary, say I 'm sad ;
>     Say that health and wealth have missed me ;
> Say I 'm growing old, but add —
>         Jenny kissed me ! "

"I wish," said Hawthorne, "that he could have had one full draught of prosperity before he died ; as a matter of artistic propriety, it would have been delightful to see him inhabiting a beautiful house of his own, in an Italian climate, with all sorts of elaborate upholstery and minute elegances about him, and a succession of tender and lovely women to praise his sweet poetry from morning to night.") "Coleridge," grumbles the philosopher, "a puf-fy, anxious, obstructed-looking, fattish old man, hobbled about with us, talking with a kind of solemn emphasis on matters which were of no interest." Milnes, one of the English friends who most appreciated him, he describes as "a pretty, robin-redbreast of a man." Of Wordsworth he says, "Franker utterances of mere garrulities and even platitudes I never heard from any man." Southey is "shovel-hatted; the shovel hat is grown to him." Thackeray is "a big, fierce, weeping, hungry man; not a strong one." Tennyson, though "a true human soul," is a man "dwelling in an element of gloom — carrying a bit of Chaos about him, in short, which he is manufacturing into Cosmos." Landor's "intellectual faculty," seemed to him "to be weak in proportion to his violence of temper; the judgment he gives about any thing is more apt to be wrong than right." Of Lamb, he says, "At his own house, I saw him once; once I gradually felt to have been enough for me." "His talk contemptibly small, indicating wondrous ignorance and shallowness, even when it was serious and good-mannered, which it seldom was." "A more pitiful, rickety, grasping, staggering, stammering tomfool I do not know." "Poor England, when such a despicable abortion is named genius." Of Basil Montagu, whose hospitality he often enjoyed, he says: "Much a bore to you by degrees, and considerably a humbug if you probed too strictly." "Washington," he writes, "is another of our perfect characters; to me, a most limited, uninteresting sort." He said to an American in a rough way, speaking of Sparks' Biography of Washington, that "the life of George Washington had yet to be written, and he would have to be taken down several pegs." He expected to meet Washington Irving at a breakfast in Paris. "I never met Washington at all," he records, "but still have a mild esteem of the good man." Accidentally, he says, he heard the famous Robert Hall preach. He thought the doctor "proved beyond shadow of doubt, in a really forcible, but most superfluous way, that God never lied." Mazzini he met, and thought "well nigh cracked by an enormous conceit of himself." "I once saw Godwin," he says, "if that was any thing." He speaks of "Macaulay's swaggering articles in the Edinburgh Review," and says, "Of Macaulay I hear nothing very good." "It seems to me of small consequence whether we meet at all." "Poor Hazlitt!" he exclaims. "He was never admirable to me." "Of no sound culture whatever." Heine he calls "blackguard Heine." "I have also seen Thomas Campbell," he says. "Him I like worst of all. He is heartless as a little Edinburgh advocate. There is a smirk on his face which would befit a shopman or an auctioneer. His very eye has the cold vivacity of a conceited worldling. His talk is small, contemptuous, and shallow."

The other sex, even, he employed his great pen in disparaging. Lady William Russell, the most cherished of his wife's titled friends, he speaks of as "a finished piece of social art, but hardly otherwise much." Old Lady Holland he "viewed even with aversion, as a kind of hungry, 'ornamented witch.'" Edward Irving's sweetheart — afterward Irving's wife — he pronounced "never quite satisfactory on the side of genuineness." "She was very ill-looking withal; a skin always under blotches and discolorment; muddy gray eyes, which for their part never laughed with the other features; pock-marked, ill-shapen, triangular kind of face, with hollow cheeks and long chin; decidedly unbeautiful as a young woman." "Spring-Rice's daughter, — a languishing patroness of mine," he refers to. Cordelia Marshall, a friend of his wife's, he sets down as "a prim, affectionate, but rather puling, weak, and sentimental elderly young lady." Mrs. Buller, who had been considerate of him, and whom he once wrote of as "one of the most fascinating women that I ever knew," becomes, on things going a little wrong, one of those "ancient dames of quality, that flaunting, painting, patching, nervous, vaporish, jiggling, scolding race of mortals." He speaks of "the honest, ever self-sufficient Harriet" Martineau. "Full of nigger fanaticisms." Her letters to his wife he calls "scrubby-

ish," "sawdustish," "Socinian didactic little notes." Of
Mrs. Sarah Austin, who did so much to introduce the
finest types of the German mind to the knowledge and
appreciation of English readers, and who as a translator
has been declared " altogether unrivaled in her own age
and country," he takes pains to record his disparaging
estimate : "' Mrs. Austin,' of these days, so popular and
almost famous, on such exiguous basis (translations from
the German, rather poorly some, and of original nothing
that rose far above the rank of twaddle)."

Of Emerson he always spoke well ; and no wonder.
There is abundant authority for the statement that for
some years Carlyle owed even his bread to the money
secured by Emerson for his earlier books, which were
published in Boston before they were printed in London.
Later, Emerson sent him seven hundred and fifty dollars,
the profits of an American edition of his French Revolution, when the profits of the English edition, to use his
own language, had been " absolutely nothing."

Arago's popularity as a lecturer on astronomy was a
result in part, it is said, of a way he had, before he commenced one of his lectures, of glancing around his audience to look for some dull aspirant for knowledge, with
a low forehead, and other indications that he was among
the least intelligent among his hearers. He kept his eye
fixed upon him, he addressed only him, and by the effect
of his eloquence and 'powers of explanation as exhibited
on the countenance of his pupil he judged of their influence over the rest of his audience. When he remained
unconvinced, the orator tried new illustrations till the
light beamed from the grateful countenance. Arago had
nothing to say to the rest of his audience. The orator
and his pupil were the Siamese twins united by an intellectual ligament. One morning, when Arago was breakfasting with his family, a visitor was announced. A gentleman entered — his pupil of the preceding evening, —

who, after expressing his admiration of the lecture, thanked
Arago for the very particular attention which he had paid
him during its delivery. "You had the appearance,"
said he, "of giving the lecture only to me."

In the midst of heavy professional work, Joseph Gri-
maldi, the incomparable clown, found time and energy to
pursue a most fatiguing hobby — the collecting of insects.
He had formed (says a writer in Temple Bar) a cabinet
which contained four thousand specimens. There was a
kind which came out in the month of June, called the
Dartford blue, for which he was particularly eager. His
enthusiasm in this pursuit may be measured by the sacrifices he made for it. After the performance was over at
Sadler's Wells he would return home to supper, then
about midnight start to walk to Dartford, a distance of
fifteen miles. He would arrive there about five in the
morning, rest and breakfast at a friend's house, then go
out into the fields ; sometimes a search for hours would
be rewarded with only a single specimen. At one o'clock
he would begin his return walk to London, reach there
in time for tea, and hurry off to the theatre. On the
same night, after the performance, he would again walk
to Dartford, re-commence his fly-hunt, return in the same
manner as on the previous day, and play again, without
rest or sleep. On the third night the pantomime was
played first, which enabled him to quit the theatre at nine
o'clock. Seemingly insensible to fatigue, he once more
started on his fifteen miles walk, and this time, arriving
at his journey's end by one in the morning, was able to
obtain a night's rest before commencing his quest. The
next day being Sunday, he had an opportunity of recruit-
ing his strength, and he must have sorely needed it.

About the only companions of the solitude of a grand
uncle of Lord Byron was a colony of crickets, which he
is said to have amused himself with rearing and feeding.
Byron used to say, on the authority of old servants of the

family, that on the day of their patron's death these crickets all left the house simultaneously, and in such numbers that it was impossible to cross the hall without treading on them.

Charles Waterton, author of that attractive book, Wanderings in South America, died at the age of eighty-three. During many years of travel in wild countries, he accustomed himself to endure every thing ; and for many years before his death "lived in a room at the top of his house, which had neither bed nor carpet ; he slept on the floor in a blanket, with an oak log for a pillow. He built a wall all round his park of two hundred and fifty acres, ranging from eight to sixteen feet in height, and modified all within to the use of birds, caring much more for their comfort than his own. His trees he watched and loved as much as his birds. It was a favorite habit of his to sit amongst their highest branches, watching birds, and reading Horace or Virgil, even after he was eighty ; and he often astonished visitors at the Hall by inviting them in perfect good faith to accompany him. He had himself, in his early manhood, twice climbed to the top of the cross on St. Peter's — once to leave his glove on the top of the lightning conductor, and again at the pope's desire (no workman in Rome being willing to risk his neck in the operation) to take it off again — so could not understand losing one's head in tree - climbing."

There are some very curious things in Charles Mathews' Memoirs about old Tate Wilkinson, the famous stage manager. He was, or rather had been, says the comedian, a great lover of good living ; his table, even after he was debarred any participation in its luxuries, was elegantly and liberally supplied, and his house the seat of hospitality. His appetite had long forsaken him, and he was very capricious in his tastes, liking to be surprised into a desire for something uncommon and unexpected. It was his custom to sprinkle about his room, between his papers and behind his books, some ratafia cakes, or any other little delicacies of the kind not liable to be spoiled by keeping, in order to detect them when he was not thinking of such a thing. Mr. Mathews more than once saw the effect of this contrivance — the old gentleman, upon the discovery, exclaiming, "Oh, here's a cake!" as if its being there was a matter of wonder to him; he would then nibble it with childish avidity, after having resisted all his wife's attempts to invite his appetite, by proposing all sorts of delicacies.

"There was a boy in my class at school," said Sir Walter Scott, "who stood always at the top, nor could I with all my efforts supplant him. Day came after day, and still he always kept the place, do what I could; till at length I observed that when a question was answered he always fumbled with his fingers at a particular button on the lower part of his waistcoat. To remove it, therefore, became expedient in my eyes; and, in an evil hour, it was removed with a knife. When the boy was again questioned, he felt again for the button, but it was not to be found. In his distress he looked down for it; it was to be seen no more than to be felt. He stood confounded, and I took possession of his place; nor did he ever recover it, nor ever, I believe, suspect who was the author of his wrong. Often, in after life, has the sight of him smote me as I passed by him, and often have I resolved to make him some reparation, but it ended in good resolutions. Though I never renewed my acquaintance with him, I often saw him, for he filled some inferior office in one of the courts of law at Edinburgh. Poor fellow: I believe he is dead; he took early to drinking."

"In the beginning of my translating the Iliad," said Pope to Spence, "I wished any body would hang me, a hundred times. It sat so heavily on my mind at first, that I often used to dream of it, and do sometimes still.

When I fell into the method of translating thirty or forty verses before I got up, and piddled with it the rest of the morning, it went on easy enough; and when I was thoroughly got into the way of it, I did the rest with pleasure."

Thoreau, in his Walden, discoursing of habitual and constitutional vices, speaks of some Spanish hides he had seen, with the tails still preserving their twist and the angle of elevation they had when the oxen that wore them were careering over the pampas of the Spanish main, — a type of all obstinacy, and evincing how almost hopeless and incurable are all such vices. " I confess," he says, " that practically speaking, when I have learned a man's real disposition, I have no hopes of changing it for the better or worse in this state of existence. As the Orientals say, 'a cur's tail may be warmed, and pressed, and bound round with ligatures, and after a twelve years' labor bestowed upon it, still it will retain its natural form.'"

One cannot bear, said Lamb, to pay for articles he has been, in the habit of getting for nothing. "When Adam laid out his first penny upon nonpareils at some stall in Mesopotamia, I think it went hard with him, reflecting upon his old goodly orchard, where he had so many for nothing."

Southey's anecdote of Master Jackson illustrates, and to some extent accounts for, an easy habit that good people sometimes fall into, that is much complained of by the parsons. "Well, Master Jackson," said his minister, walking homeward after service, with an industrious laborer, who was a constant attendant, — " well, Master Jackson, Sunday must be a blessed day of rest for you, who work hard all the week. And you make good use of the day; for you are always to be seen at church." "Aye, sir," replied Jackson, " it is, indeed, a blessed day ; I works hard enough all the week; and then I comes to church o' Sundays, and sets me down, and lays my legs up, and thinks o' nothing."

The effect of habit in self-discipline is shown in an interesting chapter from Goethe's Autobiography. "My health," says the poet, "was tolerably good; but a nervous irritability rendered me unable to endure the noise and sight of infirmities and sufferings. I could not stand on an elevation and look downwards without feeling a vertigo. I accustomed myself to noise by taking my station, at night, near the trumpets that sounded the retreat, at the risk of having my tympanum cracked by their loud braying. To cure myself of giddiness, I often ascended to the top of the Minster tower alone. I used to remain a quarter of an hour sitting on the stairs before I durst venture out. I then advanced on a small platform, scarcely an ell square, without any rail or support. Before me was an immense extent of country, whilst the objects nearest to the Minster concealed from my sight the church and the monument on which I was perched. I was precisely in the situation of a man launched into mid-air in a balloon. I repeated the experiment of this painful situation, until at length it gave me no sensation at all. Of the utility of these trials I was afterward fully sensible, when the study of geology led me to traverse mountains. When I had to visit great buildings, I could stand with the workmen upon the scaffolds on the roofs. These habits were no less useful to me at Rome, where I wished to examine the celebrated monuments of that city closely. In studying anatomy, I learned to endure the sight of those objects which at first shocked me most. I attended a course of clinical lectures, with the twofold intention of gaining an increase of knowledge, and of freeing myself of all pusillanimous repugnance. On the whole, I succeeded in fortifying myself against all those impressions of the senses and imagination which disturb the tranquillity of the soul."

Although Haller surpassed his contemporaries in anatomy, and published several important anatomical works, he was troubled at the outset with a horror of dissection beyond what is usual with the inexperienced, and it was only, it is stated, by firm discipline that he became an anatomist at all.

"Habit, in the great majority of things," says the grave and reverend John Foster, "is a greater plague than ever afflicted Egypt; in religious character, it is a grand felicity. The devout man exults in the indications of his being fixed and irretrievable. He feels this confirmed habit as the grasp of the hand of God, which will never let him go. From this advanced state he looks with firmness and joy on futurity, and says, I carry the eternal mark upon me that I belong to God; I am free of the universe; and I am ready to go to any world to which He shall please to transmit me, certain that everywhere, in height or depth, He will acknowledge me forever."

## XI

## THE HABIT OF DETRACTION.

"YES ; but " — These two little words, in this close connection — divided only by a semicolon — represent, in essence, it must be admitted, a very large part of all the conversation of all mankind. We assent, with qualification ; and the qualification, unhappily, too often ends the discussion. The shadows finish the picture. The habit we all deplore, and nearly all possess. Disparagement, detraction, — call it what you may, — that we are quick to condemn in others, we are very slow to correct in ourselves. We see it, we talk about it, we despise it, we blush at it, albeit we persist in it. The mischief goes for nothing, in effect, and we seem to look upon it as a part of life, inevitable and indispensable, to be condemned or indulged, as it disagrees or accords with our feelings or interests. Nature — human nature in this instance — goes her own way, and man is not to be made over in haste ; therefore, as a study, merely, this article is intended, without the slightest conception of reforming violently any human being. The Tigris flows through Bagdad when the caliphs are all dead.

"God," says Heine, "has given us tongues, that we may say pleasant things to our friends, and bitter truths of our enemies." "I have," he says, "the most peaceable disposition. My desires are a modest cottage with thatched roof — but a good bed, good fare, fresh milk and butter, flowers by my window, and a few fine trees before the door. And if the Lord wished to fill my cup of happiness, he would grant me the pleasure of seeing some six or seven of my enemies hanged on those trees. With a heart moved to pity, I would, before their death, forgive the injury they had done me during their lives. Yes, we ought to forgive our enemies — but not until they are hanged." "As far as I can understand the 'loving our enemies,'" said Poe, "it implies the hating our friends." When Marshal Narvaez was on his death-bed, his confessor asked him if he freely forgave all his enemies. "I have no enemies," replied the dying marshal, proudly. "Every one must have made enemies in the course of his life," suggested the priest, mildly. "Oh, of course," replied the marshal; "I have had a great number of enemies in my time, but I have none now. I have had them all shot!" You recollect the surgeon, to whom Voltaire was once compared, who not only attended a friend carefully during a last illness, but dissected him. You remember also the New Zealander who was asked whether he loved a missionary who had been laboring for his soul and those of his countrymen. "To be sure I loved him. Why, I ate a piece of him for my breakfast this morning!"

"If we quarreled," says Thackeray, "with all the people who abuse us behind our backs, and began to tear their eyes out as soon as we set ours on them, what a life it would be, and when should we have any quiet? Backbiting is all fair in society. Abuse me, and I will abuse you; but let us be friends when we meet. Have we not all entered a dozen rooms, and been sure, from the countenances of the amiable persons present, that they had been discussing our little peculiarities, perhaps as we were on the stairs? Was our visit, therefore, the less agreeable? Did we quarrel and say hard words to one another's faces? No — we wait until some of our dear friends take their leave, and then comes our turn. My back is at my neighbor's service; as soon as that is turned let him make what faces he thinks proper: but when we meet we grin and shake hands like well-bred folk, to whom clean linen is not more necessary than a clean, sweet-looking countenance, and a nicely gotten up smile for company."

Lady Mary Wortley Montagu said of the Duchess of Marlborough, "We continue to see one another like two persons who are resolved to hate with civility." Madame de Maintenon and Madame de Montespan met in public, talked with vivacity, and, to those who judged only by appearances, seemed excellent friends. Once when they had to make a journey in the same carriage, Madame de Montespan said, "Let us talk as if there were no difference between us, but on condition that we resume our hostility when we return."

The delightful deference which society obliges us to pay to those who hate us, is very much like returning thanks for injuries — a refinement in tyranny frequently practiced by the worst of the Roman emperors. Seneca informs us that Caligula was thanked by those whose children had been put to death, and whose property had been confiscated. A person who had grown old in his attendance on kings, was asked how he had attained a thing so uncommon in courts as old age? It was, replied he, by receiving injuries and returning thanks. It was on the same principle, we suppose, that Louis Philippe, unlike the great Napoleon, saw all the malicious caricatures that were made of himself, and laughed at them lustily. The young Prince Imperial, alluding to the visit of Count Bismarck to Napoleon III. at Plombières, said, "They let me laugh as much as I like ; but what I don't like is to be obliged to smile and look pleasant to men who I know are my father's enemies."

We are all sore, deficient, and vulnerable ; and by criticism, ridicule, and detraction, we supply ourselves with emollients, compensations, and weapons. Man, too, being a laughing animal, soon finds that the most laughable

object in creation is himself. He is continually blundering and stumbling, and he only learns to keep his feet
by falling. Morally as well as physically. If an invisible knocking machine tapped each one of us on the
head the instant and every time we thought evil or did
wrong, what a getting up there would be! What a scene
the street would present! To the church or to the market, the same. Verily, the world laughs; — with us, and
then at us.

Johnson uttered a conspicuously generous thing of his
friend Sir Joshua, when he said, "Reynolds, sir, is the
most invulnerable man I know; the man with whom, if you
should quarrel, you would find the most difficulty how to
abuse." "In faults," said Goethe, "men are much alike;
in good qualities they differ." We readily perceive the
faults of others by being so familiar with our own. Their
virtues are not so visible to us, for the reason that our
own are not so distinct to ourselves. The real good that
is in us is unconscious, almost occult, and blushes when
it is discovered.

It is only the very few, we hope, who, by what Hawthorne calls the "alchemy of quiet malice," concoct a
subtle poison from the ordinary experiences of life. For
the fun of the thing, more than for the mischief of it, the
world prattles on. Sometimes it is cruel; but it is the
cruelty of the thoughtless boy. It does not much concern itself about justice or injustice. To the sources it
does not much care to go if it could. It prefers to see
with its eyes rather than with its head, — by its senses
rather than by its reason. It sees outwardly, and talks
for recreation — irresponsibly, generally, and without reflection. "As for good sense," said Gil Blas, "if an angel
from heaven were to whisper wisdom in one ear, and
your cousin her mortal chit-chat in the other, I am afraid
the angel might whistle for an audience."

Boswell was thought by some of his contemporaries

to be a little dangerous; but for his love of personalities the world would not have had its best biography.
Wiser men than himself hated and feared him. "A
snapper up of unconsidered trifles," he might victimize
them. They did not know that the wise eye of Johnson
revised all that he recorded. It is said that whenever
he came into a company where Horace Walpole was, Walpole would throw back his head, purse up his mouth very
significantly, and not speak a word while Boswell remained.

Thiers' father is described as a queer, bustling, talkative little gentleman, and it is suggested that there must
have been something mischievous in his talk, or so much
pains would not have been taken by his eminent son to
keep him from his wedding. To insure the non-appear-
ance of his troublesome parent at the wedding, the minister for three weeks previously hired all the places in the
stage-coaches running from Carpentras (where he lived)
and other towns of the Vaucluse to Lyons.

Is it true, as they say, that it is the bad-tempered
people who are most apt to take to themselves and mis-
construe whatever is loosely said by the tongue of the
world, as the wasp is said to take up and convert all it
can light upon into poison? The illusory fancies of bad-
tempered people have been made the subject of much
subtle observation and analysis by mental physiologists.
It has been observed that they honestly believe that they
are the most ill-used persons on the earth, when they are
surrounded only by kindly regard and forbearing indulgence. They honestly believe that all the world is devot-
ing itself exclusively to a discussion of them, when, it
may be, the world, if it thinks or speaks of them at all,
it is only in a general way, and for the general good.
An English judge once sentenced a prisoner: "I sentence you," he said, "to die; not at all because you
have robbed this house, but in order that other people

may not rob other houses in future." The tongue is the universal policeman. It sometimes makes mistakes, and sometimes it is cruel. Good-nature is expected to forgive and submit. Virtue is its own reward.

It must be that a good deal of the evil-speaking of the world is for emphasis or for self-relief. Longinus, in his Discourse of the Sublime, commends swearing, for the reason that, now and then, on proper occasions, it adds to the grandeur and effectiveness of oratory. Old Fuseli, the painter, once said to his wife, when he found her in a tempestuous temper, "Madam, do swear a little ; you do not know how much good it would do you."

Can it be possible that a pretty general abuse of one's acquaintances was ever intended to limit one's friends ? as Lady Chantrey went into the studio with a hammer, and knocked off the noses of many completed busts, so that they might not be too common — a singular attention, it was thought, to her departed husband.

Intentionally or not, many a one's friends have been wofully reduced by the process of general offense. And the dear five hundred could not be recovered, when lost in that sweeping and unreasonable way. The offender and the offense had made it impossible. "Since I wronged you, I have never liked you," is a proverb. "The offender never pardons," is another. "No prov-erb is absolutely true," says a writer upon this subject ; "but all experience of life shows that it is the one who gives the offense, with whom it is the most difficult to make up. The reason is obvious. The offending man is secretly very angry with himself, and he has to forgive both you and himself — himself for having been unreas-onable, and you for having been in the way when he was unreasonable."

You remember Wycherley's humorous excuse for de-traction in The Plain Dealer: "Speaking well of all mankind is the worst kind of detraction ; for it takes away the reputation of the few good men in the world by making all alike." Suggesting Swift's satirical allusion to lying. He said that universal as was the practice of lying, and easy as it seemed, he did not remember to have heard three good lies in all his life.

A favorite amusement of boys is in marking out letters on signboards and in handbills — to produce what may be called wit by obliteration. A like effort it would seem is sometimes made to rub away traits of character, and laugh over the result of the prodigious performance. If such puerile wit sometimes resulted as the boys' experience with Professor John Stuart Blackie, there would perhaps be less of it. For thirty-five years he occupied the Greek chair of the University of Edinburgh. Once, we are told, on the first day of the college year he posted on the class-room door a notice that Professor Blackie would meet his classes on the 4th instant at the usual hours. A joker among the students erased the "c" in "classes," thus announcing that the Professor would "meet his lasses," etc. As class time drew near the young men gathered about to "see what Blackie would do." The Professor came, glanced at the card, touched it with a pencil, and passed in to his desk, with a grim smile overspreading his features. And the students followed him into the room, with mingled emotions of jollity and dismay, as they saw that his pencil stroke had obliterated the "l." Recalling an incident they tell of the eminent Dr. Whewell, who was a living cyclopædia. On one occasion some of his companions formed a conspiracy to trap him. A number of them read up on Chinese music from articles in old reviews. Then when they were ready they fired off their recondite knowledge on the state of music in China. For a while Dr. Whewell remained silent, and the conspirators were happy in thinking they had caught the great scholar at last. When, however, they had about emptied themselves of their curious lore, he remarked, " I was imperfectly, and to some extent incorrectly, informed regarding Chinese music when I wrote the articles from which you have drawn your information."

" I do not wonder," said Macaulay, "at the violence of the hatred which Socrates had provoked. He had, evidently, a thorough love for making men look small. There was a meek maliciousness about him which gave wounds such as must have smarted long, and his command of temper was more provoking than noisy triumph and insolence would have been."

The man who delights in giving you full credit for every excellence you possess, rather than in belittling you by an exaggeration of your foibles, is a treasure ; and the protection you feel in the neighborhood of such a man, law could not give you. He shuts your gate, he protects your child, he guards your reputation ; he does the fair and generous thing. If men were weighed and not counted, such a man would overbalance many of poorer material. Themistocles, having a farm to sell, bid the crier proclaim also that it had a good neighbor.

" Every one knows," says Goethe, " that there is no readier way to get rid of the consciousness of our own faults, than to busy ourselves about those of other people. This is a method much in vogue in the best of company. But nothing gives us so strong a sense of our independence, or makes us so important in our own eyes, as the censure of our superiors and of the great in this world."
" If we were faultless," says Fénelon, " we should not be so much annoyed by the defects of those with whom we associate. If we were to acknowledge honestly that we have not virtue enough to bear patiently with our neighbors' weaknesses, we should show our own imperfection, and this alarms our vanity. We therefore make our weakness pass for strength, elevate it to a virtue and call it zeal ; an imaginary and often hypocritical zeal. For is

it not surprising to see how tranquil we are about the errors of others when they do not trouble us, and how soon this wonderful zeal kindles against those who excite our jealousy, or weary our patience?"   "We reprove our friends' faults," said Wycherley, " more out of pride than love or charity ; not so much to correct them as to make them believe we are ourselves without them."

"It is a very ordinary and common thing amongst men," says Rabelais, in his quaint way, " to conceive, foresee, know, and presage the misfortunes, bad luck, or disaster of another ; but to have the understanding, providence, knowledge, and prediction of a man's own mishaps, is very scarce, and rare to be found anywhere.   This is exceeding judiciously and prudently deciphered by Æsop in his apologues, who there affirmeth, that every man in the world carrieth about his neck a wallet, in the forebag whereof is contained the faults and mischances of others, always exposed to his view and knowledge ; and in the other scrip thereof, which hangs behind, is kept the bearer's proper transgressions, and inauspicious adventures, at no time seen by him, nor thought upon, unless he be a person that hath a favorable aspect from the heavens."

" It is a certain sign of an ill heart," says Steele, in one of his Spectators, " to be inclined to defamation.   They who are harmless and innocent can have no gratification that way ; but it ever arises from a neglect of what is laudable in a man's self, and an impatience in seeing it in another. . . . A lady the other day at a visit, being attacked somewhat rudely by one whose own character had been very rudely treated, answered a great deal of heat and intemperance by very calmly remarking, 'Good madam, spare me, who am none of your match ; I speak ill of nobody, and it is a new thing to me to be spoken ill of.' "

One evening at a convivial gathering in Paris, where all the guests did not happen to be of the same political opinions, as they sat down to dinner, one said to the company : "Gentlemen, I should, before we begin dinner, make a little explanation of one of my peculiarities. It sometimes happens that when I have a little wine on board I take it into my head to gibe people who are not of my way of thinking in politics. I assure you that I mean nothing serious by such an action, and that if I should appear to be rude you will make a little allowance and not lay it to my account." As he seated himself, another guest, a man seven feet high, and with a hand and an arm in proportion, arose and said as courteously : "Gentlemen, I too should make a little explanation of one of my peculiarities. It sometimes happens that when I have a little wine on board and some one begins to gibe me for my way of thinking in politics I take it into my head to wring his neck or pitch him out of a second story window. I assure you that I mean nothing serious by such an action, and that if I should appear to be rude you will make a little allowance, and not lay it to my account." Not a word of politics was spoken at the table that evening, and all went merry as a dinner should.

A young lady, a member of Dr. Lathrop's church, went on a visit to a neighboring town, and while there attended a party and danced. Tidings of her sin reached home before her. On her return she was visited and called to most severe account for the disgrace she had thus brought upon herself and upon the church, and which had been found out, notwithstanding it had been done among strangers. One staid maiden was especially severe in her rebukes, and made the poor girl feel very bad. "What shall I do?" she asked. "You had better go and see Dr. Lathrop." She did go, and told him all about it. "And so, my dear, you went to the party, and danced, did you?" he said. "Yes, sir." "And did you have a good time?" "Yes, sir." "Well, I am glad of it, and I hope you will go again, and enjoy yourself. And now I want you to tell me the name of the woman who has been making you all this trouble." She told him. "Go to that woman, and tell her from me that, if she wants to get to heaven, she had better make more use of her feet, and less of her tongue."

People, it has been very truly remarked, are ever on the watch to catch their fellows tripping ; it is such comfort to find, or to fancy, one's self better than one's neighbors ; and the more favored by fortune the delinquent is, the sweeter is the pharisaical consolation we extract out of his aberrations.

Our own defects are apt to make us extremely acute in discovering the defects of others, as an infirmity sometimes seems to supply a new sense. Not long since there was living in the county of York, England, a gentleman, who, though totally blind, was an expert archer. His sense of hearing was so keen, that when a boy behind the target rang a bell, the blind archer knew precisely how to aim the shaft.

Once on a time a woman at confession told the priest that she had been guilty of slandering her neighbor. The priest gave her a thistle, and told her to go and scatter it on the fields, and then come back. On her return, the priest said, "Go now and gather up all those thistle-seeds." When she declared she could not, he said to her, "Neither can you gather up the evil words you have spoken."

Some one has said that those who utter slander, and those who believe it, ought both to be hanged, one by the tongue, the other by the ear.

In the land of Satin, Rabelais saw Hearsay, "a diminutive, monstrous, misshapen old fellow," who "kept a school of vouching." "His mouth was slit up to his ears, and in it were seven tongues, each of them cleft into seven parts. However, he chattered, tattled, and prated with all the seven at once, of different matters, and in divers languages.  He had as many ears all over his head, and the rest of his body, as Argus formerly had eyes ; and was as blind as a beetle, and had the palsy in his legs.  About him stood an innumerable number of men and women, gaping, listening, and hearing very  intently ; among them he observed some who strutted like crows in a gutter, and principally a very handsome bodied man in the face, who held them a map of the world, and with little aphorisms compendiously explained every thing to them ; so that those men of happy memories grew learned in a trice, and would most fluently talk with you of a world of prodigious things, the hundredth part of which would take up a man's whole life to be fully known."

It has been noticed in Abyssinia that an irreconcilable feud rages between the donkey and the hyena.  "I have met with my moral antipodes," says Lamb, "and can believe the story of two persons meeting (who never saw one another before in their lives) and instantly fighting." Upon one occasion Mr. Webster was on his way to attend to his duties in Washington.  He was compelled to proceed at night by stage from Baltimore.  He had no traveling companions, and the driver had a sort of felon-look, which produced no inconsiderable alarm.  "I endeavored to tranquilize myself," said Mr. Webster, "and had partially succeeded, when we reached the woods between Bladensburg and Washington (a proper scene for murder or outrage), and here, I confess, my courage again deserted me.  Just then the driver, turning to me, with a gruff voice asked my name.  I gave it to him. 'Where are you going?' said he.  The reply was, 'To Washington.  I am a Senator.'  Upon this, the driver seized me fervently by the hand, and exclaimed, 'How glad I am.  I have been trembling in my seat for the last hour; for, when I looked at you, I took you to be a highwayman.'"

Shelley somehow antagonized his neighbors ; at least,

he was always misunderstood by them and belied. He was said to be keeping a seraglio at Marlow ; and his friends partook of the scandal. This keeper of a seraglio, who, in fact, was extremely difficult to please in such matters, and who had no idea of love unconnected with sentiment, passed his days like a hermit. We have it upon the authority of his friend Leigh Hunt that he rose early in the morning, walked and read before breakfast, took that meal sparingly, wrote and studied the greater part of the morning, walked and read again, dined on vegetables (for he took neither meat nor wine), conversed with his friends (to whom his house was ever open), again walked out, and usually finished with reading to his wife till ten o'clock, when he went to bed. This was his daily existence. Yet the word " seraglio " stuck to his home like an epithet ; and you know what an epithet is. " It is by epithets," said Napoleon, "that you govern mankind."

A gentleman gave Thackeray a good illustration of the philosophy of exaggeration. Mr. —— was once behind the scenes at the opera when the scene-shifters were preparing for the ballet. Flora was to sleep under a bush, whereon were growing a number of roses, and amidst which was fluttering a gay covey of butterflies. In size, the roses exceeded the most expansive sunflowers ; and the butterflies were as large as cocked hats. The scene-shifters explained to Mr. ——, who asked the reason why every thing was so magnified, that the galleries could never see the objects unless they were enormously exaggerated. Thus pitched to their senses and apprehension, they were vehement in their applauses, and the spectacle was triumphant. Healthy criticism and sound judgment were impossible, as they always are to the excited multitude. Froude, in his sketch of Julius Cæsar, speaks of a yell which rose from tens of thousands of throats so piercing that it was said a crow flying over the Forum dropped dead at the sound of it. The Duke of Wellington would not allow the fence around his house, which had been torn down by the excited mob, to be rebuilt, because he wanted kept before him the mutability, uncertainty, and unreasonableness of all popular favor.

It is impossible to overestimate the influence of surrounding atmospheres, physical and social. Sir Rutherford Alcock, who once represented Great Britain in China, visited the Great Wall, and brought back two bricks from it. "I do not pretend to determine," says Helps, in his chapter on Social Pressure, "how many centuries these bricks had kept their form, and betrayed no signs of decay, in that atmosphere. But those centuries must have been many. Sir Rutherford put these two bricks out in the balcony of his house in London. About two years after, one of these bricks had entirely gone to pieces, being entirely disintegrated by the corrosive influence of the London atmosphere." "In Syria, and Palestine, and Egypt," says Kinglake, "you might as well dispute the efficacy of grass or grain as of magic. There is no controversy about the matter. The effect of this, the unanimous belief of an ignorant people, upon the mind of a stranger, is extremely curious, and well worth noticing. A man coming freshly from Europe is at first proof against the nonsense with which he is assailed, but often it happens that after a little while the social atmosphere in which he lives will begin to infect him, and if he has been unaccustomed to the cunning of fence by which Reason prepares the means of guarding herself against fallacy, he will yield himself at last to the faith of those around him, and this he will do by sympathy, it would seem, rather than from conviction."

Johnson, in his Preface to Shakespeare, says: "The great contention of criticism is to find the faults of the moderns, and the beauties of the ancients. While an author is yet living, we estimate his powers by his worst performance, and when he is dead, we rate them by the best." Lord Brougham conceived the brilliant idea of giving out that he had been killed in a carriage accident, to see what the newspapers would say of him. Several pages are devoted to this curious bit of history by Campbell in his Lives of the Lord Chancellors. "Whether Brougham was cognizant of this piece of bad pleasantry or not," says Lord Campbell, "he was much annoyed by the result of it. Not only was he mortified by the great preponderance of abuse which it called forth, but he discovered, to his great surprise, that he was generally suspected to be the author of it, and he knew the ridicule which he must have incurred by killing himself, and reading so many, and such unfavorable characters of himself, written when he was supposed to have gone to a better world."

Mr. Greeley used to tell a good story of the way American fabrics were once disparaged in New York city. Dr. Crosby, of New Haven, had invented an ingenious machine for the manufacture of fish-hooks, by means of which a coil of wire would be converted into a peck of fish-hooks of any size with astonishing rapidity and perfect success. It bent, pointed, barbed, and flattened the heads at lightning speed, and more beautifully than could be done by hand manipulation. Having finished a quantity he sent them down to New York. They were rejected as not of standard excellence. He sent another lot, which was also rejected for the same reason. He then sent down a third lot of hooks put on cards as usual, and said he felt sure that these would answer. The reply came, No, they would not do; they were not up to the British make. Dr. Crosby then wrote down indignantly to the New York house: "Why, gentlemen, these ought to suit you, for they are British hooks bought from your own store, and packed in my boxes to test you." That, however, did not signify, and the American hooks were still disparaged and refused.

Stanley, when voyaging down the Congo, had this significant experience: " I saw before me over a hundred beings of the most degraded, unpresentable type it is possible to conceive; and though I knew quite well that some hundreds of years ago the beginning of this wretched humanity and myself were one and the same, a sneaking disinclination to believe it possessed me strongly, and I would even now willingly subscribe some small amount of silver money for him who could but assist me to controvert the discreditable fact. . . . If the old chief appeared so unprepossessing, how can I paint without offense my humble brothers and sisters who stood around us? As I looked at the array of faces, I could only comment to myself, — ugly, uglier, ugliest. As I looked at their rude and filthy bodies, . . . and the general indecency of their nakedness, I ejaculated ' Fearful!' as the sum total of what I might with propriety say, and what indeed is sufficiently descriptive. . . . And how strangely they smell, all these queer man-like creatures who stand regarding me! Not silently: on the contrary, there is a loud interchange of comments upon the white's appearance, a manifestation of broad interest to know whence I came, whither I am going, and what is my business. The replies were followed by long-drawn ejaculations of ' Wa-a-a-antu !' (' Men !') ' Eha-a, and these are men !' Now imagine this! While we whites are loftily disputing among ourselves as to whether the beings before us are human, here were these creatures actually expressing strong doubts as to whether we whites are men! A dead silence prevailed for a short time, during which all the females dropped their lower jaws far down, and then cried out again, ' Wa-a-a-a-antu !' (' Men !')"

A charitable old woman, who afforded Mungo Park a meal and lodging, on the banks of the Niger, could not refrain, even in the midst of her kindness, from exclaiming, "God preserve us from the devil," as she looked upon him.

It has been said that we must have the same enmities to be united in spirit. That in order to love one another, we must have hatreds in common. Literature, at least, furnishes some proofs of this. We know, for instance, how, on account of the satire of Fielding, the moral Richardson and the dissolute Cibber became lasting friends. "If the Athenians were wise (Aristides is reported to have said, in the height and peril of his parliamentary struggle with Themistocles), they would have cast both Themistocles and me into the barathrum." (The barathrum was a deep pit, said to have had iron spikes at the bottom, into which criminals condemned to death were sometimes cast.) The rulers, in Heine's time, refused a residence in Prussia, and especially in Berlin, to any one who did not profess one of the positive religions recognized by the state. Tacitus, in speaking of the Germans eighteen centuries ago, says it was an indispensable duty to adopt the enmities of a father or relation, as well as their friendships. Mary de Medici, mother of Louis XIII., was extremely anxious to obtain the good graces of her son. One day she asked the prince of Piedmont, her son-in-law, "How shall I set about obtaining them?" The prince replied, "Love truly and sincerely all that he loves; these words contain the law and the prophets."

Still, according to Holmes, "Whenever two natures have a great deal in common, the conditions of a first-rate quarrel are furnished ready-made. Relations are very apt to hate each other just because they are too much alike. It is so frightful to be in an atmosphere of family idiosyncrasies; to see all the hereditary uncomeliness or infirmity of body, all the defects of speech, all the failings of temper, intensified by concentration, so that every fault of our own finds itself multiplied by reflections, like an image in a saloon lined with mirrors! Nature knows what she is about. The centrifugal principle which grows out of the antipathy of like to like is only the repetition in character of the arrangement we see expressed materially in certain seed-capsules, which burst and throw the seed to all points of the compass. A house is a large pod with a human germ or two in each of its cells or chambers; it opens by dehiscence of the front door by and by, and projects one of its germs to Kansas, another to San Francisco, another to Chicago, and so on; and this that Smith may not be Smithed to death, and Brown may not be Browned into a mad-house, but mix in with the world again and struggle back to average humanity."

Charles Young made his début at the Haymarket on the 22d of June, 1807, as Hamlet. It was an undoubted success. But from one corner of the theatre, it is said, came a persistent hiss. Young soon succeeded in detecting the malevolent person, and recognized in him his own father! It was not the first time this excellent gentleman had given public proof of animosity against his children. Once he entered a stage-coach in which one of his sons (who afterward attained some eminence as a surgeon) was sitting, and without speaking a word struck him a heavy blow in the face. The young man ordered the coach to stop, and as he alighted turned to the astonished passengers and said, "Ladies and gentlemen, this is my father!"

Douglas Jerrold has said, "Fishermen in order to handle eels securely, first cover them with dirt. In like manner does detraction strive to grasp excellence." Le Sage has said as well: "Evil tongues never want a whet. Virtue herself furnishes weapons for her own martyrdom."

"Observe," says La Bruyère, "those persons who never commend any one, who are always railing, are content with nobody, and you will find them persons with whom nobody is content." And they are not apt to be content with themselves. "How happy one would be," exclaims Madame du Deffand, "if one could throw off one's self as one can throw off others! but one is perforce with one's self, and very little in accord with one's self."

"He who will work aright," said Goethe to Eckermann, "must never rail, must not trouble himself at all about what is ill-done, but only to do well himself. For the great point is, not to pull down, but to build up, and in this humanity finds pure joy." "The man most eager to pull another down is the person who wants to get into his place. The democrat is merely a despot in disguise."

It is said that in Norway there is a superstition that if you save a man from drowning, he will serve you an ill turn, one day or another. Bourrienne said of Fouché, Napoleon's minister of police, that he never regarded a benefit in any other light than as a means of injuring his benefactor. That bitterest of all satirists, Talleyrand, being told that a certain public functionary was talking against him, exclaimed, "That surprises me. I have never done him a favor." "I never laughed more," said Voltaire to Casanova, "than when I read that Don Quixote found himself in the greatest perplexity how he should defend himself against the galley-slaves, whom, out of generosity, he had liberated."

That is good advice given by Hazlitt, "Never quarrel with tried friends, or those whom you wish to continue such. Wounds of this kind are sure to open again. When once the prejudice is removed that sheathes defects, familiarity only causes jealousy and distrust. Do not keep on with a mockery of friendship after the substance is gone — but part, while you can part friends. Bury the carcass of friendship: it is not worth embalming."

False friendship is not to be spoken of. Figured down to good federal money, about twenty-two dollars was the sum Judas received for betraying his Master.

"If what we see is doubtful, how can we believe what is spoken behind the back?" is a Chinese proverb. "Why did you say such things behind Mr. Johnson's back?" "Because," was the reply, "I would not hurt his feelings by saying them to his face." Alas, the courage it requires to defend the absent.

It is so easy to be mistaken. Eugène Sue was a boon companion of the French novelist Fromieu. The two, we are told, had one evening dined at the Café de Paris, and by reason of too generous after-dinner potations, their gayety, on issuing from the famous restaurant, was of a highly pronounced type. At once Fromieu made a false step, and falling, sprained his ankle. Sue, who in his youth had pursued a long course of medical studies, instantly lost his hilarity, hailed a passing cab, and having therein seated his unfortunate friend, proceeded in the most scientific manner to reset and bandage the dislocated bone. The operation, it was then mutually agreed upon, was a magnificent success, and the author of The Mysteries of Paris laid flattering unction on his soul, and dreamed again of splendid fees and of medals of honor. Next morning Sue came to see how his friend was progressing, when, to his surprise and horror, he discovered that he had treated the wrong ankle!

You remember the old anecdote of Blücher's admiration of London after a gorgeous city dinner: "What a splendid city it would be to sack!" cried the old Prussian to his beaming host. A fine character is often regarded in the same way by the defamer. "All hew their fagots from the fallen oak."

It is recorded that in a debate in the House of Commons, when Sir Richard Steele rose to speak, several members cried out "Tatler! Tatler!" and when he went down the house afterward, several members were heard to say, "It is not so easy a thing to speak in the house; he fancies, because he can scribble, he is fit to play the orator." This circumstance, as Lord John Russell very appropriately remarked, shows the natural envy of mankind towards those who attempt to attain more than one kind of preëminence. For it is, indeed, more often envy than prudence which has warned the cobbler not to go beyond his last, and has declared that one branch of knowledge is enough to exhaust all the energies of the human mind.

"I am Envy!" exclaims Marlowe in his play of Faustus; "I am Envy!—begotten of a chimney-sweep and an oyster-wife. I cannot read, and therefore wish all books burned. I am lean with seeing others eat. Oh that there would come a famine all over the world!—that all might die, and I live alone. Then thou shouldst see how fat I'd be!" You remember the bon-vivant who envied the beggar's staring into the cook-shop windows, and wished he could be hungry. "Alas!" pathetically exclaimed Mrs. Siddons, to the poet Rogers, "after I became celebrated, none of my sisters loved me as before." "All men," says Plutarch, "will deny envy; and when it is alleged, will feign a thousand excuses, pretending they were angry, or that they feared or hated the person, cloaking envy with the name of any passion they can think of, and concealing it as the most loathsome sickness of the soul."

Miss Sarah Pocket, one of Dickens' characters, was "a blandly vicious person." She would have lingered delightedly with Dante, to hear the wrangle of the damned spirits, and wrangled with them, if permitted. Virgil's reproaches would have gone unheeded. Abu Moslem, who rebelled against Ibraham, successor of Mahomet, was never seen to smile except on a day of battle.

There is a species of viper in India, which, in vainly attempting to bite, breaks its fangs, so that it is compelled to swallow its own deadly poison, and perish by the very means intended for the destruction of others. Malice, in the same way, often swallows the greater part of its venom.

Lady Blessington said, "We are never so severe in dealing with the sins of others as when we are no longer capable of committing them ourselves. Few people remember that they have been young, and how hard it was then to be chaste and temperate. The first thing men do when they have renounced pleasure, either out of decency, surfeit, or conviction, is to condemn it in others." In Montesquieu's Persian Letters is one from the chief eunuch, describing to his absent master his conduct of the seraglio. "I never open my mouth," he says, "but with lectures of duty, chastity, and modesty."

Few retorts are better than the pavior's to Sydenham, the great seventeenth century physician. The doctor was complaining of the bad manner in which the pavement was laid in front of his house, adding, "and now you throw down earth to hide your bad work." "Well, doctor," said the man quietly, "mine is not the only bad work that the earth hides."

There are many amiable people, it is remarked, who take a keen pleasure in dashing cold water upon any little manifestation of self-complacency in their neighbors. To find out a man's tenderest corn, and then to bring your heel down upon it with a good rasping scrunch, is somewhat gratifying to corrupt human nature. A kindly wit contrives to convey a compliment in affected satire. But the whole aim of a humorist of this variety is to convey the most mortifying truths in the most brutal plain-speaking.

Macaulay has been accused of yielding to the temptation of imputing motives, a habit which the Spectator newspaper pronounced to be his one intellectual vice — the vice of rectitude. Sterne represents Walter Shandy as "a great motive-monger, and consequently a very dangerous person for a man to sit by, either laughing or crying, — for he generally knew your motive for doing both, much better than you knew it yourself."

"Virtue is a beautiful thing in women," said Douglas Jerrold, "when they don't go about like a child with a drum, making all sorts of noises with it. There are some women (he says) who think virtue was given them as claws were given to cats — to do nothing but scratch with." Virtue, in that form, is, we suppose, what somebody has aptly called the "wrath of celestial minds."

"They who have (says Coleridge) attained to a self-pleasing pitch of civility or formal religion, have usually that point of presumption with it, that they make their own size the model and rule to examine all by. What is below it, they condemn indeed as profane ; but what is beyond it, they account needless and affected preciseness ; and therefore are as ready as others to let fly invectives or bitter taunts against it, which are the keen and poisoned shafts of the tongue, and a persecution that shall be called to a strict account." Mr. Justice Maule, in summing up a case of libel, and speaking of a defendant who had exhibited a spiteful piety, observed, "One of the defendants is, it seems, a minister of religion ; of what religion does not appear, but, to judge of his conduct, it cannot be any form of Christianity."

"Sandy, what is the state of religion in your town ? " "Bad, sir, very bad. There are no Christians except Davis and myself, and I have my doubts about Davis." Sandy was what Montesquieu might have called "a universal decider." In the Persian Letters, Rica writes to Usbek, "The other day I was at a gathering where I saw a very self-satisfied man. In a quarter of an hour he decided three questions in morals, four historical problems, and five points in physics. I have never seen such a universal decider." Such complacency is illustrated in the Turkish story book. One night, seeing the moon reflected in a well, Nasr-Eddin (the Turkish Joe Miller) thought it had tumbled in ; so he lowered a bucket to pull it out. The rope getting entangled, he pulled so hard that he broke it and fell backwards. When he came to after the shock, he saw that the moon was all right in the sky. "God be praised and thanked!" quoth he ; "I 've hurt myself, but the moon is put back in her place."

At the grand academy of Lagado, the metropolis of Balnibari, Gulliver "heard a warm debate between two professors, about the most commodious and effectual ways and means of raising money, without grieving the subject. The first affirmed, 'the justest method would be, to lay a certain tax upon vices and folly ; and the sum fixed upon every man to be rated, after the fairest manner, by a jury of his neighbors.' The second was of an opinion directly contrary : 'to tax those qualities of body and mind, for which men chiefly value themselves ; the rate to be more or less according to the degrees of excelling ; the decision whereof should be left entirely to their own breast.'"

Mr. Gregory told Caroline Fox that, going by steamer from Liverpool to London, he sat by an old gentleman who would not talk, but only answered his inquiries by nods or shakes of the head. When they went down to dinner, he determined to make him speak if possible, so he proceeded, "You 're going to London, I suppose?" A nod. "I shall be happy to meet you there ; where are your quarters?" There was no repelling this, so his friend, with the energy of despair, broke out, "I-I-I-I 'm g-g-g-going to D-D-D-Doctor Br-Br-Br-Brewster to be c-c-c-cured of this sl-sl-sl-slight im-impediment of sp-sp-sp-sp-speech." At this instant a little white face which had not appeared before popped out from one of the berths and struck in, "Th-th-th-that's the m-m-m-man wh-wh-who c-c-c-c-c-cured me !"

"Judge not thy fellow-man," says the Jewish Talmud,

"till thou art similarly situated." The wisdom whereof is feelingly expressed in the story of Plutarch. A Roman having repudiated his wife, his friends reproached him, remonstrating that she was fair and good, and had fine children. To which the husband replied by showing his foot, and saying, "This shoe is new, and well made ; but none of you know where it pinches ; I do."

Garrick kept a book of all who praised and all who abused him. Franklin, in his autobiography, mentions a gentleman who, having one very handsome and one shriveled leg, was wont to test the disposition of a new acquaintance by observing whether he or she looked first or most at the best or worst leg. "He who cannot see the beautiful side," says Joubert, "is a bad painter, a bad friend, a bad lover ; he cannot lift his mind and his heart so high as goodness." "There are heads," says the same wise aphorist, "that have no windows, and that daylight cannot strike from above. Nothing comes into them from the side of heaven." Who has read and not enjoyed the Life of John Buncle, Esq.? the model husband of seven perfect wives. The curious book is a treasure. It is romantic. It is optimistic. It is wholesome. So full of good animal spirits. The geese are all swans. The houses all have libraries and observatories and conservatories and laboratories. The women are all learned and beautiful. The religion inculcated is without cant. The style is delicious. Many of the paragraphs end with short sentences, that suggest for all the world the licking of overladen lips, after "the hungry edge of the appetite" is cloyed. The flavor the queer book has! No wonder it has lived.

It was the fashion of old, when an ox was led out for sacrifice to Jupiter, to chalk the dark spots and give the offering a show of unblemished whiteness. "There goes Fritz," said one soldier to another, as the king went by. "What a shabby old hat he has on!" "Yes," said the other, "but you do not see what a fine head it covers." On one occasion Louis XIV. asked Bourdaloue, the famous orator of Notre Dame, his opinion of Ornorato, the great jocular capuchin. "Sire," was the reply, "that preacher tickles indeed the ear, but also pricks the heart. People return at his sermons the purses they steal at mine."

"Gil Blas (said his master), leave our neighbors to discourse as they please, but let not our repose depend on their judgments. Never mind what they think of us, provided our own consciences do not wince." "There will always be some to hate you," said Publius Syrus, "if you love yourself." "Do well," Rubens would say, "and people will be jealous of you: do better, and you confound them."

My grandfather Titbottom "lived much alone, and was what people called eccentric — by which I understand, that he was very much himself, and, refusing the influence of other people, they had their revenges, and called him names."

It is a very serious thing to do as you like. "The man, and still more the woman," says John Stuart Mill, "who can be accused of either doing 'what nobody does,' or of not doing 'what every body does,' is the subject of as much depreciatory remark as if he or she had committed some grave moral delinquency. Persons require to possess a title, or some other badge of rank, or the consideration of people of rank, to be able to indulge somewhat in the luxury of doing as they like without detriment to their estimation. To indulge somewhat, I repeat: for whoever allow themselves much of that indulgence incur the risk of something worse than disparaging speeches — they are in peril of a commission de lunatico, and of having their property taken from them and given to their relations."

"Men of true wisdom and goodness," remarks Fielding, "are contented to take persons and things as they are, without complaining of their imperfections or attempting to amend them ; they can see a fault in a friend, a relation, or an acquaintance, without ever mentioning it to the parties themselves or to any others; and this often without lessening their affection : indeed, unless great discernment be tempered with this overlooking disposition, we ought never to contract friendship but with a degree of folly which we can deceive ; for I hope my friends will pardon me when I declare, I know none of them without a fault ; and I should be sorry if I could imagine I had any friend who could not see mine. Forgiveness of this kind we give and demand in turn : it is an exercise of friendship, and perhaps none of the least pleasant, and this forgiveness we must bestow without desire of amendment. There is perhaps no surer mark of folly, than an attempt to correct the natural infirmities of those we love : the finest composition of human nature, as well as the finest china, may have a flaw in it ; and this, I am afraid, in either case, is equally incurable, though nevertheless the pattern may remain of the highest value."

An amiable feature in Edmund Burke's disposition, we are told, was a dislike to any thing like detraction, or that insinuation against private character too often tolerated even in what is called good society, which, without amounting to slander, produces nearly the same effects. When this occurred in his own house by any one with whom he was familiar, he would directly check it, or drop a hint to that effect : "Now that you have begun with his defects," he would say, "I presume you mean to finish with a catalogue of his virtues ;" and sometimes said, though mildly, "Censoriousness is allied to none of the virtues." When remarks of this kind were introduced by others whom it might have been rude to interrupt, he took the part of the accused by apologies, or by urging a different construction of their actions, and, as soon as he could, changed the subject; exemplifying the advice he once familiarly, but wisely gave to a grave and anxious acquaintance, who was giving vent to some querulous lamentations, " Regard not trifles, my dear sir ; live pleasantly."

It is best, wisely concluded Thackeray, on the whole, for the sake of the good, that the bad should not all be found out. You don't want your children to know the history of the lady in the next box, who is so handsome, and whom they admire so. Ah me, what would life be if we were all found out, and punished for all our faults ? Jack Ketch would be in permanence ; and then who would hang Jack Ketch ?

## XII.

### THE ART OF LIVING.

The eminent Theodore Parker, not long before his death, wrote from Rome, "Oh, that I had known the art of life, or found some book or some man to tell me how to live, to study, to take exercise, etc. But I found none, and so here I am." Alas! The art of life! We all sigh for it. If only some one knew it, and could impart it, how we should all flock to him to learn! "There is nothing so handsome and lawful," says Montaigne, "as well and truly to play the man; nor science so hard as well to know how to live this life. . . . We say, 'I have done nothing to-day.' What! have you not lived? 'T is not only the fundamental, but the most illustrious of your occupations. . . . 'T is an absolute, and, as it were, a divine perfection, for a man to know how loyally to enjoy his being." To enjoy life, to relish it, without the transport of some passion, or the gratification of some appetite. To live to have the fewest regrets. Some such admonitory words as a wise man once caused to be written on his tomb, one would think, would be in every mind's eye, — "Think on living." Yesterday — to-day. "We are all going to the play, or coming home from it." The past is dead, the present is without memory, the future is not assured; we are to be, in a sense, as if we had never been. If only we could live to-day upon the experience of yesterday, something like foresight would be given us, and to-morrow might be easier and more joyful. "Foolish man!" exclaims Goethe, "who passes the day in complaining of headache, and the night in drinking the wine that produces it." "Comedy is crying," said little Lucy Triplett to Pegg Woffington. "Father cried all the time he was writing his one." "Nobody," says Hawthorne, "will use other people's experience, nor has any of his own till it is too late to use it." Experience! "To most men," said Coleridge, "experience is like the stern lights of a ship, which illumine only the track it has passed." Strange! that any thing so common and so useful should be of so little use as heads. Every body has one. It is not strange that we should do foolish things; but that we should do the same foolish things, over and over, is more than strange — it is incomprehensible. In homely phrase, we follow our noses, and not our judgments. "When we subtract from life infancy (which is vegetation), — sleep, eating, and swilling — buttoning and unbuttoning — how much," asks Byron, "remains of downright existence? The summer of a dormouse." "Youth," says Beaconsfield, "is a blunder, manhood a struggle, old age a regret." "To those who think," says Horace Walpole, "life is a comedy — to those who feel, a tragedy." "We must laugh at man," said the great Napoleon, "to avoid crying at him."

It was a profound thought of Arthur Helps that if the object of the arrangements of the universe was to make man happy, he would have been gifted with at least five minutes' foresight. "Heavens!" exclaimed De Quincey, . . . "if life could throw open its long suites of chambers to our eyes from some station beforehand, — if, from some secret stand, we could look by anticipation along its vast corridors, and aside into the recesses opening upon them from either hand, — halls of tragedy or chambers of retribution, simply in that small wing, and no more, of the great caravanserai which we ourselves shall haunt, — simply in that narrow tract of time, and no more, where we ourselves shall range, and confining our gaze to those, and no others, for whom personally we shall be interested, — what a recoil we should suffer of horror in our estimate of life ! . . . Death we can face : but knowing, as some of us do, what is human life, which of us is it that without shuddering could (if consciously we were summoned) face the hour of birth ? "

Dr. Johnson, whose one enthusiasm was " an enthusiasm of sadness," pronounced the world in its best estate to be nothing more than a larger assembly of being, combining to counterfeit happiness, which they do not feel, employing every art and contrivance to embellish life, and to hide their real condition from one another.

The lives of those who in England were loudest in exclaiming, All is for the best, did not prove the truth of their doctrine. Shaftesbury, who first brought it into fashion, was a very unfortunate man. " I have," says Voltaire, " seen Bolingbroke a prey to vexation and rage, and Pope, whom he employed to put his wretched system into verse, was the man most to be pitied of any I have known ; misshapen in body, dissatisfied in mind, always ill, always a burden to himself, and harassed by a hundred enemies to his very last moment. Let those at least be fortunate and prosperous who tell us, All is for the best."

They have a legend in Spain that Adam made a visit to the earth a few years ago, to see how his farm was getting on. He alighted in Germany, and found schools, and colleges, and books, and the people intent on learning. He soon left it for France, where the people dressed in fantastic styles, and were mad upon works of art and improvements unknown to our great ancestor. Disgusted with all he saw, he went down to Spain, and, with delight, exclaimed, " This is just as I left it ! " But the legend stops short of telling us that Spain herself was particularly happy in her condition.

" People always fancy," said Goethe, laughing, " that we must become old to become wise ; but, in truth, as years advance, it is hard to keep ourselves as wise as we were. Man becomes, indeed, in the different stages of his life, a different being ; but he cannot say that he is a better one, and, in certain matters, he is as likely to be right in his twentieth, as in his sixtieth year. We see the world one way from a plain, another way from the heights of a promontory, another from the glacier fields of the primary mountains. We see, from one of these points, a larger piece of the world than from the other ; but that is all, and we cannot say that we see more truly from any one than from the rest."

" All places," said old Burton, " are distant from heaven alike ; happily the sun shines as warm in one city as in another ; and to a wise man there is no difference of climes ; friends are everywhere to him that behaves himself well, and a prophet is not esteemed in his own country."

" There are to-day at Naples," said Montesquieu, " fifty thousand men who live only upon herbs, and whose only possession is the woolen habit which they wear ; yet these people, the most miserable upon the earth, fall down with fear at the least smoking of Vesuvius : they have the foolish apprehension of becoming miserable."

" I believe," says Thoreau, " that men are still a little afraid of the dark, though the witches are all hung, and Christianity and candles have been introduced." All over England, it is stated, the peasants believe still that the spirits of unbaptized children wander in the wind, and that the wails at their doors and windows are the cries of the little souls condemned to journey till the last day. It is said that amongst the curiosities in the India-House, is the dream book of Tippoo Sahib, in which he daily wrote his dreams and their interpretation with his own hand, and to which he, like Wallenstein, might mainly have ascribed his fall. Cambyses, for having dreamt that his brother should be one day King of Persia, put him to death ; a brother whom he tenderly loved, in whom he had always confided. Cowper communicated his waking dreams to a poor mendicant schoolmaster, and consulted with him about them, as a person whom the Lord was pleased to answer in prayer. Tycho Brahe maintained an idiot, who lay at his feet whenever he sat down to dinner, and whom he fed with his own hand. Persuaded that his mind, when moved, was capable of foretelling future events, the great astronomer carefully marked every thing he said. Cromwell, Napoleon, Johnson, Pascal, and many other great personages, were peculiarly prone to superstition. The fact is, some one has said, that men who deal with enormous, incalculable forces, as statesmen and generals do, have the same temptations as gamblers to indulge in superstition. Beyond what we can see and know remains the province in which we can guess, and our unacknowledged guesses are often as irrational as those of the savage who fancies that the paddle-wheel of a steamer is licked round by the tongue of a great serpent.

Many years ago, we are told, before the days of railways, a nobleman and his lady, with their infant child, were traveling in the depth of winter across Salisbury Plain. A snow-storm overtook them ; their child became ill from the cold, and they were forced to take refuge in a lone shepherd's hut. The wild shepherd and his wife drew near the child in awe and silence. The nurse began undressing it by the warm cottage fire. Silken frock and head-dress did the baby wear. One rich baby-dress came off to reveal another more beautiful. Still the shepherd and his wife looked on with awe. At last the process of undressing was completed, and the now naked baby was being warmed by the fire. Then was it, when all these wrappings and outer husks were peeled off, that the shepherd and his wife, relieved of their superstition, broke silence, exclaiming, "Why, it 's just like one of ours ! "

Allston, the artist, when he was in England, told Coleridge an anecdote of a youth in America who took it into his head to convert a free-thinking companion by appearing as a ghost before him. He accordingly dressed himself up in the usual way, having previously extracted the ball from the pistol which always lay near the head of his friend's bed. Upon first awaking, and seeing the apparition, the youth who was to be frightened very coolly looked his companion the ghost in the face, and said, " I know you. This is a good joke; but you see I am not frightened. Now you may vanish ! " The ghost stood still. " Come," said the other, " that is enough. I shall get angry. Away ! " Still the ghost moved not. " By ——," ejaculated the man in bed, " if you do not in three minutes go away, I 'll shoot you." He waited the time, deliberately leveled the pistol, fired, and with a scream at the immobility of the figure, became convulsed, and afterward died. The very instant he believed it to be a ghost, his human nature fell before it.

In our purblind and crippled state, our superstitions and prejudices are our most convenient crutches. The more ignorant we are, the more necessary they seem to us. Poor auxiliaries, we may say, but better than nothing, in our many extremities. Something we must have to hold to, as we feel our way in the obscurity of our intelligence and reason ; and these poor aids come down to us as a part of the general inheritance of ignorance from the generations that groped before us. To whatever extent we may conceal them, or deny them, or be ashamed of them, in extremity they show themselves, as in death the family likeness comes out which is obscured by individual peculiarities during active life. The old lithograph printer at the Riverside Press told us that it not unfrequently happens that the picture, thought to have been completely ground out of the stone, reappears to contest its successor and confound the printer.

Alas! our ignorance. Our transgressions are quite as often blunders as sins. The Japanese do not swear at one another; they say "Fool!" Cave, who was jailer during the two years Leigh Hunt was a prisoner, had become a philosopher by the force of his situation. He said to Hunt one day, when a new batch of criminals came in, "Poor ignorant wretches, sir!" The Chinese have a profound saying which expresses it: "He who finds pleasure in vice and pain in virtue is a novice in both."

We are told of a traveler who once went all the way from New Zealand to see London. He landed at Poplar, where he stayed till it was time to take ship back again, which he did under the firm belief that he had seen London in all its grandeur. Linnæus considered that a small quantity of moss that could be covered by the hand might be the study of a lifetime. It is asserted that in the very advanced and ramified science of chemistry, fourteen years are required by the student to overtake knowledge as it now stands. That is to say, that to learn what is known, before you can proceed to institute new experiments, fourteen years are necessary — twice the time which the old law of England exacted of an apprentice bound to any trade. It is pronounced by De Quincey to be one of the misfortunes of life, that we must read thousands of books only to discover that we need not have read them. "The modern precept of education very often is (says Sydney Smith) 'Take the admirable Crichton for your model; I would have you ignorant of nothing.' Now my advice on the contrary is, to have the courage to be ignorant of a great number of things, in order to avoid the calamity of being ignorant of every thing." So too, when somebody, in eulogizing a distinguished member of one of the English universities, observed that "science was his forte," Sydney retorted, "and omniscience his foible."

It is true, as a quaint old writer puts it, that the greatest part of our felicity is to be well-born — of parents, in other words, with sound bodies, sound minds, and correct principles, and to inherit the same. Especially, if it be true, as Hazlitt asserts, that "no one ever changes his character from the time he is two years old ; nay, from the time he is two hours old. We may, with instruction and opportunity, mend our manners, or else alter them for the worse, 'as the flesh or fortune shall serve ;' but the character, the internal, original bias remains always the same, true to itself to the very last — 'and feels the ruling passion strong in death.' . . . The color of our lives is woven into the fatal thread at our births ; our original sins and our redeeming graces are infused into us ; nor is the bond, that confirms our destiny, ever canceled."

Nevertheless, against all odds, humanity hopefully exerts herself to overcome every neglect and effect. "This afternoon," says a late writer, " I went into the New England Hospital for Women and Children, and the head physician, a woman, with a rare blending of sweetness and light in her face, took me round through the wards. Presently, we entered that of the children, where were, perhaps, half a dozen little ones of from two to five, with their attendants. How the eyes beamed and the hands began to wave when they saw the welcome face ! In the middle of the floor lay a warm blanket, on which was sprawling a chubby-cheeked, flaxen-haired little fellow of two and a half or three. 'Let me show you how he can help himself on to his feet,' the beaming doctor said. And sure enough, when she had encouragingly reached him her hands, he worked himself up erect in such creditable fashion that I did not wonder at the banners of triumph hung out from his proud little face. 'Two months ago,' she went on to say, 'he was brought here diseased and half-starved. No bones, gristle only, through lack of proper food. But I 'll make a brave little man out of him yet ! ' And her face glowed a look of such genuine delight over her blessed work that I felt an instinctive thrill."

" There are more diminutive and ill-shapen men and women in Rome," says Hawthorne, " than I ever saw elsewhere, a phenomenon to be accounted for, perhaps, by their custom of wrapping the new-born infant in swaddling clothes." Speaking of the customs of the Moravians, Southey remarks : " The system of taking children from their parents, breaking up domestic society, and sorting human beings like cabbage-plants, according to their growth, is not more consonant to nature than the Egyptian method of hatching eggs in ovens : a great proportion of the chickens are said to be produced with some deformity, and hens thus hatched bear a less price than those which have been reared in the natural way, because it often happens that they will not sit upon their eggs,— the course of instinct having been disturbed."

It is stated that when the poet Wordsworth was engaged in composing The White Doe of Rylstone, he received a wound in his foot, and he observed that the continuation of the literary labor increased the irritation of the wound, whereas by suspending his work he could diminish it, and absolute mental rest produced a perfect cure. "Constitution," says Dr. Holmes, in his remarkable Elsie Venner, "has more to do with belief than people think for. I went to the Universalist Church, when I was in the city one day, to hear a famous man whom all the world knows, and I never saw such pewsfull of broad shoulders and florid faces, and substantial, wholesome-looking persons, male and female, in all my life. Why, it was astonishing. Either their creed made them healthy, or they chose it because they were healthy."

If only full-grown men and full-grown women, with sound bodies and sound minds, were suffered to marry ! But conscience, integrity, and reason, have little to do with the divine relation. "A youth marries in haste," says Emerson; "afterward, when his mind is opened to the reason of the conduct of life, he is asked what he thinks of the institution of marriage, and of the right relation of the sexes? 'I should have much to say,' he might reply, 'if the question were open, but I have a wife and children, and all question is closed to me.'" A young man came to say he was about to be married, and to ask what was thought of it. The reply was, "You say you are going to be married; that settles the matter for you. If you had told me you thought of marriage, I might have had something to say of it." "More misery," says an eminent married woman, "comes from the antagonism between man and woman than from all other causes put together; for each starts in life worshiping an ideal being who has no existence in this world." "That so few marriages are observed to be happy," says Montaigne, "is a token of its price and value. If well formed, and rightly taken, 't is the best of all human societies. We cannot live without it, and yet we do nothing but degrade it. It happens as with cages; the birds without despair to get in, and those within despair of getting out." "Did you ever hear my definition of marriage?" asked Sydney Smith. "It is that it resembles a pair of shears, so joined that they cannot be separated; often moving in opposite directions, yet always punishing any one who comes between them." You remember the conceit of the great French satirist, of the man who had been made deaf by his physician, that he might not hear the scoldings of his wife, whose tongue the utmost skill of the surgeon had previously failed to cure of its violence. "Some time after, the doctor asked for his fee of the husband; who answered, that truly he was deaf, and so was not able to understand what the tenor of his demand might be. Whereupon the leech bedusted him with a sort of powder, which rendered him a fool immediately, so great was the stultifying virtue of that strange kind of pulverized dose. Then did this fool of a husband, and his mad wife, join together, and falling on the doctor and the surgeon, did so scratch, bethwack, and bang them, that they were left half dead upon the place, so furious were the blows which they received." "I am well aware," wrote Schiller to Körner, "that of ten men who marry, there are nine who choose their wives to please other people — I choose mine to please myself." Madame de Staël's marriage, like most marriages of policy, was far from being a happy one. When she became a mother, she used sorrowfully to say, "I will force my daughter to make a marriage of inclination."

"The most important thing in life," said Pascal, "is the choice of a profession; yet this is a thing purely in the disposal of chance." And we never stop to consider the effects of occupation upon mind and character. Rösch and Esquirol affirm from observation that indigo-dyers become melancholy, and those who dye scarlet, choleric.

"The high prize of life," says Emerson, "the crowning fortune of a man, is to be born with a bias to some pursuit, which finds him in employment and happiness."

Quin was very proud of his vocation. A peer, who, at least, had wit enough to enjoy Quin's society, had the ill-manners to say, "What a pity it is, Mr. Quin, you are an actor." "Why," said ever-ready James, "what would you have me be? — a lord?"

It has been very truly said that the man who would raise himself to be a power must begin by securing a pecuniary independence. Michelet describes a French peasant on a Sunday morning, walking out in his clean linen and unsoiled blouse. His wife is at church, and this simple farmer paces across his acres and looks fondly at his land. You see him in solitude, but his face is illuminated when he thinks his farm is his own, from the surface of the globe to its centre, and that the climate is his own from the surface of the earth up to the seventh heaven. You find that man, if a stranger approaches him, withdrawing, that he may enjoy his affection in solitude; and as he turns away from his Sunday walk through his own pastures, you notice that he looks back over his shoulder with affection, and parts with regret. He is not at work; he is not out to keep off interlopers; he is out simply to enjoy the feeling of ownership, and to look upon himself as a member of responsible society. His dear possessions are without encumbrance. He owes no man any thing. That hated thing, mortgage — from two French words, meaning death-pledge (death-grip) — does not affright him. Ah! if only every land-owner realized its derivation and full meaning. In the time of Solon a pillar was erected on every piece of mortgaged land, inscribed with the name of the lender and the amount of the loan. Every debtor unable to fulfill his contract was liable to be adjudged as the slave of his creditor, until he could find means either of paying it or working it out; and not only he himself, but his minor sons and unmarried daughters and sisters also, whom the law gave him the power of selling.

The feeling of ownership, which comes of possessing what is the representative of so much toil and painstaking fidelity — of so much self-denial and so much self-sacrifice — amounts to a steady and supporting emotion — it is fruition; and its good effect upon the character, when freed of any feeling of avarice, is hardly estimable, and is not to be depreciated. That nature, somebody has said, is the nearest complete which has the delicate touch, the sheltered fineness, and the sweet calmness of good circumstances, with the robust habit of exertion, and experiences of the realities of poverty; and such natures we believe to be found especially in America.

"I affirm," says Sterne, in one of his sermons, "that

it is not riches which are the cause of luxury, — but the corrupt calculation of the world, in making riches the balance for honor, for virtue, and for every thing that is great and good ; which goads so many thousands on with an affectation of possessing more than they have, and consequently in engaging in a system of expenses they cannot support. In one word, 't is the necessity of appearing to be some body, in order to be so, which ruins the world."

" Pay as you go," said John Randolph, " is the philosopher's stone." " I always say to young people (says Sydney Smith), Beware of carelessness ! no fortune will stand it long ; you are on the high road to ruin the moment you think yourself rich enough to be careless." " Economy," said Voltaire, " is the source of liberality." Thackeray, commending Macaulay's frugality, admonishes : " To save be your endeavor, against the night's coming, when no man may work ; when the arm is weary with long day's labor ; when the brain perhaps grows dark ; when the old, who can labor no more, want warmth and rest, and the young ones call for supper." Crabb Robinson was industrious and frugal that he might withdraw from his profession in time (as Wordsworth expressed it) " for an autumnal harvest of leisure." An aged husbandman, according to the German allegory, was working in his rich and wide-spread fields, at the decline of day, when he was suddenly confronted by a spectral illusion, in the form of a man. " Who, and what are you ?" said the astonished husbandman. " I am Solomon, the wise," was the reply, " and I have come to inquire what you are laboring for ?" " If you are Solomon," said the husbandman, " you ought to know that I am following out the advice you have given. You referred me to the ant for instruction, and hence my toil." " You have," said the apparition, " learnt but half your lesson ; I directed you to labor in the proper season for labor, in order that you might repose in the proper season for repose."

An economist, or a man (says Emerson) who can proportion his means and his ambition, or bring the year round with expenditure which expresses his character, without embarrassing one day of his future, is already a master of life, and a freeman.  Lord Burleigh writes to his son that one ought never to devote more than two-thirds of his income to the ordinary expenses of life, since the extraordinary will be certain to absorb the other third.

A good illustration of the ethics of debt is to be found in Haydon's life-long habit, which was, "to scheme a great work, requiring years of labor, without money of his own to carry him on a month; to borrow, right and left, as he went on, leaving, at the same time, his landlord and his tradesmen unpaid; to defy or pacify, as best he could, the clamor of creditors who thus gathered round his painting room; and then, when the work was finished and sold, to clear off as much of his debt as the price would allow, leave himself penniless, or nearly so, and begin the same process over again.  The result was forty years of ceaseless braggardism and unrest, and a wreck at last."  Cooke, who translated Hesiod, lived twenty years on a translation of Plautus, for which he was always taking subscriptions.  Paschal, historiographer of France, was continually announcing titles of works he was preparing for the press, that his pension for writing on the history of France might not be stopped.  When he died, his historical labors did not exceed six pages!

It was a saying of Aristotle, that some men are as stingy as if they expected to live forever, and some as extravagant as if they expected to die immediately.  In the buried city of Pompeii, near the temple of Isis, was found a prostrate skeleton, and in its hand were clutched three hundred and sixty coins of silver, forty-two of bronze, and eight of gold, wrapped securely in a cloth. He had stopped before his flight to load himself with the treasures of the temple, and was overtaken by the shower of cinders and suffocated.

It has been remarked by an acute writer, that as to the individual it may sometimes be questioned, whether a prudent temperament secures as much of happiness, taking all the years of life together, as a careless and impulsive one. Of all dreary disillusions, the dreariest must be that of the rich old man, who has denied himself every pleasure while he had senses and emotions to taste it, and sits down to partake at the eleventh hour of the feast of life, when appetite is dead, and love has fled, and disease lays its grip on him, and reminds him that it is time to go to that bed which all his balance at the banker's can unfortunately make neither more warm nor soft. But however it may be for the man himself, there can be no doubt that the fewer prudent and frugal persons there are in any country, so much the less prosperous that country will be ; and thus it comes to pass that the land where the principle of wine to-day, water to-morrow, has too many adherents, is (other potent causes aiding to the result) in the condition Ireland has been for centuries back.

A man is said to be rich in proportion to the number of things which he can afford to let alone. You remember the remark of the old philosopher, when passing through the crowded bazaar where every thing attractive and costly was displayed for sale : "How many things there are in this world that I do not want!" A certain Chinese mandarin, who delighted in covering his richly dressed person with precious stones, was one day accosted in the streets of Pekin by a priest of the sect of Fohi, who, bowing very low, thanked him for his jewels. "What does the man mean?" cried the mandarin. "I never gave thee any of my jewels." "No," replied the other; " but you let me look at them, and that is all the use you can make of them yourself; so there is no difference between us, except that you have the trouble of watching them, and that is an employment I do not want." You recollect the odd way the old bookkeeper had of enjoying the vast possessions of the rich old merchant. Bourne owned the fences and the dirt, Titbottom the sky and the landscape. "I don't hesitate to say," said Thomas Hughes (adopting an observation of John Sterling), "that the worst education which teaches simplicity and self-denial is better than the best which teaches all else but this."

"Get of gold," says the Koran, "as much as you need, of wisdom all that you can." With all that you can command of either, happiness will not abide. "Who can tell where happiness may come; or where, though an expected guest, it may never show its face?" A well-known divine, in his wise old age, once said to a newly married pair: "I want to give you this advice, my children — don't try to be happy. Happiness is a shy nymph, and if you chase her you will never catch her; but just go quietly on, and do your duty, and she will come to you."

To enjoy the present, without regret for the past or solicitude for the future, appeared to Goldsmith to be the only general precept respecting the pursuit of happiness that can be applied with propriety to any condition of life. "The whole art of life," wrote Sir William Hamilton, "is really to live all the days of our life; and not with anxious care disturb the sweetest hour that life affords, — which is the present."

"Moderation and prudence in conduct," says La Bruyère, "leave man obscure. To be known and admired, 't is necessary to have great virtues, or, what is perhaps equal, great vices." Boswell's servant, who went with him and Dr. Johnson to the Hebrides, had traveled over a great part of Europe, and spoke many languages.

Johnson, who seldom applied the epithet to any one, pronounced him a " wise man." It has been said by a man of a genius and a renown so great as to render his saying the more remarkable, that if we could become thoroughly acquainted with the biography of any one who has achieved fame, we should find that he had met with some person to fame unknown, whose intellect had impressed him more than that of any of the celebrated competitors with whom it had been his lot to strive. A startling effect is produced upon us, it has also been truly observed, when we suddenly become acquainted with a remarkable person whom we have never seen or heard of, yet who has been long living in the world and long laboring in it ; and who, as we feel at once, must have exercised for all that time a strong intellectual influence in circles of which we did not know the existence.

Forecast is as good as work, is an English proverb. A man should know his opportunity, and seize it when it comes. " A dwarf may be carried on the crest of a wave to the top of a cliff, which a giant could not climb from the beach." Vigilance and adaptability are nearly all to the ordinary man. The Persians have it that a poor man watched a thousand years before the gate of Paradise. Then, when he snatched one little nap,— it opened and shut. Sir James Mackintosh returned with broken health to England from India, where he had been judge of the admiralty court, and recorder of Bombay. " He had been to El Dorado, but had forgotten the gold ; and was obliged to confess to his friends that he was ashamed of his poverty, since it showed a want of common sense." " My opinion is," said Gargantua's instructor, " that we pursue the enemy whilst the luck is on our side ; for Occasion hath all her hair on her forehead ; when she is past you may not recall her, — she hath no tuft whereby you can lay hold on her, for she is bald in the hinder part of the head, and never returneth again."

"It is a maxim worthy of all acceptation," says Emerson, "that a man may have that allowance he takes. Take the place and attitude which belong to you, and all men acquiesce. The world must be just. It leaves every man with profound unconcern, to set his own rate." "So soon as you feel confidence in yourself," said Mephistopheles to Faust, "you know the art of life." Half the failures in life, it is affirmed, arise from pulling in one's horse as he is leaping. We are pusillanimously afraid of ourselves. Alexander perceived that the fury of Bucephalus proceeded merely from the fear he had of his own shadow, whereupon, getting on his back, he ran him against the sun, so that the shadow fell behind, and by that means he tamed the animal. "Walking along Piccadilly with Sheridan," says Kelly, "I asked him if he had told the Queen that he was writing a play. He said he had, and he was actually about one. 'Not you,' said I to him; 'you will never write again; you are afraid to write.' 'Of whom am I afraid?' said he, fixing his penetrating eye on me. I said, 'You are afraid of the author of the School for Scandal.'" But it is recorded of Guido, whose paintings were much sought after, that from mere good-nature and a desire to help unsuccessful artists, he allowed imitations to be made of his works, to which he added one or two touches, that they might be sold as his productions. Is there any where to be found such another instance of liberality at the risk of a great reputation?

Character and powers, early and late, do not much vary. The inspiration of purpose, and work, very soon establish personality. Can any man remember when the radically distinguishing things he stands for first took root within him? Nathaniel Hawthorne, when he was sixteen years old, sent forth, we are told, the first number of The Spectator, a small but neatly printed and well edited paper. A prospectus had been issued only the week before, setting forth that The Spectator would be issued on Wednesdays, " price twelve cents per annum, payment to be made at the end of the year." Among the advertisements on the last page was the following : " Nathaniel Hawthorne proposes to publish, by subscription, a neat edition of The Miseries of Authors, to which will be added a sequel containing facts and remarks drawn from his own experience." The Hawthorne of The Scarlet Letter already existed. An oration delivered by Daniel Webster, July 4, 1802,— then twenty years old, and principal of Fryeburg Academy,— was recently discovered in a mass of the author's private papers which had found their way into a junk shop. The last speech made by Mr. Webster in the Senate, July 17, 1850, concluded with the same peroration with which he closed the Fryeburg oration, forty-eight years before !

Do you remember the words that young Carlyle wrote to his brother, nine years after he had left the University of Edinburgh as a student, forty-three years before he returned as its Rector ? " I say, Jack, thou and I must never falter. Work, my boy, work unweariedly. I swear that all the thousand miseries of this hard fight, and ill-health, the most terrific of them all, shall never chain us down. By the river Styx it shall not. Two fellows from a nameless spot in Annandale shall yet show the world the pluck that is in the Carlyles."

" There are three things, young gentleman," said Nelson to one of his midshipmen, " which you are constantly to bear in mind. Firstly, you must always implicitly obey orders, without attempting to form any opinion of your own respecting their propriety. Secondly, you must consider every man your enemy who speaks ill of your king. Thirdly, you must hate a Frenchman as you do the devil."

A young student asked Sir Vicary Gibbs how he should learn his profession. Sir Vicary : " Read Coke upon

Littleton." Student: "I have read Coke upon Littleton." Sir Vicary: "Read Coke upon Littleton over
again." Student: "I have read it thrice over." Sir
Vicary: "Thrice?" Student: "Yes; three times over
very carefully." Sir Vicary: "You may now sit down
and make an abstract of it."

"What a wedge, what a beetle, what a catapult," exclaims Thoreau, "is an earnest man! What can resist
him?" In 1849, at the time of general depression in
Garibaldi's Italian Revolutionary army, he issued this
proclamation: "In recompense for the love you may
show your country I offer you hunger, thirst, cold, war,
and death; who accepts these terms, let him follow me."
"The Puritans," says Macaulay, "even in the depths of
the prisons to which Elizabeth had sent them, prayed,
and with no simulated fervor, that she might be kept from
the dagger of the assassin, that rebellion might be put
down under her feet, and that her arms might be victori-
ous by sea and land. One of the most stubborn of the
stubborn sect, immediately after one of his hands had
been lopped off by the executioner for an offense into
which he had been hurried by his intemperate zeal,
waved his hat with the hand which was still left him, and
shouted, God save the Queen!"

While General Jackson was President, the small-pox
broke out among his servants, and nearly every body
fled; but the President remained in the White House,
and waited on black and white with unremitting attention.
He did not leave them wholly to the protection of Providence and inefficient help — he helped them himself.
Just before going into battle, Nelson wrote to his wife:
"The lives of all are in the hands of Him who knows
best whether to preserve mine or not; my character and
good name are in my own keeping." After a day's weary
march, Mahomet was camping with his followers. One
said, "I will loose my camel and commit it to God."
"Friend, tie thy camel, and commit it to God."

"**In manners,**" said Madame de Maintenon, "tranquillity **is the** supreme power." Goethe, in a note to Eckermann, refers **to that** "state of tranquil activity, from which views of the world and experiences are evolved in the surest and purest manner." It so often happens, it is observed, that mere activity is a waste of **time,** that people **who** have **a** morbid habit of being busy **are often terrible** time-wasters, whilst, on the contrary, **those who** are judiciously deliberate, and allow themselves intervals **of** leisure, see the **way before** them in those **intervals,** and save time by **the accuracy of** their calculations.

**The** self-possession which distinguished Romilly is an **invariable** characteristic of a truly great mind. Lord Chesterfield used **to say** of a person in a hurry that **he** plainly showed his business was too much for him. **The** Duke of Newcastle, **commemorated** in Humphry **Clinker,** was always in a hurry. It used to be said of him **that** he had lost one hour **in the morning which he was look-**ing for during the rest **of** the day. When Nelson had finished his famous despatch to the Crown Prince **of** Denmark, at the battle of Copenhagen, a wafer was given **him to seal it** with ; but **he ordered** a candle to be **brought from** the cock-pit, and **sealed the letter** with wax, affixing **a larger seal than he** ordinarily used. "This," **said he, " is no time** to appear hurried and informal." "I **remember a** small Mussulman boy," says an officer, in **his** published Recollections of Military Service in India, "**one of our** servants, lying on **the** veranda, apparently **asleep,** when, to our horror, we saw a cobra creep out **of a lot of boots** lying near, which the boy had **been clean-**ing. **The cobra** passed over his face, and actually **darted** his fork in **and** out of his open mouth. The **boy** never stirred, and we remarked how providential it was that he was fast asleep. **The snake after a** time glided off, when the boy jumped up, **and** seized a stick, and killed it. He had been awake **all the** time."

Mirabeau is described by Carlyle as a man stout of heart ; whose popularity was not of the populace, whom no clamor of unwashed mobs without doors, or of washed mobs within, could scare from his way. Dumont remembers hearing him deliver a Report on Marseilles : " every word was interrupted by abusive epithets ; caluminator, liar, assassin, scoundrel : Mirabeau pauses a moment, and, in a honeyed tone, addressing the most furious, says : 'I wait, Messieurs, till these amenities be exhausted.'" "Oliver Cromwell, when that agitator serjeant stept forth from the ranks, with plea of grievances, and began gesticulating and demonstrating, as the mouthpiece of thousands, expectant there, — discerned, with those truculent eyes of his, how the matter lay,— plucked a pistol from his holsters ; blew agitator and agitation instantly out. Noll was a man fit for these things." "It is false," said Napoleon, "that we fired first with blank charge ; it had been a waste of life to do that. . . . The French Revolution is blown into space by it." It is stated that at one of the judicial sittings in Tunis, a Moor approached the throne silently, holding a large sack in his hand, out of which rolled two human heads, bleeding, one a man's, the other a woman's. The Bey looked first at the heads, then at the Moor, and without saying a word, made the sign which meant acquittal. It was simply a husband who discovered his wife was deceiving him.

"A stream," says Landor, "is never so smooth, equable, and silvery, as at the instant before it becomes a cataract. The children of Niobe fell by the arrows of Diana, under a bright and cloudless sky." Mark the quiet of an animal before the fatal spring, and how serene and fair is the complexion of determined rage.

Genuine repose is unconscious. Leigh Hunt said of Sir William Temple, "I believe he talks too much of his ease, to be considered very easy. It is an ill head that takes so much concern about its pillow."

Barnes, editor of the Times newspaper, related to Crabb Robinson that at Cambridge, having had lessons from a boxer, he gave himself airs, and meeting with a fellow sitting on a stile in a field, who did not make way for him as he expected, and as he thought due to a gownsman, he asked what he meant, and said he had a great mind to thrash him. "The man smiled," said Barnes, " put his hand on my shoulder, and said, 'Young man, I 'm Cribb.' I confessed myself delighted ; gave him my hand ; took him to my room, where I had a wine-party, and he was the lion." Cribb was at that time the champion of England! The same writer refers, in his Diary, to another "most interesting party" at Lord Kenyon's. " The lion of the party," he says (on that occasion, of quite another sort), "was Daniel Webster, the American lawyer and orator. He has a strongly marked expression of countenance. So far from being a Republican in the modern sense, he has an air of Imperial strength, such as Cæsar might have had." When Jenny Lind was in Boston, Mr. Webster called upon her. It is said he talked sound sense to her, with dignity and stately courtesy. When he was gone, Jenny jumped up, walked the floor excitedly, clasped her hands, and with indescribable earnestness, exclaimed, "Oh! that is a man! that is a man! I never saw a man before! I never saw a man before!"

How the "godlike Daniel" would have been stirred by the ecstatic praises of the sweet songstress! We all like to be appreciated. Sterne, in replying to the panegyrics of a person who called himself Ignatius Sancho, says very truly, "'T is all affectation to say a man is not gratified with being praised. We only want it to be sincere." It is a maxim of Vauvenargues', "If men did not flatter one another there would be little society ;" and it is a meanness, we say, to be suspecting the motive.

"It was a maxim with Foxey, our reverend father," said Brass (in Old Curiosity Shop) to his sister Sarah, —

"'Always suspect every body.' That's the maxim to go through life with." Dickens moralizes upon the detestable character he was delineating: "It will always happen that men of the world, who go through it in armor, defend themselves from quite as much good as evil; to say nothing of the inconvenience and absurdity of mounting guard with a microscope at all times, and of wearing a coat of mail on the most innocent occasions." The very bad or desperately vicious, fortunately, is exceptional. Interest, instinct, and reason are united against it. God and nature forbid it. It must be rare, and it must generally fail of its purpose, if man and society are to exist and be secure. Courage and virtue, therefore, are not diverted by it or alarmed. Some time before the battle of Dunbar, as Cromwell, accompanied by a number of his officers, was visiting the ground, a Scotch soldier, who had hidden behind a wall which surrounded the field, fired at him, missing his mark. Without being alarmed, and without increasing the gait of his horse, Cromwell went toward the Scotchman, and said, "Bungling rogue! if one of my soldiers had failed in an end so important, he would soon be judged by a council of war."

Flattery, that is evil, and conspiracy, are illustrated in the manner in which the Arabs capture the hyena. Its subterranean abode is described as so narrow as not to permit of the animal turning about in it; and hence, to use the Arabian phraseology, it has "two doors," by one of which it enters, and by the other goes out. The Arabs, lying concealed in the vicinity of one of these dens, watch the particular hole by which the hyena enters, and then proceed to place a strong rope net over the opposite hole, — whilst one of their fraternity, skilled in the business, and prepared with a rope, works his way in by "the door" which the animal has entered. As he nears the brute (which cannot turn upon him) he "charms it," saying, "Come, my dear little creature, I will lead you to places where many carcasses are prepared for you — plenty of food awaits you. Let me fasten this rope to your beautiful leg, and stand quiet while I do so." This sentence, or something very similar to it, is repeated until the operation is effectually achieved; when the daring son of the Sahara gores the brute with a dagger till he is forced to rush out, and he is caught in the net, and either killed on the spot or is carried off alive. If any blunder happens, however — as is sometimes the case — through which the hyena is enabled to struggle and re-enter its abode, the "charmer," in spite of his charming, falls a victim to its savage rage, and frequently his companions can scarcely contrive to get clear without feeling something of its effects.

It is pronounced a characteristic of wisdom not to dispute things. "There is," says Sherlock, "no dispute managed without passion, and yet there is scarce a dispute worth a passion." A modern English writer is said to have been very fond of controversy for its own sake, and once at dinner to have roared out to some one at the end of the table, "I totally disagree with you. What was it you said?" On one occasion, when they were together, Dr. Campbell said something, and Dr. Johnson began to dispute it. "Come," said Campbell, "we do not want to get the better of one another; we want to increase each other's ideas." Johnson took it in good part, and the conversation then went on coolly and instructively. When the erudite Casaubon visited the Sorbonne they showed him the hall in which, as they proudly told him, disputations had been held for four hundred years. "And what," said he, "have they decided?" On first nights, in the time of Voltaire, when partisans were unusually excited, each spectator was asked, as he entered the parquette, "Do you come to hiss?" "Yes." "Then sit over there." But if he answered, "I come to applaud," he was directed to the other side. Thus the two belligerent bodies were massed for more effective action.

The young Smiths, we are told, employed their information in disputing with one another. "The result," says Sydney, "was to make us the most intolerable and overbearing set of boys that can well be imagined, till later in life we found our level in the world." Franklin relates that he had contracted in youth the same litigious habit by reading the controversial books on religion which formed his father's little library. "Persons," he adds, "of good sense, I have since observed, seldom fall into it, except lawyers, university men, and generally men of all sorts who have been bred in Edinburgh." It would perhaps have been juster to say, that persons of good sense, like himself and Sydney Smith, soon discover that the practice is displeasing, and lay it aside. "We are told," says Sydney further, "'Let not the sun go down on your wrath.' This, of course, is best; but, as it generally does, I would add, Never act or write till it has done so. This rule has saved me from many an act of folly. It is wonderful what a different view we take of the same event four and twenty hours after it has happened."

"I asserted that the world was mad," exclaimed a poor philosopher, "and the world said that I was mad, and, confound them, they outvoted me." In Hawthorne's American Note-Books a memorandum is made of a sketch to be given of a modern reformer. "He goes about the streets haranguing most eloquently, and is on the point of making many converts, when his labors are suddenly interrupted by the appearance of the keeper of a mad-house, whence he had escaped."

A thick-headed squire being worsted by Sydney Smith in an argument, took his revenge by exclaiming: "If I had a son that was an idiot, by Jove, I'd make him a parson." "Very probable," replied Sydney; "but I see your father was of a very different mind."

An anecdote which Robert Hall told of himself is instructive. He set out to defend the doctrine of the Trinity, in a series of sermons. In prosecuting the discussion, he attacked the various forms of heretical dissent from the orthodox opinion. At the conclusion of his discourses, much to his surprise, he discovered that there was a small party in the congregation for each of the heresies which he had combated, but which most of his hearers had probably never heard of before he made his onset upon them. One should be sure, before he raises the devil, that he is able to lay him.

Many people work themselves up by disputation somewhat as Macready worked himself up for his great parts on the stage. "Mr. Macready, you know," said a director of Her Majesty's Theatre, "when engaging his dresser, whom I knew very well, arranged that when he shook him he should pay him double wages, and when he struck him his pay should be trebled. I think that dresser used to get treble wages all the while Macready was at Drury Lane. I went once to Macready's dressing-room during the performance. The tragedian had the dresser in the corner and was nearly choking him. He was rehearsing his part. He afterward rushed upon the stage and startled his audience by his brilliant acting."

You doubtless recollect Voltaire's definition of a physician — an unfortunate gentleman, expected every day to perform a miracle, — namely, to reconcile health with intemperance. Emerson speaks of the unhappy condition where brains are paralyzed by stomach. A celebrated French physician, the first time he was called into a house, always began by running into the kitchen, embracing the cook, and thanking him for a new patient. "There was a Lord Russell," said Pope to Spence, "who, by living too luxuriously, had quite spoiled his constitution. He did not love sport, but used to go out with his dogs every day, only to hunt for an appetite. If he felt any thing of that, he would cry out, 'Oh, I have found it!' turn short round and ride home again, though ·

they were in the midst of the finest chase. It was this lord, who, when he met a beggar, and was entreated by him to give him something because he was almost famished with hunger, called him a ' happy dog ! ' and envied him too much to relieve him."

Kinglake describes a " savagely happy " party he saw, as he lay one night on the banks of the river Jordan. " A little distance from me," he says, " the Arabs made a fire, round which they sat in a circle. They were made most savagely happy by the tobacco with which I supplied them, and they had determined to make the whole night one smoking festival. The poor fellows had only one broken bowl, without any tube at all, but this morsel of a pipe they passed round from one to the other, allowing to each a fixed number of whiffs. In this way they passed the whole night."

In that land of monotony and poverty, a very little thing is a great event. It is said there are artisan families in India, and also in Damascus, who have worked at the same work day by day for a thousand years ; peasant families who have not only tilled the same fields, but have gone into them and left them at the same hour, according to the season, from a period before the birth of Christ. They have no wish for change, no ambition to do better, no inclination to roam, no sense of failure because they are as their forefathers were, and as their sons will be. With such a people, any extreme is but natural — it is philosophical. " If we throw a silver coin upon a table," says Sir Charles Bell, "and fix the eye upon the centre of it, when we remove the coin there is, for a moment, a white spot in its place, which presently becomes deep black. If we put a red wafer upon a sheet of paper and look upon it, and continue to keep the eye fixed on the same point, upon removing the wafer, the spot where it lay on the white paper will appear green. If we look · upon a green wafer in the same manner and remove it, the spot will be red ; if upon blue or indigo, the paper will appear yellow. These phenomena are to be explained by considering that the nerve is exhausted by the continuance of the impression, and becomes more apt to receive sensation from an opposite color."

"The most exquisitely delicate artists in literature and painting," says a writer upon The Intellectual Life, "have frequently had reactions of incredible coarseness. With the Châteaubriand of Atala there existed an obscene Châteaubriand that would burst forth occasionally in talk that no biographer would repeat. I have heard (he says) the same thing of the sentimental Lamartine. We know that Turner, dreamer of enchanted landscapes, took the pleasures of a sailor on the spree. A friend said to me of one of the most exquisite living geniuses : 'You can have no conception of the coarseness of his tastes ; he associates with the very lowest women, and enjoys their rough brutality.' "

It has been remarked, that the chief lesson of the lives of Byron, or Shelley, or Burns, is how much their inspiration cost ; but we do not admire the inspiration less because it was visibly at the cost of the life.

Matthew Bramble, in Humphry Clinker, writing to his old friend, Dr. Lewis, says : " I begin to think I have put myself on the superannuated list too soon, and absurdly sought for health in the retreats of laziness. I am persuaded that all valetudinarians are too sedentary, too regular, and too cautious. We should sometimes increase the motion of the machine, to unclog the wheels of life ; and now and then take a plunge amidst the waves of excess, in order to case-harden the constitution. I have often found a change of company as necessary as a change of air, to promote a vigorous circulation of the spirits, which is the very essence and criterion of good health." Madame de Sévigné wrote to her daughter, " Be not uneasy about my health ; the rule I observe at present is, to be irregular." Luther advised a young scholar, perplexed with foreordination and free-will, to get well drunk.

The night air was thought to be detrimental to the health of Theodore Hook, and his method of avoiding it was peculiar. Planché refers to it in a pleasant manner. "It was day-break," says the dramatist, "broad daylight, in fact, before we separated. I had given an imitation of Edmund Kean and Holland, in Maturin's tragedy of Bertram, which had amused Hook; and, as we were getting our hats, he asked me where I lived. On my answering ' at Brompton,' he said, ' Brompton ! — Why that 's in my way home — I live at Fulham. Jump into my cabriolet, and I will set you down.' The sun of a fine summer morning was rising as we passed Hyde Park Corner. ' I have been very ill,' said Hook, 'for some time, and my doctors told me never to be out of doors after dark, as the night air was the worst thing for me. I have taken their advice. I drive into town at four o'clock every afternoon, dine at Crockford's, or wherever I may be invited, and never go home till this time in the morning. I have not breathed the night air for the last two months.' "

It is reported by Suidas that there was a great book of old, of King Solomon's writing, which contained medicines for all manner of diseases, and lay open still as the people came into the temple ; but Hezekiah, King of Jerusalem, caused it to be taken away, because it made the people secure, to neglect their duty in calling and relying upon God, out of a confidence in those remedies. God's remedies are temperance, exercise, and air. "Oh, temperance !" apostrophizes healthy John Buncle. "Divine temperance ! Thou art the support of the other virtues, the preserver and restorer of health, and the protracter of life ! Thou art the maintainer of the dignity and liberty of rational beings, from the wretched inhuman slavery of sensuality, taste, custom, and example ; and the brightener of the understanding and memory ! Thou art the sweetener of life and all its comforts, the companion of reason, and guard of the passions! Thou art the bountiful rewarder of thy admirers and followers, thine enemies praise thee, and thy friends with rapturous pleasure raise up a panegyric in thy praise." Andrew Tiraqueau, to whom Rabelais wrote some of his epistles, is said (by his biographer), "yearly to have given a book, and by one wife, a son to the world, during thirty years, though he never drank any thing but water."

"For my part," says the venerable William Howitt, "seeing the victims [of society and late hours] daily falling around me, I have preferred the enjoyment of a sound mind in a sound body, the blessings of a quiet, domestic life, and a more restricted, but not less enjoyable circle. I am now fast approaching my seventieth year. I cannot, indeed, say that I have reached this period, active and vigorous as I am, without the assistance of the doctors. I have had the constant attendance of four famous ones — temperance, exercise, good air, and good hours. Often, in earliest years, I labored with my pen sixteen hours a day. I never omit walking three or four miles, or more, in all weathers. I work hard in my garden, and could tire down a tolerable man at that kind of thing. During my two years' travel in Australia, when about sixty, I walked, often under a burning sun, of from one hundred and twenty to one hundred and thirty degrees at noon, my twenty miles a day for days and weeks together; worked at digging gold in great heat and against young, active men my twelve hours a day, sometimes standing in a track. I waded through rivers — for neither man nor nature had made many bridges — and let my clothes dry upon my back; washed my own linen, made and baked my own bread, slept constantly under the forest tree, and, through it all was hearty as a roach. And how did I manage all this, not only with ease, but with enjoyment? Simply because I avoided spirituous liquors, as I would avoid the poison of an asp."

"A year or so ago," said Chief Justice **Parsons**, "while conversing with Dr. James Jackson, I happened to remark that, at my age, I felt as if one's days must be few, and the capacity of usefulness well-nigh exhausted. 'You mistake there,' said he. 'At sixty, a man in fair health may enter upon a series of years equal in usefulness and happiness to those of any period, provided proper precautions are taken and proper habits formed.' And upon further inquiry into these essentials or conditions, I found he summed them up in 'employment without labor; exercise without weariness; temperance without abstinence.'"

It was the opinion of Grattan that the most healthy exercise for elderly persons was indolent movement in the open air.

"Nervousness," said Hunt, "I learned to prevent by violent exercise. All fits of nervousness ought to be anticipated as much as possible with exercise. Indeed, a proper, healthy mode of life would save most people from these effeminate ills, and most likely cure even their inheritors."

Carlyle records one of his walks. "At 8 p. m. I got well to Dumfries, the longest walk I ever made, fifty-four miles in one day." Professor Wilson once walked as much as seventy miles in the same time. Dickens was a great pedestrian — walking again and again from his place at Gad's Hill to London and back again in a day. Lord Macaulay's long afternoon walks through every part of London are familiar to all.

Gibbon took very little exercise. He had been staying for a length of time with Lord Sheffield in the country; and when he was about to go away, the servants could not find his hat. "Bless me," said Gibbon, "I certainly left it in the hall on my arrival here." He had not stirred out of doors during the whole of the visit.

Plato thought exercise would almost cure a guilty conscience. Sydney Smith said, "You will never break down in a speech on the day when you have walked twelve miles."

There is a story in the Arabian Nights' of a king who had long languished under an ill habit of body, and had taken abundance of remedies to no purpose. At length, says the fable, a physician cured him by the following method: he took an hollow ball of wood, and filled it with several drugs; after which he closed it up so artificially that nothing appeared. He likewise took a mall, and after having hollowed the handle and that part which strikes the ball, he inclosed in them several drugs after the same manner as in the ball itself. He then ordered the sultan, who was his patient, to exercise himself early in the morning with these rightly prepared instruments, till such time as he should sweat; when, as the story goes, the virtue of the medicaments perspiring through the wood, had so good an influence on the sultan's constitution, that they cured him of an indisposition which all the compositions he had taken inwardly had not been able to remove. This Eastern allegory is finely contrived to show us how beneficial bodily labor is to health, and that exercise is the most effectual physic. We ought to be ashamed of an indigestion which brisk movement out of doors would effectually drive out through the two or three million pores in two or three hours.

Professor Smith, at one time in the medical chair at Dartmouth, gave the last ten years of his life to the poor. The Professor, in talking with Mr. Webster about his experience with the diseases of the poor, said that he thought there was more suffering from want of proper ventilation than from disease itself. He added, that it had been very much impressed upon his mind that people did not know the value of good ventilation. He often had been called to cases of fevers and the like among poor people; and, upon arriving at the house, he would find, perhaps, nobody but a child in attendance, — the husband and sons being away at work. He had often, before even feeling the pulse of the patient, gone to the woodshed, taken wood and split it up, carried it in-doors in his own arms, built a fire, and thrown open the windows; and he could see the patient begin to revive before he had thought of medicine.

Had God Almighty intended we should stint ourselves in air, is it at all likely he would have poured it out all round the world forty miles deep?

The Persians express a taste for out-doors very forcibly. In Bombay the Parsees use the Victoria Gardens chiefly to walk in, — as they express it, "to eat the air." Their enjoyment of it is more than animal — it is super-sensual.

We take care of our health; we lay up money; we make our roof tight, and our clothing sufficient; but who, asks Emerson, provides that he shall not be wanting in the best property of all, — friends? The question was once put to Aristotle how we ought to behave to our friends; and the answer he gave was, "As we should wish our friends to behave to us." "I look (says Emerson again) upon the simple and childish virtues of veracity and honesty as the root of all that is sublime in character. Speak as you think, be what you are, pay your debts of all kinds. I prefer to be owned as sound and solvent, and my word as good as my bond, and to be what cannot be skipped, or dissipated, or undermined, to all the éclat in the universe." "No man," said Sir Walter Raleigh, "is wise or safe but he that is honest." "There is scarce any character so rare," says Sterne, in one of his sermons, "as a man of real, open, and generous integrity; — who carries his heart in his hand, — who says the thing he thinks, and does the thing he pretends. Though no one can dislike the character, yet discretion generally shakes her head, and the world soon lets him into the reason." When you find a person a little better than his word, a little more liberal than his promise, a little more than borne out in his statement by his facts, a little larger in deed than in speech, you recognize, says Holmes, a kind of eloquence in that person's utterance not laid down in Blair or Campbell. It is said that coming into the presence of the Apollo, the body insensibly assumes a nobler posture. It seems that there are moral and intellectual natures of such purity and elevation and strength, that one insensibly assumes a more upright and noble attitude in the serene presence of their spotless lives. The homage we unconsciously pay to worth is illustrated by the sensitive plant of South America. When a large surface of ground is covered the effect of walking over it is said to be impressive. At each step the plants for some distance round suddenly droop, as if struck with awe, and a broad track of prostrate herbage, several feet wide, is distinctly marked out by the different color of the closed leaflets.

Washington Allston, called, in Rome, the American Titian, on one occasion, when crippled in resources in London, having sold a picture for a considerable sum, as he sat alone at evening, the idea occurred to him that the subject, to a perverted taste and prurient imagination, might have an immoral effect ; he instantly returned the money and regained and destroyed the painting. There is an account of an old merchant, who, on his death-bed, divided the results of long years of labor. " It is little enough, my boys," were almost the last words of the old man ; " but there is n't a dirty shilling in the whole of it." A gentleman that had a trial at the assizes sent Sir Matthew Hale a buck for his table ; so, according to Bishop Burnet, his biographer, when he heard the man's name, he asked if he were not the same person that had sent him venison ; and, finding he was the same, he told him he could not suffer the trial to go on till he had paid him for his buck. To which the gentleman answered, that he never sold his venison ; that he had done nothing to him that he did not do to every judge that had gone that circuit, which was confirmed by several gentlemen then present; but all would not do, for the lord chief baron had learned from Solomon, that a gift perverteth the way of judgment, and therefore he would not suffer the trial to go on till he had paid for the present ; upon which the gentleman withdrew the record.

Albert Gallatin held the office of Secretary of the Treasury through three presidential terms, under Jefferson and Madison, till 1813. Amongst the special missions of importance to which he was appointed was one to England in 1818. While in this office he rendered some essential service to Alexander Baring in the negotiation of a loan for the French Government. Mr. Baring in return pressed him to take a part of the loan, offering him such advantages in it that without advancing any funds he could have realized a fortune. " I thank you," was Gallatin's reply ; " I will not accept your obliging offer, because a man who has had the direction of the finances of his country as long as I have should not die rich." Which memorable answer is not more memorable than a sentence in a private letter written to the author of this composition by the daughter of Robert W. Tayler, Comptroller of the Treasury for sixteen years, from 1862 till the day of his death, and through whose hands passed the vouchers for thousands of millions. "At father's death," says Miss Jennie, " we were left dependent upon ourselves. I speak of this because you were his friend, and because it is something of a matter of pride with me, that he lived and died a poor man."

"As things are," says Froude, "we have little idea of what a human being ought to be. After the first rudimental conditions we pass at once into meaningless generalities ; and with no knowledge to guide our judgment, we allow it to be guided by meaner principles ; we respect money, we respect rank, we respect ability — character is as if it had no existence. How little respect do we pay to the breach of this or that commandment in comparison to ability? So wholly impossible is it to apply the received opinions on such matters to practice, to treat men known to be guilty of what theology calls deadly sins, as really guilty of them, that it would almost seem we had fallen into a moral anarchy; that ability alone is what we regard, without any reference at all, except in glaring and outrageous cases, to moral disqualifications."

Joubert had a bad opinion of the lion when he learned that his step is oblique. It is Machiavelian morals, that virtue itself a man should not trouble himself to obtain, but only the appearance of it to the world, because the credit and reputation of virtue is a help, but the use of it is an impediment.

Thackeray once lost a pocket-book, containing a passport and a couple of modest ten-pound notes. The person who found the article ingenuously put it into the box of the post-office, and it was faithfully restored to the owner; but somehow the two ten-pound notes were absent. It was, however, a great comfort to the great novelist to get the passport, and the pocket-book, which was worth about nine pence.

The cunning of Louis XI. admitted to one or two peculiar forms of oath the force of a binding obligation, which he denied to all others, strictly preserving the secret, which mode of swearing he really accounted obligatory, as one of the most valuable of state mysteries.

"I heard Le Sage say," said Spence, "I thank God, I don't wish for any one thing that I could not pray for aloud." Madame du Deffand objected to praying not to be led into temptation, on the ground that she had found temptation very pleasant. She also disliked praying to be made good, for fear that she should be taken at her word. She did not believe with Jerrold, that conscience, be it ever so little a worm while we live, grows suddenly to a serpent on our death-bed. "My lord cardinal," said Anne of Austria to Richelieu, "there is one fact which you seem to have entirely forgotten. God is a sure paymaster. He may not pay at the end of every week or month or year; but I charge you, remember that he pays in the end."

There are three sorts of lies, in the judgment of Mahomet, which will not be taken into account at the last judgment: 1st, one told to reconcile two persons at variance; 2d, that which a husband tells when he promises any thing to his wife; and, 3d, a chieftain's word in time of war. Joe Gargery made no exceptions. "Lies is lies," he said to Pip. "Howsoever they come, they did n't ought to come, and they come from the father of lies, and work round to the same. Don't you tell no more of them, Pip. . . . Lookee here, Pip, at what is said to you by a true friend. Which this to you the true friend says. If you cah't get to be oncommon through going straight, you 'll never get to do it through going crooked. So don't tell no more on 'em, Pip, and live well and die happy." Lying, in the opinion of Leigh Hunt, is the commonest and most conventional of all the vices. It pervades, more or less, every class of the community, and is fancied to be so necessary to the carrying on of human affairs, that the practice is tacitly agreed upon; nay, in other terms, openly avowed. In the monarch, it is kingcraft. In the statesman, expediency. In the churchman, mental reservation. In the lawyer, the interest of his client. In the merchant, manufacturer, and shopkeeper, secrets of trade. There is no lie, said John Sterling, that many men will not believe; there is no man who does not believe many lies; and there is no man who believes only lies.

It is the conclusion of Professor Venable, that many

teachers of morality destroy the good effect of judicious counsel by too much talk, as a chemical precipitate is redissolved in an excess of the precipitating agent. If you would convince a man that he does wrong, said Thoreau, do right. But do not care to convince him. Men will believe what they see. Let them see. Dr. Telfair, a philosopher and a Christian, used to insist that the doctrine of the Golden Rule is not to be preached, but only to be announced. It is for self-application — to be received and acted on by each one, and not to be taught by him to another. A rule, some one has said, which you do not apply, is no rule at all. " My father," said the Attic Philosopher, " feared every thing that had the appearance of a lesson. He used to say that virtue could make herself devoted friends, but she did not take pupils ; therefore he was not anxious to teach goodness ; he contented himself with sowing the seeds of it, certain that experience would make them grow." "Goodness," said Lamb, "blows no trumpet, nor desires to have it blown." "I hoped for much advantage," said Leslie, "from studying under such a master as Fuseli, but he said little in the Acad my. He generally came into the room once in the course of every evening, and rarely without a book in his hand. He would take any vacant place among the students, and sit reading nearly the whole time he stayed with us. I believe he was right. For those students who are born with powers that will make them eminent, it is sufficient to place fine works of art before them. They do not want instruction, and those that do are not worth it. Art may be learnt, but cannot be taught."

Plutarch says of Julius Cæsar that he won all his battles by saying to his soldiers, "come," rather than "go." So it is in morality, thought James Freeman Clarke. Who are those who have done us good? Who but those whose goodness has inspired us with love of virtue? Not denunciation, but example, touches the heart. That is why the martyrs' blood is the seed of the church. We had been denouncing slavery as sin, with small apparent effect, but when John Brown went down into Virginia, and died on the scaffold out of love for the slave, there came a sudden inspiration to us all. The brave Sir Jacob Astley's prayer, immediately before the advance, at the battle of Edgehill, was short and fervent. "O, Lord, thou knowest how busy I must be this day. If I forget thee, do not thou forget me. Come on, boys!" At one time Nelson's ship, the Boreas, was full of young midshipmen, of whom there were not less than thirty on board; and happy were they whose lot it was to be placed with such a captain. If he perceived that a boy was afraid at first going aloft, he would say to him in a friendly manner, "Well, sir, I am going a race to the mast-head, and beg that I may meet you there." The poor little fellow instantly began to climb, and got up how he could, — Nelson never noticed in what manner; but when they met at the top, spoke cheerfully to him; and would say, how much any person was to be pitied who fancied that getting up was either dangerous or difficult.

Humanity — human nature — within and without — is well illustrated in the baobab-tree of Africa. Dr. Livingstone, in his Missionary Travels, describes it. The description is interesting in itself, and interesting for the purpose we use it. "No external injury, not even fire, can destroy the tree from without; nor can any injury be done from within, as it is quite common to find it hollow. Nor does cutting down exterminate it, for I saw instances in Angola in which it continued to grow in length after it was lying on the ground. Those trees called exogenous grow by means of successive layers on the outside. The inside may be dead, or even removed altogether, without affecting the life of the tree. The other class is called endogenous, and increases by layers applied to the inside ; and when the hollow there is full, the growth is stopped — the tree must die. Any injury is felt most severely by the first class on the bark — by the second on the inside ; while the inside of the exogenous may be removed and the outside of the endogenous may be cut, without stopping the growth in the least."

In Dickens's Miss Havisham, "the vanity of sorrow had become a master mania, like the vanity of penitence, the vanity of remorse, the vanity of unworthiness, and other monstrous vanities that have been curses in this world." Holmes describes the widow Rowans in "the full bloom of ornamental sorrow. A very shallow crape bonnet, frilled and froth-like, allowed the parted raven hair to show its glossy smoothness. A jet pin heaved upon her bosom with every sigh of memory, or emotion of unknown origin. Jet bracelets shone with every movement of her slender hands, cased in close-fitting black gloves. Her sable dress was ridged with manifold flounces, from beneath which a small foot showed itself from time to time, clad in the same hue of mourning. Every thing about her was dark, except the whites of her eyes and the enamel of her teeth. The effect was complete. Gray's Elegy was not a more complete composition."

"You once observed to me," wrote Dr. Channing to Lucy Aiken, "that every where the Sovereign is worshiped ; with us, that sovereign is an idol called Gentility, and costly are the offerings laid upon the altar. Dare to make conversation in the most accomplished society something of an exercise of the mind, and not a mere dissipation, and you instantly become that thing of horror, a Bore."

That caustic satirist, Jerrold, says, "There are a good many pious people who are as careful of their religion as of their best service of china, only using it on holiday occasions, for fear it should get chipped or flawed in working-day wear." "Eve," says the same wicked wit, "ate the apple, that she might dress."

Emerson, in one of his Essays, expresses the opinion that "The end of all political struggle is to establish morality as the basis of all legislation. 'T is not free institutions, 't is not a democracy that is the end, — no, but only the means. Morality is the end of government. We want a state of things in which crime will not pay, a state of things which allows every man the largest liberty compatible with the liberty of every other man." Man, it is very truly said, will not be made temperate or virtuous by the strong hand of the law, but by the teaching and influence of moral power. A man is no more made sober by act of parliament than a woman is made chaste.

"They that cry down moral honesty," said old John Selden, "cry down that which is a great part of religion, my duty towards God, and my duty towards man. What care I to see a man run after a sermon, if he cozens and cheats as soon as he comes home." "If thou hadst but discretion, Sancho, equal to thy natural abilities, thou mightest take to the pulpit, and go preaching about the world." "A good liver is the best preacher," replied Sancho, " and that is all the divinity I know." "Or need know," responded the Don.

"There are," said Miss Spence, in John Buncle, "heavenly-mindedness, and contempt of the world, and choosing rather to die than commit a moral evil. Such things, however, are not much esteemed by the generality of Christians: Most people laugh at them, and look upon them as indiscretions; therefore there is but little true Christianity in the world. It has never," she said, "been my luck to meet with many people that had these three necessary qualifications."

One day, when some one remarked, "Christianity is part and parcel of the law of the land," Rolfe, afterward Lord Chancellor of England, whispered to a barrister near by, "Were you ever employed to draw an indictment against a man for not loving his neighbor as himself?"

An eminent German saw a poor old woman at a station of a calvary in Bavaria, who was crawling on her knees up the hill. She told her story. A rich lady who had sinned was required by her confessor to go on her knees as many times up the calvary; but she might do it by deputy. She paid this poor woman 24 kreutzers (17 cents) for a day's journey on her knees, "which," said the woman, "is poor wages for a day's hard labor; and I have three children to maintain. And unless charitable souls give me more, my children must go half fed."

Every body is familiar with a class of assassins in British India (now happily nearly exterminated), organized into a society, with chiefs, a service, a free-masonry, and even a religion, which has its fanaticism, and its devotion, its agents, its emissaries, its assistants, its moving bodies, its passive comrades who contribute by their subscriptions to "the good work." Comte de Warren describes it in his work on British India. "It is a community of Thugs, a religious and working confraternity, who war against the human race by exterminating them, and whose origin is lost in the night of ages. The foundation of the Thuggee confraternity is a religous belief, the worship of Bohwanie, a dark divinity who loves nothing but carnage, and hates especially the human race. Her most acceptable sacrifices are human victims, and the more of these are offered up in this world, the more will you be recompensed in the next by joys of the soul and the senses, and by females always young, fresh, and lovely. If the assassin should meet with the scaffold in his career, he dies with enthusiasm, a martyr whom a palm awaits. To obey his divine mistress, he murders, without anger and without remorse, the old man, the woman, and the child. To his colleagues he must be charitable, humane, generous, devoted, sharing all in common, because they, as well as he, are ministers and adopted children of Bohwanie."

"The fasts of the Greek church," Kinglake tells us, "produce an ill effect upon the character of the people, for they are carried to such an extent, as to bring about a bonâ fide mortification of the flesh ; the febrile irritation of the frame operating in conjunction with the depression of spirits occasioned by abstinence, will so far answer the object of the rite, as to engender some religious excitement, but this is of a morbid and gloomy character, and it seems to be certain, that along with the increase of sanctity, there comes a fierce desire for the perpetration of dark crimes. The number of murders committed during Lent is reported greater than at any other time of the year."

As an instance of the little influence the religion of the Italians had upon their morals, Hiram Powers told Hawthorne of one of his servants, who desired leave to set up a small shrine of the Virgin in her room — a cheap print, or bas relief, or image, such as are sold every where at the shops — and to burn a lamp before it ; she engaging, of course, to supply the oil at her own expense. By and by her oil-flask appeared to possess a miraculous property of replenishing itself, and Mr. Powers took measures to ascertain where the oil came from. It turned out that the servant had all the time been stealing the oil from him, and keeping up her daily sacrifice and worship to the Virgin by this constant theft. Hawthorne's wife came in contact with a pickpocket at the entrance of an Italian church ; and, failing in his enterprise upon her purse, he passed in, dipped his thieving fingers in the holy-water, and paid his devotion at a shrine. Missing the purse, he said his prayers, in the hope, perhaps, that the saint would send him better luck another time.

"It is easier," says a thoughtful English writer, "to be a learned man than a good man. Why morals should be so difficult, stirs another and a deeper question ; for we must suppose that there is a wisdom in the fact. A question of creeds is but a petty question at any time. The real question lies deeper."

In England, Theodore Parker met an Episcopal clergyman whose liberal sentiments enticed him into conversation. "I asked him," said the American divine, "if it were not possible for all classes of Christians to agree to differ about theological symbols, ceremonies, disciplines, modes, and the like, while they fell back on the great principles of religion and morality; in a word, on religion and morality themselves; and I told him that I had aimed in my humble way to bring this about. He said he liked the plan much, and did not see why all should not unite on these principles as they were expressed in the Thirty-Nine Articles." When Oliver Cromwell was contending for the mastery, he besieged a certain Catholic town. The place made a stout resistance; but at length, being about to be taken, the poor Catholics proposed terms of capitulation, among which was one stipulating for the toleration of their religion. The paper containing the conditions being presented to Cromwell, he put on his spectacles, and, after deliberately examining it, cried out, "Oh, yes; granted, granted, certainly; but," he added, with stern determination, "if one of them shall dare be found attending mass, he shall be instantly hanged!"

It is not improbable, if the disposition of a great part of the clergy continues, to give less and less attention to what the world esteems as morals, apart from what they esteem religion, that a system of schools will arise, in which radical morals, as an essential part of religion, will be taught to the people. Attempts to divorce them, only tend to weaken and confuse the public conscience, while they diminish the influence of spiritual leaders.

The time may come also, we opine, when chairs of common sense will be set up in the universities. The trouble may be to fill them ; but suitable men, when wanted, will be found. The distinction between scholarship and usefulness will be better defined. Boys will more and more be educated for the uses of education; and so much that must be unlearned will give place to what may be applied.

The sculptor Chantrey pointed out to one of his friends the bad effects of light from two windows falling on a column in the Louvre, and said, " The ancients worked with a knowledge of the place where the statue was to be, and anticipated the light to which it would be exposed." In like manner, education should be adapted to the character and wants of each individual, anticipating, as far as practicable, occupation and position in life.

" What is true by the lamp is not always true by the sun," says Joubert. The bad effect — perhaps the only bad effect — of education is what has been called " its inflating tendency — to turn the educated into a clique or caste who think of those who have no education as the Pharisees thought of the 'accursed' people who knew not the law."

The boy should be taught to have some apprehension of the diffusion and universality of intelligence ; that no man has it all, but every man a little ; that the average is always worthy of respectful consultation ; that the education of the schools is but as the scaffolding and tools to the builder (bearing in mind all the time that the building that is to endure is not made with hands) ; that the hodman and the farm hand must teach him many things he must know ; that the Commentaries of Cæsar — valuable enough for culture — and the maxims of philosophy, must give way again and again, and without humiliation, to the commonest experience of the meanest man, whom he would despise till he has fairly put his mind and fact to his in the conflict of affairs ; in fine, that he must surrender his self-conceit, be put upon his feet with the crowd, **and totally** unlearn and forget **very** much that he **has learned before he can** begin to be truly **sensible and wise.**

Sensible men, it is truly said, are very rare. A sensible man does not brag, avoids introducing **the names of his** creditable companions, omits **himself as habitually as** another man obtrudes himself **in the discourse, and is** content with putting his **fact** or theme simply **on its ground.** Conduct **is** three-fourths of life, **thought** Matthew Arnold, and a **man** who **works** for conduct, therefore, **works for more** than a man who **works** for intelligence. **"I always feel** happy near Meyer," said Eckermann, **"probably because** he is a self-relying, satisfied person, **who** takes but little **notice of** the circumstances around him, but at suitable intervals exhibits his own comfortable soul. At the same time, he is every where well grounded, possesses the greatest treasures **of** knowledge, and **a** memory to which the most remote **events** are as present as if they happened yesterday. He has a **preponderance** of understanding which might make us **dread him,** if it **did not** rest upon the noblest **culture ; but, as it** is, his **quiet presence** is always agreeable, always instructive."

**Life should teach** us **our** deficiencies, and our industry should supply them. **The Moravian** missionaries very **soon found out and acknowledged that they** must teach **their converts to count the number three before** they **taught them the doctrine of the Trinity.**

Immorality, **as before affirmed, is often only ignorance.** **A set of constituents** once **waited upon the member of** parliament **whom** they had **chosen, to request that he** would **vote against the** Minister. **"What !"** he answered, with **an oath ; "have I** not bought you **? and do you think** I will **not sell you ? "**

**How to** live with **unfit companions, is an** important **part of** education ; **for, with such, said a** wise man, life is **for the** most part spent : **and** experience teaches little better than our earliest instinct of self-defense, namely, not to engage, not to mix yourself in any manner with them; but let their madness spend itself unopposed.

A sensible man considers his situation, and is careful not to over-estimate himself. His ears, his eyes, and his reflection make him circumspect. He is not apt to be in the predicament of the man who was anxious to be introduced to a deaf woman, but when he was presented, and one end of her ear-trumpet was put into his hand, had nothing to say. " Nature, I am persuaded," says Rabelais, " did not without a cause frame our ears open, putting thereto no gates at all, nor shutting them up with any manner of inclosures, as she hath done upon the tongue, the eyes, and other such outjutting parts of the body. The cause, as I imagine, is, to the end that every day and every night, and that continually, we may be ready to hear, and by a perpetual hearing apt to learn."

Common sense, with common reflection, is not apt to suffer from the confusion, in common matters, of cause and effect, which certain ignorant islanders once displayed, referred to in Boswell's Johnson. They invented all sorts of superstitions to account for their being seized with colds in their heads whenever a ship arrived, until it occurred to an intelligent reverend gentleman to find the cause in the fact that a vessel could enter the harbor only when a strong north-east wind was blowing. And in a certain part of Scotland the servants on a farm suffered every spring from fever and ague, which was received as a judgment of God upon their sins, until with proper drainage of the land the disorder disappeared.

Big words, where little ones were better, generally arise from an ignorant misapprehension of means to ends. A good story is told of a senator, staying at a hotel in St. Louis. He saw from his window that, just across the street, a house was on fire. He instantly raised the window, and began to shout to the people, as they passed along, in stentorian tones, "Conflagration ! conflagration ! conflagration !" But to his utter amazement, the people paid no attention to him whatever. Finally, becoming exasperated, he threw away the word conflagration, and began to shout at the top of his voice, " Fire !" The people understood at once, and the fire was put out.

A great advantage of common sense with education is to enable us to see the direct way to an object or result. There is an incident of a well-known Oxford man, who one day saw a favorite pupil who was within an hour to take his place in the school for final examination. " I 'm in for Butler's Analogy," said the student, " and have not had time to read it through." " All Butler's governing ideas," mildly remarked the tutor, "are reducible to four. You can learn them in a quarter of an hour, and you must manipulate them as well as you can." The pupil passed a capital examination in Butler. Short cuts are good, if you know how to take them.

Rufus Choate and Daniel Webster were once opposed to each other as lawyers in a suit which turned on the size of certain wheels. Mr. Choate filled the air with the rockets of rhetoric, and dazzled the jury, but Mr. Webster caused the wheels to be brought into court and put behind a screen. When he rose to speak the screen was removed, and his only reply to Choate's eloquence was, " Gentlemen ! there are the wheels ! "

At Palermo, Lord Dundonald met with Lord Nelson, and through life adopted as his own the injunction he received from the victor of Trafalgar : " Never mind manœuvres ; always go at 'em."

The prime mischief of modern education, mental and moral, is " cramming." Fuseli did not attempt to make all his pupils alike by teaching. He saw in Wilkie, Mulready, Etty, Landseer, and Haydon, peculiar talents, and through his " wise neglect," they became distinguished. Coleridge opposed the system of " cramming " children, and especially satirized the moral rules for juvenile readers, lately introduced. "I infinitely prefer," he said, "The Seven Champions of Christendom, Jack the Giant-Killer, and such like : for at least they make the child forget himself : but when in your good-child stories, a little boy comes in and says, 'Mamma, I met a poor beggarman, and gave him the sixpence you gave me yesterday. Did I do right?' 'Oh, yes, my dear; to be sure you did.' This is not virtue but vanity. Such lessons do not teach goodness, but, if I might hazard such a word, goodiness."

Sainte-Beuve, it is related, as he grew older, came to regard all experience as a single great book, in which to study for a few years ere we go to heaven ; and it seemed all one to him whether you should read in chapter XX., which is the differential calculus, or in chapter XXXIX., which is hearing the band play in the gardens. As a matter of fact, an intelligent person, looking out of his eyes, and hearkening in his ears, with a smile on his face all the time, will get more true education than many another in a life of heroic vigils.

The motto to Leigh Hunt's Indicator is a description of a bird in the interior of Africa, called the bee-cuckoo, or honey-bird, whose habits would rather seem to belong to the interior of Fairyland, but they have been well authenticated. It indicates to honey-hunters where the nests of wild bees are to be found. It calls them with a cheerful cry, which they answer ; and on finding itself recognized, flies and hovers over a hollow tree containing the honey. While they are occupied in collecting it, the bird goes to a little distance, where he observes all that passes ; and the hunters, when they have helped themselves, take care to leave him his portion of the food.

A happy man or woman, some one has said, is a better thing to find than a five-pound note. He or she is a radiating focus of good will ; and their entrance into a room is as though another candle had been lighted. We need not care whether they could prove the forty-seventh proposition ; they do a better thing than that, they practically demonstrate the great theorem of the reasonableness of life.

You remember the immortal fireside saint, St. Jenny, created and canonized by Jerrold. " St. Jenny was wedded to a very poor man ; they had scarcely bread to keep them ; but Jenny was of so sweet a temper that even want bore a bright face, and Jenny always smiled. In the worst seasons Jenny would spare crumbs for the birds, and sugar for the bees. Now it so happened that one autumn a storm rent their cot in twenty places apart ; when, behold, between the joints, from the basement to the roof, there was nothing but honeycomb and honey — a little fortune for St. Jenny and her husband, in honey. Now, some said it was the bees, but more declared it was the sweet temper of St. Jenny that had filled the poor man's house with honey."

As solace alone, books are very much to many ; "but the scholar only knows," says Washington Irving, "how dear these silent, yet eloquent, companions of pure thoughts and innocent hours become in the seasons of adversity. When all that is worldly turns to dross around us, these only retain their steady value. When friends grow cold, and the converse of intimates languishes into vapid civility and commonplace, these only continue the unaltered countenance of happier days, and cheer us with that true friendship which never deceived hope, nor deserted sorrow."

We are told of an Indian bird, which, enjoying the sunshine all the day, secures a faint reflection of it in the night, by sticking glow-worms over the walls of its nest. And something of this light is obtained, it is observed, from the books read in youth, to be remembered in age. " Summer's green all girded up in sheaves."

At the battle of Edgehill, the Prince of Wales and the Duke of York, then ten and twelve years old, were on the hill. "They were placed," says Lord Nugent, "under the care of Dr. William Harvey, afterward so famous for his discoveries concerning the circulation of the blood, and then Physician in Ordinary to the King. During the action, forgetful both of his position and of his charge, and too sensible of the value of time to a philosophic mind to be cognizant of bodily danger, he took out a book, and sat him down on the grass to read, till, warned by the sound of the bullets that grazed and whistled round him, he rose, and withdrew the princes to a securer distance."

Scott (one of his biographers tells us) received a letter from his old friend, Sir Adam Ferguson, captain in the 58th regiment, then serving in the Peninsula. The gallant soldier had just received a copy of The Lady of the Lake, and had it with him when his company was posted on a piece of ground exposed to the enemy's shot. The men were ordered to lie prostrate, and, while they kept that attitude, the captain, kneeling at their head, read aloud the description of the battle of Beal' an Dhuine, in the sixth canto, and the listening soldiers only interrupted him by an occasional huzza as the French shot struck the bank above them.

It has been said, that of all the toils in which man engages, none are nobler in their origin or their aim than those by which he endeavors to become more wise. We may say, as well, that no one should be discouraged by this discovery, that "the more there is known, the more it is perceived there is to be known;" for, it is also true, that "the infinity of knowledge to be acquired runs parallel with the infinite faculty of knowing, and its development." The possibilities of infinite culture can be only imperfectly anticipated on this "shoal of time." Heaven orders that our intellects can be employed only in part.

The human brain is wonderfully constructed ; but it has its limitations. The mental physiologist tells us that a fragment of the gray substance of it, not larger than the head of a small pin, contains parts of many thousands of commingled globes and fibres. Of ganglion globules alone, according to the estimate of the physiologist Meynert, there cannot be less than six hundred millions in the convolutions of a human brain. They are, indeed, in such infinite numbers that possibly only a small portion of the globules provided are ever turned to account in even the most energetic brains. Dr. Maudsley contrasts the fifteen thousand words which Shakespeare employs for the expression of his ideas with the hundreds of millions of brain globules that must have been concerned in the production of this intellectual harvest. The little that we can know here, is, at best, only the alphabet of the course progressive and unending. What we cannot see now, will be apparent hereafter to our improved vision, as the high-flying birds, twenty thousand feet above the earth, and countless stars of heaven, are seen clearly by the telescope. The parchment used by the ancients, from which one writing was erased, and on which another was written, was called a palimpsest. "What else than a natural and mighty palimpsest," exclaims De Quincey, "is the human brain ? Everlasting layers of ideas, images, feelings, have fallen upon your brain softly as light. Each succession has served to bury all that went before. And yet, in reality, not one has been extinguished." Doubtless it will appear, at the great restoration, that enough has been impressed, in one short earthly existence, to more than compensate for all its ills, and hopefully to encourage a start in the life that is illimitable.

Yet, in the here, we long for the fruition of the hereafter. The sigh and the longing are irrepressible. The San Carlos Theatre at Naples was so placed that Vesuvius might be seen from the royal box. Ah! if only it were possible, in the drama of **this life,** to be so disposed as to have occasional visions of the Eternal.

**One** day a good **old man** saw a **bird** fluttering **in** the **road before** him. **He took it up,** and found **it was a** robin, whose plumage was **so filled** with the burs **of the** fields that it could not fly. He **picked out** the burs tenderly, and the creature flew away. **Alas!** the clogs, entanglements, and limitations. But how glorious the emancipation!